Only Her

By Allie Everhart

Only Her
By Allie Everhart

Copyright © 2015 Allie Everhart
All rights reserved.
Published by Waltham Publishing, LLC
Cover design by Okay Creations
ISBN: 978-1-942781-05-9

CHAPTER ONE

RACHEL

It's been over three years since I left my old life behind and started a new one here in Italy. I still live in the same tiny village. I used to love this village. The beautiful scenery. The friendly people. The delicious food. And those things still make this town a nice place to visit, but it's not where I want to live. Not anymore. This was only supposed to be temporary. I was supposed to live here a few months, maybe a year. Just until Pearce came to get me.

But he never came, and now I've grown to hate the town I once loved. It's a constant reminder of my old life. Of Pearce. And the time we spent here.

This is where Pearce and I came for our honeymoon. I'll never forget that trip. Everything about it was perfect. When we found this tiny village, we both fell in love with it. It was Christmas, and sparkling lights lined the streets and the storefronts. We stayed in a small hotel that I now walk past every day to get my groceries. If I look up, I can see the balcony where Pearce and I sat on Christmas night, discussing our future. A future that got cut short when I found out people were trying to kill me.

Sometimes I think I should've just stayed in America and went back to Pearce and told him what really happened. But I didn't, because I was terrified that doing so would put both him and Garret at risk, and I couldn't do that. If anything ever happened to either of them, I couldn't live with myself.

"Are you ready to go?" Celia asks in her strong Italian accent. She speaks fluent English but sometimes with her accent it's hard to understand her. I'm used to it now, but when I first met her, I had to try to guess what she was saying.

"Yes. I'm ready," I tell her.

She turns to leave but then stops suddenly. "The ovens! I have to check. Wait here."

Celia is forgetful and always has to double and triple check that she turned the ovens off before she goes anywhere.

Today she's going to Naples to visit her sister and she agreed to let me go with her. We're staying overnight. I offered to get myself a hotel room but Celia wouldn't allow it. She insisted I stay with her and her sister.

When Jack sent me away, he told me to never go into big cities or tourist areas because they have cameras everywhere that link to large security networks that use facial recognition software to locate people. He said the organization can hack into these systems to find people they're looking for, so if they ever suspected I was alive, they could find me through the cameras. They could put an image of my face into the system so that if the cameras ever caught me, whoever was looking for me would be alerted and I'd be in danger.

I'm willing to take the risk. I'm done sitting around waiting for Pearce. I don't know why he hasn't shown up, but it's been over three years and I can't keep waiting. I have to do something.

Every day since I've been here, I've considered going back, but then I hear that warning in my head from Jack, saying that if I went back, they might harm Garret or Pearce. I've wanted to call Pearce, and almost have, several times, but then remembered that Jack said Pearce's phone could be bugged, and if it was, then the organization would know I'm alive. They'd trace the call and come here and kill me.

So I've done as Jack said, and remained in this small remote village, and not contacted anyone from my former life. But my patience is up. I can't do this anymore. I have to take action.

I'm not sure what my plan is yet. First, I need to find out whatever I can about Pearce that might explain why he hasn't come to get me. Did something happen to him? Or is he still trying to figure out how to get me home without them killing me?

I don't know what I'll find out today, but I'm hoping to get at least some answers out of this trip.

"Let's go." Celia walks quickly out the door to the street. I follow, and she locks the door behind us. Our bags are already in the car.

We get into her tiny two-door Fiat and she takes off. Celia is 68 years old so you'd think she'd drive slow and with caution, but no. She drives like a crazy person. She goes way too fast on these small roads, and if someone cuts her off in traffic, she yells at them and shakes her fist out the window. Given her driving skills, I'm not confident we'll make it to Naples alive, but she's my only option.

"You still going in the city?" she asks.

"Yes. You can just drop me off and pick me up later. We can decide on a meeting place when we get there."

She shakes her head. "You shouldn't go to the city alone. It's dangerous."

Celia reminds me of my mom, who was always so overprotective of me.

"I'll be fine," I assure her. "I'll be surrounded by tourists."

"Speak Italian so they don't know you're American. The Americans are targets."

I smile. "Celia, I'll be fine. You don't have to worry about me."

She reaches over and pats my hand. "I worry. You're a nice girl. Bad people live in the city." She whips around a corner with only one hand on the wheel, veering into the other lane. I hold my breath, then release it when she veers back into her lane.

I'd offer to drive but I don't have a license, and I can't get one without a real identity and documents to support it. My fake identity limits me from doing a lot of things, like get a job. That's why I still work for Celia and still tutor. Those jobs pay me cash under the table.

Celia has never questioned why I don't have official documents. I think she knows I'm running from something. She probably thinks I escaped from an abusive husband or boyfriend.

3

Given what an emotional mess I was when I first arrived here, she knows something bad happened to me, but thankfully, she's never forced me to tell her.

"You going shopping?" she asks.

"Yes," I lie. "I haven't been shopping forever and I miss it."

"What are you buying?"

"I'm not sure." I gaze out the side window. "Maybe a new scarf. I'm tired of this one." I adjust the scarf I'm wearing, making sure it covers my head. My scarf and a pair of sunglasses are all I have to hide my identity from the cameras. Wearing a wig would've caused Celia to be suspicious about what I was up to and I didn't want her asking questions.

She reaches for her wallet on the dashboard. I hold my breath again because she only has one hand on the wheel and we're heading toward a very tight curve on the edge of a cliff.

"Let me get it," I tell her, taking the wallet.

She rounds the curve, then grabs the wallet from me and fumbles with it until she grasps a few bills. She holds them out to me. "Here. You buy something nice."

"Celia, no. I can't take your money."

She nods, shoving the money at me. "You take it. Buy something pretty."

I take the money just so she'll put her eyes back on the road.

"Thank you," I say.

I don't need the money. I'm not going shopping. And if I were, I'd use my own money. I have some saved up. The past three years I've spent as little money as possible, trying to save enough to buy a plane ticket back to the U.S. Actually, I have enough money for a ticket, but I haven't bought one yet because I don't have a plan. And I'm worried that if I leave Italy, Pearce won't be able to find me. But he's had over three years to find me, so why hasn't he shown up? Why hasn't he tried to contact me? Or sent someone here to give me a message?

I need answers, or at least some clues that will hint at what's going on with Pearce, although I'm a little nervous about what I'm going to find out.

When we arrive in Naples, Celia pulls over to the side of a very crowded street. There are people and cars everywhere. I'm not used to all this activity. The town where I live is so quiet and has so few people.

"Where do you want to go?" she asks.

"Somewhere with shops. Take me where the tourists go."

"Tourist shops are expensive. I'll take you somewhere else."

She pulls out of the parking space and speeds off.

"No, I really want to go to the tourist area."

She looks at me funny. "You sure?"

"Yes."

She sighs as she makes a sharp right down a narrow street. "Tourist areas are dangerous."

"I'll be okay."

We reach a street that's even more congested than the one we were on before. Crowds of people line the sidewalks. We pass some stores and then I spot what I'm looking for. An Internet cafe. I knew they'd have one here. There's no Internet service in the town where I live and there probably won't be for years. Only big cities have Internet access, so I knew Naples would.

"Just drop me off here," I say.

She yanks the wheel into a parking spot, nearly hitting a light pole.

"Remember. Speak Italian," she says. "And don't talk to any men. City men are no good."

I smile as I get out of the car. "Okay. I'll stay away from them. Should we plan to meet here in a few hours?"

She nods. "Sí. Two hours. Plenty of time to shop."

"Thank you, Celia."

As soon as I shut the door, she speeds off. She's a terrible driver. I hope she makes it to her sister's house.

I go into the Internet cafe. There are two public computers to use, or people can hook up their own. Both of the public computers are taken, so I'll have to wait for someone to leave. The place is very crowded and everyone looks like a tourist, loaded up with backpacks and cameras. It seems like almost everyone in here is American, with English being spoken all around me with no foreign accents. It's comforting to be around Americans again. It makes me feel at home. It also makes me *miss* home. God, I miss home. I miss my family. I want them back.

I get a coffee, then find an empty chair near the door and sit down. I check to make sure there aren't any security cameras. There aren't, so I take my sunglasses off.

A man holding a laptop sits in the chair next to mine.

"Waiting for a computer?" he asks. He must've noticed me intently staring at the people at the computers, willing them to leave.

"Yes," I say.

"I'm Brian." He holds his hand out. He's about my age with jet black hair and tan skin. He's wearing a suit and tie and sounds American. He's probably here on business.

"Jill," I say, shaking his hand.

"Are you here on vacation?" he asks.

I pause, not sure how to answer. I wasn't expecting people to talk to me and now I don't have a story prepared.

"Yes," I lie. "I'm visiting my aunt. She moved here a couple years ago."

He smiles and pivots his body toward me. "Where are you from? I assume you're from the States."

"Um, yes. I'm from Texas."

"Really? You don't have an accent."

"I grew up in California. I moved to Texas when I was older." I turn away from him. This guy seems nice enough but I have no interest in talking to him.

"Where in California? I'm from LA."

"Would you excuse me a minute?" I hop up from my chair and go up to the young girl who works the cash register. She's also American, probably here as an exchange student.

"I really need to use one of those computers," I tell her, pointing at the public computers. "Do you know how much longer they'll be?"

She shrugs. "You'll have to ask them. There isn't a time limit. As long as you pay for your time, you can be there as long as you want."

I sigh. "Okay."

I walk over to the people using the computers. A guy and a girl. I think they're a couple. They're both in their twenties and dressed all in black with piercings on their faces. They're wearing headphones so probably won't hear me.

"Excuse me." I nudge the girl's arm. She looks at me, annoyed, chomping on her gum. She doesn't remove her headphones. "Could you tell me when you might be done with the computer?"

She rolls her eyes, then looks back at the computer screen. Then the guy next to her turns toward her and pulls her face to his and they start kissing. So I guess I'm not getting an answer.

I return to my chair to wait.

"Would you like to use mine?" Brian asks, offering me his laptop.

Should I take it? If I use it, he'll know what I was looking up. That could be bad. Then again, he's a total stranger and has no idea who I am, so why would he care what I'm researching?

I glance at him. He seems normal. And he's from LA, so nowhere near my old life. It's probably risky to do this, but I'm desperate and I'm guessing the teenagers making out at the public computers will be there a while.

"Thank you," I say, taking the laptop from him.

He has the Internet open to a news website and I find myself scanning the headlines to see what's going on in the U.S. I feel so disconnected to everything there. There's a small TV in my apartment, but it only gets the local channels so I occasionally hear news about the U.S., but not much.

I notice Brian watching me. I turn so he can't see what I'm looking up on the computer.

"I'll try to hurry," I say so he'll stop staring.

"Oh, no. Don't worry about it. Take your time." He pulls out a business book from his laptop bag and begins reading.

I focus back on the computer and click on the search bar. I have so many questions and need so many answers that I'm not sure where to start. I decide to start with myself. I type in my old name. Thousands of search results pop up. The first page is all articles about the plane crash. I click on one from a news website.

The story is about how the plane crash may not have been an accident. There are quotes from various people who say that the plane was tampered with in order to kill Senator Wingate, but they don't say who might have tampered with it.

I'm not surprised people are questioning the crash. Whenever a prominent person dies in a small plane, it seems like people are always suspicious, especially reporters. But I'm sure they'll never find anything to prove the plane was taken down. The organization will make sure nobody learns the truth.

I click on another article. This one describes the crash in more detail and lists the people who died, including me.

Brian clears his throat and I check my watch and realize I've been using his laptop for 20 minutes now. I'm desperate to read more but I need to hurry up.

Next I type in 'Pearce Kensington.' Tons of search results pop up, which makes sense since Pearce is well-known in the business world. In fact, the first few pages of results are all business-related. According to the articles, Pearce is now CEO of Kensington Chemical. Holton must've retired. I continue to search, but see nothing about Pearce's personal life. I go up to the search bar and type 'Pearce Kensington's wife' to see if I get different results than what I got from typing in my name.

When the search results pop up, I gasp and almost drop the laptop. The whole first page is filled with articles about Katherine Seymour.

Who is now Katherine Kensington.

Pearce's wife.

CHAPTER TWO

RACHEL

"Oh my God." I cover my mouth with my hand.

Brian catches the computer before it slips off my lap. "Is everything all right?"

I'm unable to answer. I can hardly breathe.

Pearce married Katherine? No. That can't be true.

"Jill." Brian touches my arm and I glance over and see him staring at me. "Are you okay? You don't look well. I think you might be hyperventilating."

I hear my quick shallow breaths and think he might be right. My chest feels weighted down, my lungs struggling for air. I feel dizzy, to the point that I might pass out. Maybe this is what a panic attack feels like, because I'm definitely panicking. I loosen my scarf, but it still feels tight.

"I'll get you some water." Brian sets the laptop down and jumps up from his chair. Moments later he appears with a glass. I have to hold it with both hands so I don't drop it. My body feels paralyzed from the shock. Like I can't move. Can't think.

"Oh my God." I say it again, staring straight ahead.

"Drink some water," Brian says. "You're really pale. Maybe you're dehydrated."

I take a tiny sip, just so he'll leave me alone, then hand him the glass.

Katherine is married to Pearce. That can't be right. There must be some mistake. He wouldn't marry her. Never in a million years. Her father, Leland, tried to kill me! Pearce wouldn't marry his daughter. It would never happen.

9

Even if she wasn't Leland's daughter, Pearce wouldn't marry her. He doesn't even like her. He used to say how immature she was. How fake she was, and shallow, and deceitful like her mother. He couldn't stand the way she'd follow him around at parties, infatuated with him. So how could he be married to her? This doesn't make any sense. He's married to me! He can't marry someone else when he's married to me.

"I need to see that." I point to the laptop. Brian is still staring at me like I'm going to pass out, which is a real possibility.

He slowly hands me the computer. He's probably concerned I'm going to drop it. I sit up straighter and set it on my lap. I click on the first article. It's about a charity auction held in New York last week. There's a photo of Pearce and Katherine. Pearce is wearing a tuxedo and looks as handsome as I remember. My heart aches seeing him again. It's been so long. I wish I could print out a picture of him and take it with me. I have no photos of him. Only memories. Memories of what used to be. Those memories are what get me through each day, giving me hope that I'll be reunited with my family. But now, I don't know if I will. Pearce is remarried. To Katherine.

As I look closer at the photo, I notice there's something different about Pearce. His eyes. They look empty. Emotionless. Dead. I could always tell how Pearce was feeling by his eyes. They always gave him away. But I never saw them look this way. This is not the Pearce I know. He's not smiling in the photo. He's just staring straight ahead with those lifeless eyes.

"What happened to you?" I whisper as my finger touches Pearce's face on the screen.

My eyes move to Katherine, who's wearing a royal blue evening gown, her blond hair pulled up and back, huge diamonds on her ears and along her neck. She has her arm wrapped around Pearce's arm. I look at her left hand and see a large diamond ring. There's a smirk on her face. Not even a smile. A smirk. Like a spoiled child who got what she wanted and is rubbing it in my face.

The caption below the photo says, 'Pearce and Katherine Kensington.' The article is about the auction, not them specifically, and their photo is one of many on the page. I go back to the search results and scan the headlines. They're all stories covering various charity events.

I type in 'Katherine Seymour's wedding' and find out that she married Pearce almost two years ago. I sink back into my chair. How could he do this to me? How could he marry her? The daughter of the man who wanted me dead?

Maybe they forced him to marry her. Jack said members have to marry the daughters of other members. And Leland is a member. So is that what happened? Is that why Leland tried to kill me? So his daughter could marry Pearce? Is Katherine that damn spoiled that her father would kill someone to give her what she wants?

What about Garret? Oh, God. She's his stepmother. No! I won't allow it. I will not allow that woman to raise my son. I scan the articles and see nothing about Garret. It's like he wasn't even at the wedding. I don't see any photos of him. Where is he? Did something happen to him?

I search his name but don't get much for results. It's mostly stories about the plane crash and how he was my only child. After three pages of results, there's something more recent. Swim meets he competed in. I smile, tears welling up in my eyes. Garret's swimming. He's still swimming. And he's on a team. My little boy is on a swim team. But he's not a little boy anymore. He's 13. A teenager. And I've missed all these years of his life. I feel wetness on my cheeks as tears stream down my face.

"Jill, are you sure you're okay?" Brian asks. He was pretending to read his book but he's really been watching me out the side of his eye.

I wipe my cheeks. "Yes. I'm fine. I'm sorry I'm taking so long."

"I'd let you continue using it, but I need to leave in a few minutes. I have a meeting across the street."

I nod. "Okay."

What else should I look up? *Think, Rachel. Think.*

Jack! I quickly type in his name. I almost drop the laptop again when I see the results.

A heart attack. Jack had a heart attack the night of the plane crash. He was found in his car. The article says he had a heart attack while driving and the car went in a ditch. He was dead by the time someone found him. They found the car just five miles from our house.

Tears continue down my cheeks. He's dead. Jack is dead. He went to tell Pearce and died before he made it there. He was so close. Just five miles away. But he never made it.

Pearce was never told. He thinks I'm dead. He has this whole time. He hasn't been looking for me. Hasn't been trying to find a way to get me back. Instead he's moved on with his life. He's married to Katherine. The enemy. Whose father tried to kill me.

And I have no idea what has happened to my son. If he's okay. Or if he's suffering, living with that witch of a woman. Forced to be part of the Seymour family.

Oh my God. Pearce doesn't know. He doesn't know what Leland did. He doesn't know because Jack was never able to tell him. Pearce has no idea he's married to the daughter of the man who tried to kill me.

I close the Internet and get up and set the laptop on my chair.

"I have to go," I say to Brian. "Thank you for letting me use your computer."

"Yeah. Sure." He's looking at me like I'm crazy, which isn't surprising. I'm crying. My breathing is erratic. I'm shaking. I'm a mess. I have to get out of here.

When I get outside, I squeeze through the crowds of people, searching for a quiet place where I can sit for a moment and think. But there's no place to go. It's noisy and people are everywhere. Bumping into me. Pushing me along. I find myself at the edge of a busy intersection, wedged within the crowd. Across the street I spot some benches around a fountain. It's not quiet, but at least it's somewhere to sit, and I need to sit. I'm feeling very light-headed.

As I'm waiting for the light to turn, I glance up and see a camera aimed directly at me. Shit! I reach up to make sure my scarf is covering me but it's not there. It must've fallen off. I search the area all around me but I can't find it. And then I realize my sunglasses are also missing. I must've left them at the cafe. The light changes and people are pushing me to move forward. I keep my head down and hurry across the street to the fountain and find an open bench.

That camera definitely saw me. I looked right at it. Dammit!

It's fine. Nobody's after me. Everyone thinks I'm dead. So why would anyone be looking for me? They wouldn't. I'm fine.

My mind returns to what I just read online. Pearce and Katherine are married. And my son is living under their roof. Oh, God. I think I might throw up. I lean over, clutching my stomach, which is twisting and churning and cramping all at once. My throat is burning as I try to hold back my tears, but I'm not doing a very good job because they're still streaming down my face.

I sit up a little and focus on the fountain and take some deep breaths. I need to relax so I can figure out what to do.

I watch the water flowing in the fountain and it calms me enough to think. I will NOT let this happen. I will not let that woman take my family from me. I have to stop this. I have to go back there. I'll disguise myself. I'll fly to a small town in the middle of nowhere and hide out. I'll contact Pearce and tell him what happened. And when he finds out I'm alive, he'll divorce Katherine and we'll be together again. We'll be a family.

It won't be that simple. I know it won't. I'll be risking a lot by doing this, but I have to try. I can't let this continue. I've been waiting here in Italy for nothing! For no reason. Nobody's been looking for me. Jack is dead, and Pearce has moved on with his life.

I take a few minutes to calm down, then go back across the street to find my scarf, keeping my eyes aimed at the ground so the cameras won't see my face. I search everywhere for my scarf but it isn't there. It's gone. I go inside the Internet cafe to get my glasses but they're also gone. Someone must've taken them.

I return to the bench by the fountain and wait until it's time for Celia to pick me up. She's late and I'm stuck standing in front of the Internet cafe, where there is yet another camera that I hadn't noticed earlier. I keep my head down and stare at the ground. My hair is long again, so I look more like myself than I

13

did when I arrived here years ago. I should've gone in a store and bought another scarf but it's too late now.

A scarf. Shit! I forgot to get a scarf. Now Celia will wonder why I went shopping and didn't buy anything. Why didn't I buy one? I'm so distraught over what I found out about Pearce that I can't even think straight.

Twenty minutes later Celia finally shows up, nearly knocking over a trash can as she pulls in the spot. I quickly get in the car.

"My sister is ill. We're going home." She squeals out of the parking space, almost sideswiping a car. She seems angry.

"I'm sorry to hear she's ill. Will she be okay?"

Celia rolls her window down and yells obscenities in Italian at the man in the car next to us and shakes her fist at him. I don't even know what he did wrong. She's usually so sweet and mild-mannered, but get her on the road and she turns crazy.

She rolls her window up. "She's not sick. We fought. We always do. This is why our visits never last for more than a few hours."

"Oh. That's too bad. I thought you liked her."

"Of course I like her!" She throws her hands in the air, leaving the steering wheel unattended. Her hands return to the wheel. "She's my sister. I love her. But then she starts arguing with me and soon…" She continues her rant, speaking in both Italian and English. She's gesturing with her hands and I'm getting nervous. There's too much traffic. She needs to keep her hands on the wheel.

I keep quiet and let her drive. We can talk about this later. Now that I think about it, I do remember this happened the last time she came to Naples. She said she'd be gone a couple days but was back the same day she left.

Celia talks to herself the entire drive back. She's talking really fast in Italian, likely replaying the argument with her sister.

I just sit back and close my eyes and wait for us to get home. When we arrive there, it's after dark. I take my small travel bag from the back seat and tell Celia I'm tired and going up to my room. She motions me to go, still mumbling to herself.

Back in my apartment, I lie in bed, staring at the cracks in the ceiling which are illuminated from the street light that shines through my window.

Am I really doing this? Why do I even ask? Of course I'm doing it. I have to. I have to get back to my family. I have to get them away from Katherine and Leland. I know it's risky but I can't sit here and do nothing.

The decision is made. I'm leaving. I'm flying back to the U.S. If Celia can't drive me to the airport, I'll take a cab. I have just enough money for a plane ticket, cab ride to the airport, and bus fare to wherever I end up going when I get there.

Maybe I'll leave tomorrow. I know I haven't thought this through, but what's there to think about? There's no need to stay here. I'd be better off hiding out in a tiny rural town in America than here. At least I'd be closer to my son.

My son. Garret. I smile just thinking about him. I can't believe I've gone this long without seeing him. Without hugging him. Without telling him I love him.

But I'm going to see him again soon. Very soon.

The next morning, I take my suitcase from the closet, and just the sight of it gets my blood pumping with excitement. I'm leaving. I'm finally leaving. I'm going back home. Back to America and back to my family.

I empty my closet, putting all the clothes on my bed and folding them up. I don't have many clothes. Just enough to fill the suitcase. Next, I get out my passport, which is hidden under my mattress, along with my stash of money. I take the money out too. A few thousand dollars. It's all I have.

There are no banks in this town, and even if there were, I wouldn't open an account. Before I came here, Jack told me to avoid any kind of paper trail, meaning don't have things like a bank account, credit card, driver's license, or car registration. I didn't think it was possible to get by without those things, but I've done so successfully for three years now, and I'm hoping I can do the same when I get back to the U.S. Even with my new identity, I'll need to remain hidden and untraceable.

15

I've decided to leave first thing tomorrow. I'll spend today preparing for the trip, and then I'll go to bed early so that I'm well rested and alert for what will likely be a long and possibly dangerous trip.

"Good morning." Celia comes up and gives me a quick hug as I walk in the kitchen. She's a hugger, like me, which is what made me instantly like her when we first met. "The dough is already made." She points to it on the counter.

Usually I make the dough, so I say, "Why did you make it so early?"

"I couldn't sleep." She walks back and forth through the kitchen, her arms flailing as she talks. "That Maria. She drives me crazy!"

Maria is the sister she went to visit yesterday. Celia stops abruptly in front of me. "She has a new man in her life. Twenty years younger!"

So that's why Celia was so upset? Is she jealous? Or just worried for her sister? Her sister's 75. I don't think Celia needs to worry about her sister dating a 55-year-old man. Or maybe the younger man was just part of the reason for the fight.

She storms out of the kitchen into the restaurant. I know she's upset, but I need to talk to her.

"Celia," I say, getting her attention. She's taking the chairs off the tables and setting them upright on the floor. I walk over to her. "Can we talk for a moment?"

"Sì." She pulls a chair out for me and we both sit at one of the small tables.

"I was wondering if you could take me to Naples tomorrow."

She cocks her head to the side. "You're going shopping again?"

"No. I need a ride to the airport."

She eyes me with concern. "Where are you going?"

"I'm leaving. Going back home."

I can tell she wants to ask why, but she's always respected my privacy so I hope she continues to do so now. Because if she questions me, I don't know what to tell her. I haven't had time to come up with a story.

16

"You're leaving for good?" she asks.

"Yes. For good. I'm not coming back." I feel sad as I say it, because as much as I want to leave, I *will* miss Celia. And she'll miss me. I can already see the loss in her eyes.

She nods. "I will take you. What time do we leave?"

"In the morning. Before the restaurant opens. I can make tomorrow's dough later today so it'll be all ready for you when you get back."

She stands up. "I'll close the restaurant. Take you to the airport, then maybe go back and see my sister." She hurries off to the kitchen and I know it's because she was about to cry. She doesn't like people seeing her cry. She'll get angry and yell and scream, but she's not one to cry, at least not in front of other people.

I feel bad leaving her, but I have to leave. I have to get back to my family. This isn't my home. My home is with Pearce and Garret.

Later that day, I ask Celia to tell the parents of my students that I had to leave and won't be coming back. I didn't want to tell them myself. They'd just ask me questions I don't have answers to, so it's better if Celia tells them I'm gone once I've already left.

At eight, I go to bed because we're leaving at five in the morning. But I'm unable to sleep. I'm excited, but also nervous and scared and worried something will happen that will prevent me from making it home. Like maybe there will be a problem at security and they won't let me through to the gate. Or maybe I'll get to customs and they won't accept my passport.

No. None of that will happen. Everything will be fine. I need to stay positive. I used to always be positive, but the day of the plane crash everything changed. I no longer see the world the way I used to. Before the crash, I was always hopeful. Always seeing only the good in people. But now? I view the world with a much darker lens. I'm much more cautious around people. I'm suspicious of their motives. I don't trust people the way I used to.

After everything that's happened to me, it's a struggle to remain positive, but it's what I need to do to get through this. I can't give up hope. If I do, I'm letting my enemies win.

After a few hours of staring at the ceiling, I finally drift off to sleep, dreaming of Pearce and Garret and being reunited with them after three very long years.

My blissful dreamland suddenly turns dark when it's overtaken by a nightmare that seems so real I feel like I'm actually living it. Everything's black and I hear deep voices and then feel something covering my mouth. It jars me from my sleep and I awake to find that there really is something over my mouth. A piece of duct tape. And there's a large man hovering over my bed.

Panic overwhelms me, fear seething through my veins.

This isn't a nightmare. This is real. It's all real.

CHAPTER THREE

RACHEL

I try to sit up, but I can't. The man is holding my shoulders down. I try to kick at him, but my legs won't move. I look down and see another man holding down my ankles.

Oh, God. Are they going to rape me? Then kill me?

Out of instinct, I start thrashing around, trying to escape their hold, but they're much bigger and stronger than me and my efforts barely faze them. I notice the man at my legs is now tying my ankles together. So I guess they're not raping me. But why is he tying my legs? Are they kidnapping me? Taking me somewhere to rape me later? Or selling me? They could be human traffickers.

Their faces are covered in ski masks so I can only see their eyes and mouths. They're dressed all in black. Black pants, black jackets, and black leather gloves. The room is dimly lit and they look like dark shadows surrounding me.

I'm gasping for breath but the tape has made a tight seal over my mouth. I focus on breathing from my nose, trying to get some air. The man holding my shoulders yanks me up to a sitting position and forces my arms behind my back. The other man comes over and ties my wrists together, then shoves me back against the wall, so I'm sitting up. He sits next to me, while the other man remains at the end of the bed.

"Shut the fuck up," the man next to me says. "No one can hear you."

I notice the muffled sounds coming from my throat as I try to scream. I didn't even know I was doing it until he said that. I'm completely panicked. My survival instinct has kicked in to the

19

point that I'm not even fully aware of what I'm doing. I halt my screams and focus on trying to breathe.

"This is a warning," the man says in a deep steady voice. He takes something from his coat pocket and holds it in front of my face. It's a cell phone. His finger presses the screen and a video appears.

"Hello, Rachel."

Oh my God. It's Holton.

The video is from Holton. He looks the same as he did three years ago. With that same smirk on his face that he always had when he got away with something he shouldn't have. Like when he took Garret out of school that day. Pearce wouldn't let me get mad at Holton, saying it would just make things worse. So I held my tongue, and the next time I saw Holton, he had that damn smirk on his face. The one I'm looking at right now.

"I assumed you were alive." The smirk disappears and his expression turns dark. "Jack betrayed us. I don't know how he was able to get you out of the country, but then again, he's always been resourceful when it comes to matters of life and death." Holton grins. "In case you're wondering, Jack is dead. Before the plane crash, I discovered that Jack had been talking to my son for years, despite strict orders not to do so. I found the phone he'd been using to call Pearce. That was all the evidence I needed to prove that Jack would betray us. And he did. I followed him that night of the crash. When he stopped within miles of your house, I knew he was there to tell Pearce something, and given the timing, I assumed he was telling Pearce something about you. Perhaps that he'd saved you and was hiding you somewhere. So I killed him before he could tell Pearce the news. I shot him in the head." He laughs a little. "It was quite satisfying. I always hated that man."

I'm shaking. My entire body is shaking. What does this mean? He's going to shoot me next? Is he here? Is he going to appear as soon as this video ends and shoot me in the head, like he did to Jack? Those articles said Jack had a heart attack, so did Holton somehow cover up what he did? Did he hire people to tell the media that Jack died from a heart attack?

Holton takes a drink of something from a short fat glass. Probably bourbon, his favorite liquor. "I had my men keep an eye out for you, just in case you were alive. For years you never turned up, and I thought perhaps you really were on that plane. But then you turned up on a street corner in Naples, Italy." He chuckles to himself. "I'm surprised Jack didn't warn you about the dangers of cameras. All that work to help you escape and then he leaves out that very important detail." Holton takes another drink, then sets the glass down. "Jack didn't know this, but the plane crash was my idea. I requested it be done as punishment for Pearce marrying you. The punishment was approved, but instead of doing it right away, I asked them to wait. There were things I needed to get in order before it happened, such as waiting for Katherine to be an appropriate age to marry my son."

So Holton did this. He did all of it. Planned my death. Planned the timing of it. He must've forced Pearce to marry Katherine. He must've threatened him. It's all making sense now.

"I had to do what's best for my family." He narrows his eyes and leans closer to the camera. "And YOU are not what's best for this family. YOU were a destructive force that came into our lives and ripped my family apart. Humiliated us. Disgraced the family name." He leans back and picks up his glass and takes a drink. "I should kill you. I should have those men in your room kill you right now and end this." He pauses, and my eyes dart to the two men, checking to see if they have guns pointed at my head. They don't. They're still standing there, motionless, waiting for the video to finish.

"But killing you," Holton says, "would put you out of your misery. It would be far better for you to remain there and suffer, knowing your family has gone on without you. Knowing that Katherine has replaced you. Knowing that *she's* the one now sleeping in Pearce's bed. Having his child." He grins. "They had a girl."

He pauses to take another drink. Is he lying just to hurt me? Or did Pearce really have a child with Katherine?

"Contrary to your plans," he says, "you will not be returning home tomorrow. Or at any time in the future. You will never set foot on U.S. soil again. You will remain where you are, and that is where you will live the rest of your days. I will keep watch on you, and if you even attempt to leave, or attempt to contact anyone from your former life, there will be consequences. Consequences for Garret."

I try to rip my arms free so I can take the phone and slam it against the wall. How dare he threaten Garret! His own grandson!

Holton is the most evil man I've ever met. I always knew he was bad, but I didn't know he was this evil. I didn't know anyone was capable of being this evil. He's sick in the head. Completely deranged.

My efforts are useless. I can't free my arms. I can't scream at Holton. I can barely move or breathe. I just have to sit here and listen to his hateful message.

"If you want your son to be safe, you'll heed my words. Don't attempt to contact him, or Pearce, or anyone else. To everyone here, you are dead. No one knows you're alive except for me and the men in your room. You should've died in the plane crash, and perhaps now, you wish you had. But since you didn't, I will leave you to live in your own personal hell. And I will take pleasure in your suffering. It's what you deserve for interfering with my family and disgracing my family name." He smirks again. "Before I go, I should mention that your parents' deaths weren't an accident." He looks right at the camera, his smile gone, his eyes narrowed. "No one plays father to my son. I am the only father he will ever know." He pauses. "Heed my words. Or I will go there and kill you myself. And your son will—" The video cuts off.

I frantically look up at the man holding the phone, nodding at the screen. My son will *what*? What was he going to say? My son will *die*? Why did the video cut off like that?

The man takes the phone back and slips it in his pocket. I'm writhing on the bed, trying desperately to get free. The other man comes up beside me. I see a long needle in his hand.

"No!" I scream, but no sound comes out. Then I feel the prick in the side of my neck and everything goes black.

I awake to my alarm going off. It's four a.m., which is the time I set it for. I yank at my arms and notice they're no longer tied. I move my legs and notice they're not tied either. I turn on the light by my bed, then shove the covers back just to make sure I'm not imagining this. I'm not. My legs are free and so are my arms.

I touch my mouth. There's no tape there and there's no sticky residue on my cheeks.

Was that all just a nightmare? But it seemed so real. The two men standing by my bed. Holton talking on that video.

As I glance around the room, nothing seems out of place. There are no signs of a break-in. The lock on the door is still locked. The windows are closed. My suitcase is still there on the floor.

I go in the bathroom and check my face. There are no marks where the tape was ripped off. I check my wrists and my ankles. No marks. So it must've just been a nightmare. A horrible nightmare.

I exhale a sigh of relief, then wash my face and dry it with the towel. I go out to where my suitcase is sitting, on the floor just outside the closet. My clothes remain as I left them, neatly folded in the suitcase.

Celia will be taking me to the airport soon. I need to shower quick and get dressed. I grab a pair of jeans and a black sweater, but notice my envelope of money is sticking out the edge of my suitcase. Last night, I tucked the envelope under my clothes. At least I think I did, but maybe I didn't.

When I go to hide it back under my clothes, I notice the envelope is too light and too thin. I open it up and see that the money is gone. All of it.

"No," I say quietly, my shoulders sinking in despair. "It can't be. It was just a nightmare. It wasn't real."

There's something else in the envelope. I reach in and pull out a gold chain. Tears fall from my eyes when I see what it is. It's the necklace Pearce gave me when I came home from the hospital after having Garret. There are two heart lockets hanging from the chain; one big and one small. I open the big heart. It used to contain a photo of Pearce and me, but now there's a tiny slip of paper in it that reads, 'heed my words.' My hands are shaking as I

23

open the smaller locket. It still has the photo I put in there. It's a photo of Garret as a baby.

Oh, God. It *was* real. It wasn't a nightmare. Those men were here. They showed me a video. A message from Holton.

It was all real.

But where did Holton get this necklace? It was in my bedroom, hidden in my jewelry box. Did he steal it right after the plane crash?

It doesn't matter how he got it. What matters is that last night really happened. Holton threatened me. And he threatened Garret. Maybe he was bluffing about Garret. Saying it just to scare me. He wouldn't really hurt Garret, would he? I don't know. I really don't.

That's why he said it. He knows I'd never put Garret at risk. He knows how much I love my son. That's why Holton made a threat he knew I couldn't test the validity of.

He also knew that giving me this locket would nearly kill me. That it would break my heart all over again. Now, every day, I'll look at this photo of my sweet baby boy and wish I was with him. I'll agonize over the fact that he's living with Katherine and having family dinners with Leland. I'll have to live with the guilt and regret over the decision I made to come here years ago. I never should've left. I should've stayed and contacted Pearce right away.

Now it's too late. I'm stuck here. Being watched. Threatened. Unable to go home. Unable to see my family.

Holton is beyond evil. There aren't words to describe someone as evil as him. Maybe he wasn't bluffing. Maybe he really would kill his own grandson. He tried to kill ME. And he killed Jack. And my parents. Oh my God. He killed my parents! He admitted it. He killed them.

I collapse onto the floor, sobbing, the locket still in my hand.

I'll never get out of here. I'm trapped in this tiny town, having to pretend to be someone else. Living a life that's not my own. And hating every second of it. All because of Holton.

Suddenly it hits me that this isn't forever. Holton will eventually die. He's in his sixties. He won't live forever. And once he's gone, I'll go back.

That small remnant of hope gives me the strength to sit up and wipe my tears. I sift through my suitcase to make sure Holton didn't leave me anything else. There's nothing there. Just my clothes and my—

I rifle through my clothes, tossing them out of the way. It's not there. Where is it? I clear out the entire suitcase, then search the outside pockets. It's not there either. I check my dresser drawers, the nightstand, and all around the small studio apartment. But it's not there. He took it.

Holton had those men take my passport so I'll never be able to leave.

I have no money. No passport. He took everything. And left me with a reminder of what I'll never have again. My son.

"Jill." There's a knock on my door. It's Celia. "Are you ready?"

It's now four-thirty and I'm still in my pajamas. I wipe the wetness from my face and answer the door.

"I decided not to go," I say, putting on a fake smile. "I'd miss you way too much."

She sees my face and my red eyes and I can tell she doesn't believe me. But as usual, she doesn't come right out and ask what's wrong.

"Are you sure about this?" she asks, in a tone that's inviting me to tell her more. But I can't. Doing so would put her at risk.

"Yes. I'm sure. I'm sorry I made you get up so early. You can go back to bed. I'll go down and get the bread baking."

She reaches for my hand. "You know I would help you. If you need money for—"

"No." I quickly shake my head. "I don't need money. But thank you for offering. I should get ready." I fake an even bigger smile. "The early birds will be arriving soon. I need to get the bread in the oven."

She stares at me, knowing I'm hiding something, but simply nods, and then leaves.

I shut and lock the door, then fall to my knees, sobbing over what could've been. I was so close. I should've left yesterday. If I had, I'd be back in the U.S. right now. Why did I wait?

Now I have no money. No passport.

I'm left with a necklace and the looming threat that Garret will be harmed if I even attempt to leave.

Holton was right about one thing. I'm living in my own personal hell. And I can't escape it.

CHAPTER FOUR
Two Years Later

GARRET

"Garret," I hear my dad yelling from the bottom of the stairs. Instead of actually walking to my room to speak with me, he has to yell at me from downstairs. Maybe if he didn't make us live in such a huge house, he could actually make it up to my room.

"What?" I yell back. It seems like all we do in this house is yell.

"I need you to come down here and get your sister."

Seriously? This is so fucking ridiculous. Why the hell did he even have a kid if he wasn't going to take care of her? I'm only 15 and I'm the one always taking care of his kid.

There's no way Katherine would take care of her. She doesn't like toddlers. She thinks they're too messy and too loud. Of course she'd never admit that to her friends, but at home I've heard her say it. When Lilly is older and able to take care of herself, then maybe Katherine will pay attention to her, but for now, she tries to push her parenting responsibilities onto me and my dad, and sometimes my grandmother.

We used to have a nanny, but then the woman tried to steal Lilly and my dad had to pay to get her back. She was just a baby, and after that, my dad wouldn't hire another nanny.

I go down the stairs. My dad is holding Lilly. He's still in his suit. He must've just got home from work. Usually he stays there until nine or ten at night but tonight he's home early because Katherine's parents are in town and they're coming over for dinner. My grandparents are coming too.

Normally, I'd have to sit there and suffer through dinner with all of them, but I got out of it because of Lilly. I'm eating in the kitchen with her because apparently nobody wants a toddler at a dinner party, which maybe I could understand if other people were coming over. But this dinner party is all family; my dad, Katherine, and Lilly's grandparents on both sides. Why the hell wouldn't they want her there? I know why they don't want *me* there. Everyone thinks I'm a screw-up. But they still have hope for Lilly, so you'd think they'd allow her to eat with them.

"Can you take her upstairs?" My dad hands her to me.

She started reaching for me as soon as she saw me. I spend so much time with her, I think she likes me better than she likes her parents.

When I take her, she smiles and grabs the drawstring on my hooded sweatshirt, twirling it around in her hand.

"Hello, Garret." It's Leland, Katherine's father.

He comes up behind me and I cringe when he touches my shoulder. I hate him about as much as I hate Katherine. The apple didn't fall far from the tree. They're both conniving, back-stabbing, lie-to-your face people who are only concerned with themselves.

I turn toward him, so that his hand falls off my shoulder. I don't bother saying hello to him. Why play this fake nice act when we both know we hate each other?

"Are you still swimming?" he asks, a phony grin on his face.

"I've been swimming my whole life," I say, hoisting Lilly up in my arms. "Why would I stop?"

"You wouldn't." He's staring at me with this odd expression. Like he's hiding some kind of secret. I always feel like he's up to something but I can never tell what. "You obviously take after your mother. I hear she was quite an excellent swimmer."

I look at my dad to respond. He gets furious whenever someone brings up my mom. He likes to pretend she never existed, which is one of the many reasons he and I don't get along.

"Leland," my dad says. "Perhaps we should go get a drink."

Usually he'd get much angrier than that. Katherine must've told him to behave tonight. He has a hard time controlling his temper around Leland. The two of them don't get along. Actually, they hate each other.

"I'm going upstairs," I say, not wanting to be around Leland.

"Charles said your dinner will be ready within the hour," my dad says as I go up the stairs.

I take Lilly to her room. She has an all pink room. It's too much pink for me, but all her toys are in here so it's easier being in here than in my room.

We sit on the floor and I try to set her down but she won't let go of me.

"No," she says, her tiny hands clutching my shirt, her cheek pressed into my shoulder.

She does this all the time. She clings to me because she doesn't get enough affection. Truthfully, I don't either. Not that I need it at the age of 15, but a hug now and then from my dad would be nice. But unfortunately, the only hugs I get are from Lilly. Or the girls at school, which are a different kind of hug. A much different kind.

"Garrah," Lilly says. That's what she calls me. She can't say my name yet. She has trouble with the t.

"Garret," I say, emphasizing the t.

She tries to repeat it. "Garrah."

That was Lilly's first word, except it was more like "gah-rah" so she's improved a lot since then. Katherine was furious that her daughter's first word was my name. But what did she expect? Katherine doesn't spend any time with her. I've never seen her play with her. Not once.

Lilly's second word was 'dada,' which just shows that even my dad, who's never home, spends more time with Lilly than Katherine does. At least when my dad's around, he doesn't completely ignore her.

Lilly's no longer gripping my shirt so I set her down in front of me.

"Garret." I say it slow. "Try it again."

"Garrah." She giggles and claps her hands. "Garrah."

I laugh. She's so damn cute with her bright blond curls and blue eyes and little pink dress.

"Garrah! Garrah!" She's cracking herself up, giggling and clapping.

I pick her up and hug her and kiss her cheek. "You're funny."

When I found out my dad was having another kid, I was pissed. I didn't talk to him for weeks. I thought I'd hate my new brother or sister, but then Lilly came home from the hospital and was so tiny and sweet, there was no way I could hate her. And now I love her. She's my baby sister and I will always take care of her and look out for her.

I complain about having to babysit her, but I actually like spending time with her. She makes living here somewhat tolerable. She's the only person in my family who actually acts like she wants me around.

Lilly toddles over to her basket of stuffed animals and grabs a white bear. She toddles back over to me and drops the bear in my lap. Then she goes back and gets a pink bear for herself. She always does that. She always gives me something before she gets something for herself. I don't know anything about toddler psychology, but to me, that says there's hope she won't turn out like her mom. Katherine is completely selfish and wouldn't dare do anything for anyone else unless it somehow benefitted her.

I'm trying to make sure Lilly never acts that way. That she doesn't become Katherine. The last thing the world needs is another Katherine.

"Garret!"

Speak of the devil. I look up and see Katherine standing above me, her hands on her hips, which means she's about to yell at me.

I ignore her and watch Lilly take another stuffed animal from the basket.

"Why is she playing on the floor?" Katherine asks. "It's unsanitary, and an inappropriate place to play. She's not an animal!"

"She's only two," I say. "Where exactly do you expect her to play?"

She points to the miniature white table and chairs on the other side of the room. "She should be sitting in the chair."

"She won't sit in the chair for more than two seconds. She wants to run around and play on the floor."

"Because you're teaching her to do so."

"I didn't teach her that. It's just what kids her age do, which you would know if you actually spent time with her."

"Don't you dare talk down to me!" she hisses.

"As you can see, I'm talking up to you," I say, being a smart ass as I look up at her from the floor.

"You're such a child! I'm counting the days until you leave for college."

"Yeah. Me too. Believe me, I'd go right now if I could."

Lilly toddles toward me at a running pace. I open my arms and she slams into my chest.

I fall back onto the floor, letting her think she tackled me. "You got me!"

She laughs and hugs my chest. "Garrah."

Katherine huffs. "Make sure she eats her dinner." She storms out of the room.

"She should get the worst mother of the year award," I say to Lilly. She giggles, which makes me laugh. Thank God for Lilly. I'd never laugh if it weren't for her.

I hear the front door open downstairs. My grandparents must be here.

"Holton, good to see you again," I hear Leland say. He has the loudest damn voice. I'm all the way upstairs and can still hear him.

My grandfather is friends with Leland. My dad said Katherine's family and our family have been friends for years. My parents used to go to parties at their house. I've always wondered what my mom thought about them, but I don't dare ask my dad or he'd kill me. *Don't talk about your mother,* he says, whenever I ask about her.

I'm sure my mom didn't like them. I wonder what she thought of Katherine. I bet Katherine was a bitch to my mom. Katherine hates poor people, and although my mom didn't grow up poor, she wasn't from this high society world I now live in, which means Katherine would never accept her.

Katherine was only a teenager when my parents got married. And now she's married to my dad. If my mom knew that, she'd be pissed, especially if she knew how Katherine treats me.

My phone rings and I sit up, setting Lilly next to me on the floor. I yank my phone out and answer it. "Yeah."

31

"Hey. You coming over?" It's Decker, one of my friends from school.

"Later. I have to watch Lilly."

"When can you leave?"

"I don't know. It's a school night, so technically I'm not supposed to go out. But my dad's having a dinner party, so he probably won't even notice I'm gone. Lilly will be in bed by eight. Can you pick me up?"

"Yeah. Blake's having his driver pick everyone up and we're all going over to his house."

"Why do we have to hang out with Blake? You know I hate that guy."

"Yeah, but his parents don't care if we drink. Oh, and Ava's going to be there."

Ava's a girl at my school. She's a short brunette with big breasts who flirts with me all the time. We've made out and taken things pretty far, but we haven't had sex yet. She's 15, like me. I think she's still a virgin. I'm not. I slept with a girl last summer at camp. My first time wasn't great but I'm ready to try again. I'm just not sure I want to do it with Ava. I think she's one of those girls who could turn psycho if you start dating and then break up with her. And I don't need that shit. I have enough problems to deal with.

"Tonight could be the night," Decker says. "Blake's house has plenty of open rooms. You think you'll do it with her?"

Lilly's running around the room and I'm trying to keep an eye on her. This probably isn't a conversation I should be having while babysitting my little sister.

"No, not tonight," I say.

"Why not? You know she wants it. She was practically begging you for it at the party last weekend."

"That's why I'm not really into her. She's too needy. I like a challenge. A girl who makes me work for it."

"Shit. I can't believe you'd turn her down. I wouldn't turn any girl down. But I guess if I had girls lining up to be with me, like you do, I could be picky."

Decker has trouble getting girls. He hasn't even kissed a girl yet. As for me? I've lost track of how many girls I've kissed. Decker wasn't exaggerating. I have girls lining up to date me. I don't know why. Maybe because I play sports and work out a lot.

Lilly starts climbing on me. "I have to go," I tell Decker. "Get here at eight. I'll sneak out if I have to."

We hang up and I play with Lilly until it's time for dinner. Then I take her downstairs. On my way to the kitchen, I run into my grandparents.

"There's my girl," my grandmother says, taking Lilly from me. Ever since Lilly was born, my grandmother has lost all interest in me. I guess she likes granddaughters better than grandsons. Or maybe she just doesn't like teenagers.

"Garret," my grandfather says.

"Hello, Grandfather."

My grandfather is a strange man. He's so formal. It's like he never relaxes. Not even when he's around family.

"Your father said you made the honor roll," he says.

"Yes." I'm surprised my dad told him that. He pays so little attention to me that I didn't think he even knew I made the honor roll.

"Keep it up," my grandfather says. "You'll need top grades to get into Yale. The Kensington name will only get you so far."

I just nod. I don't want to go to Yale, but according to my grandfather, it's my only option. I haven't even thought about where I want to go to college, but Yale is too close to home. I need to go somewhere far away. Maybe California.

"Holton, don't pressure the boy," my grandmother says. "He's only 15."

"He's not a child, Eleanor. I had Pearce working at the company at 16. It's time Garret stepped up and started taking on more responsibility."

"What's everyone discussing out here?" my dad asks as he meets us in the hall.

"Garret's future," my grandfather says. "We need to get him working at the company after school and on weekends."

My dad puts his arm around me, which he rarely does. "He's not working there, Father. He's only 15. He needs to focus on school."

"He'd have time to work there if he wasn't wasting all his time on sports and in that damn pool."

"Holton!" Eleanor says, shielding Lilly's ears. "Don't use such words around the children."

"Why don't you two go into the dining room?" my dad says. "Dinner will be starting shortly." He takes Lilly, and my grandparents go down the hall and into the dining room.

My dad kisses Lilly's cheek. "Thank you for taking care of her tonight," he says to me.

"After I have dinner with her, I have to go."

"Go where?"

"To Blake's house. He's having Decker and some other people over."

"You're not allowed to go out on school nights."

"And yet you make me *babysit* on a school night. And you don't even pay me for it. The least you could do is let me hang out with my friends for an hour or two."

He sighs. "Is your homework done?"

"Yes." It's not entirely true. I still have math problems to work on.

He considers it, then says, "Will Blake's parents be there?"

"Yeah. You can call them if you don't believe me."

My dad has no idea that Blake's parents actually encourage him and his friends to party and drink. Blake's dad is the state attorney general so my dad assumes the guy is really strict, but he's not at all. But I'd never tell my dad that.

He sighs again. "Fine. But you need to be home by ten." He hands me Lilly, then goes back to the dining room.

Lilly and I go down to the kitchen. Charles has dinner plated and waiting on the kitchen table.

"Hi, Garret." He smiles. "How was your day?"

Charles is the only one who ever asks me that. On most days, I talk to Charles more than I talk to my dad.

"It was okay. I got a B plus on that English paper."

34

If I said that to my dad, he'd have no clue what I'm talking about.

"That's great! I know you spent a lot of time on it." He wipes the counter down. "How was swim practice?"

"Awesome." I set Lilly in her high chair and she kicks and screams. She always wants to eat sitting on my lap. I lift her out of the chair and sit down at the table with her. She's happy again now that she's on my lap. I reach over and take her plate off the high chair tray and set it next to mine.

"I beat my own time today at practice," I say to Charles. "Coach said if I get just a little faster, I'll break a school record."

I reach around Lilly to cut my piece of chicken. Hers is already cut into small chunks and she's eating it with her fingers. It's hard to eat my meal with a constantly moving toddler on my lap, but it's better than having her scream.

Charles sits across from us. "The English paper? Your swim times? That's a lot of accomplishments in one day."

I shrug. "Wish my dad thought so," I mumble, but I'm sure Charles heard.

"If your mother—" He stops, because he's not supposed to talk about her. He gets up and goes to the sink.

"If my mother *what?*" I ask him. "My dad's not here. You can say it."

He turns to me and smiles. "She'd be very proud of you. And if she knew you were still swimming…well, it would make her very happy."

"Yeah." I gaze down at my plate. I'm not really hungry anymore.

Thinking about my mom always makes me miss her, and when I miss her, I feel sick. I want her back. I want to go back in time and save her. I almost stopped her from going on that trip, and I always tell myself that if I'd just tried harder, maybe she never would've gone. Then she'd be alive, and my dad would be happy, and I'd be happy, and we wouldn't live in this giant house with that bitch, Katherine.

Why did the plane crash have to happen? Everything was so perfect, and then it all ended and it's never been the same.

"Garrah!" Lilly's holding a piece of carrot up to my face. I pretend to bite her fingers as I take it from her. She laughs and falls back on my chest.

"Come on, Lilly." I point to her plate. "You need to eat your dinner."

She sits up again and picks at her chicken. But I've lost all interest in mine.

"Remember that day?" I ask Charles. "When I asked her to stay?"

That day is still so fresh in my mind. Like it happened just yesterday. My mom, Dad, and I had gone out for pancakes in the morning, then went to my basketball game in the afternoon. Charles was at our house that day, making cookies for a bake sale.

He sets his dish rag down, his face serious. "Yes. I remember. But I'd already left when you asked her."

"But before you left, my mom seemed happy, right? I mean, she wanted to go?"

"Garret." He comes back to the table. "You shouldn't relive this. You can't go back and change it."

"I know. But just tell me."

"Yes. She wanted to go. She was excited about it. She and your dad hadn't been on a trip together, just the two of them, for a long time."

"Dad won't tell me anything about that weekend. I've asked him, but he won't tell me."

"It's hard for him to talk about."

"It's been five years. By now, he should be able to tell me." I set my fork on my plate. "I don't even have a photo of her."

Charles sighs. "Your father never should've thrown those out."

"I went online and printed out the ones I could find of her. There weren't that many, but at least it's something. Don't tell my dad."

"I won't." He pauses. "Garret, maybe you should see someone again."

"I'm not going to counseling again. I've talked about it enough. Like you said, I can't change the past."

36

Katherine storms into the kitchen. "Charles, the potatoes were completely overcooked!"

He rolls his eyes as he stands up, but he's facing me so only I could see his eye roll. I laugh.

"What's so funny?" Katherine asks.

"You. Complaining about the potatoes, when millions of people are starving right now."

"What is she doing?" Katherine points to Lilly, who's stuffing a piece of chicken in her mouth.

"Eating her dinner," I answer, knowing that's not what she's asking. But I like pissing Katherine off. I used to try to get along with her, but it was completely pointless. No matter what I say, she finds a way to turn it into a fight.

"What is she doing on your LAP instead of in her CHAIR?" she asks, her voice raised.

"She didn't like the chair," I say casually, as I take a bite of potatoes. "They're not overcooked," I say to Charles. He gives me a smile, but Katherine can't see it because he's facing the sink.

"She needs to be in her high chair, Garret. It is unacceptable for…"

She keeps talking but I just ignore her. I check the clock. It's almost eight. Lilly has eaten most of her dinner, so I push my chair back and get up and take Lilly over to Katherine.

"She's all yours." I hold her in front of me.

She steps back, motioning to her white dress. "I can't take her. Her hands are a mess."

"You're saying you won't hold your own daughter?"

Charles comes over and takes her. "I'll clean her up." He takes her to the sink and starts wiping her hands.

I turn to leave and hear Katherine yelling at me, "Where are you going? You have to watch her!"

"I'm going out. Dad said it was okay."

"But we have two more courses to be served!" she yells as I walk away. She cares more about her dinner party than her daughter. Worst. Mother. Ever!

I go up to my room and change clothes and put on some cologne. I'm only going out tonight so I can drink. I've been drinking a lot lately and my dad doesn't even care. Not that I want him yelling at me about my drinking. No kid wants that. But the fact that I can come home completely drunk and he doesn't even say anything just proves that he's given up on me. He doesn't even care enough to save me from my own destructive habits. So I just keep doing them.

If I keep drinking this much, I'll probably become an alcoholic before I even get to college, especially since no one's trying to stop me. Part of me keeps hoping that one of these days, my dad will notice what I'm doing and ground me or punish me some other way. At least that would show that he cared.

When I get back downstairs, I go outside and see Blake's driver waiting for me. I was expecting to see a car, but it's a limo. The driver opens the door for me and I get inside.

"Garret!" the girls yell all at once.

There are four girls in the limo, including Ava. Blake and Decker are also there, along with two other guys from my school.

Ava crawls over one of the girls and sits on my lap. She's wearing a very short skirt. So short that I'm sure her exposed ass is touching my jeans right now. She wraps her arms around my neck. "Hey." She bites her lip, then leans closer and whispers in my ear, "I'm all yours tonight if you want me."

See? It's too easy. I like more of a chase. But I'm not stupid. I'll take sex if she's offering. But I'm not going to be her boyfriend. I never want a girlfriend. Or a wife. Marriage equals misery. Just look at my dad and Katherine. Couldn't get more miserable than that.

My dad got lucky with my mom. She was his soulmate, and he somehow found her. But that almost never happens. And losing her almost killed him. He hasn't been the same since she died. So falling in love? Getting married? It's not for me. I'm going to be a bachelor forever.

Ava is kissing me now, trying to shove her tongue down my throat. She needs to work on her kissing. Again, she's too aggressive. She needs to let the guy make the moves.

I back away.

"What's wrong?" she asks.

I nod toward the rest of the limo. "I don't like an audience."

She smiles. "Oh." She turns toward them, but remains on my lap.

One of the other girls is hanging all over Blake while Decker sits next to them, looking depressed that he can't get a girl. He'll drink his sorrows away tonight, and by tomorrow he'll be fine.

We get to Blake's house, which is huge, but not nearly as big as mine. He takes us to a big open room with couches, a pool table, two giant TVs, and a bar.

"Line up for shots." Blake starts pulling liquor bottles out from behind the bar.

I'm first in line and do three shots of vodka, one after the other. I need to get wasted tonight. I can't handle the pain I'm feeling right now. This is why my dad won't talk about my mom. It's too hard. It brings back memories, and those memories make the pain even worse.

Why didn't I work harder to get her to stay home that weekend? Why didn't I cry and scream and beg her to stay? It's my fault she's dead right now. It's all my fault. If I'd just tried harder.

The guilt. The pain. It's too much. I need to bury it before it consumes me.

Blake keeps pouring shots and I keep drinking them, the pain gradually going away and my mind drifting off into a hazy state of consciousness.

I feel Ava on top of me, kissing me, and I hear her asking me to go into a room. Maybe I will later. But not right now.

For now, I just want to keep drinking. Letting the pain slip away. The memories. Memories of my mom. My old life. Before it all went to hell.

CHAPTER FIVE

PEARCE

"Pearce." Katherine appears in the dining room, holding Lilly. "Your son just took off and now we have no one to watch Lilly." Katherine says it as though having to care for her own daughter is a huge inconvenience and something she has no interest in doing.

"Just give her to me," I say. "She can sit here while we have dessert."

"A toddler cannot be at a dinner party, Pearce," she says.

"I agree," my father says. "We can't have an adult conversation with a crying child present."

My father was the same way when Garret was a baby. He didn't want him around. He can't stand being anywhere near a child who's under the age of ten, or any child who can't sit still and be quiet.

"She's not crying," I say. "She'll be fine if I hold her."

"Pearce." Katherine uses her warning tone. "Take her upstairs. It's her bedtime. She's all wound up because of your son and you're the only one who can get her to sleep when she's like this."

"I can take her upstairs," my mother offers.

"It's HIS child," Leland says. "HE should do it."

I'm trying to control my temper, but I'd like to strangle Leland. He's made rude comments about me all through dinner, but I've kept quiet because I told Katherine I wouldn't argue with him tonight. But it's difficult to keep quiet when all he does is put me down. Between him and my father, the insults have been nonstop all through dinner. And now Leland is ordering me to take care of Lilly when his daughter is perfectly capable of doing it herself.

40

"I don't mind," my mother says as she pushes her chair out.

"Eleanor," my father says. "It is not your job to put that child to bed."

I don't want this escalating into a family fight, so I say, "I'll take her upstairs. Go ahead and have dessert without me."

I get up from my chair and take Lilly from Katherine, glaring at her as I do. The woman needs to stop neglecting our daughter and embrace her role as a mother. But she refuses to do so. When I'm not around, she makes Garret take care of Lilly, which isn't fair to him. He's not a live-in babysitter. He loves Lilly, and he's very good with her, but it's not his job to watch her all the time.

"Daddy." Lilly hugs me as we're going up the stairs.

When we get to her room, I get her pajamas out of the dresser and set her down to change her out of her dress.

"No, Daddy." She won't let me go. She clings to me, probably because she never sees me.

It reminds me of when Garret was a baby. The first year of his life, I worked all the time and hardly ever saw him, so in the rare times that I did, he'd cling to me just like Lilly is doing now. He was desperate for me to spend time with him, yet I kept working all those hours. It wasn't until Rachel almost threatened to leave me that I finally woke up and put my family before my job.

Now I can't seem to do that. I know Lilly needs me. I know Garret does too. Yet I keep working a hundred hours a week. I can't stop myself, and Katherine will never tell me to work less. She likes not having me around. I could be gone for weeks and she wouldn't even notice or care.

I'm doing my best to get along with Katherine but it's nearly impossible. She starts a fight over every little thing. After everyone leaves tonight, she'll fight with me over the fact that I allowed Garret to go out with his friends instead of babysitting Lilly. And instead of keeping quiet, I'll fight back, because I'm sick and tired of her ordering my son around like he's her servant. We'll argue until I eventually give up because I can't take it anymore.

That's one reason why I work so much. To get away from Katherine and the constant fighting we do. I try not to fight with her but she knows which buttons to push to set me off. Those buttons are either Garret or Rachel. Katherine knows I can't control my anger when she says bad things about my son or my wife.

I still consider Rachel to be my wife. She's not my dead wife. She's just my wife. She always will be. She's the only woman I'll ever consider my wife. Both my first wife and Katherine were arranged marriages so the 'wife' title is meaningless. Rachel was my real wife. The only woman I have ever loved and *will* ever love. My heart will always belong to her, even though she's gone.

I still think about her all the time. I dream about her. I even sometimes talk to her in my head. I miss her to the point that I can't even say her name. It hurts too much. I put all the photos of her in a box so I wouldn't have to look at them, but I still do. I keep them hidden away in my office, and when I need to see her, I take one out and just stare at the woman who still owns my heart.

Garret thinks I threw her photos away. I told him I did because it would be too hard for him to see them. He misses her as much as I do and I'm trying to help him move on. *I* never will, but maybe he can.

"Daddy." Lilly is now in her pink pajamas and lying on my chest as I sit in the white upholstered chair next to her crib. She's playing with my tie but her eyes are getting sleepy. If I keep holding her, she'll eventually fall asleep, then I'll put her in her crib.

"Go to sleep, honey." I kiss her head and rub her back.

She's a sweet little girl and very affectionate. She's always trying to hug people. I'm sure Garret taught her that. He's always hugging her, just like Rachel used to do with him. He's still so much like Rachel that I struggle just being around him sometimes. He'll say something or do something that she would do, and it sparks a memory of her. Garret can't help that. It's not his fault that he's like her, and I need to stop blaming him for it and pushing him away because of it.

A few minutes later, Lilly's asleep. I consider staying up here with her so I don't have to go back downstairs. But if I take too much longer, Katherine will be up here yelling at me. I set Lilly in her crib and put the blanket over her, then quietly leave the room.

When I get back to the dining room, everyone's having after-dinner drinks.

"What took so long?" Katherine asks. She's definitely in a fighting mood. I might have to go back to the office tonight just to avoid her.

I return to my seat at the end of the table. "I wanted to make sure she was asleep before I put her in the crib."

"If Garret hadn't riled her up, she would've gone to sleep right away."

The room is quiet as my parents and her parents look at us both. They know we don't get along. They know this marriage is a business arrangement. They also know we can't get divorced, so they just smile and act like nothing's wrong. Our parents don't care if we're happy or not, especially our fathers.

After I married Katherine, Leland used his connections with the military to help Kensington Chemical win several large government contracts. We didn't need them. The company has already experienced substantial growth since I took over as CEO, but my father is chairman of the board and feels the need to interfere where he shouldn't. He worked with Leland directly to get these government contracts, not even telling me it was being done. I was furious that he did that, but my father thinks I should thank him for it. I never did and I never will.

"So Pearce, have you started looking at colleges yet?" Leland asks.

I was just about to suggest we end the dinner, but then Leland had to open his mouth again.

"Are we talking about colleges for Garret?" I ask.

He laughs. "Well, obviously, given that Lilly is only two."

"I realize that, but you normally don't ask about Garret."

"Pearce," Katherine scolds. "Be polite."

When she scolds me in public like that, I want to strangle her.

"Garret is going to Yale," my father says. "It's where I went and where Pearce went."

"Maybe he's more suited to Moorhurst," Leland says, dabbing his mouth with his napkin.

Katherine glares at him. "What are you saying, Father?"

43

"I'm saying that not everyone can go to Yale. But Moorhurst is a fine alternative."

Katherine and her sister are very competitive when it comes to pleasing their father, and Katherine is currently losing the battle. Caroline, Leland's other daughter, went to Yale and graduated with honors. Katherine went to Moorhurst and barely graduated. So Caroline is currently Leland's favorite child, but that doesn't stop Katherine from trying to win that title.

"My grandson is NOT going to Moorhurst." My father is trying to control his temper, but we can all see his anger as his face tightens and his eyes narrow. "He is going to Yale."

Leland smirks. "We'll see."

My father hits the table with his fist. "That boy has a future! There are plans for him!"

"What plans?" I ask.

My father clears his throat. "I'm simply referring to the fact that Garret will someday be CEO of Kensington Chemical. A future CEO does not attend a school like Moorhurst."

Katherine's pouting at the other end of the table. She's just been insulted by both our fathers. Good. Now she'll know what I feel like on a daily basis.

"I think it's time for us to go," my mother says. "That last drink made me very tired, and it's getting late."

"Yes." I stand up. "We should call it a night. But thank you all for coming. I hope you enjoyed your dinner."

"The potatoes were overdone," my father says as he rises from his chair. "You need to hire a different cook."

"I could recommend one," my mother says.

"Please do," Katherine says. "We've been looking to replace Charles for months now."

"We are NOT hiring a new cook," I say forcefully.

Everyone stares at me. I guess I said it more forcefully than I thought. But I am not firing Charles. And for the record, the potatoes were not overcooked.

"Mother." I offer her my arm and lead her out of the room so that the others will follow.

"Give Lilly a kiss for me," she says as we walk to the door. "I didn't get to say goodbye to her."

"I will. But you also didn't say goodbye to Garret."

We're in the foyer now and everyone is getting their coats from the maid.

My mother pulls me aside. "You need to get that boy under control. One of these days he's going to do something to embarrass the family."

"He's just struggling right now. He's still adjusting to not having his mother around and to all the changes he's had to deal with."

"That's no excuse. Death happens to everyone. It's a part of life. And it's been five years since she died. You can't continue to let her death be an excuse for Garret to behave this way."

She's referring to his drinking. He's been drinking with his friends and been drunk a few times. I don't know how she knows this, but I'm assuming one of her friends told her. Their grandchildren go to Garret's school and perhaps he's getting a reputation there that is spreading to the parents and grandparents.

"Eleanor," my father says, holding her coat.

"Yes. I'm coming." She puts her coat on and we say our goodbyes.

Then Leland and Audrey leave. Luckily they're not spending the night. Leland has a meeting in Manhattan tomorrow morning so they're spending the night there.

As soon as the door shuts, Katherine whips around, her hands on her hips. "We need to discuss the incident with Garret tonight. He ruined our entire dinner!"

She sounds like a spoiled child. Next she'll be stomping her foot and sticking her tongue out.

"Garret did not ruin dinner. It is not his job to babysit our daughter. He's still a child himself, and he should be doing his homework or out with his friends, not caring for a toddler. Lilly is our responsibility, not his. And I'm sick and tired of you not doing your job as a mother."

"I'm here with her all day!" she yells. "And all night because you're never around!"

"You make the maids or Charles take care of Lilly during the day. And you make Garret take care of her at night."

She pauses, probably wondering how I know this. I know because Garret told me. When I'm not home, he said Katherine treats the maids as if they're nannies, even though childcare is not their job. And she makes Charles feed Lilly her meals.

"This isn't about me," she says. "This is about Garret. He was supposed to watch Lilly tonight and instead, he just took off. You need to deal with him, Pearce, or I'm sending him off to boarding school again."

"Garret is not going to boarding school. He will continue to live with us and you will stop ordering him around. He does not work for you. He is not an employee. He is my son, and he is part of this family."

"He is an irresponsible brat! And I'm not letting—"

"Stop!" I scream it so loud it echoes in the foyer. I go up to her and hold her shoulders, my eyes on hers. "You are DONE putting him down. Ordering him around. Fighting with him. It all ends now. Do you understand me?"

"I'm not taking orders from you. Just because Rachel was submissive to your demands doesn't mean I will be. I'm stronger than she ever was."

I clench my jaw, trying to control my temper, but it doesn't work. I turn and storm into my office and slam the door and lock it.

Another fight, instigated by Katherine. She said Rachel's name and insulted her, two things she knows will make me furious. And she does this after insulting my son.

Her heels click on the tile as she walks away, likely with a big smile on her face for getting a reaction out of me. She loves making me angry.

I turn on my computer and try to do some work, but now my mind's on Rachel. She's all I can think about.

Hours pass and Garret still isn't home. I told him to be home at ten and it's now almost eleven-thirty. I'm worried. What if something happened to him? He won't answer his phone if he sees I'm the one calling him. I'll have to call Blake's parents. As I'm looking up their number, I hear a car outside.

I leave my office and see Garret stumbling in the front door.

"Garret?" I close the door behind him, then help him to the stairs. He can barely walk. I've never seen him this drunk.

"Dad," he mumbles.

"How much did you drink?"

He shrugs. "I don't know."

"Let's go to your room." I get a firm grip on him and drag him up the stairs.

How did this happen? Why is he so drunk? He said Blake's parents would be home, but they obviously weren't. I should've called them before he left to make sure they were there.

"Garret, we need to talk about your drinking." I help him onto his bed.

He lies facedown, his arms spread out on both sides. I remove his shoes and get a blanket from his closet. He's too drunk to change clothes or get under the covers. I lay the blanket over him. His eyes are closed. I'll have to talk to him about this tomorrow, although I don't know when I'll have time. I have meetings from early in the morning until late at night.

My life is such a mess. Work is out of control. Katherine is out of control. My son is out of control. And I can't seem to make any of it better.

If Rachel were here, she would be ashamed of me. She would never let Garret drink like this, or even drink at all. And she'd never let him stay out this late on a school night. He probably wouldn't even want to go out if she were here. He used to like being home with us, but now he hates being home.

"Dad?" I hear Garret mumble.

I sit next to him on the bed. "Yes, Garret."

"I'm sorry," he whispers.

"About what?" I start to panic, thinking maybe he did something illegal or got into some other kind of trouble. "Did something happen?"

"I'm sorry...about Mom." His eyes are closed and he's slurring his words.

I'm not sure why he said that, but people say strange things when they're drunk.

"I'm going to let you sleep this off." I get up from his bed. "We'll talk tomorrow."

He starts mumbling again. "I'm sorry I didn't stop her."

I sit down again. "What are you talking about?"

"I should've stopped her. I tried, Dad. I really tried. But she still left."

Stopped her? What does he mean?

"Garret, I don't understand what you're saying. Stopped her from what?"

He turns on his side, his eyes still closed. "From going to DC. I told her not to go, but I didn't try hard enough. And now she's dead."

He blames himself for her death? How the hell could he even think that? It's not his fault.

The day Rachel and I flew to DC, Garret was only 10 and he begged her not to go. I couldn't figure out why he was acting like that. He didn't usually get that upset when we went somewhere. But that day, it's almost like he knew. Like he sensed something bad was going to happen, so he begged her not to go.

"Garret, look at me." I hold onto his shoulder and wait for his eyes to open. "It was not your fault. Don't even think that."

"It WAS my fault. I should've stopped her and I didn't. I killed her, Dad." Tears stream down his face. "It was all my fault."

I pull him up from the bed and force him into a hug. "Don't say that, Garret. Don't you ever say that again. It was not your fault. It was nobody's fault. It was an accident. It was just an accident."

"She wouldn't have been on the plane if I'd stopped her. I screwed up. And now she's dead."

Is that really what he thinks? That he could've prevented it from happening? Does he live with this guilt every day? God, I hope not. Because I already live with it, and it nearly kills me. I keep blaming myself for her death. Telling myself it's my fault she got on that plane. I'm the one who suggested she take that earlier flight. I encouraged her to do so. If anyone's to blame, it's me.

"It's not your fault, Garret." I hug him tighter.

"I'm sorry, Dad." He sniffles. "I'm sorry."

He's been hiding this from me for all these years. The guilt. The false idea that he somehow had control over what happened.

Maybe I should get him into counseling again, but I know he won't agree to it. And now that he's older, it's harder to force him to do things.

I don't know how to help him. I'd like to think that spending time with him would help, but our relationship has become so strained the past few years that we fight whenever we're together. Or we just don't talk. Or I ask him questions and he gives me the silent treatment. I don't know how to get through to him. I feel like I've already lost him and it's too late. Tonight is the first time in years that I've felt like we're connecting.

After a few minutes, I lower him back down to the bed. He's falling asleep so I cover him again with the blanket. I don't think I should leave him in here alone when he's this drunk. He might get sick and need help. So I take the chair from his desk and sit next to the bed and just watch him sleep. Just like I used to do when he was an infant. After a stressful day at work or after an assignment, it used to calm me to watch him sleep. Even now, I find it calming. He's my son and I love him and he's my only connection to Rachel, and all of that is calming to me.

If only I hadn't been forced to marry Katherine. Garret and I would've been much better off on our own. Just the two of us. But then I wouldn't have Lilly. She's the only good thing that came out of my marriage to Katherine.

I remain at Garret's side, falling asleep in the chair. Around four a.m., he wakes up with a hangover. I wait in the bathroom while he throws up, then I get him some water and aspirin. I thought he'd tell me to go away, like he always does, but he didn't. He goes back to sleep and I go to my room to get ready for work.

Katherine wakes up when I enter the bedroom. "Where have you been all night?" She uses a tone that implies I was out cheating on her.

"I was helping Garret. He got sick in the night."

"Because he was drunk again? If he's that drunk, then let him suffer in his own vomit. It'll teach him a lesson for once. You can't keep rescuing him, Pearce."

I go in the bathroom and shut and lock the door. She's trying to start another fight, but I won't do it. I'm exhausted and I'm not going to waste energy fighting with her.

After I'm showered and dressed for work, I go down to Lilly's room to check on her. She's sound asleep, looking adorable with her pink pajamas and blond curls.

I gently touch her head. "Goodbye, honey. I'll see you tonight."

Next I go to Garret's room. He's awake, tossing and turning.

"Garret." I sit next to him on the bed. "How are you feeling?"

"Like my head's going to explode."

"Yes, well, you'll probably feel like that until this afternoon."

"I can't go to school."

"You're going to school."

"I can't. My head hurts too bad."

"Which is why you're going. Suffering through a day of high school with a hangover will make you never want to drink again."

"So you're punishing me? But I'm sick."

"I'm looking out for you. I don't want you getting drunk like that again."

He sighs and turns away from me.

I nudge his back. "Hey."

"What?" he groans.

"Turn around."

He reluctantly rolls back over until he's facing me. "What?"

"Do you remember what you said to me last night?"

"Yeah," he says softly.

"Is that really how you feel? Do you blame yourself?"

He closes his eyes. "I don't want to talk about it."

"It's not your fault, Garret. I don't know why you ever thought that it was, but you need to know that she wanted to go with me on that trip. You wouldn't have been able to stop her."

He opens his eyes and looks at me. "She would've stayed if I'd begged her not to go."

50

Maybe I shouldn't tell him this. I wasn't going to because I didn't think he needed to know. But if it will help relieve his guilt in any way, then I need to tell him.

"Garret, your mother wanted to go with me that weekend. We'd been planning it for months."

"Why? It was just a dumb political thing."

"The fundraiser was not the only reason we went. That Sunday was a special day for us. We were celebrating. That's why she wanted to go."

"What were you celebrating?" Garret sits up, leaning against the headboard.

"If I tell you this, you can't tell anyone. Only a few people know this. So will you keep this a secret?"

"Yeah, okay."

"That Sunday was our wedding anniversary. The real one. The wedding we had in March was fake. It was just for show. Your mother and I got married in November, right before Thanksgiving."

"Why would you have a real wedding and a fake wedding?"

"Your grandparents didn't approve of your mother, so if we'd told them we were getting married, they would've tried to stop us."

"What are you saying? You eloped?"

"Yes. We flew to Las Vegas and got married and didn't tell anyone."

"Are you serious?"

"Yes."

"Why didn't you tell me this?"

"Your mother and I planned to tell you when you were older. But after hearing how you feel about that day we left, I think now is the right time to tell you. It was our anniversary trip, Garret. We had it all planned. Your mother wanted to go. You couldn't have stopped her. So please, don't blame yourself. Stop feeling guilty about this."

He nods.

I lean over and hug him. "I need to get to the office. Are you okay?"

"Yeah." He's gazing down at the blanket, but then looks up again. "Wait. So you only knew each other three months before you got married?"

"Yes."

"That's really fast."

"I didn't need more time. I knew she was the one. I knew from the day I laid eyes on her." I smile thinking of that day she walked in late to my speech. "I'll see you tonight." As I'm walking to the door, I say, "I'll be calling the school later to see if you're there. And if you're not, I'll be taking you there myself."

"Dad, I can't go."

"You can go. Get in the shower. And drink some water. You need to learn never to do this again. Goodbye, Garret."

I leave feeling like I actually acted like a father for once. Now if I could just keep it up.

CHAPTER SIX
Four Years Later

RACHEL

It's October. I used to love October. Pearce and I would take Garret to buy pumpkins. We'd have scary movie marathons. I'd bake my famous apple cobbler, which was Pearce's favorite dessert. I'd make pumpkin-shaped sugar cookies and Garret and I would decorate them. Then right before Halloween, I'd take Garret to the mall to pick out his costume.

Every year, I looked forward to October, but now it's just another month. Another passage of time in this place that is not my home. I've tried to leave. Several times. But each time I've tried, they've stopped me.

The first time was a week after I got that video message from Holton. I wanted to see if he really had people watching me, or if he just said that to scare me. I packed my bag and was going to go to Naples and stay at a hotel near the airport, as if I was really leaving. I called a taxi and left late at night.

The taxi drove out of town, then stopped suddenly on the side of the road in a desolate area. It was dark and I was scared, unsure what the driver was doing. I asked him why he stopped but he didn't answer. He just sat in the front seat, not saying anything. The back door opened and a man in a black ski mask yanked me out of the taxi and shoved me into a black sedan.

"What did he tell you?" the man yelled at me. He sounded like one of the men who came to my room that night I got that message from Holton. "Answer me!" the man yelled from the front seat, his gloved hands gripping the steering wheel.

I was shaking and stammering. "I...I don't know who you're talking about."

"Do you want to live?"

"Yes. Of course."

"Then answer me! What did he tell you?"

"Not to...not to try to leave."

The man started the car and drove away. I wasn't sure where he was taking me, but then he turned around and drove the other way, back toward my apartment.

"Do you know about my son?" I asked. "He's not going to hurt him, is he? Please, tell me what—"

"Shut the fuck up!" he barked. I kept quiet until we got back. He stopped in front of my building. "Don't try it again."

But I didn't listen. I tried again a few months later, except that time, I attempted to leave with Raul, a man who works at the meat market in town. He supplies meat for Celia's restaurant so I see him all the time. One day, I heard him tell Celia he had to take his sister to the airport the following day. I asked if I could ride along. It was spring, and it's a beautiful drive, so I just told him I wanted to go on a drive. He agreed to it, happy to have some company for the drive back.

The night before I was supposed to go, I found a note on my dresser saying that if I went with Raul, there would be consequences. Someone had broken into my apartment and left the note. So I told Raul I couldn't go.

Ever since then, I've felt trapped. I can't even leave this tiny village. Holton is keeping me isolated within a five mile radius so that I can't get any information about my old life. This town doesn't have Internet access, so I can't look anything up. I can't check on Pearce or Garret to make sure they're okay, or to see their photos, or see what's going on in their lives.

I can't even call them. I've tried, several times, but each time I do, the phone goes dead. I even tried to call Martha but the call wouldn't go through. I don't know how Holton does it. He must have some kind of sophisticated equipment that blocks all outgoing calls I try to make. After repeated attempts to call home, I got a warning letter in my room saying Pearce, Garret, or I would be hurt if I tried calling home again. So I haven't. I'm too scared of what Holton might do.

Holton has me imprisoned here, with no way to contact anyone. And I'm sure he's loving every minute of it. He's probably sitting in his mansion right now with that smirk on his face, pleased with himself for what he's done.

Celia is getting more and more worried about me because I never go anywhere. It's been years since we took that trip to Naples, and since then, I haven't left this town. I used to tell her how much I love traveling and going to new places, so she keeps offering to take me to Rome for a weekend, or to Sicily, but I have to keep turning her down. She asks why, but I don't give her an answer. I can't. She can't know what's going on. If I told her, I'm sure Holton's men would kill her.

Celia also keeps inviting me to go to Naples with her, and every time she asks, I have to tell her no. Last month, I finally just said yes to see if I'd get another note. I didn't tell anyone I was going. Only Celia knew. And yet, a warning note was there on my dresser the day before we were supposed to leave. That's when I realized they were listening in on my conversations. They had the restaurant bugged and probably my apartment as well.

Despite all this, I haven't given up. I'm determined to see Pearce and Garret again. That determination is what keeps me going. Holton has to die eventually, and when he does, maybe those men will stop watching me. But I'm worried Holton may have told someone else to watch me after he dies, like maybe Leland, who has a vested interest in keeping me away since his daughter is married to Pearce. But I'm still going to try to escape. I just don't know when.

How will I know when Holton dies? I have no way of knowing. I could ask someone to look it up for me the next time they're somewhere that has Internet access, but the person would think I'm crazy for asking such an odd question. And I know I'd be caught just for asking. They'd hear me ask and then send me another warning. Or I'd be punished. So as of now, I haven't figured out what I'm going to do. The only thing I know is that I'm not giving up. As long as I'm alive, I'm going to keep trying.

55

"Can I get you another coffee?" I ask the customer I'm waiting on.

I still work at Celia's restaurant and I still rent out the studio apartment upstairs. I also still tutor English. Nothing has changed in years. It's like I'm living the same day over and over again.

"I suppose I could have one more," the man says.

He's American. He told me he's from New York. He's in Italy on business, but had some free time so decided to take a drive, which led him here. I don't even know this man and yet I feel a connection to him because he's American.

We don't get many American tourists so when I heard his New York accent, my heart sped up a little. I got this sudden spark of hope. It's because of a dream I had a few nights ago. In the dream, I told an American tourist to contact Pearce, and he did, and then Pearce came here and got me and finally brought me home.

What if I actually did that? What if I asked this man to contact Pearce? He might find it odd, but who cares? I don't get many opportunities like this. I could just ask. The man could always say no.

I get his coffee, and when I bring it back I notice he's reading a financial newspaper. He looks like he's in his fifties. He's wearing a gray suit and a very expensive watch.

"Do you work in finance?" I ask him.

He looks up from the paper. "Yes. Banking. On Wall Street."

"That must be very interesting."

"At times it is." He smiles. "Are you from the U.S.?"

"Yes."

"How did you end up in Italy?"

"I came here on vacation and fell in love with this town and ended up moving here."

"How long have you been here?"

Years ago I would've been afraid to tell him. But now? I don't care. I'm desperate to get out of here and this man may be able to help me.

"I've been here about nine years. If you'd like a quick tour of the town, I'd be happy to give you one."

"Actually, yes, that would be nice." He says it flirtatiously and smiles even wider.

Does he think I was flirting with him? Maybe this is a bad idea. But I have to try to get a message to Pearce, and I can't talk to this man in the restaurant, where I know Holton's men could be listening.

"I'm Michael, by the way."

"Jill." I shake his hand as he gets up. "Just let me tell my boss." I hurry back to the kitchen. "Celia, one of the customers wanted a quick tour of the town. I'll just be gone a few minutes."

She smiles. "The handsome American?"

Handsome? I don't think he's handsome.

"Yes, the American."

She waves me on. "Go ahead."

"Okay," I say to Michael, motioning him to the door.

As we walk down the narrow street, I describe the architecture of the old buildings and the history of the town. I know everything there is to know about this place after living here for so long. If we had more tourists, I actually could give tours.

"You know your history," he says as we're walking back. "You should be working in a museum, not a restaurant."

If he only knew. Maybe he'll remember this and tell Pearce.

"Actually, I studied history back in college. I even have a graduate degree in it."

"Where did you go to grad school?"

"Hirshfield College." I'm nervous just saying it. This is the first time I've told anyone the truth about me since I got here. But I need to give him details. Details he can give Pearce.

"In New Haven?" he asks.

"Yes. Do you someone who went there?"

"The daughter of one of my business associates goes there. She's a freshman. So if you have a history degree, why aren't you giving tours at a museum? I heard you speaking Italian earlier. It sounds like you're fluent in it."

"I am, but I really wanted to live in this town and, as you can see, it doesn't have any museums. Besides, I studied American History in college."

"Are you from Connecticut?"

"No. I grew up on a farm in Indiana, in a really small town. About the only thing there is a country bar." I know this guy would never remember the town's name, so I mentioned the country bar where Pearce and I went, hoping it might be something he'll remember to tell Pearce.

"Do you ever go back there?"

"No. My parents died in a car accident so it's not really home anymore."

I need to tell him something else. These are all facts he could've just looked up. I need to tell him something that will get Pearce's attention. Because I can't just come out and tell this man who I am. For one, he probably wouldn't believe me. Everyone thinks I'm dead. And if *did* believe me, he'd probably tell the media, and then Holton would order his men to kill me before anyone could save me. Even if I instructed Michael to only tell Pearce, and no one else, I don't trust that he'd listen to me. I just met this man and I don't trust him enough to tell him the truth. I'm almost certain he'd tell the media and then I'd be dead. So I can't tell him who I am. But I *can* give him clues to give Pearce.

We're almost back at the restaurant. I need to come up with something else to say. Something only Pearce would know.

"I'm sorry about your parents," Michael says. "Do you have any other family back home?"

"No, but I have a close friend that I'd love to see again. I haven't talked to him in years."

"You should call him."

"I would, but he's married now, and his wife gets extremely jealous if a woman calls, even if it's just an old friend." I stop walking and so does he. "Is there any way you could maybe call him just to tell him I said hello? I think he'd get a kick out of hearing that you ran into me in this tiny town in Italy."

I take a few steps back, worried there might be microphones hidden outside the restaurant.

"Um, I don't know," he says. "He might find that rather odd, having a stranger calling him."

58

"You could just say that we're friends. I know we just met, but we're fellow Americans and I served you breakfast and gave you a tour, which kind of makes us friends, right?"

He smiles. "I suppose it does. So what is this man's name?" He gets his phone out.

"No." I cover his phone with my hand. "Don't put it in there."

If Holton's men are watching and see this man typing something into his phone, they'll get suspicious.

Michael's holding his phone, giving me a strange look.

I smile. "What I mean is that you don't need to write it down. His name is Pearce Kensington."

He slides his phone into his pants pocket. "Are you talking about THE Pearce Kensington? The CEO of Kensington Chemical?"

"Yes, that's the one. So you know who he is?"

"Of course. Everyone in the business world does. I've heard him speak at conferences many times. He's an excellent speaker. And a brilliant businessman."

My heart soars hearing him talk about Pearce. This is the closest I've felt to him in years. It's like I'm connecting with him through this man.

"Can you please call him for me?"

He laughs. "I'm afraid I can't. Someone like Pearce Kensington wouldn't even answer my call. I'm sure his secretary screens all his calls."

"Please just try. Tell him thank you for the Christmas ornament. He gave me an angel that I used to keep on the mantel after my parents died."

Now he's looking at me like I'm crazy. "Um, I'm just going to get my things and head out." He walks off.

I catch up to him. "Please. I can't call the U.S. from here. The infrastructure here is so dated that the phones barely work, even for local calls. Please just call him. Tell him you saw me here. Please."

"Yes, fine." He says it like he's brushing me off.

Shit. I totally screwed this up. And they probably heard me talking and are going to punish me for doing so. Or maybe they'll do something to this man to make sure he never talks to Pearce. Oh, God. I hope they don't kill him. Maybe they didn't hear us.

Michael drops some bills on the table and gives me a quick courtesy wave as he goes out the door. He's not going to tell Pearce. He probably thinks I don't even know him. That I'm just some crazy woman making up stories. Dammit!

I grab a rag and spray bottle and nervously wipe down the tables.

"Is something wrong?" Celia asks.

"No. I'm just cleaning up. Did you need help in the kitchen?"

"Jill." She holds my arm. "What's wrong? Was it the American? Was he being inappropriate with you? Did he say something to upset you?"

"No. Not at all. He was fine. He had to get to a meeting."

She watches me as I wipe down another table. She knows something's going on with me. But I can't tell her anything. She couldn't help me, so why put her at risk by telling her?

She goes back to the kitchen and I continue cleaning up out front. Michael's car is gone now. He'll probably never come back. And I know he'll never tell Pearce. I had my chance to get him a message and I blew it.

Every day, I remind myself to have hope. To stay positive. But with each passing day, that gets harder and harder to do.

CHAPTER SEVEN

GARRET

I knock on her door. "Jade, hurry up. You're taking too long."

She's laughing as she opens the door. "What do you expect me to do? Come running the second you knock?"

"Yes," I say, being very serious. "That's exactly what I expect. In fact, running isn't fast enough. I'd prefer that you sprint to the door."

She shuts it behind me. "That's not going to happen. In fact, from now on, I'm going to mosey to the door."

I take her hand and pull her toward me. "Do you even know how to mosey?"

"Of course I do. I mosey all the time."

"I've never seen you mosey. Saunter, maybe, but not mosey."

She rolls her eyes. "Anyway, why are you here, and why are you in such a hurry?"

I put my arms around her waist and kiss her cheek. "I'm here because it's Saturday night, which is the night I always spend with you." I kiss her other cheek. "And I'm not in a hurry. At least not now."

"Why not now?"

"Because now I'm here with you."

"So you're saying you were in a hurry to see me?" She gives me her shy smile. It's adorable. I have to kiss her cheek again, so I do.

"Yes. I was in a hurry to see you. I missed my best friend."

She tilts her head, which is also adorable. "Am I really your best friend? You have a lot of friends, Garret."

"Fake friends. You're my real friend. And my best friend."

61

Jade and I are more than just friends, but she refuses to be my girlfriend. She says she's not ready for that yet. So for now, we remain just friends. Friends who sometimes kiss. And hold hands. And flirt constantly with each other.

"You're my best friend too," she says quietly, looking down.

"I know," I say in a cocky tone so the mood isn't so serious.

"Hey!" She pushes on my chest. "Watch the ego, buddy, or I'm not hanging out with you."

"You *have* to hang out with me. We have a deal. Every Saturday night. It's tradition. Just like Sundays at Al's Pancake House. You can't break tradition, Jade." I lead her to the bed and set her down on my lap. "So are you ready to go out?"

"Go out? But we usually stay in."

It's true. We usually hang out in my room and watch movies. Given that we're in college, we should be at a party on Saturday night, but we're not because Jade doesn't drink and she doesn't like being around alcohol.

I don't drink either. I used to, but I stopped because of Jade, but also because I was turning into an alcoholic and it scared me. I was drinking to numb the pain of losing my mom and to forget about the fights I'd have with my dad. But the alcohol wasn't helping. My mom is dead, and I need to accept that and deal with the pain rather than numb it. As for my dad? He hates me and probably wishes he never had me, but getting drunk won't change that or make it better.

"I don't want to stay in," I say. "Let's go out."

She loops her arms around my neck. "Where do you want to go?"

"Dinner and a movie. You can pick the movie."

"But it's only 4:30. That's too early for dinner."

"Then we'll go to the mall first."

"The mall? We've never gone to the mall."

"Then we definitely need to go. Friends always hang out at the mall. We can't call ourselves friends if we haven't done this."

She laughs. I love making her laugh. She has the cutest laugh. "There aren't any malls in this town."

"I have a car, Jade. We're not limited to this town. There's a mall like twenty minutes from here. We'll go there and walk around, then we'll go to dinner and a movie."

"I can't afford all that." She gets up and goes over to her desk. "Let's just watch a movie here."

Jade only has enough money to do laundry. She has no spending money. And Frank, the guy who took her in after her mom died, can't afford to give her money. He has MS and all his money goes to pay his medical bills. Even though Jade is broke, she doesn't like it when I pay for stuff. But I've slowly been convincing her to let me pay for things like dinners or movies, because if I didn't, we'd never go anywhere.

"We're going out." I take out my wallet, pull out some bills, and drop them on the floor as she looks for something in her desk. "You can pay this time."

"I'm paying for both of us?" She turns around. "Then I guess we'll be eating out of a vending machine and sneaking into the movies for free."

"You have money right there." I point to it on the floor. "Just use that."

She reaches down and picks up four $20 bills. "Take it back, Garret."

I put my hands up. "It's not mine."

"Yeah, it is. Come on. Take it." She holds the bills out to me.

"Jade, I swear. It's not mine. Maybe it's from the tooth fairy. Did you lose some teeth recently? Let me see." I try to open her mouth, but she swats my hand away, laughing.

"Okay, fine. I'll pay." She pauses. "Thank you."

"For what? I told you that money wasn't mine."

"Not for the money. For spending Saturday nights with me."

I pull her back onto my lap. "You don't have to thank me for that. I love our Saturday nights. I look forward to them every week."

"But you should be—"

"No," I say, cutting her off. "I don't want to be at a party, Jade. I want to be with you."

From her expression, I can tell she doesn't believe me. It's something I need to work on with her. She grew up in such a shitty home that she doesn't think she's worthy of anything. Even friendship. She thinks she can't count on anyone, and that if she gets close to someone, they'll leave her. That's why she's afraid to get close to me. She's starting to open up more, but it's like one step forward and two steps back. As soon as I make progress with her, she takes a step back. It's a process. A frustrating process, but I want to help her work through it. Because she's my closest friend. And because she's kind, and caring, and a beautiful person. And because...I love her.

"Let's go." She stands up and offers me her hand.

I take it and pull her toward me. "Can I have a kiss first?"

"For what?" she asks kiddingly. "I'm already buying you dinner and a movie. If anything, you owe ME a kiss."

I smile, because I don't think she realizes what she just asked for. Before she can figure it out, I lean in and press my lips to hers. Then I slowly back away.

She's blushing and trying not to smile. "You weren't supposed to do that."

"I wasn't? Then why did you tell me to?"

"I didn't. I was just making a reference to the fact that some men expect a goodnight kiss, or more than a kiss, after paying for a date. Which is wrong, by the way. They shouldn't expect anything. Neither should a girl who pays."

"So you won't be expecting me to kiss you at the end of this evening?"

"No. And just to be clear. This isn't a date. We're just two friends hanging out."

I look her in the eye. "Are you ever going to go on a date with me, Jade?"

She shrugs. "I suppose it will happen eventually."

"But not tonight?"

"No. Not tonight."

"Damn, I was really looking forward to that kiss." I stand up, then lean down by her ear and say, "I think you were too." I walk past her. "Let's go."

On the drive to the mall, she asks me about my day and then tells me about hers. I keep looking over at her and smiling. She makes me smile for no reason at all. Sometimes I don't even know I'm doing it until she asks me why I'm smiling.

As she's talking I reach over and hold her hand. Even though we're not dating, I still hold her hand. I like touching her. I just wish she'd let me touch more of her than her hand. I'm used to moving much faster with girls. I've even had a few one-night stands. But I'm taking things slow with Jade. Very slow.

"This is it," I say, pulling into a parking space. "It's not a big mall, but we can still walk around."

"Aren't you worried about people seeing us?" she asks, as we go in the mall entrance.

"Jade, I told you. I'm done listening to my dad." I hold her hand as we walk.

"Yeah, but if he knew we were still friends, he might take my scholarship away."

"He won't. Stop worrying about it."

My dad has been trying to keep me away from Jade ever since he found out we were friends. He says a Kensington can't be seen with a girl like Jade, and definitely can't date someone like her. I'm only supposed to date girls he picks out for me, which in the past have all been snobby bitches I can't stand. But I'm done letting him control my life, especially my dating life.

I can't believe he's being such an ass about Jade. Just because she grew up poor is not a reason to ban me from being friends with her. My mom didn't come from a rich family and yet he still married her. So I don't understand why he's so against me being with Jade.

"What stores do you want to go in?" I ask her.

"Well, I can't buy anything so it's kind of pointless to shop."

"You can still look." I smile at her. "And maybe your friend will buy you something."

She smiles back. "My friend is not buying me anything. My friend is already paying for dinner and a movie."

"Since when?" I feign surprise. "I thought *you* were paying."

She laughs. "Yeah, that's right. I forgot. Come on. Let's go in here."

It's a place that sells new and used movies on DVD. I didn't know they still had these stores. I haven't been to this mall in years. It's the same mall my mom and I used to go to. My dad doesn't like to shop, so he usually wouldn't come with us.

As Jade's looking at movies, I check my phone to see if there are any messages from my dad. Even though I told Jade I'm not worried he'll find out about us, the truth is I am. If he finds out I'm with her, he'll try to forbid me from seeing her.

"There's nothing here," Jade says. "Should we go?"

"Yeah." I take her hand again as we leave the store.

"Want to look in the Halloween store?" She points to it.

"No." I lead her away from it.

It's the place my mom used to take me to get my Halloween costume when I was a kid. It's October, and that store is only here for a month, then it turns into a Christmas store. Every year, my mom would take me there to get my costume. I could never decide what I wanted to dress up as, so I'd wait until the last minute and then my mom would have to drive me all the way here the day before Halloween to get it.

Going in there now would bring back too many memories. Those memories shouldn't bother me anymore, but they still do. I want to remember her, and yet I don't. Because when I do, I miss her and it hurts, and I'm tired of hurting.

"So what can I get you?" I ask Jade, putting my arm around her.

"You're not getting me anything. You already bought me those lights for my room."

"That was a birthday gift. This is a first-time-together-at-the-mall gift."

She smiles. "I didn't know that was a special occasion. But you're still not buying me anything."

We pass in front of a candy store. "I know what to get you." I pull her inside and take one of the plastic bags next to the bins and hand it to her. "Fill it up with whatever you want."

She checks out all the bins of candy, her eyes wide, her face lit up. Jade loves candy, and this store has every kind imaginable.

She reads the sign that's next to the candy bins. "I don't know, Garret. This could get expensive. You have to pay by the pound."

"Just fill up the bag. Don't worry about what it costs."

"Are you going to eat some of it?"

She asks because I rarely eat sweets. My dad doesn't either. I inherited his lack of a sweet tooth.

"Yes. I'll have some." I probably won't, but if I tell her I will, she'll let me pay for it.

"Okay, then I guess we'll get some." She opens a bin and scoops out two gum balls and puts them in the bag.

"Jade, you have to get more than that. We're not leaving here until that bag is full."

She scoops out some more gum balls.

My phone rings. "Keep filling it up. I'll be right back."

It's my dad calling. Shit.

I leave the store as I answer my phone. "Yeah, Dad. What do you need?"

"I was just checking in. How are things going?"

He never calls me so I don't know why he's calling now.

"Everything's fine. Where are you?"

"In Tampa. I have to give that speech tomorrow."

"Yeah, that's right." I pretend I knew that, but I really didn't. I never know where he is. He's gone so much, I can't keep track of where he goes. "What kind of conference is it?" I ask, purposely trying to put the focus on him instead of me.

"It's a business conference aimed at people in the finance and banking industry. Garret, I didn't call to talk about the conference. Tell me about school. Are your classes going okay?"

"Yes. I told you, everything's fine."

"What are you doing tonight?"

"Hanging out with some guys who live on my floor."

"What are their names?"

"It doesn't matter. You don't know them." I can't stand it when he does this. He calls me, acting like he wants to know how

I'm doing, then turns the call into an inquisition about my personal life.

Some girls walk by me, talking really loud.

"Who was that?" my dad asks.

"Just some people walking by. I'm at the mall getting a new charger for my phone."

"Are you going to a party tonight?"

"I don't know. Maybe. Dad, I have to go. I'll talk to you later."

"Garret, I—"

I hang up, and luckily he doesn't call back. I had to get off the phone because I knew he was getting ready to ask about Jade and if I'd been hanging out with her. I'd lie, of course, but sometimes he can tell when I'm lying so I couldn't risk it.

I go back in the candy store and see Jade's only filled a fourth of the bag. I come up behind her, my arms going around her waist. "If you don't have that bag full in two minutes, I get to kiss you later tonight."

She spins around. "There's no way I'm agreeing to that." She spins back around and opens the gummy bear bin. "We're friends, Garret. Friends do not kiss."

"Some friends do. Haven't you heard the expression 'a friendly kiss'? That's a kiss between friends."

"No, it's not. You're just making stuff up." She puts a few gummy bears in the bag.

"My God, Jade. We'll be here all night." I take the scoop from her hand and fill it up and dump it in the bag.

"Garret, that's too many. I don't want that many."

"Yeah, you do. You love gummies." I grab the bag from her. "I'm taking over. You're too slow. What else do you want?"

We finish filling the bag, then I shoo her away as I pay so she won't see the price. It ended up being four pounds of candy so it cost over thirty dollars, which is nothing to me, but Jade would make me put it all back if she knew it cost that much.

"I've had enough mall time," I say. "How about you?"

"Yeah, I'm done," she says, chewing on a gummy worm. "Thanks for the candy."

"You're welcome." I take her hand as we walk out of the store.

When we're almost at the mall exit, a woman passes me and I do a double take. I glance back to see her again. She looks just like my mom. Well, not exactly, but close. Tall and thin with dark brown hair and a similar face.

This happens sometimes. I see a woman who resembles my mom, and for a moment, I think it's her. I think she's still alive. Obviously she's not. It's just my mind playing tricks on me, wishing she were still here.

"Garret, do you know that woman?" Jade asks.

I realize I've stopped walking and am still looking back at that lady.

"No. I thought I did, but I don't."

"Then should we go?" She's holding the door for me, smiling at me with that beautiful smile and those big green eyes.

I smile back. "Yeah. Let's go."

If my mom were alive, she would love Jade. I know she would. Jade is the type of girl my mom would've liked to see me marry someday. And maybe someday, I *will* marry Jade. But my mom won't be there to see it. Just like she wasn't there to see my swim meets. Or my basketball games. Or my football games. Or my birthdays. Or my high school graduation. I wished she'd been there for all those things.

Even nine years after her death, I still miss my mom. I miss her every day.

I always will.

CHAPTER EIGHT

PEARCE

"Katherine, we are not fighting about this," I say as I pace the floor of my hotel room. "I told you I will deal with this issue with Jade. You will not interfere."

"You're never home, Pearce. How do you expect to take care of this if you're never home?"

"I will be home next week, and I will deal with it then."

"That's too late. Clarissa just called and said she and her daughters were at the mall and they saw Garret there with Jade."

So Garret lied to me. I shouldn't be surprised. He refuses to let Jade go.

"Pearce. Did you hear me?" Katherine raises her voice. "Your son was out with that trashy girl in public! And people we know saw them together! Do you know how bad that makes us look?"

"I will take care of it when I get back," I say forcefully. "Until then, you will stay out of it."

"What could he possibly see in that girl, anyway? She's white trash. Raised by an alcoholic, drug-addicted mother. She probably does drugs. Or sells them. Is that really the type of girl you want around our family?"

"Jade does not do drugs, nor does she sell them. She doesn't even drink alcohol. She's a nice girl. She's just not the right girl for Garret."

"We have a deal with the Hamiltons. Garret has to be seen with Ava. If he's not, her parents will be furious."

"I understand that. But there aren't any events coming up for them to appear together at, so Ava's parents have no reason to get upset."

"You don't even care, do you? Our reputation is being destroyed by some little tramp you had to give a scholarship to, and you don't even care!"

"Katherine, we are done discussing this. I need to go. Give Lilly a kiss for me. Goodbye."

She continues to yell at me, but I end the call. After years of fighting with Katherine, I've learned it's best to walk away or hang up on her, and not allow the fight to continue. We still fight, but not nearly as much as we used to.

You would think by now there would be nothing left for us to fight about, but Katherine always finds something. And the current hot button issue is Jade. Ever since we found out Garret's been seeing her, Katherine has been furious. She hates Jade, because Jade isn't from our high society world. It's the same reason she hated Rachel.

I have my own concerns about Jade, but not because of her background. It's because of who her father is. Jade doesn't know it, but her father is Royce Sinclair. Years ago, Royce told me he had an affair with a woman, and that the woman had a child. That child is Jade.

After she was born, Royce assured me that he gave Jade's mother plenty of money to live comfortably and take care of her child. But it was a lie. He never gave her money. Jade's mother had to drop out of college. She became addicted to alcohol and prescription drugs so couldn't get a job. She abused Jade and didn't take care of her, and Royce never stepped in to help. Even when Jade's mother committed suicide when Jade was 15, Royce still did nothing. So Frank, a man Jade's mother used to know, took Jade in and cared for her until she left for college.

Despite her difficult childhood, Jade made a success of herself. She worked hard and was valedictorian at her high school. But that wasn't the reason I gave her the Kensington Scholarship. I gave it to her as a favor to Royce. He asked me to keep watch on her during his presidential campaign. He wants me to make sure she never finds out about him, and if she does, he wants me to keep her quiet so she doesn't tell the media and ruin his chance for the presidency. The organization would never allow him to be president if they found out about Jade. And he'd be punished for not telling them this secret from his past.

Jade goes to Moorhurst College, which is about a half hour from my house, so it's easy to keep an eye on her. Garret is also a freshman at Moorhurst, but I never thought he'd end up pursuing Jade. But when I think about it now, it's not surprising he likes her. Unlike the rich, self-absorbed people he's used to being around, Jade is more like the people Garret grew up with before his mother died. His friends back then were just normal children with normal parents. Now his friends all come from billionaire families like ours, and are chosen for him based on how their families will benefit us. Many times this benefit is simply a rise in social status that comes from being seen with the right people.

That's the world I grew up in, so I used to think nothing of it. But after I met Rachel and lived in her world, I decided I didn't want my son growing up like I did. And yet, he's been living in that high society world for the past nine years. I didn't give him a choice. At times I feel guilty for that, but then I tell myself it's for the best. After what I went through with his mother, I know from experience that choosing a girl like Jade will make his life extremely difficult. And being with Jade, specifically, is even worse, because she's the daughter of Royce Sinclair.

Just as I'm thinking that, my phone rings. It's Royce.

"Hello, Royce," I answer.

"Pearce. How are the plans for the fundraiser coming along?"

In November, I'm hosting a political fundraiser for Royce at my house. It's a dinner and dance and Royce will be giving a speech. A lot of the media will be there.

The organization is making me support Royce's campaign, so I've had to travel the country going to his speeches. It's another reason I haven't been home. It seems like I haven't been home in months, which is why I'm having a hard time keeping Garret away from Jade.

"The fundraiser is already planned, Royce. Katherine and my mother will handle any last minute details. You don't have to worry about it."

"Do you have the guest list yet?"

"Yes. I already sent it to you."

"My staff must have it. I don't remember seeing it. Add Sadie to the list. She's bringing her boyfriend, Evan, so that's two more guests."

"That's fine. We have plenty of room and plenty of food ordered."

"What about our other problem?" he asks.

Royce refers to Jade as a 'problem.' He feels no fatherly connection to her, which I suppose makes sense since he didn't raise her, but she's still his daughter so calling her a 'problem' always irritates me.

"She goes to her classes and studies in her room. She's not a problem, Royce."

"She will be if she tells someone."

"She doesn't even know about you. And she never will. Even if she did, she doesn't seem like someone who would run to the media."

"Don't be an idiot, Pearce. Of course she'd go to the media. She'd sell her story to every magazine and newspaper in the country and come out a millionaire. And then she'd come after *my* money."

"Which you should have given her in the first place."

"I didn't want her, remember? You're the one who talked me into leaving her mother alone. And now I'm stuck having to deal with her."

"You're not dealing with her. *I* am. And I promise you, she will not be a problem. She's a nice girl. Very intelligent. If you met her, you'd like her."

"I have no interest in meeting her. And you better not be getting attached to her, Pearce. You are to treat her like she's a problem to be dealt with, just as we'd deal with a problem at the organization."

I shudder when he says it, because a 'problem' at the organization is someone who will end up being killed.

"Jade is not that type of problem and she will not be dealt with in that way. She's an innocent girl. She knows nothing about us."

"She will if your son keeps seeing her."

"Garret doesn't know about the organization. And he doesn't know about your connection to Jade. He has nothing to tell her."

"You might let something slip. Or he might overhear us talking. If Jade ever found out about me—"

"She won't. She'll never know."

"She could find out about the organization. Your son's been around you long enough to know that you're part of something. He may not know what that something is, but he knows it exists. And if he tells Jade—"

"He will not tell her anything. As I said, Garret knows nothing about it."

"Some of the young men are being initiated at the age of 19. Garret is already 19."

"Yes, I know." I don't need Royce reminding me of this. I'm already worried sick about it. I've been trying to get the rules changed for years now, along with some of my fellow members who want the same thing. We've formed a committee to look into recruiting members from the outside rather than forcing our sons to join, but it's still in the discussion stage. We haven't been able to change the rules yet. Right now, sons still have to be members.

"You need to end this, Pearce. Garret cannot be around her. And he shouldn't be. She's not one of us. It looks bad. I can't believe you'd even let him be seen with her."

He sounds like Katherine. Talking as if Jade is trash. He says this about his own daughter, who actually IS one of us. She's a Sinclair, and she wouldn't have grown up the way she did if he had just helped her mother like he said he was going to do.

"I will take care of it, Royce. Garret will not be seeing her anymore."

"Don't be feeling sorry for that girl. It will cloud your judgment. I need you to see this for what it is. Jade cannot find out our secrets, and if she does, she will need to be taken care of. And if you don't do it, I will find someone who will."

"What are you saying, Royce? You'd hurt your own daughter?"

He chuckles. "Of course not. I'm a father, Pearce. You know how much I love my girls."

"Not *all* of your girls."

He chuckles again. "You've always had such a dark sense of humor. I've always liked that about you. We'll talk soon. Goodbye, Pearce."

After he hangs up, I consider calling Garret again and reminding him that he is not allowed to see Jade, but it wouldn't do any good. I need to be there in person in order to keep them apart. And right now, I'm in Tampa for a conference. But when I get back, I will put an end to Garret's relationship with Jade. It's not what he wants, but it's for the best.

The next morning I go to the ballroom at the hotel to give my speech, which is about developing a business strategy. I've given this speech so many times I could probably do it in my sleep. As the CEO of a major corporation, I'm often asked to speak at business conferences. I get so many requests that I have to turn most of them down or I wouldn't have time to run the company. But I agreed to do this conference because I need to make some new connections in the banking industry that might offer me more competitive financing options as I continue to expand our operations.

"Pearce, welcome." A man greets me on stage as another man checks the microphone. "We're thrilled to have you here."

I shake his hand. "Thank you. I was happy to do it."

"We'll introduce you in a few minutes. You can wait here if you'd like." He points to a chair.

"No. I'm fine." I don't like sitting before a speech. Standing keeps my energy level up and I like to have a lot of energy when giving a speech. Otherwise it becomes dull and people lose interest.

Sometimes when I'm giving these speeches, I imagine Rachel walking in, like she did when I gave that speech at Yale. I imagine her looking older, but still as beautiful as ever, with those bright blue eyes and that smile that lights up a room.

When I first saw her at that speech all those years ago, I couldn't take my eyes off her. That was the worst speech I ever gave. It started out okay, but as soon as she walked in, I stumbled on my words, forgot what I was saying, and my throat was so dry I had to keep stopping to take a drink of water. I used to tell Rachel that she made me speechless that day, as in I couldn't give my speech. She always used to laugh about that. I miss her laugh.

"...pleased to introduce, Mr. Pearce Kensington."

I was so deep in thought I missed my entire introduction. I go up to the podium and deliver my speech. It goes smoothly and, as always, it's well received. People seem to like this particular topic, which is why I'm repeatedly asked to give this speech.

When it's over, the conference attendees spill out into the hallways and lobby of the hotel. I remain in the ballroom, letting the crowds disperse before I go. As I wait, I check some of the hundreds of unread emails I have on my phone.

"Mr. Kensington?"

I look up and see a man coming toward me. He's older than me, wearing a gray suit and conservative tie, like all the other conference attendees. People in the finance industry tend to all dress the same.

"Yes." I stand up and shake his hand.

"Hello. I'm Michael Cloustin. It's nice to meet you. I've heard you speak many times. I always learn something new."

"I'm glad you found it useful. Are you a banker?"

"Yes. I work on Wall Street." He hands me his card.

"Did you have a question?" I ask.

He hesitates, then says, "This is going to sound very strange, and maybe I shouldn't even be telling you this, but..."

"What is it?" I'm now intrigued by what he has to say.

"A few weeks ago, I was in Italy for business and had some time to kill so I took a drive. I ended up in this tiny town." He goes on to describe it.

It's the same town where Rachel and I spent part of our honeymoon. We spent Christmas there and loved it so much we even talked about retiring there someday. How odd that this man has been to that same town. And why is he telling me about it?

"I had breakfast there," he says, "and was talking to the waitress. She's American, and maybe she missed the company of another American because she wouldn't stop talking. She even gave me a tour of the town."

"Is there a reason you're telling me this?" I ask.

"Yes. The woman said she knew you. She wanted me to tell you hello."

"What's her name?"

"Jill. I didn't get a last name."

"I don't know anyone named Jill."

"She talked as though you two used to be good friends."

I can't think of who this would be. I meet a lot of people, so it's possible I know her and just don't remember her, but we certainly weren't good friends, as she claims.

"What did she look like?" I ask.

"She's probably a couple years younger than you. Tall. Thin. Dark brown hair. Blue eyes. She's very pretty. She's originally from Indiana but said she went to college in Connecticut at um..." He pauses to think. "What's the name of that small college in New Haven? Begins with an H. Hirshfield! That's the one. She went to graduate school there and studied American History. Is any of this ringing a bell?"

I'm staring at him, taking in each word, trying to figure out what the hell is going on here. He just described Rachel. Why would he do that? Is this some kind of sick joke?

"Who put you up to this?" I ask in a harsh, angry tone.

"I don't understand. What are you talking about?"

He seems sincere, and very serious, so maybe he's just the messenger. Maybe someone hired him to do this. But why would he agree to it? He seems like a normal man. And if he really is a banker on Wall Street, he wouldn't take part in some sick joke.

"Where in Indiana?" I ask, wanting to know what else he knows about Rachel.

"She didn't tell me the name of the town, but she did say something about a country bar. I don't know what that has to do with anything but—"

I grab his arm. "Who told you to tell me this?"

He glances down at my hand on his arm and I let him go. "The woman I talked to. Jill. The woman in Italy."

"There IS no woman in Italy. You're making this up! Now tell me who sent you here! Was it Royce?"

It sounds like something Royce would do. If anyone has a dark sense of humor, it's him, not me.

"Royce?" Michael looks confused. "Royce who?"

This man is either a very good liar or he's some lunatic that looked up information about Rachel online and for whatever reason decided to use that information to make up this story about some woman named Jill.

"She must've confused you with someone else," he says. "I'm very sorry I wasted your time."

He turns and walks away. He doesn't seem like a lunatic. So what is going on here? I feel like I want to ask him more, but then it would encourage him and I shouldn't do that. But then I do.

"Did she say anything else?"

He turns back. "No. That was it." He takes a couple steps then turns back again. "Actually, she *did* say something about..." He thinks for a moment, then shrugs. "I can't remember what it was. Sorry."

"It's fine. Thank you."

This is obviously some kind of hoax. This man may not knowingly be in on it, but he was sent here to say those things about my dead wife for a reason I do not understand.

What kind of person would do something like that? If it wasn't Royce, maybe it was Leland. He hates me because I don't treat his little princess, Katherine, the way he thinks she deserves to be treated, which would entail agreeing to her every demand. Leland has a sick sense of humor so it could've been him. Or one of the other members.

But why would they do this to me? Is this part of my punishment? Make me think my wife is still alive when she's really not? Or do they just want to torture me for their own amusement?

For a moment there, I really did think Rachel might be alive. But that's ridiculous. She was on the plane. There were no survivors. And if Rachel were alive, she wouldn't be living in Italy. She'd be here. With me. And with her son.

I'm not going to mention this to Leland or the other members. I'm not going to give them the satisfaction of knowing their sick joke affected me in any way.

I take Michael's card from my pocket and throw it in the trash. Then I return to my room to pack my suitcase to go home. Before I start packing, I sit on the bed and close my eyes and try to get that man's words out of my head. But I can't do it. Because his words describe the dream I've had many times the past nine years. I've dreamt that Rachel was out there somewhere, waiting to be with me again. It's a foolish thought, and I shouldn't even let my mind entertain the idea.

She's gone. Rachel is gone. But I still love her. I will always love her.

CHAPTER NINE
Two Months Later

PEARCE

The past couple months I've been on edge every second of every day, and it's all because of Royce. His presidential campaign has been ramping up and he's determined to be the frontrunner, even though he knows the organization will make sure he wins. But winning isn't good enough. He wants to be the center of attention in the media for the entire year leading up to the election. He wants the public to adore him. The press to praise him. And his fellow running mates to hate him because he's so far ahead of them in the polls.

Royce isn't at that place yet and probably never will be, but that hasn't stopped him from trying. He'll do everything possible to get ahead, and he won't let anyone stand in his way. That's why he's been threatening Jade since October. He hasn't done it himself. He hired people to scare her into keeping quiet.

There was no need to keep her quiet because Jade didn't even know who Royce was back then, but when I told him that, he didn't believe me. Then Garret brought Jade to the political fundraiser I had for Royce last month, and Royce was furious. He said I purposely had Jade at the party to expose his secret to the world and destroy his campaign. He accused me of being jealous that the organization chose him instead of me for the role of president, despite knowing how much I despise the whole political system.

It just shows how irrational Royce has become and how paranoid he's getting about people trying to take him down and ruin his image and prevent him from being president. He's even accused some of the members of sleeping with his wife, Victoria, saying they're doing it to harm his image of having the perfect family.

I've been trying to control Royce the best I can, but he's a loose cannon. The organization has been too lenient with him, so now he thinks he doesn't have to follow the rules. And the truth is, he doesn't. Every time I think he'll get in trouble for something, Dunamis looks the other way instead of punishing him. So Royce just continues on, doing whatever he pleases.

But if the members found out about Jade, they might not be so forgiving. Royce should've disclosed this secret years ago. Dunamis wouldn't care that he had an affair with Jade's mother. Our members have affairs all the time. But having a child with the woman is a different story. Dunamis would want to know that, and if they found out, Royce would definitely be punished for not telling them. *I* can't tell them because I'm afraid of what they might do to Jade. She's technically a Sinclair, but she didn't grow up in our world so I fear the members would see her as a risk and might try to harm her.

This is why I've been so on edge the past few months. I'm trying to control Royce, while also protecting Jade. I'm also trying to keep Garret safe. He's putting himself at risk by dating Jade, but no matter what I do, I can't get him to stop seeing her. He reminds me so much of myself and how I was with his mother. I risked everything to be with her, and once I had her, there was nothing anyone could do or say to convince me to give her up. Garret is the same way with Jade, which is why I stopped trying so hard to break them up.

But now I'm back to thinking I need to, because being with Jade is just too dangerous. Royce is now targeting Garret. He's convinced Jade will find out the truth about him the more time she spends with Garret and our family. What Royce doesn't know is that Jade already knows he's her father. She found out just the other day, while she was home in Iowa, visiting Frank in the hospital. Frank, in his drugged-up, post-operative state, told Jade about Royce. Apparently, Frank knew that Royce was Jade's father. Jade's mother told Frank this years ago.

If Royce found this out, he'd kill both Jade and Frank, and maybe Garret as well. A few days ago, I didn't think Royce would take things that far, but now? I know he would, because he damaged the brakes on Garret's car, almost killing Jade and Garret yesterday when they were driving home from the airport. Now I'm so worried about their safety, I have both Jade and Garret staying at my house, until I can figure out what to do with Royce.

The phone rings as I'm sitting in my office. I'm at Kensington Chemical, where I've been all morning, trying to figure out how to handle Royce. I check the phone and see that it's him calling. After what he did, I don't think I'll be able to control my anger toward him, but I answer anyway.

"Pearce, we have a problem," he says.

"That's a fucking understatement," I reply.

"What is that supposed to mean?"

"You damaged the brakes on Garret's car." I don't raise my voice. I remain calm. Doing so always throws Royce off. He likes getting a rise out of people, and when he doesn't, it confuses him.

"Why would you accuse me of such a heartless crime?" He laughs a little as he says it. "Garret is your son. I have no interest in harming the boy."

"And yet you tampered with his brakes, hoping he'd get into an accident and die. Along with Jade, who was also in the car."

"Perhaps if you'd broken the two of them up like I told you to months ago, Garret's car trouble would never have occurred."

I pick up a pen and tap it on my desk, my eyes watching it rise and fall in a steady pattern. It's a technique I use to keep my anger in check. My father does the same thing, which should make me not want to do it, but I do it anyway because it works.

"You will never attempt to harm my son again," I say. "Do you understand me?"

"I don't follow orders. You should know that by now."

"You will when it comes to this. Because I promise you, if you ever try to harm Garret again, I will kill you. I will not hesitate. I will not give you warning. This right now? This is your one and only warning. You will not harm him."

"If he gets in my way, I can't control what happens to him. He's collateral damage. Do what needs to be done for the greater good. It's the first thing they teach us as members. You should know that more than anyone. Your father lives by that rule."

"Killing my son is not for the greater good. But killing *you* would be." It's not just a threat. I really will kill Royce if he continues to threaten Garret.

"I don't like your attitude, Pearce. If anyone should be asking for forgiveness here, it's you. You said you'd take care of this. You said you'd keep Jade in line and keep her away from Garret. But you didn't. You lied, and now you have to deal with the consequences."

"You also lied. You told me it was an affair, when the truth is that you raped Jade's mother, then beat her until she was nearly dead."

Jade told me this yesterday. If I'd known this twenty years ago, I would've tried to help Jade's mother. But I trusted that Royce was telling me the truth. I believed him when he said it was an affair. Given his history of abusing the associates, it's not surprising Royce raped a woman, but I had no way of knowing he'd raped Jade's mother. He's good at covering up his sins, which is exactly what he did with the rape.

The phone is quiet, then Royce says, "So she knows. She knows it was me her mother wrote about in that letter."

He's referring to a letter Jade's mother wrote to her years ago. The letter mentioned the rape, but never said who the man was who did it. When Royce found out about the letter, he panicked. He was certain Jade would find out it was him. And she did.

Dammit. I didn't think Royce would automatically assume it was Jade who told me what happened to her mother. I thought he'd assume I got this information from a police report or a hospital record.

"It wasn't Jade," I say. "I did some research and found an old police report filed that night."

"You're lying! There IS no police report! I got rid of it, along with all the other evidence. The only evidence that's left is HER!" Through the phone, I hear something slamming against the wall, followed by the sound of glass breaking. "The bitch knows! She knows I'm her father! Fuck!" More sounds of glass breaking.

"Royce, calm down. It wasn't her. That's not how I found out."

He's breathing hard. "Then who was it? Who else knows? Garret?"

"No. Jade and Garret don't know anything. It was someone else who told me."

"Who?" He yells it.

"Let's meet somewhere and I'll tell you." I need to calm him down before he does something drastic.

"You're lying again!" he yells. "Lying to protect that bitch! She's just like her mother. Trying to destroy me. I should've killed her mother when I had the chance. Why did I listen to you? I could've got rid of them both years ago if it weren't for you! When I'm done killing Jade, I'm killing you next, Pearce. For destroying my life and making me risk everything for that bitch and her bastard child."

"Royce, I promise you, Jade doesn't know about you. Let's meet somewhere and talk. Where are you right now?"

He doesn't answer.

"Royce?" I glance at my phone and see that he ended the call.

Shit! I don't know where he is right now. He should be in Iowa, campaigning, but I don't trust that he's there."

I call his house in Virginia.

The maid answers. "Sinclair residence."

"Yes, is Royce home?" I leave my office and head to the parking garage.

"Mr. Sinclair is out of town."

"Do you know where he is?"

"No, Sir, I don't."

"Put Victoria on the phone."

"She and the girls are in Florida. Can I take a message?"

"No." I hang up and hurry to my car.

I should've asked Royce where he was before we started arguing. Then again, he probably would've lied. What if he's in Connecticut? If he is, he'll go to the house. Given his constant

84

state of paranoia, I'm sure he's having Jade followed, which means he knows she's at my house.

I call Garret on his cell phone, but he doesn't pick up.

He's safe, I tell myself. Jade and Garret are both safe. Royce can't get in the house. He'd have to get past the gate and the security guards and the locked front door. But the security guards think Royce and I are friends, so they might let him past the gate. They shouldn't, knowing I'm not home, but Royce is good at talking people into doing things.

As I'm driving, I call the security guards. Neither one of them answers. That's not a good sign. I call the house phone, but it's busy. Who the hell is on the phone? Katherine is at her parents' house with Lilly, and Garret never uses the home phone.

I'm now speeding down the road, heading to the house. *Royce isn't there*, I say to myself. *He's in Iowa, campaigning. He's scheduled to be there all week.*

It's true, but it doesn't reassure me. Royce is unpredictable. He does what he wants. And right now? He wants to kill Jade.

When I arrive at the house, the gate doesn't automatically open like it normally would when the guards see me approach. That's concerning. There are two guards and they never go on break at the same time.

I punch the code into the gate, and when it opens, I hit the gas, racing down the long entrance to the house. Right away I see the black Mercedes. It's not one of mine. It's Royce's.

I slam on the brakes and get out of my car and go around to the trunk. As I'm doing so, my eyes catch the sight of two bodies lying on the grass. Royce shot my security guards, multiple times, killing them.

I grab my handgun from the trunk, check that it's loaded, and run to the front door. I slowly open it and immediately hear Royce's voice. He's standing in the foyer, just outside the study. His back is to me and his gun is in his hand, aimed at whoever is in the study.

As I step into the foyer, I hear Garret talking. "Royce. Don't do this. I'm begging you. I'll take her far away. We'll move overseas. You'll never see or hear from us ever again."

I raise my gun and aim it at Royce, but before I can shoot, his gun goes off. I fire my gun directly into his back, right over his heart. He collapses onto the tile floor with a loud thud.

I run into the study. "Garret! Jade!" Jade is lying there with Garret covering her. I kneel down beside them, setting the gun on the shelf next to me. "Are you okay?"

"Yes." Jade pushes on Garret. "Garret, get off me." He doesn't move, and that's when I see the blood on Jade's shirt. But it's not coming from her. "Garret." She pushes on his shoulder and blood rushes out of his chest, spilling all over the floor.

"No!" Jade screams. "Help him!"

I gently rotate Garret onto his back. His shirt is soaked in blood and it continues to flow from the upper part of his chest. Jade is panicking, screaming and crying, but I remain perfectly calm, as if the bleeding, unconscious young man lying before me isn't my son.

As soon as I saw the blood, something happened and I became someone else. The person I am when I do my assignments. The person who detaches all emotion from the situation and does what needs to be done.

Jade's screaming at me. "Do something! Call the ambulance!"

I rip Garret's shirt down the center, exposing his chest. Blood is pouring out from the area just below his shoulder where the bullet went in.

"Do something!" Jade's frantic, her whole body shaking. "Please! Hurry!"

"Jade, I need you to pull yourself together so you can help me," I say in a calm, even tone, my eyes on hers. "Garret's losing a lot of blood. I need you to hold your hand here and apply pressure." I pick up her hand and set it over Garret's chest, right over the bullet hole. "I'm going in the other room to call for help."

As I leave, I turn back and see Jade leaned over Garret, pressing as hard as she can on his chest, trying to stop the bleeding. I hear her talking to him.

"It's gonna be okay," she says, still shaking, tears streaming down her face.

My cell phone is in my hand and I've already dialed the number as I hurry to the bathroom to get a towel.

Logan answers. "What is it, Pearce?"

"Garret's been shot." I grab a towel from the linen closet. "He's here at the house, in the study. He's losing a lot of blood."

"What the hell happened?"

"I'll tell you later. "You need to get a team here right away."

"Yes, of course. Just a minute." I hear Logan talking to someone but I can't make out the words. Then I hear footsteps and doors opening and closing. "We're in the van. We'll be right there."

"You're coming too?"

"I've been working at the Clinic in Connecticut this week. They needed someone to fill in."

"How fast can you be here?"

"We're less than ten minutes away. We'll be there shortly."

"Ten minutes away? Where are you?"

"There was a Clinic meeting offsite today. You're lucky it was close to your house. We'll be there soon."

"Thank you." I hang up and immediately dial nine for the clean-up crew. "Get to my house right away," I say when they answer.

"The house in Connecticut?"

"Yes." I now have several houses so I should've been clearer.

"Is this a freelancer?"

"No. It's a member. This is a cover-up. Send your top team."

"Yes, Sir."

I shove my phone in my pocket and hurry back to the study. Jade is now covered in blood. Her clothes, her hands, her arms. She's shaking so much her teeth are chattering. She needs to relax so she can understand what I'm about to tell her.

She slowly backs away as I kneel down next to Garret and press the towel against his chest.

"They'll be here any minute," I say to Jade. I set my eyes on her. "Listen to me, Jade. Listen to me very closely. What happened to Garret was an accident. He was cleaning his gun and didn't

87

realize there was a bullet left in it. That's what happened here. Do you understand?"

"Um, no. Why wouldn't you tell the police the real story?"

"The police aren't coming. I'm telling you this in case you're ever asked about this incident. The story I just told you is the only story you know. Now do you understand?"

She nods, tears running down her face.

"The people coming to take Garret are not paramedics," I say. "And he's not going in an ambulance. A van will arrive instead. It's a mobile medical unit and it has a team of physicians. They'll take care of him. He'll be okay."

"How do you know?" She looks down at Garret.

"I just know."

Jade looks as though someone just tore her world apart, taking away everything she ever loved and cared about. And by 'everything' I mean Garret. He's her everything. I see it now. It's as clear as day. I kept saying this relationship between Jade and my son was just a teenage crush. But I knew it was more than that, at least on Garret's end. I wasn't sure about Jade's feelings for Garret because I never see the two of them together. But now, as I watch Jade, I see that she loves Garret as much as he loves her.

Jade leans down over Garret's face. "Your dad said you'll be okay." She places her hand across his forehead and gently kisses his cheek.

"You really love my son, don't you?"

She leaves her eyes on him. "More than I can even describe."

This is a girl who has never known love, but she found it with Garret. And he loves her more than anything. Since meeting Jade, Garret has stopped drinking, his grades have improved, and he's happy. He's finally happy. So why do I keep trying to break these two apart? Maybe they could make this work. It would be difficult, but being with Rachel was difficult and yet it's the best decision I ever made.

"He feels the same way about you," I say to Jade.

She looks up at me. Our eyes lock and I try to express without words that I won't get in the way anymore. That she and Garret can be together. It will be difficult, and may not work out, but I'll at least give them a chance to try to make it work.

Jade seems to understand. I see the hope in her eyes.

Maybe I shouldn't put that hope there, knowing what might lie ahead for Garret's future. But for now, I'm going to believe that they can be together, and let Jade believe so too.

CHAPTER TEN

PEARCE

Moments later, Logan, and the other doctors from the Clinic, storm through the front door, going right past Royce's body as they enter the study. They know better than to ask questions or look too closely at the situation. Their job is to deal with medical issues, not issues of the organization. It will be *my* job to deal with Royce. I'll soon have to report this to the members, and together, we'll cover it up so that the public never knows what really happened.

The doctors take Garret out of the room on a stretcher and walk quickly to the front of the house.

Logan and I follow behind.

"It appears that the bullet is lodged in his upper chest," Logan says.

"But he'll be okay, correct?"

We're now in the foyer, and I go to the door and watch as they load Garret into the back of the van.

"We'll know more once we get him into surgery."

I turn back to Logan. "That's not the answer I wanted."

He sets his hand on my shoulder. "The bullet is a safe distance from his heart. Right now, our biggest concern is the bleeding." Logan nods at one of the doctors who's waiting by the van. "Pearce, we have to go."

"Yes. Please keep me updated."

"I will. I'll call you as soon as we get there."

They drive off just as the first members of the clean-up crew arrive. Two men come in and take Royce's body out to their van.

Then they come back into the house and one of them asks me, "Where do we take him?"

"To his house in Virginia. His family isn't home. There shouldn't be anyone there."

"And then what? Where do we leave him?"

"Someone will call and let you know. Make sure you have a body bag and people who can be on camera. This will be all over the news."

They nod and go back outside. There's no need to explain. They've faked a suicide before. Not with someone who was slated to be president, but they've done it with other high-profile people.

I'm assuming the members will want to go with the suicide story. Royce couldn't handle the pressure of the campaign so he flew home and took his own life. It's a believable story and people will feel sorry for him, which means Victoria and the girls will be treated well by the press. I feel horrible taking the girls' father away, but I had to do it. He was going to kill Garret. And Jade. And anyone else he thought might pose a threat to his campaign.

The second part of the clean-up crew arrives, the ones who will actually clean the room. There are eight of them, but I stop them before they go in the study.

"Don't go in there yet," I say. "Wait until I tell you."

They remain outside the door, all dressed in the same white uniforms.

"I need a garbage bag." I point to a box one of the men is holding.

He pulls out a bag and hands it to me and I return to the study. Jade hasn't moved from the floor.

"Jade, you need to get up now." I help her stand up. "I need you to listen very carefully to what I'm about to say. Royce Sinclair was never here. You have no connection with him. He's not your father. You know nothing about him. Am I clear?"

She nods.

"Over the next few days and weeks, you'll hear what happened to Mr. Sinclair. You'll hear it on all the news channels and the radio. You'll read it in the papers. The story you hear or read about is the only one that happened. Do you understand?"

91

"Yes," she says quietly. "I understand."

"This is over now. You and Garret are safe. Frank and Ryan are also safe and they will remain safe."

Ryan is Frank's son and like a brother to Jade. She cares about Frank and Ryan very much. They're not related to her, but they're the only family she knows.

"What are you saying?" Jade asks. "Was Sinclair planning to do something to Frank and Ryan? How do you know that? Why didn't you tell me that before?"

"Never ask questions, Jade. That's the number one rule." I wait until I know she understands. She nods, and I continue. "I don't want you calling Frank or Ryan until tomorrow. You need to calm down and get your head clear before you talk to anyone. Now take this and go clean up." I hand her the garbage bag. "Put all of your clothes in there and leave it outside your room when you're done."

I glance back at the men standing just outside the door and signal them to get to work. They come filing in with spray bottles, towels, and brushes.

Jade and I walk out of the room and I watch as she goes up the staircase. "Welcome to the family, Jade."

She pauses a moment, then continues up the stairs.

She doesn't know what I meant just now, but that was intentional. My comment was a message. I can't explain the meaning behind the message, but she doesn't need to know that. She only needs to know that she's part of this. She's seen too much today, and because of that, she's now part of this family. Part of our world. Even if she breaks up with Garret someday, she'll still have to keep our secrets, which makes her one of us.

Dunamis won't know that. I'll never tell them about Jade. I won't tell them what she saw today, or that she's Royce's daughter. But if she stays with Garret, she could be in danger, especially if I can't get him out of being a member. If I can't, then Dunamis will forbid Garret from being with an outsider like Jade, and if he doesn't listen, they'll threaten to hurt her. If that happens, he'll have to break up with her. But I'll do what I can to keep that from happening.

Garret loves her and she makes him happy. Since the day he was born, all I've ever wanted is for him to be happy and find love. He has both love and happiness with Jade. She's the one for him. I can see it in his eyes when he looks at her. And now I know Jade feels the same way about him. When I saw her today, sobbing over Garret, panicking when she thought she might lose him, it was clear how much she loves him.

As I watched her, I wondered why I wasn't reacting the same way. I love my son more than anything, and yet I saw him there, bleeding all over the floor, and felt nothing. No emotion. No panic. Nothing. My son could've died and I felt nothing.

What does that say about me? That I'm turning into my father? A cold, heartless, emotionless man who doesn't even care about his own son? That's not the man I want to be. And yet I feel like that's who I've become ever since Rachel died. I work all the time. I never see my children. I turn off all emotion so I never have to feel anything.

I'm a hollow shell of a man, just like I was before I met Rachel. I said I'd never be that person again, but that's who I've become. And I realized it today when I saw Jade sobbing over Garret. She's known him for just a few months and yet she showed more care and concern for him than I did. Instead of acting like his father, I acted like he was just some stranger I was helping out until the doctors arrived.

If Rachel had been here today, she would've been like Jade, sobbing and begging for Garret to be okay. So why is it that I felt nothing? Am I that detached from human emotion that I can't even feel something when I see my son almost dying?

Things have to change, starting today. I'm going to be a better father, and I'm not just saying that, like I have in the past. This time, I'm actually going to do it. I'm committed to being a good father, but I need help to get there. I need to talk to someone. I need to get into counseling and finally deal with Rachel's death so I can move past it and get over my grief and be a father again to Garret and Lilly. Truthfully, I've never been much of a father to Lilly, but I'm not going to let that continue. Lilly is only six, so it's not too late. I still have time to be a father to her.

As for Garret? He's in college now, so maybe it's too late to fix our relationship, but I'm still going to try. I love my son and I want to be a father to him again.

Around midnight, I call the Clinic. I've been calling them several times an hour to check on Garret. They're probably getting annoyed with my calls, but I'm worried about him and I have to know that he's okay.

"Pearce, it's Logan," I hear him say. I called the main number so I'm surprised he picked up. Usually one of the nurses answers.

"How is he?" I ask.

"He's resting. There's no change since the last time you called."

"So he's doing well?"

"Yes, very well. We'll continue to monitor him overnight."

"I'm coming to see him."

"Right now? But it's the middle of the night and a forty-minute drive."

"I don't care. I need to see him. I need to see that he's okay."

"Good." He pauses. "It's good you're coming. I'll see you soon."

Logan knows I've been a terrible father since Rachel died, but he's never said anything to me about it. Logan and Shelby still live in New York in a town that's just across the border from Connecticut. We meet about once a month for lunch, but we're not good enough friends that he would comment on my lack of parenting skills.

On my way to the Clinic, I call the various members assigned to cover up Royce's death. I'm not in charge of the cover-up but I keep checking in to see how it's coming and to make sure it's being done right. I don't want to risk anything being traced back to me.

The story I told the organization is that Royce came to my house and accused me of sleeping with Victoria. He's accused several members of this, so it's a story I knew they'd believe. I told the members that I denied the affair, but that Royce didn't believe me and threatened to shoot Garret if I didn't admit to sleeping with Victoria. So I told them I admitted to it, just to get Royce to leave, but that instead of leaving, Royce became so enraged that he shot Garret, and that's when I shot Royce.

The organization believed my story and immediately began the cover up, going along with the fake suicide story I suggested. Royce's body is now in Virginia and Dunamis has already filmed footage of the body bag being taken out of the house, and the video has been relayed to all the major news networks, along with a press release. Victoria and her daughters have received the news and are on their way back to Virginia from Florida, which is where they were vacationing when all of this happened. They will only know the fake story, not the real story. Royce's body will never be seen or examined. We'll make whatever fake reports need to be made, ruling it a suicide, and then the body will be cremated and services will be held.

"Follow me," Logan says as he greets me at the nurse's desk. I just arrived at the Clinic and Logan was waiting for me. "He's right in here."

I go into Garret's room and see him hooked up to machines. It reminds me of when I came to see Rachel, right after she had Garret. She was lying in a hospital bed after nearly dying, hooked up to monitors, looking pale and weak. Garret doesn't look pale or weak, but I still hate seeing him in a hospital bed.

"I'll be in the office down the hall," Logan says. "Come get me if you need me."

"You're not going home?"

"No. I'm going to stay here tonight." He motions to Garret. "Keep an eye on him."

"You don't have to do that. I saw Dr. Cauldwell when I got here. He said he has the night shift."

"Pearce, we've been friends for a long time. Dr. Cauldwell is an excellent physician, but I'm not going to leave your son here under the care of someone else."

I nod. "Thank you."

"You're welcome." He goes out the door, leaving me alone with Garret.

I take one of the chairs in the room and place it next to Garret's bed. I sit down and pick up his hand and hold it in mine. He's sleeping, so can't hear me, but I talk to him anyway.

"Garret, I'm sorry about what happened today. I should've stopped him long before he was able to do this. The warning signs were all there, but for whatever reason, I didn't take them seriously. I didn't think he would take things this far." I lower my head and close my eyes, pinching the bridge of my nose. "I'm also sorry for abandoning you after your mother died. I'm sorry I haven't been there for you all these years. And I'm sorry that I'm such a bad father."

All the emotion I'd been bottling up comes to the surface, flooding my eyes with tears. I haven't cried like this for years. The last time I did was that night I was in the kitchen, a few months after the plane crash. I was standing over the sink, remembering Rachel, and the tears just broke loose. Garret caught me crying and tried to help me, but I pushed him away. I've been pushing him away ever since, which is what got us to the place we're at now. My son is an adult and I feel like I don't even know him.

"Dad." I hear his voice. It's very faint, and when I look up at his face, I see his eyes are closed.

"I'm right here, son."

His eyes attempt to flicker open but then close again.

"Don't go," he mumbles. He's heavily drugged on painkillers and his words are slurred.

"I won't." I rub his hand. "I'll stay right here." He's too out of it to understand what I'm saying, but I continue. "But I have to leave in the morning. I have to wrap up some things and I need to be at the house when Jade wakes up."

"Jade," he whispers.

Maybe he *can* understand me. If so, he probably won't remember this tomorrow.

"Where's Jade?" I feel him tense up, but his eyes remain closed.

"Jade is fine," I tell him. "She's at the house. She's safe. She wasn't hurt."

He relaxes again.

"Garret, I know how much you love Jade. And I know how much she loves *you*. You two are good for each other. It reminds me of your mother and me. We brought out the best in each other and had the kind of love that only comes around once in a lifetime. I think you have that love with Jade. So I will do what I can to help you be with her, but it's not going to be easy. And if it comes to the point where your life, or Jade's life, is threatened, I won't allow you to continue seeing her. I want you to be happy and I want you to have love in your life, but I won't allow you to be with her if it means putting your life at risk. Or hers. But I will do whatever I can to prevent that from happening."

I take a deep breath and slowly let it out. "I hope you can forgive me, Garret, for not being a father to you all these years. I hope you'll give me another chance. I'm not just saying it this time. I'm committed to this. I'm going to get help. I'm going to see someone and address this grief that's consumed me since your mother died. It's not going to be an easy or quick process, so I can't promise you I'll be a new man by tomorrow or next week or even next month. But I *can* promise you that I will no longer be the absent father you've known for so long. I want to be part of your life again, and I hope you'll allow me to do so."

He didn't hear me. He's sound asleep, his breathing slow and steady.

I lean down over his bed and kiss his head, like I did when he was a child. "I love you, son."

I haven't told him that for years. I haven't been able to and I'm not sure why. Even now, if he were awake, I don't think I could've said those words. It proves that I need help. I need to work through whatever's keeping me from connecting with my children and being the father they need.

After a few minutes, I leave Garret's room and go down to the office and find Logan doing paperwork at the desk.

"Are you leaving?" he asks as he stands up.

"No. I'm going to stay here until morning. Do you think Garret could come home tomorrow?"

97

"Tomorrow? I don't know, Pearce. That might be too soon. He's doing better, but I think it's best if we keep him here a few days."

"I don't want him here. It's too far away. I want him at home."

Logan thinks for a moment. "I suppose we could send a nurse home with him so she could care for him and monitor his condition."

"Yes, that'll work. She can stay in one of the guest rooms. I want the best nurse you have. I'll pay whatever it costs."

"I'd volunteer to stay there too, but Shelby just called and said our youngest is sick so I told her I'd be home tomorrow sometime."

"Does that mean Dr. Cauldwell will be taking over?"

"Yes. As I said before, he's excellent and lives here in Connecticut, about a half hour from your house. If you need anything, just call him. Or you can always call me. I can come and check on him after I check on things at home."

"No, you need to be with your family. I've worked with Dr. Cauldwell before. I trust him to care for Garret."

"I'll need to reassess him in the morning before we make any decisions about sending him home. If he's not ready, I can't release him."

"I understand. Thank you, Logan, for staying here tonight."

He nods. "You're welcome. I'll see you in the morning."

I return to Garret's room and sit on the chair by his bed. And that's where I remain until morning.

As I'm driving home, I tell myself it's a new day. A new beginning. I'm going to change, for good this time. I'm going to be the man I used to be. The man Rachel helped me become. The man she would be proud of if she were still in our lives.

Rachel is gone. I've lost her, and my refusal to accept that nearly destroyed my relationship with my son. But I won't let that happen.

I've lost Rachel, but I will not lose Garret.

CHAPTER ELEVEN
Six Years Later

RACHEL

I'm on my break at the restaurant. A family just walked in. They look like tourists; parents with two teen girls, each with a backpack. They might be Americans. If they are, I should see if they'll give Pearce a message. But I've tried this so many times and failed that I don't know if it's even worth doing again.

For fifteen years I've been trapped in this tiny town and tried almost everything to escape. But the past few years, I admit, I've pretty much given up. I'm constantly being monitored so it's no use even trying to leave. And I don't have a passport, so even if I could leave this town, I couldn't leave the country.

My break is over, so I rise up from my chair, put on a smile, grab some menus, and approach the table with the family.

"Salve," I say, greeting them in Italian.

The husband raises his hand. "We don't speak Italian. Do you speak any English?"

"Yes. I'm American."

His wife smiles. "So are we. We're from New Hampshire. These are our girls, Maddie and Emma."

"Hi," I say, but they're staring at their phones. Maddie looks to be around 16 and Emma is maybe 18. It's the middle of May, so they're probably on summer break and this is the big family vacation.

"Mom, there's no cell service in this town," Maddie says.

"No Internet either," I add.

"Dad, let's leave," Emma says. "We have to find someplace where I can check my phone."

"We're having lunch," he says. "You'll live without your phone for an hour."

"Dad!" both girls cry out at once.

He ignores them and talks to me. "So where are you from?"

"Texas," I lie, because from past experience, telling the truth has earned me a warning letter delivered to my room. That was a few years ago, and ever since then, I've gone back to lying about my past. I know they're listening to everything I say. "I'll give you some time to look at the menu."

"Could you recommend something?" the husband asks. "We can't read the menu in Italian."

"Yes. Of course." I give them some options and let them decide.

I put their order in, and as they're waiting for their food, I try to decide what to do. Should I attempt to get another message to Pearce? Doing so will earn me another warning letter from whoever is watching me. Or maybe they'd do something to hurt me. I'm sure they're tired of me not following orders, although I haven't even attempted this in years. Still, I know I'll get in trouble if I even bring up Pearce's name.

I don't care. I'm desperate. I have to do something. But what if these people don't believe that I know Pearce? Or what if they don't give him the message? If they're like everyone else I've asked, they'll find it to be an odd request, and chances are they'll never tell him. Maybe if Pearce was a regular person they would, but people are too intimidated to call up a well-known billionaire.

When I bring out their food, Emma is looking at a magazine. It's one of those celebrity magazines with lots of pictures.

"Maddie, look!" Emma points to a page in the magazine. "Prep School Girls starts in two weeks!"

Maddie shrugs as I set her food down in front of her. "This one won't be as good as the one in Connecticut. That was the best season out of all of them."

Emma smiles, her eyes dreamy. "Only because of Garret." I wait for her to move the magazine, then lay her plate down.

"Garret who?" I ask.

"Kensington," they both say, and then start giggling.

100

I almost drop their mom's salad but I quickly set it down before I do.

"Who's Garret Kensington?" I ask innocently, but I think my voice sounded shaky. I clear my throat, then say, "I've never heard of him."

Emma looks at her sister and smiles. "He's the world's hottest guy."

"Definitely," her sister agrees. "Emma has pictures of him all over her room."

They must be talking about a different Garret Kensington. My son wouldn't be on a TV show.

"Is he an actor?" I ask Emma.

"No. Prep School Girls is a reality show. Garret was on it a few years ago, back when he was in high school. The show followed him and his girlfriend around, along with some other couples. Then they did a reunion show when he was in college."

Their mother laughs. "Don't get them started. They could talk about that boy all day."

Maybe it *is* him. The boy they're describing would be around Garret's age and he *does* live in Connecticut, at least he used to.

I smile at the mother, then turn back to the girls. "Where is he now? Still on TV?"

"No," Emma says as she adjusts her ponytail. "You don't hear much about him anymore. The rumor is that he lives somewhere in California. People have seen him in Santa Barbara. I heard he's married but I don't believe it. He's too young to be married, and besides, he's supposed to be with Ava and she's still single. Ava was his girlfriend on the show. They were totally in love."

"You know those shows aren't real," their father says. "Those two probably never even dated in real life."

Maddie rolls her eyes. "Whatever, Dad."

"Do you have children?" he asks me.

I almost say yes, but then catch myself. "No. No children."

"Imagine if you did and he was on a reality show." He laughs. "It must've been a real nightmare for his father, especially since he's in such a serious profession. I'm sure he was embarrassed having his son on some reality show."

"Honey, here's your napkin." His wife hands it to him.

"Who's his father?" I ask.

"Pearce Kensington. The billionaire CEO. Have you heard of him?"

A nervous flutter takes over my stomach but I try to remain calm. "I think so. He owns a chemical company?"

"Yes, that's him." The man bites into his sandwich.

I should let these people eat but I have to know more. I decide to play dumb. "I thought his father was the CEO."

"His father died five years ago," the man says, wiping his mouth with his napkin. "He had a stroke and went into a coma and died."

It takes a moment for my mind to process what he said, but when I do, I feel my heart racing in excitement.

"I'll be back to check on you," I say, then quickly walk away.

Holton is dead? He's really dead? I want to go outside and jump up and down and scream to the world that I'm free. I'm finally free!

The bell in the kitchen rings, alerting me that an order is ready. I race over to get it and practically skip on my way to deliver it to the customers waiting at table five. They look at me funny. They've probably never seen anyone look so happy or smile so wide, but I can't hide it. I'm free! I'm finally free!

Then my happiness plummets as I realize I don't have a passport and I don't have the right documents to get one. Why didn't Jack give me anything when I left? A fake birth certificate? Fake ID? Then again, if I'd had those things, Holton's men would've stolen them years ago.

Holton's men. I almost forget about them. Are they still watching me? That man said Holton died five years ago. Oh my God. He died five years ago! I could've left here five years ago! But I didn't know. I had no idea he was dead.

I quickly think about the last five years. I haven't really tried to leave town in those five years. Last year, I road my bike outside the town limits one day and nobody stopped me, but I thought that was just because they assumed I wouldn't get very far on a bike.

102

But maybe they didn't stop me because they weren't here. Because they stopped watching me after Holton died.

What if this whole time, I could've left town and didn't even know it? I race into the kitchen and go up to Celia, who's taking rolls out of the oven.

"Can I borrow your car?" I ask her.

She sets the baking sheet down on the counter. "You can't drive. You don't have a license."

"I'm not going far. Just a few kilometers outside of town. Then I'll come right back."

She turns to me and feels my forehead. "Are you ill? Your face is flushed and you're acting very odd."

"I'm not ill. Please, Celia. I just need to borrow your car."

She's staring at me like she knows something's up. She pulls her keys out and hands them to me. "I'll watch your customers for you."

I hug her. "Thank you!"

She keeps her eye on me as I run off. I'm going to miss her when I leave. *When I leave.* It's been years since I've even thought those words in my head. I guess because I'd given up hope, assuming I'd never get out of here.

I drive down the narrow road. It feels strange to drive a car again. I haven't driven a car in fifteen years. I haven't done a lot of things in fifteen years.

When I reach the end of town, I get nervous but I keep going. I go a kilometer and no one stops me. Then I go another, and another one after that. I drive five kilometers out of town without anyone chasing me or running me off the road. I pull off to the side and take a deep breath and cry tears of joy. They're gone. Holton's gone. Those men are gone. I'm finally free!

Back at the restaurant, I drop the keys off with Celia and return to work. Celia keeps watching me, but she doesn't say anything. When my shift is over, I go up to my apartment. A few minutes later, I hear a knock on the door.

I panic for a moment, thinking it's Holton's men, but they wouldn't knock.

"Who is it?" I ask.

"It's Celia."

I open the door. "Come on in." She walks in and I shut the door. "Is something wrong?" I ask because she seems more serious than usual.

"Sit down." She leads me to the bed.

"What's this about?"

"Are you going back home? To America?"

That's an odd question. She's never asked me that before.

"Um, I don't know." I don't look at her. If I do, I might tell her things I shouldn't.

"Are you afraid to go home?" she asks.

Another strange question. I keep quiet.

"Jill." She wraps her hands around mine. I look back at her and she looks directly in my eyes. "I have never once asked you about your past. I don't ask, because I don't want to be asked about mine. But I know you're hiding something. Something from your past. That's why you came here. You had to get away."

I swallow hard. "Why would you say that?"

"Because I've been in your shoes. Scared. Alone. Afraid to trust people. I've watched you for fifteen years. I've seen the sadness in your eyes. The fear. The loneliness. I've seen you gradually lose hope. You used to have hope, Jill. I don't know what you were hoping for, but there was a light in you that kept you going. Then that light went out and I haven't seen it in years. Until today." She squeezes my hand. "That hope is back, and I don't want to see you lose it again."

I nod. "You're right. I heard something today that gave me hope."

"Hope that you'll be able to go home?"

I hesitate. "Yes."

"But you can't, because there's someone there you're afraid of. Someone who might hurt you."

"No. Not anymore."

"Tell me, Jill. Tell me why you've been hiding here all these years."

I shake my head. "I can't.

104

How does she know I've been hiding? Is it that obvious? I guess it is. A woman from America shows up here with nothing more than a suitcase, and stays here for fifteen years? I would find that suspicious too. And yet, Celia has never asked me this before.

She releases my hand and sits back a little. "I'm going to tell you a story, but you need to keep this a secret, okay?"

"Yes." If she only knew how many secrets I'm keeping.

"When I was 22, I married a man who I thought was the love of my life, but after we were married, his love turned into an obsession to control me. He wouldn't let me leave the house, not even to go to the market. If I tried, he beat me. He made me a prisoner in my own home. This went on for over a year and I knew that eventually he would kill me. He drank too much and had a bad temper. One night he came home drunk and accused me of cheating on him and put a gun to my head. The gun slipped out of his hand so I grabbed it and shot him, multiple times to make sure he was dead."

My eyes are glued on her as she tells the story. I had no idea she'd been abused like that. And she killed him? She really killed her husband? I wonder if she's ever told anyone this.

"Then what happened?" I ask.

"My brother took care of it. He made it look like my husband was killed by street thugs and left to die in an alley."

Covering up a murder? It sounds like something the organization would do.

"How did your brother do that?" I ask.

"I'll tell you after you tell me more. I told you my story. Now I'd like to know yours. Why did you come here, Jill? What are you running from? Were you being abused?"

"No. I was being threatened by some very powerful people." I stop, afraid to tell her more. But I trust Celia, so I continue, but keep it vague. "If these people found me, they might kill me, so I had to hide out. But then one of them *did* find me, but instead of killing me, he's held me hostage here. He's had people watching me, and every time I tried to leave, his men would come after me and stop me."

"And now this man is gone?" she asks.

"Yes, and so are the men he hired. At least I think they are. That's why I took your car today. I left town, and for once, I wasn't stopped."

She doesn't seem surprised by this. Her expression hasn't changed at all since I told her.

"Celia, I expected you to be more shocked by what I told you."

She shakes her head. "Nothing shocks me. I've seen too many things over the years." She sees my questioning look and says, "My brother, Marco, is a criminal. He works with a group in Rome."

"A group? You mean like organized crime?"

"Yes. He's been working with them for years. So I'm familiar with threats being made by powerful people."

"Do you still talk to your brother?"

"All the time. Despite what he does, he's still my brother. He's chosen that lifestyle and I can't change him. It's not my place to judge him."

I almost laugh because I find it funny that she judges her sister for the men she dates, but she doesn't judge her brother for being a criminal.

"Does he kill people?"

She shrugs. "Probably. I don't ask. As far as I know he mostly works the streets, stealing from tourists. Wallets. Cell phones. Laptops. That's why I warned you about going to tourist areas. Criminals roam the streets and it can be dangerous." She pauses. "Those men. The ones you said were watching you. What did they look like?"

"I'm not sure. They always wore masks. But they were big guys. And tall, with deep voices."

"They're dead," she says calmly.

"What? How do you know that?"

"A few years ago, I noticed some men lurking behind the restaurant. I saw them when I went to dump the garbage. I'd seen them a few times before, also late at night, hiding behind the restaurant. I told my brother, and he came here and looked into it. He found that the men lived on the outskirts of town. He searched their apartments and found a stash of weapons and surveillance equipment. He did a sweep of the restaurant and

106

discovered listening devices hidden everywhere. We assumed someone found out what I'd done to my husband and hired those men to spy on me and perhaps capture some kind of evidence they could use to charge me with the crime. But I could never figure out who would do that or why. My husband didn't have many friends and his family wouldn't care enough to go to all that trouble, especially all these years later." She looks off to the side. "Now it all makes sense. Why those men were here. It wasn't about me. It was about you."

"So your brother um…took care of them?"

"I didn't ask," she says abruptly. "All I know is that they're dead. And no one has shown up to replace them."

"When did this happen?"

She shrugs. "Maybe five years ago?"

Five years ago. The same year Holton died. So did he know what happened to those men? Or was Holton already dead when it happened? Did he pay those men enough money to keep watch on me forever? Even once he was gone?

Celia gets up and walks around my room, her eyes searching the floor.

"What are you doing?"

She kneels down in the far corner of the room where there's a crack in the wall, so small it's barely noticeable. She takes the pencil from her apron and slips it in the crack and a tiny silver object falls out onto the floor. She holds it up. "It's the same as we found downstairs."

"A microphone?"

"Yes. And I'm sure there are more."

"We shouldn't be talking in here," I whisper.

"They're not listening. They're gone, and my brother took all their equipment."

"But someone else could be—"

She holds her hand up, silencing me. Then she leaves the room and I hear her go downstairs. She returns with a metal wand-like device and waves it around the room and the furniture and the walls. It must detect hidden microphones.

She shakes her head. "Nothing. I'm sure there are more in here but they're no longer working. Nobody is listening."

I let out a heavy sigh. "All this time...I didn't know...if I had, I could've..." My voice trails off. I can't do this to myself. I can't beat myself up about this, blaming myself for not knowing this sooner. Because how was I to know? I've been trapped in this tiny town with no access to information of any kind. And how could I have possibly known those men were dead and no longer watching me? And that Celia's brother got rid of them? She never even talks about her brother.

Celia sits beside me on the bed. "Those men are gone. And if that other man you were fearful of is no longer a threat, then you should go."

My shoulders slump in disappointment. "I can't. He stole my passport. And I don't have the necessary documents to get a new one."

"This is why it's good to have a brother like mine." She pats my knee. "I'll get you a passport."

I look at her. "Are you serious?"

"It's simple. He could have it to me in a day."

I'm so excited I jump up from the bed. "He could really do that? And it would work? I could get through customs?"

"Yes. You'd have no problems."

My heart swells with joy as I consider the possibility that I might actually get home. That this might finally happen.

I give her a hug. "Celia, you have no idea how happy you've just made me!"

"What about money?" she asks.

"I have some saved, but not much. How much does he want for the passport?"

"You don't need to pay for the passport. I'll take care of it. I was asking about the plane ticket."

"I have enough to buy the ticket."

"You'll need more than that. That's not enough. You'll need money for when you get there. Where will you be staying?"

"I don't know. I guess I'll find a hotel. I'm not even sure where I'm going. That family I talked to earlier said my son—" Damn. I didn't want to tell her that.

Her expression is pained as she slowly rises from the bed and stands in front of me. "You have a son?"

I nod, tears filling my eyes.

"You haven't seen your son in fifteen years," she says quietly, as if she's saying it to herself.

"I miss him so much," I say, tears running down my face.

"Oh, Jill." She puts her arms around me and hugs me. I hear Celia sniffling. She never cries, but the fact that I've been away from my son for so long has brought her to tears.

We break apart and both wipe our eyes.

"How old was he?" she asks. "When you left?"

"Ten." I squeeze my eyes shut, trying not to cry, but the tears still fall. "He was only ten."

She holds my hand. "So he thinks you left him?"

I sniffle. "I can't tell you what happened. I love you, Celia, and I trust you, but the more I tell you, the more I put you at risk. And I don't want them ever coming here and hurting you."

She nods. "We need to get you out of here. You need to go see that little boy."

I smile and wipe my tears. "He's not so little anymore. But yes, I want to see him as soon as possible."

"I'll call Marco and tell him we need the passport right away. I'll even have him drive us to the airport, just in case we run into any trouble. His car is more secure than mine. Bulletproof glass. Tinted windows. And he has a gun. I do too, but he has better aim than I do."

How did I never know this about her? She's shot a gun? Killed her husband? Has a brother who's a criminal? I guess we've both been keeping secrets. I just can't tell her mine.

"You need money," she says. "I'll give you the equivalent of three thousand American dollars. Will that be enough?"

"Celia, that's too much money."

She waves her hand around. "What do I need money for? It's yours."

"I'll pay you back. I promise."

She pauses, like she's thinking. "I need to get your ticket. I doubt they take cash at the airport. Even if they did, buying a last-minute ticket with cash would draw suspicion. I'll have Marco get the ticket. Where do you want to go?"

"Um, I'm not sure."

If I went to Connecticut to see Pearce, I'd risk running into people I know who might recognize me. And he may not even be there. He could be traveling for business. Those teen girls said Garret might be living in California. They said he was seen in Santa Barbara, but that doesn't mean he lives there. Still, it's a start, and at least I don't know anyone in Santa Barbara. I've never even been to California.

"Santa Barbara, California," I tell her.

"Santa Barbara," she repeats as she walks to the door. "Pack your suitcase. If Marco can get this done, you might be leaving tomorrow."

Once she's gone, I race around the room packing the few possessions I have. I'm excited, but also scared. Scared of making it through customs with a fake passport. Scared of someone coming after me if I make it to the U.S. Scared of putting Pearce and Garret in danger by showing up there.

I'm also scared because the last time I packed my suitcase to leave, those men showed up in my apartment and I saw that video of Holton. What if someone else is watching me? What if Leland is? Or one of the other members? Will I really be able to leave? Or will someone stop me again?

CHAPTER TWELVE

RACHEL

In the morning, I hear knocking on my door. It's 5:15, which is when I usually get up for my job at the restaurant.

I race to the door and open it. Celia's standing there.

"Marco will be here at noon. We'll go straight to the airport. You should be home by tomorrow sometime."

Tears fall again. I can't help it. I'm so happy. So relieved. So shocked that this is really going to happen. Fifteen years. Fifteen excruciating years I have waited for this moment and now it's finally here.

I hug her and don't let go. "Thank you. Thank you so much."

She pats my back. "You have to promise to write me. Or call me. Let me know you're safe."

"Yes. I will. I promise." I step back and see her smiling.

"Your face." She holds it between her hands. "You finally look happy."

"I am. I can't even tell you how happy I am."

"Get dressed, then come downstairs. We'll have breakfast together one last time."

"But you have to open the restaurant and make the bread."

"I called Mona. She's taking care of it." Mona is the waitress that works the dinner shift. "And the bread's already in the oven. I'll see you downstairs."

She leaves, and I hop in the shower, get dressed, and meet Celia in the restaurant. We have breakfast, and as we sit there by the window on this beautiful spring morning, I look out at the storefronts lined with flowers and remember when I used to love this town. How I wanted to retire here with Pearce. But now, I don't think I could ever come back here, not even to visit. There are too many bad memories. This is a part of my life I want to put behind me. I've been someone else the past fifteen years. Rachel wasn't the person living here. It was Jill, and I never want to be Jill again.

Marco arrives just before noon, wearing black dress pants and a white cotton shirt. He has dark gray hair that's slicked back and his skin is very tan. He doesn't look like a criminal. He looks like a distinguished older man, which probably makes it easier for him to steal from people. They'd never suspect someone like him to be a criminal, so they let their guard down around him. It's a good reminder for me not to trust anyone as I begin this journey back home. Looks can be deceiving and I have to keep a careful watch on everyone around me.

Marco gives me the passport of an American woman who looks very similar to me. Her name is Andrea. I feel bad that this woman had her passport stolen. What a nightmare it would be to have to replace that while in a foreign country.

As I take a closer at the picture, I see that it's not some woman who looks like me. It's actually me. Celia must've taken my picture when I wasn't looking. Maybe it was during her birthday party last year. She was taking a lot of photos that day.

I thought this was a stolen passport, but Marco must've made it himself. The edges are worn and there are stamps inside so it looks very real.

Celia sees me looking at it. We're riding in the back seat of the car as her brother drives us to the airport.

"It's real," Celia whispers, nodding toward the passport in my hand. "He just changes the photo. It will work. I promise."

I nod. So it *was* stolen. I'm leery of Marco, knowing he steals and commits other crimes. It's a world I like to pretend doesn't exist. Just like the world Jack told me about years ago in which a secret organization controls things, like presidential elections. I've tried not to think about that over the years because I don't want to believe Pearce is part of it. Or that Garret is part of it.

Celia reaches over and holds my hand. She knows I'm nervous, so she lets me sit quietly while she talks to her brother in Italian.

As we approach the drop-off area, I store my passport in the small travel bag Celia gave me. It's a thin, square purse that has a strap that I wear across my body.

"Be sure to write," Celia says, as we hug on the curb next to the drop off area.

"I will." I bite my lip to keep from crying. "Thank you. For everything."

She gently pushes me back and holds my shoulders, looking me in the eye. "Don't be afraid. You can do this." She smiles. "Go back and see your son."

She hugs me once more, then gets in the car and they drive away. People are scurrying past me with their luggage. I take my suitcase and go into the airport terminal.

I made it. I actually made it to the airport. Now if I can just make it onto the plane. The check-in process goes smoothly. I show them my passport and smile and pretend I'm Andrea. Next is the security line. Again, I try to act natural, even though I'm a nervous wreck. I make it through security with no problems, then wait at the gate.

I feel sick to my stomach, fearful that someone will try to stop me before I board. There are cameras all over this airport. What if someone sees me? Holton's gone, but what if someone else is looking for me? What if Holton told someone I'm alive?

An announcement comes over the speakers that translates to 'looking for passenger Jill Smithfield. Please return to...' I relax. I heard the name 'Jill' and then 'Smith' and panicked. Now my heart is beating lightning fast. I take some deep breaths, trying to calm down so I don't draw attention to myself.

After almost two hours of waiting, I board the plane. It's a huge plane and it takes forever to get to my seat. As I sit there, I nervously tap my foot, anxious for the plane to take off.

"You don't like flying?" the man next to me asks. He's about my age, wearing a suit and tie. He sounds American. I look over and see him smiling at me.

I immediately stop tapping my foot and smile back. "I don't mind flying. I just get a little nervous right before takeoff."

He nods. "My ex-wife was the same way."

This guy better not be a talker, because I really don't want to talk to anyone. I turn away from him but I'm stuck in a middle seat with people on both sides. The person on my other side is an older man who I've just noticed has bad body odor, so I turn and face forward again and close my eyes.

I hear the sound of paper crinkling and peek open my eyes to see that the guy in the suit is now reading a newspaper. The safety announcements start on the speakers above me and then I feel the plane moving. As it takes off, I close my eyes and smile. I made it. I made it on the plane. The first step in getting back home.

There isn't a direct flight from Naples to New York so we have a short layover in Rome. I get nervous again as I change planes, but make it safely on the next one and feel relieved when it takes off.

Ten hours later, we land at JFK airport in New York. I'm happy to be back in the U.S., but I feel sick again as I wait in the long line at customs. What if they find out my passport has been tampered with? What if this Andrea person put out an alert saying her passport was stolen?

It takes almost an hour to reach the front of the line, and when I'm finally there, I hand my passport to the man and answer his questions as calmly as possible.

He looks at my passport, staring at the photo. He holds it up, glancing at me and then the photo. What's taking so long? He didn't do this with anyone else.

There's something wrong. This isn't going to work. I made it this far and now I'm not going to make it into the country.

He motions another worker to come over.

Oh, God. This is bad. They know the passport was stolen. Now what? Will they take me to jail? Send me back to Italy?

The other man takes my passport and runs his finger over the photo. He looks at me, then sets the passport down.

"It's just worn edges," he says to the other guy. "She can go."

He walks off and I breathe again. I was holding my breath that entire time.

The man hands me my passport. "Next," he says to the person behind me.

I walk through the airport and find a place to exchange my money for American dollars. Then I continue on to the terminal and wait to board the plane.

I'm so tired. It's now the middle of the night and last night I didn't sleep much. And I didn't sleep on the long flight here. I was too nervous, afraid I'd wake up and this would all be a dream. Now I have another long flight, all the way across the country to LA, followed by another layover, and then a short flight to Santa Barbara. Maybe I should try to sleep on the plane. I need to be alert when I get there.

An hour later, we're boarding. It's another huge plane that takes a long time to board. As I'm waiting in line, I look over at the other gates. The one across from mine is going to Paris and leaves in an hour. I've always wanted to go to Paris, but after being stranded in Italy for fifteen years, I may never leave the U.S. again.

The line moves up a little. A man walks past me, talking loudly on his phone. I freeze because the voice sounds very familiar. But it couldn't be him.

The line inches forward and I glance behind me and see the man with the familiar voice. He's in a black suit, his back to me, standing in line at the check-in desk for the Paris flight. He's still on the phone, talking with his hands, and when he turns slightly, I see that it's him. It's Leland Seymour!

I quickly turn around so that I'm facing my gate. Leland didn't see me. I'm sure he didn't. He was too busy talking on his phone. But I can't risk having him see me. I need to get on the plane. And fast!

The people in front of me are mumbling and pointing to the gate. There seems to be a problem with the machine that scans the boarding passes and now we're not moving.

Hurry up! I yell inside my head. One of the airline workers goes to help the woman who was running the machine, but he can't get it to work. He goes back to the check-in desk and makes a call.

115

Hurry! I plead inside my head. *Please, hurry. Please, please, please.*

The worker hangs up the phone, then picks up the loud speaker. *No, no, no! Leland will hear the announcement and look over here. Dammit!*

"I got it," the woman running the machine says. "It's working now."

I breathe again, my stomach doing flip-flops from all the stress. Or maybe it's because I haven't eaten anything for almost twenty-four hours. I should probably eat something, but I feel too sick to keep anything down.

The line finally begins moving again. I don't dare look back. I can't risk it. Leland could be looking this way. A few minutes later, I'm on the plane, stuck in another middle seat. There's a teenage girl on one side of me, and a guy in his twenties on the other. They both have headphones on and are staring at their phones. They don't seem like talkers, so that's good.

The plane takes off and I end up falling asleep, waking up an hour outside of LA. I feel a little better from the sleep, but my stomach is growling. The flight attendant is walking by and I ask her for a soda and some nuts. When she brings them, I devour them, realizing I'm more hungry and thirsty than I thought.

I change planes in LA, and on the short flight to Santa Barbara, I try to figure out what I'm going to do when we land. I'll have to get a rental car, then find a hotel. After that I'll have to find a library where I can look up information on Garret and Pearce.

What if Garret doesn't live in California? Maybe those girls were wrong and he still lives in Connecticut. I should've had Marco or Celia look that up before I came here. But I couldn't tell them Garret's name. I don't want them knowing I'm a Kensington. I trust Celia, but I don't trust Marco or the people he works with.

When we land, I get my luggage and go straight to the car rental place that has the shortest line.

"I need a car," I say to the man at the desk. "An inexpensive one."

He holds his hand out. "ID and credit card."

116

"Oh, um, I don't have a credit card. I'm paying with cash."

"We require that a credit card be on file in case the car is damaged or stolen."

"I…I'm not going to damage or steal it." I sound nervous. I need to calm down.

"We still need a credit card on file." He seems annoyed, his eyes on the line of people behind me.

"Do all the rental companies require a credit card?"

"Yes. It's standard policy."

That's just great. So now I can't drive anywhere.

Wait a minute. I don't have a license. I can't rent a car without a driver's license. What was I thinking? I'm so tired and hungry and stressed that I'm not thinking straight.

"Ma'am, I have a line of people waiting."

"Yes. I'm sorry." I pick up my suitcase and exit the line and go outside to where the taxis are lined up.

One of the drivers sees me waiting and jumps out of the car.

"Where are you going?" he asks. He has an Italian accent and it throws me. For a moment I thought I was back in Italy. "You want a ride or not?" he asks, holding the door open.

"Yes." I get in the back seat and he closes the door.

He puts my suitcase in the trunk, then gets in the front seat and starts the meter. "What's the address?"

"Just take me to a hotel. Someplace not too expensive in a decent part of town. Maybe next to a grocery store."

He glances back at me, giving me a strange look. "You don't have a hotel reservation?"

"No. I don't know the area that well so I wasn't sure where to stay."

"Most people have a reservation," he mumbles as he drives off.

He's right. Most people would. He keeps checking the rearview mirror, looking at me with suspicious eyes. I need to make up a story.

I scoot to the end of my seat so he can hear me better. "I'm surprising my boyfriend. He just moved here and I haven't seen him in two weeks and I wanted to surprise him, so on a whim, I got the first flight here and didn't even bother to find a hotel. I

117

didn't want to just show up at his place after being on the plane. I want to go to a hotel and freshen up."

He smiles and nods. "That's nice. Very romantic."

He believes me. That's good.

"You need a nicer hotel," he says. "I know where to go."

"I can't afford much. I need something moderately priced."

"This is an expensive town. Nothing's cheap around here."

We're driving down a street that has homes hidden behind iron gates. I didn't realize Santa Barbara was such an exclusive area.

He turns right, onto a street that has restaurants and gas stations. I spot a hotel, and next to it is a small grocery store.

"Take me to that one," I say, pointing to it.

"That'll be expensive. All the rich people live around here."

"That's fine. I won't be here long."

He pulls into the hotel. It doesn't look that fancy. It's a single-level hotel with a white stucco exterior and flowers in large pots lining the entrance. I pay the driver, get my suitcase, and go inside to the check-in.

"I need a room for the night," I say to the woman behind the desk. "The cheapest one you have."

She types into her computer. "The ones we have available are $250 a night plus tax."

Wow. That's expensive.

"Okay. I'll take it. Just one night." I'll find something cheaper for tomorrow night, but right now, this will have to do. I'm too tired to find something else and my cab is already gone.

The woman holds her hand out. "Credit card."

"I'm paying with cash."

"We need a card on file in case there are damages to the room."

Again? This is so ridiculous. Can't anyone do anything without a credit card?

"I don't have a credit card. My wallet was stolen and all I have is cash."

She sighs. "Then call the credit card company and have them give us your number."

"Could you please just let me have the room? I promise you, I won't damage it."

She rolls her eyes. "Yeah, we've heard that before. Which is why we require a card."

Now I'm getting angry. "Do I look like someone who would damage the room?" I stand back, motioning to myself in my conservative black slacks and beige blouse. "I would never damage a hotel room."

"It's our policy to require a credit card."

"Can I speak with your manager, please?"

"I AM the manager," she says, annoyed.

"So I can't have the room? Even if I pay you double for it?"

"I need a credit card." She sighs again and crosses her arms over her chest.

"Then I guess I'm leaving. Are there any hotels you know of that don't require a credit card to check in?"

She laughs. "Maybe one of those pay-by-the-hour hotels they have next to the truck stop just off the freeway."

"Thanks for your help," I mumble. I wheel my suitcase out the front doors, then stand there, just outside the entrance.

What am I going to do? I have no place to stay. I can't get a hotel room. And I don't have a car.

CHAPTER THIRTEEN

RACHEL

I'm starving, so I decide to go to the grocery store, which is closer than any of the restaurants on this street.

It's a very small grocery store and everyone stares at me as I walk in rolling a suitcase behind me. They probably think I'm homeless, which I guess I am. I have no place to go. Where am I going to sleep tonight?

As I wander through the produce section, I say a little prayer, begging God to help in any way possible. And then begging my parents to help me. I know they're keeping watch on me. If they weren't, I would have gotten on that plane years ago and be dead now. Or Holton would've killed me after he found me in Italy. But I'm still alive, and there has to be a reason for that. I have to believe that reason was so that I could be with my family again.

I place a few bananas in the shopping cart. Fruit sounds good so I get a couple apples too, and some oranges. Maybe I'll get some nuts. They're filling and portable and easy to eat. As I'm rounding the corner of the aisle, pushing my cart and dragging my suitcase behind me, I run right into someone else's cart.

"I'm sorry," I say.

"It's no problem, dear," I hear an older woman say as I check that my suitcase didn't fall over.

She goes around me and I look up and smile at her. She smiles back, then stops abruptly. She's staring at me. Why is she staring at me? Does she think she knows me?

Do I know *her*? She does look familiar. I'm guessing she's in her seventies. Maybe she was a friend of my parents. But none of their friends lived in California, unless this woman retired here.

"Could I ask your name?" she says.

"Um, it's Jill…I mean Andrea." Great. I just gave her two names, as if I don't even know my own name.

She knows I'm lying. The name mixup is a dead giveaway.

"I have to go," I say, but I can't get past her. It's too tight of a turn around the aisle with her cart right next to mine.

"Rachel?" she asks.

She knows me? How does she know me? Maybe she thinks I'm a different Rachel.

"I'm sorry, but could you please move your cart?"

I feel her staring at me. "Rachel Kensington."

"No." I shake my head, my heart racing. "You must have me confused with someone else. My name is Andrea."

"No, it's you. Rachel…" Her voice drifts off. "But how could that be? You were on the plane." She glances at my suitcase, then back at me. "Where have you been?"

"I…I don't know what you're talking about." I try to maneuver my cart around the tight corner.

She holds my arm. "Do you remember me? Grace Sinclair."

My eyes dart to her face. That's why she looks familiar. Grace Sinclair. Royce's mother. She looks so much older now that I didn't recognize her at first. "Grace?" I say without realizing I even said it out loud.

"Yes." She nods. "Grace Sinclair. We used to know each other."

I don't know what to say. Do I admit who I am? Can I trust Grace? She's part of the organization. Or at least her husband and sons are, according to what Jack told me years ago. What if she turns me in? They'll come after me. They'll kill me!

"Rachel." She's holding my hand now, lightly rubbing it to get my attention.

Her voice is soft, soothing. And I get a gut feeling that I can trust her. I always liked Grace and Arlin. I thought they were nice people. But then why was Arlin part of that group? Because he

121

was forced to be part of it. I have to keep reminding myself of that. It's not a choice. Pearce was forced to be a member, and so was Arlin.

"Honey, are you okay?" Grace asks in a motherly tone. And she called me 'honey' just like my mom used to do. She looks concerned. "Maybe we should go sit down. You're white as a ghost."

"I'm a little light-headed," I say, noticing how dizzy I suddenly feel. "I haven't eaten much the past couple days."

"You should sit down." She checks the area around us, but there's no place to sit. "Is someone with you?"

"No. I'm here alone."

"Where do you live?"

"I, um…" I close my eyes until the dizziness passes, then open them again. "I don't live anywhere. I…I just got here. I just got off a plane."

"Oh, dear." She sounds worried. "We need to get you home. Do you have a car?"

"No. I walked here. I mean, I took a taxi."

She pushes my grocery cart aside and stands next to me, taking my arm. "Let's go to the car. My house is just a few blocks from here."

I agree to it because I'm not sure what else to do. She's offering to help me and right now I need help, so I'm going with my gut and trusting her.

As we're walking away, I say, "What about your shopping cart? Don't you want to check out?"

"It's fine. I didn't need much. I'll come back and get it later."

She leads me out to the parking lot, holding onto my arm the entire time. We stop next to a silver Mercedes. She pops open the trunk and I put my suitcase in there, then get in the car.

This is so surreal. I arrive in a town I've never been to, go to a tiny grocery store, and run into Grace Sinclair? I feel like I'm dreaming this.

"I normally have bridge club on Saturdays," she says as we're driving down the street. "That's why I'm here. But I'll call and tell them I won't be there."

Her words run together in my head. What did she say? Something about bridge? I'm not sure. I'm so out of it. I need to eat. And I need some water. I don't feel good.

Grace's house is one of the ones behind the gate that the taxi drove past on the way here. When the gate opens, we're surrounded by flowers. It reminds me of my wedding. The second one. The ballroom where the reception was held was covered in flowers.

"This is beautiful," I say as I lower my window, the scent of the flowers surrounding me.

She smiles as she parks in front of the house. "I enjoy flowers."

"Me too," I say. "I love flowers."

Her house looks like a country cottage, with stone on the outside and a white bench on the porch and flowers everywhere.

We go inside her house. It's bright and cheery, with a yellow sofa in the living room and windows all along the back wall that let the sun in.

"I love your house." I walk over to the windows. Her back yard is huge and full of every kind of flower imaginable, separated by stone walking paths and a gazebo in the middle. "Your flower gardens are beautiful. I could live out there."

She takes my arm again. "We'll go out there later. Let's go to the kitchen and get you something to eat."

As Grace makes me a sandwich, I drink three big glasses of iced tea. Then I devour the sandwich, and when I'm done, I feel much better.

"Thank you for the lunch," I say, taking another drink of iced tea.

"You're very welcome. I'm just glad I was in town and ran into you."

"You don't live here?"

"No. I own the house, but I don't live here. But I like to come down here sometimes and visit my flowers. And as I said, I have bridge club on Saturdays, twice a month."

"Where do you live?"

"About an hour north of here." She looks like she wants to say something, but then she doesn't.

"I don't want to inconvenience you. If you need to go, that's fine. But maybe you could just help me get a hotel. I tried to—"

"Honey, you're not staying at a hotel." She rubs my hand. "You're staying with us. Isn't that why you're here? To see him?"

What is she talking about? Stay with us? Who's 'us'? The Sinclair family? We were kind of friends, but not really.

"I'm not sure what you mean."

"Oh." She looks concerned. "I guess you don't know. I just assumed you were here to see Garret."

My heart takes off just hearing his name. "Garret is here? It's not just a rumor? He's really here in California?"

"Yes. He and his wife, Jade, live about an hour north of here, in a house along the coastline. And I live next door to them."

I smile, tears falling down my face. "Garret's only an hour away?" I cover my mouth with my hand. "And he's married?"

"Yes. To Jade. Jade is my granddaughter."

"My son is married to your granddaughter?"

"Yes. She's Royce's daughter. It's a long story. I think it's best if Jade and Garret tell you. In fact, I'd rather have them tell you everything. It might be best if you talked to Garret alone first. Why don't I call and see if he could come down here?"

I nod quickly. "Yes. Please. I'm desperate to see him. I've waited so long. I have to see him."

She gets up from the table and goes over to her phone, which is in the kitchen. She calls him, and I'm tempted to run over and grab the phone from her, but I don't. Knowing I'm alive is going to be a huge shock to him. It's better if our reunion happens face-to-face.

"Hello, Garret." Grace smiles at me as she puts the phone on speaker.

"Hi, Grace." I hear the voice, but don't recognize it. He has a deep voice, like a man, not the little boy voice I remember. "Aren't you supposed to be playing bridge?"

"Yes, but something came up so I decided not to go. Garret, I was wondering if you could come down here?"

"Why? Is something wrong?"

"No, I just wanted to have some friends over this afternoon and I need the patio furniture taken out of storage. It's too heavy for me to move myself."

"Yeah, don't do it. You'll hurt yourself. I'll do it. Do you want me to come down right now?"

"If you could, then yes."

"Let me tell Jade. She's not quite ready to leave."

"Jade doesn't need to come. It won't take long to do the furniture."

"Okay. Are you coming back tonight or staying there?"

"I'm sure I'll be back tonight."

"All right. I'll see you soon."

"Thank you, Garret."

"No problem. Bye, Grace."

Grace ends the call and takes a box of tissues from the counter and brings it over to me. "Rachel, I'm sorry. I thought you'd want to hear his voice."

I take a handful of tissues because I'm a crying mess. "I *did* want to hear it. He just sounded so different than I remember. I can't believe my little boy is now a man. He sounds so mature."

She sits next to me. "Garret has grown up to be a wonderful young man. He's polite. Responsible. Always willing to help. Any mother would be proud to have a son like him."

I grab more tissues and dab my eyes. "Tell me more. I want to know everything about him."

"Let's wait. I'd rather have him tell you himself."

I nod. "What about Pearce? Where does he live?"

"He still lives in Connecticut." Her brows furrow in concern. "Rachel, where have you been all this time? Why do you not know these things about Pearce and Garret? I thought you would've perhaps gone on the Internet and—"

"I didn't have access to the Internet." I set my tissue down. "I was in a very remote town. I can't say where. I've always liked you, Grace, and I want to trust you, but after what I've been through, I don't really trust anyone. I'm sorry, but I'm not ready to tell you everything."

She pats my hand. "I understand."

"Can you tell me anything else about Pearce?"

"I'd prefer if Garret did. The two of you have a lot to talk about."

"I *do* know that Pearce married Katherine."

"Yes." She sits back. "But it wasn't a good marriage."

"*Wasn't?* You mean they're no longer married?" My voice is rushed, excited.

Grace notices and smiles slightly. "They divorced five years ago. He's been single ever since. But he has custody of Lilly." She sees the pained expression on my face and says, "Oh. Rachel, I'm sorry. I assumed you knew he had another child."

"I did. I just…I hadn't thought about it for a while." Actually, I thought Holton might've been lying when he said Pearce had a child with Katherine. "So how old is his daughter?"

"Lilly is 12. She's a very sweet girl. But again, you should ask Garret about all of this. I don't feel right being the one to tell you."

I'm quiet for a moment as I let this sink in. Garret is married. Pearce is divorced and has custody of his daughter. What else has happened? I don't ask Grace, because she'll insist that I wait for Garret, so I ask her about herself instead.

"Is Arlin here?" I ask.

She smooths the tablecloth with her hand. "Arlin passed away six years ago."

"Grace, I'm so sorry. I shouldn't have asked."

"It's all right, dear. You didn't know." She pauses, her eyes on the tablecloth. "Royce is gone too. He died a few months before Arlin did."

I reach for her hand. "Grace, I'm so very sorry. That's devastating to lose them both in one year."

I wonder how they died. Arlin would've been old, but Royce is Pearce's age. So why did Royce die at such a young age?

"How are Victoria and the girls?" I ask.

"They're doing well. It was hard on them at first, but they've adjusted to life without him."

"And how about you? How are you adjusting?"

She smiles softly. "I'm doing well. After Arlin died, Pearce checked in on me, making sure I was okay. And Jade called me almost every day. And of course, I have William, but he travels so much for work and has...other obligations." Her voice trails off.

What does she mean by 'other obligations'? Does she mean obligations for that secret organization? I want to ask her about it, but I'm not sure if I should.

"Is William part of it?" I blurt out before I can stop myself. I know he's part of it, so why did I ask?

"Part of what, dear?"

"I know about that secret group." I watch her reaction, but she doesn't have one. Her expression hasn't changed. "I know Pearce is a member and I know Royce was, so I assume William is too?"

"Yes," she says quietly.

"Do you know much about it?"

"It's another topic we shouldn't discuss. You should ask Pearce about it."

"I need to know, Grace. Do they really make their members do horrible things? Like...hurt people?"

She sighs. "It's changed a lot the past few years. I can't say much more than that."

"Do you think Pearce has...done things? Bad things?"

"Rachel. Please don't judge Pearce based on what he's done in the past. He was not given a choice. He did what they told him to do. Pearce is a good man. Just like Arlin was a good man. I know it's difficult to overlook what they've done, but you need to see that side of them as someone else. The Pearce you know is the real Pearce. The one you fell in love with." She smiles. "We've done enough talking. I'm sure you'd like to clean up a little after traveling. If you'd like to take a shower or change clothes, there are several guest rooms down the hall."

"Yes, a shower would be good." I get up from the chair, then lean down and hug her. "Thank you again, Grace. I don't know what I would've done if I hadn't run into you."

She pats my back. "Go get ready. Garret will be here soon."

I shower and put on a dress, then wait in the living room with Grace. I'm excited, but also nervous to see Garret. I don't know how he's going to react.

We hear a car pulling into the driveway.

"That's him," Grace says. "Let me talk to him first before I bring him inside."

"Are you going to tell him I'm here?"

She pauses to think. "No. But I will let him know he's not here to take out the patio furniture." She smiles. "Relax, Rachel. Everything will be fine."

I rise from the couch and smooth the wrinkles from my dress, feeling even more nervous. What if Garret gets mad at me for leaving? Or what if he's angry that I showed up here again? Am I putting him in danger by coming back? God, I hope not. If I am, I'll leave again. I would never do anything to put my family in danger.

Grace goes out the front door and I hear her saying hello to Garret.

This is it. The moment I've been waiting for for fifteen years. I will finally see my son again.

CHAPTER FOURTEEN

GARRET

"Hey, Grace." I get out of the car, which is parked behind hers. "So what time are your friends coming over?"

She stops me as I'm walking up to the house. "I'm not really having friends over. I just said that because I needed you to come here."

"To take out the patio furniture?"

"No." She glances at the house, then back at me. "There's someone inside who wants to see you."

"Who is it?"

"Someone from your past."

"Grace, what is this about? You're making me nervous."

"Don't be nervous. But keep an open mind."

"An open mind? What are you talking about?"

"You'll see." She gives me a quick hug. "I'm going to run to the store to give you two some time alone."

"Time alone? Grace, tell me who's in there."

"You need to see for yourself." She holds her hand out. "May I have your keys? You blocked my car in. I'll just take yours, if that's okay."

"Yeah, that's fine." I hand her the keys and she walks off and gets in my car.

This is very strange. Who is she hiding in the house? She said it's someone from my past. I have no clue who it would be or why this person would come here to see me.

I go into the house. "Hello?"

Nobody answers. I walk through the foyer and stop when I reach the living room. There's a woman standing by the couch. I'm not good with ages, but I'm guessing she's maybe in her mid- to late-forties. She's tall and thin, wearing a casual navy dress with a white cardigan sweater.

"Garret." She says it softly, her voice trembling.

"Who are you?" I remain where I'm at as she slowly walks toward me. She looks familiar. Really familiar. Eerily familiar. In fact, I'm getting this strange feeling because she looks so familiar.

She keeps walking until she's right in front of me. She's crying, tears pouring down her cheeks. "It's me."

She has shoulder-length, dark brown hair and bright blue eyes. Seeing her up close, she almost looks like—no, that's crazy.

"Do I know you?" I ask.

"Yes." Tears continue down her cheeks as she smiles.

I focus on her smile, and the way her eyes smile along with her mouth. My mom's face did the same thing. People were always drawn to my mom because of her smile.

My heart's pounding and I'm breathing fast. This isn't right. I must be seeing things.

"Garret, honey." She reaches for me. "It's me. Your mom."

I step back. "No! Stop! Who are you? Tell me."

She doesn't come any closer. "Garret." She speaks softly, her eyes on mine. "I'm your mother. Rachel."

Who the hell is this woman and why is she saying this shit? My mom is dead. She died fifteen years ago. I saw the plane, burning in the field. There was nothing left of it.

I should turn and walk out the door. And yet I can't take my eyes off her. She looks so damn familiar. I'm studying her face. The shape of it. And her eyes. They're the exact same color as mine.

"I had to leave," she says. "They forced me to. I had no choice. If I didn't, they would've—" She squeezes her eyes shut and more tears fall down her face, her body trembling.

This is so messed up. I don't know what to do. Why is this woman here? Why did Grace let her into her house?

130

"Hey." I touch her arm to get her attention. She looks up at me and I stop breathing for a moment. Her eyes. God, they look so much like my mom's eyes.

She reaches in the pocket of her sweater and pulls something out. "I wasn't sure if you'd recognize me after all this time." She wipes the tears from her cheek and sniffles. "So I wanted to show you this. So you'd know it was me."

She lifts her hand up, holding it in front of me. Then she slowly opens her fist, and lying on her palm is a gold chain with two heart-shaped lockets hanging from it; one big and one small.

My eyes focus on the necklace. My mom had one just like it. She wore it almost every day.

I point to it, my heart pounding. "Where did you get that? Where did you fucking get that?"

"Honey, you know where I got it. Your father gave it to me when I came home from the hospital after you were born." She opens the small heart locket and shows it to me. Inside is a photo of a baby. "That's you, Garret." She closes the locket. "When your father gave this to me, I was—"

"Stop it!" I swallow hard and try to catch my breath. "Why do you have that? Who the fuck are you?"

Now I feel my own tears forming and it's pissing me off. Who the hell does this woman think she is? Pretending to my mom? And why does she have that necklace? It's not hers. It belongs to my mom!

"Why are you doing this to me?" I scream it at her, my voice shaky. "Why are you pretending to be her? My mom is dead! She died fifteen years ago. And to this day—" I'm sobbing now and I don't know why. Or maybe I do but I can't accept it. I can't accept this could possibly be real. "To this day, I'm not over her death. I still miss her so damn much…it fucking hurts."

"Oh, honey, I'm so sorry." She's crying too, even more than before. But she won't stop looking at me. And I can't take my eyes off her either.

"You can't do this to me! You can't come here and pretend she's alive. Pretend you're her. You can't do that to me!"

131

She sets the necklace on the table and reaches her hand out toward me. "Garret, just let me—"

"You look like her. You really do. And I don't know how you got that necklace, but you shouldn't have it. That was hers! Dad gave it to her and she wore it almost every damn day until the day she—" I cover my tear-soaked face with my hands and rub my eyes. "Until she was gone."

I feel her arms around me. I should yank away from her. But I don't. Because this feels familiar. The way she's hugging me feels familiar. Why does it feel familiar? What the fuck is going on here?

"Garret." She's crying so hard, she can barely say it. "I'm so sorry. I'm so sorry I left you."

I can't even speak. My mind is such a mess right now. What she's saying can't possibly be true, but the way she looks, her voice, the way she's hugging me. It's all so damn familiar that I have no other explanation.

She pulls away, her hands on my arms, her eyes on mine. "I didn't want to leave you. I didn't want to leave my little boy. My only child. I loved you and your father more than anything in this world. I still do."

I shake my head and yank away from her. "No! You're not her. It's not possible."

"I know it's hard to believe." She wipes her eyes. "And I know you're upset. I was worried about coming back. I wasn't sure if you'd accept me back into your life. But when I found out he was gone, I had to come see you. I've thought about you every second of every day since I left. And so when I knew I could, I had to come back. I had to see you again."

I don't understand this. If it's really her, how is this possible?

"You weren't on the plane," I say.

"No."

"Why? Why weren't you on the plane?"

"Because someone warned me."

"Who?"

"A friend of ours."

I look at her. "What friend? Who was it?"

132

"It was…it was Jack. Do you remember Jack? He was like a grandpa to you. And his wife, Martha? She loved you. She used to come over all the time to see you."

Jack and Martha. I remember them, but it was so long ago. And then they moved and we never saw them again.

"So Jack was part of the organization?" As soon as I ask, I realize she doesn't know about the organization. Or at least she didn't before.

"Yes. He's the one who told me about it." She holds my arm. "You're part of it now, aren't you? They make you do things. They make you—"

"No. I'm not part of it. They let me out."

Her brows rise. "But I thought—"

"It's a long story. A really long story. And not one I want to tell right now."

How does she know all this? How does she know about Jack and Martha? How does she know my parents were friends with them? That's not something you could look up online.

She's staring at me, her eyes still teary. "You're so grown up."

"I'm 25."

"I know. I celebrated every one of your birthdays, even though I wasn't here." She smiles.

It's the smile I'd see in my head whenever I thought about her. The smile that was always on her face when she picked me up from school. The smile I saw across from me at the dinner table every night. The smile I saw the day she left for DC for that fundraiser, which was the last time I saw that smile. Until today.

My head is finally getting this. Realizing this isn't some kind of hoax. It's real. This woman really is my mother. Holy shit!

I step up to her and wrap my arms around her. "It's really you, isn't it?"

"Yes." Her arms wrap tightly around me. "And I'm so sorry. I'm so sorry for putting you through that. Leaving you. It was the hardest thing I've ever had to do. I love you, honey. And I love your father. I love you both so much."

She's crying and so am I. I can't believe this is happening. That she's really here.

133

"I thought you were gone." I keep my arms around her, not wanting to let go. I'm afraid if I do, she'll disappear and I'll find that this was all just a dream. "I saw the plane. I thought you were dead."

"I know." She holds me closer. "I'm so sorry."

We remain there until our tears have stopped and then we finally let go of each other. We both step back and wipe our faces.

"Let's sit down." She takes my hand and leads me to the couch.

I have so many questions I don't know where to begin. "Where were you? Where have you been all these years?"

"In Italy. In a small village your dad and I went to right after we got married. We loved it so much that your dad said we should live there when he retired. So when I had to pick a place to hide, I picked that same village. Jack said he'd tell your father where to find me. I kept waiting for your father to show up, but he never did. Months went by, then years, so I went to a place that had Internet access and did some research and found that Jack died the night he went to tell your father about me. So your father never knew. Jack wasn't able to tell him I was alive." More tears spill down her cheeks.

"Mom, why? Why did you leave? If you knew about the plane, why didn't you tell Dad? He would've kept you safe. He would've—"

"Garret, there was an order to kill me. I saw it. It was from the organization."

"I know, but—"

"How did you know?"

"They told me a few years ago when they were trying to force me to be a member. They showed me the order. And then Grandfather—" I stop, not sure if she knows that part of the story.

"Yes. I know it was your grandfather's idea." She takes a deep breath. "I know Holton wanted to kill me. And I knew if I went back to you and your father after the plane crash, that I'd be killed."

"Dad would've never let that happen. He would've done anything to protect you."

134

"He couldn't protect me from the organization. I know how they operate. They're all about rules. They follow orders. And if there's an order to kill, they do it. And I worried that in their efforts to kill me, you could be harmed. I couldn't put you at risk. I would never do that." She rubs my arm. "Honey, more than anything I wanted us to be a family again. But I knew that wouldn't happen if I went back home. I knew my only chance of seeing you and your father again would be to go into hiding and wait until your father could find a way to keep me safe."

"When Dad didn't show up, and you found out he never got the message, why didn't you leave? You could've at least hidden out here in the U.S. At least you would've been closer to us and then—"

"Garret, I tried. I tried to leave, but Holton stopped me."

"What do you mean he stopped you? He knew you were alive?" I feel heat burning inside me. It's rage. Pure rage toward my grandfather and all the things he's done to destroy our lives. "What did he do?"

"He threatened me. He said if I tried to leave, or tried to contact anyone from my old life, that there would be consequences. Consequences for you, Garret. I was so scared. I didn't know if he'd hurt you, but I couldn't take the chance."

If my grandfather were alive, I'd kill that bastard right now. He knew my mom was alive, but he didn't tell us? How could he do that to us? All those years, he saw my dad and me grieving. Saw how her death destroyed us and tore us apart. And my grandfather still didn't tell us. He purposely kept her from us.

"Holton was determined to keep me there," she says. "He hired some men to keep watch on me, day and night. I couldn't even leave the town. I was a prisoner there, and it was such a small rural town that it had no Internet access. I couldn't get any information about you or your father."

"Why didn't you call him? I know you were worried about what Grandfather would do, but couldn't you have at least tried to call Dad? At least once?"

She nods. "I did. I dialed your father's number, but the call wouldn't go through. Holton or his men were somehow able to block it. Then I tried calling Martha and the same thing happened. The call was blocked. After I made those calls, I got a warning letter delivered to my apartment, telling me never to do it again. So I tried a different approach to reach your father. Instead of calling him, I tried to get a message to him. Whenever Americans would come to the restaurant I worked at, I would ask them to call your father and tell him about me, but none of them ever did. At least, I don't think they did."

What is she saying? That she thinks my dad wouldn't try to get her if he knew she were alive? That's crazy.

"If Dad knew," I say, "he would've been over there the second he found out."

"But he was married, so maybe—"

"No. He would've dropped everything and went to get you."

She nods, but she looks like she doesn't believe me.

"So Grandfather had those men watching you, but what happened when he died? Did they leave?"

"No. They um…they robbed a bank in Naples and were shot and killed by the police." She looks down as she says it and it makes me think that's not the real story. "But I didn't know they were gone until just recently, after I found out about Holton. I didn't know Holton was dead until just a few days ago. When I heard the news, I wanted to leave but I didn't have a passport. Holton's men stole it a long time ago. Luckily, a friend of mine was able to get me a fake one so I could get home."

My head is aching from all the thoughts running through my mind. I have so many questions and so much to tell her.

CHAPTER FIFTEEN

GARRET

"So you haven't talked to Dad yet?" I ask.

"No. I just arrived here today. I had planned to find a library so I could go online and look up information about you and your father, but then I ended up running into Grace at the grocery store. If I hadn't, I'd still be looking for you."

"How did you know to come to California?"

"An American family came into the restaurant I worked at in Italy and the two daughters were talking about you, saying you were on some TV show. I asked them about you and they said you lived in California. They thought you lived in Santa Barbara but they weren't sure. I thought it would be safer to come here than to go to Connecticut where I might run into people who know me. If one of those people happened to be a member, I was afraid of what they might do to me."

I wonder how much she knows about the organization. If she knows what they do, what does she think of my dad? He's had people killed and done it himself. And he lied to her all those years. But she just said she loved him, so does that mean she's forgiven him?

"So you didn't know about the organization until Jack told you?"

"No, I never knew. And at first I didn't believe Jack, but the more he told me, the more it made sense. I could never figure out why your father would sometimes leave late at night. Or why he always had these secretive phone calls he didn't want me to hear. Or why he'd sometimes become very withdrawn and distant. I'd ask him what's wrong and he wouldn't tell me. And the next day he'd be fine."

"You never asked him about those things?"

"He always blamed everything on work. And given how demanding your grandfather was, I assumed your father was telling me the truth. But now I know it was all because of this group. I assume your father's still part of it?"

"Yes, but he's not as involved as he used to be. He doesn't have to do their assignments anymore. He just has to give them access to the company."

"But you're not part of it?"

"No. I'm out of it. Forever."

"I don't understand. Sons are forced to join. It was never a choice before. Did they change the rules?"

"Like I said before, it's a long story. And probably one I shouldn't tell you. You're better off not knowing."

She nods. We both know how this works. The secrets, and why they must be kept, even from each other.

"Mom, how do you feel about Dad? I mean, knowing what you know, does it change anything?"

"Your father is the only man I've ever loved, and that will never change. As for what he's done, I know he wasn't give a choice but—"

"Mom, he never wanted to do those things. After being with him all those years, you know he's not the type of person who would willingly do those things."

"Yes, I know, but I still don't like it. But I've had a lot of time to think about this and I understand that your father did what he had to do to keep them from harming us, or himself."

"So you don't hold it against him?"

She shakes her head. "No. Although it hurts me to know that he lied to me all those years."

"He didn't have a choice. If he'd told you anything, they would've come after you. Dad was just trying to protect you."

"I know that, honey, but it's still hard when the person you love lies to you, even if they're forced to do so. Your father was living this whole other life that I didn't even know existed."

138

I don't know how my dad hid it from her for that long. How do you keep something like that from your wife? He had to, but still, I don't know how he did it. Back when I was dating Jade, I found it nearly impossible to keep my family's secrets from her, and I only knew part of them. Even after we were married, I tried to hide things from Jade in order to protect her, but it killed me to do it. I hated lying to her.

"I heard your father has a daughter," my mom says.

"Yeah, Lilly. She's 12. Dad has custody of her. Grace told you he's divorced, right?"

"Yes. And I know he was married to Katherine."

"It was an arranged marriage. He never loved her. They fought all the time. Now she's remarried. He hardly ever talks to her."

"And your dad's okay? He's happy?"

"Yeah, he's okay."

She holds my hand. "And how about you? Are you happy, Garret?"

"I wasn't for a long time, but I am now." I smile. "I'm married."

"That's what Grace said." She smiles. "When did you get married?"

"When I was 19."

She laughs a little. "Nineteen? That's so young."

"It's not what I planned, but you can't always plan this stuff. Her name is Jade. We met in college. You'd love her, Mom. You two are a lot alike."

"And it wasn't arranged?"

"No. She's from Iowa. She never had money. She grew up without anything. Sometimes she didn't even have food. But she got through all that and did really well in school and Dad gave her a scholarship to the same college I went to."

"I don't understand. Grace said Jade is her granddaughter. So how could she grow up without money?"

"Jade didn't know she was a Sinclair until she was in college. Royce had an affair with Jade's mom when he was in Iowa working on a political campaign." I'm not ready to tell my mom the real story, about how Royce raped Jade's mom, then tried to cover it

139

up. It'll take too long to tell her all that, and really, it's Jade's story to tell, not mine. "Royce didn't help Jade's mom out financially so she struggled to pay their bills."

"That's so sad. The Sinclairs have more than enough money. I can't believe Royce would be that selfish."

"Royce was more than just selfish. He's—never mind. He's dead now. I assume Grace told you that."

"Yes. So does Jade ever see her mother?"

"Her mom committed suicide when Jade was 15."

"Oh, that's terrible."

"Yeah, but Frank took her in. He went to college with her mom. He's like a dad to Jade. He walked her down the aisle at our wedding."

She puts her hand to her mouth, and tears fall from her eyes. "I missed your wedding."

I hug her. "I know. But I imagined you there. And I know Dad did too."

"I missed your graduation. Both of them." She pulls away. "You finished college, right?"

"Yes. Jade and I both graduated." I glance down, then look back at my mom. "And I have a daughter."

"You're a father?" More tears fall down her face.

"Yeah." I smile. "You have a granddaughter. Her name is Abigail."

She's smiling as she wipes her tears. "How old is she?"

"She just had her first birthday. And, um...I haven't told anyone this but—" I smile even more just saying it. "We're having another one. Jade's pregnant. We just found out."

"Oh, honey. That's wonderful. Congratulations."

"Yeah. We're really excited."

"I'm so happy for you, Garret. All I ever wanted is for you to be happy and it sounds like you are."

"I *am*. And I'm even happier knowing you're alive. I still can't believe this. Dad's not going to believe this either. We need to call him and let him know. Or, actually, it would probably be better if we tell him in person." I get my phone out. "He needs to get here right away."

140

"Wait." She stops me before I make the call. "I don't know if I'm ready to see him."

"Why not?"

"Because everything is so much more complicated now. Just a few days ago, I honestly never thought I'd see him again, and now here I am, and I'm not sure what to say to him."

"Just tell him how you feel." I set my phone down on the table that's in front of the couch. "You still love him, right?"

"Yes. With all my heart."

"Then tell him that."

"But if he doesn't feel the same way then—"

"Mom." I hold her shoulders. "Dad still loves you. He still thinks about you and talks about you all the time. He has pictures of you in his office and on the dresser in his bedroom. He misses you. If he knew you were alive, he'd be here as fast as possible. And he'd never let you go."

"Garret, you don't know that. A lot has happened in fifteen years."

"Yes, he was married and he has another child, but that doesn't change the fact that he still loves you. Mom, I swear to you, he would do anything to have you back in his life. When you died, or when we thought you died, he shut down. He buried himself in work, trying not to think about you. And he—" I stop before I tell her how he gave up being a father to me. She doesn't need to know. It'll just upset her. And it's the past. He's a great father now.

"He what?" she asks. "What were you going to say, Garret?"

"That Dad hasn't been the same since you left. He still misses you." I pause. "Do you want to get back together with him?"

"Yes. But I don't know if it's possible."

"Why wouldn't it be?"

"Because things are different now. I know things I didn't know before. Things about your father that I have to learn to get past."

"He's not doing that stuff anymore. He's not even allowed to go to the meetings."

"Yes, but he's done things. Bad things."

"But he didn't want to. He only did those things because they made him. Mom, you just said you were okay with this."

141

"I'm not okay with it. I've just told myself I have to accept it."

"Are you mad at him?"

"I'm upset that he kept this from me all those years, but no, I'm not mad. I was angry when I first found out, but enough time has gone by that I've forgiven him. But I worry that I might feel differently about him when I see him again, now that I know he has this whole other side."

"That other side isn't him. It's like when you left here and lived in Italy. You became someone else, right?"

"Yes, but I didn't hurt anyone." She glances down.

"I'm just saying that you can become someone else if you have to. If you're forced to. Mom." I wait until she looks at me. "If you love him and want to be with him, then don't let this get in the way."

"It's not just me, honey. Your father has to want this too." She pauses. "And maybe he won't."

"Are you kidding? Dad loves you. I told you, he would do anything to get you back. He's going to be so freaking happy when he sees you. But…"

"But what?"

"When he finds out you know about the organization, he'll be afraid you won't want to be with him. That's why I'm asking if that's what you want. If you really want to be with Dad. Because I don't think he'll survive having you back and then having you leave again."

"Garret, I want to get back together with your father. There are just so many things he and I have to talk about, and so many things we have to figure out in order to make this work. For one, everyone thinks I'm dead. Your father can't be seen with his deceased wife."

"You're not deceased. You're alive, and we'll find a way to explain why. We'll make a fake story to tell the media. Believe me, it's been done before."

"We also have to deal with the organization. If they know I'm alive, they might try to kill me. Or do something to you or your father. I don't want to put either of you in any kind of danger."

"Nobody is going to come after us. Grandfather is dead. And William Sinclair will make sure they don't harm you. I don't know if you know William but—"

"Yes, I know William. But I don't know how he could help."

"William is now at the highest level at the organization. He won't let any of the members come after you. All I have to do is make a phone call and he'll take care of it. They'll never bother you."

She looks as if she doesn't believe me. I don't either. I'm not sure if William can protect her, but for now I'm going to pretend that he can.

"Still, I can't be seen with your father. He's well known and he can't have the media seeing him with me."

"We'll worry about that later. For now, just let me call him and get him out here. You two need to talk."

She nods. "Okay."

I pick up my phone and call him. "Dad, what are you doing right now?"

"Catching up on some paperwork. Why?"

"I need you to get out here. Where's Lilly? Is she with you?"

"No, she's with Katherine for the week. School ended yesterday and Katherine wanted to have Lilly visit now instead of in June as we'd planned. I wasn't going to agree to it, but Katherine's decided to spend the summer in France, so this is the only time she'll see Lilly until the fall."

"Then head to the airport. You need to leave right away. Call me when you get here."

"What's wrong?" He sounds panicked. "What happened?"

"Nothing's wrong. I just need you to get out here."

"Garret, I can't just drop everything and fly out there."

"Dad, I'm serious. You need to get out here. You don't have to worry. This isn't bad. It's good."

"Are you and Jade having another baby?"

I laugh. "Shit, how did you know that?"

"I didn't. I was just guessing. Congratulations. That's wonderful."

"Yeah, it is, but that's not why I called you."

143

"Is Jade okay? Is Abigail okay?"

"Yes, everyone's fine. And if you come out here, you'll get to see your granddaughter, so there's another reason why you need to get out here. But that's not the main reason."

He sighs. "Fine. I'll call my pilot and have him get the plane ready. Am I staying for more than a day?"

I look at my mom. "I hope so. Or maybe you'll go somewhere else. I don't know. Just get here and we'll figure it out later. Call me when you land. Bye, Dad." I end the call before he can change his mind.

My mom's biting her lip, which she always used to do when she was nervous.

I put my hand on her shoulder. "Mom, calm down. There's nothing to worry about. He's going to be happy to see you."

She nods. "I hope you're right."

"I'm always right," I say jokingly.

"You sound just like your father. You look like him too." She hugs me. "Oh, honey. I've missed you so much."

"I missed you too." When we break apart, I sit back and see tears on her face again. "Mom, what's wrong?"

"I'm just so happy to see you. I never thought this day would come. I can't believe I finally made it back here and that I'm sitting here with you. I've spent the past fifteen years thinking about you, worrying about you, wondering if you're okay, and praying that I would someday see you again. And now here you are, all grown up. I missed all those years with you. I missed watching you grow up." Her voice is shaky. She's trying not to cry but she can't seem to stop.

I hold her hand. "Mom, it's okay. It's the past. And you're here now. That's all that matters. Let's go to my house. We can talk some more there. Have you eaten?"

"Yes." She takes a tissue from the table and dabs her eyes. "Grace made me a sandwich."

As she says it, the front door opens. My mom and I stand up as Grace comes in, carrying a shopping bag. She sets it down and her eyes bounce between my mom and me. "Seeing you two together again...it's just..."

144

"A miracle," my mom says, hugging me into her side. She laughs. "He's so tall. I always wondered if he'd be as tall as Pearce."

"Not quite," I say. "Dad's still taller than me."

"Have you called him?" Grace asks me.

"Yes. He's flying out here but I didn't tell him why."

She smiles at my mom. "He's going to be overjoyed when he sees you."

"Grace, we were just getting ready to head back," I say. "Why don't you follow us?"

"I think I'll stay for the weekend and work in the garden. Rachel could use the guest house if she'd like."

"No, she's staying with us." I smile as I motion her to the door. "Come on. Let's go."

On her way out, my mom stops to hug Grace. "Thank you so much for all your help."

"You're welcome." She lowers her voice, but I hear her say, "Forgive him, Rachel. He's a good man. And he loves you very much."

Grace is talking about my dad. My mom must've asked her about his involvement in the organization.

When we're outside, she says, "I forgot my suitcase. It's in the guest bedroom."

"I'll get it." I go back inside and find it sitting on the floor. It's not a very big suitcase. And yet this is all she has. All her possessions fit inside one small suitcase. Is this how she's been living all this time? With nothing? Before she left, she was married to a billionaire and could have whatever she wanted. But the past fifteen years she's had nothing. And my grandfather knew it and kept her away from us. I seethe with anger as I think about that. God, I hated that man. I still hate him, even though he's dead.

I zip up the suitcase and go back out to the driveway. My mom's leaning down, sniffing the roses. The driveway is lined with flowers on both sides. My mom always loved flowers. She planted them all around our old house and in the window boxes and in pots on the porch.

"It's nice, isn't it?" I put her suitcase in the trunk.

145

"Yes." She walks over to the car and I open her door for her. "I love all the flowers."

"Did she take you out back?" I ask as I get in the car.

"No, but I could see it from the windows. Her flower gardens are beautiful."

"Yeah, she likes flowers as much as you do." I back out of the driveway. "We'll come here again and you can spend time in the back yard. She has all kinds of different flowers back there. She even has those same pink flowers we used to have in front of our house. I don't remember the name of them but you always planted them every spring."

"You remember that?" she asks, her voice sad.

"Of course I do." I glance at her. "Why wouldn't I?"

"After what happened, I thought maybe you'd want to forget. It had to have been hard on you to hold onto those memories."

"That's all I had left of you. There's no way I'd forget."

She gazes out the front window, and I notice a tear sliding down her cheek. I reach over and hold her hand.

"Mom, are you okay?"

"I missed so much of your life. I wasn't here for you. I feel sick about it."

"It wasn't your fault. It was *his*. Grandfather did this. And the organization."

"I just wish I'd done things differently. Maybe if I'd—"

"Mom, don't." I squeeze her hand. "You can't change the past. You did what you felt was your only option. Don't blame yourself for any of this. The past is over. Let's just focus on the future."

"Can I ask you about the past? About what happened after I left?"

"What do you want to know?" I let go of her, putting my hand back on the steering wheel.

"How long did you and your father live at our house after I left?"

"About a year."

"And then you moved when your dad got married?"

146

I grip the steering wheel tighter. That was such a rough time in my life that I try to forget it. Just thinking about it makes me tense up.

"Yeah. Dad married Katherine and she insisted we live in a mansion. Dad still lives there."

"Did you have to go to a different school?"

"Yes." I don't want to talk about this because it'll just make her angry. And if she knew Dad sent me to boarding school, she'd be furious. She may not want to get back together with him if she knew how he treated me after she left. "I don't want to talk about this right now. Could we talk about something else?"

"Of course. Why don't you tell me about your wife." She smiles. "And my granddaughter."

I smile back. "I can't wait for you to meet them."

As I tell her about them, I feel like I'm in some kind of dream.

I'm in the car with my mom. My mom! Holy shit! I still can't believe it.

CHAPTER SIXTEEN

RACHEL

I'm riding in a car with my son. Driving to his house. And soon I'll meet his wife and daughter.

My son has a wife and a daughter. He's no longer my little boy. He's a grown man. And a husband. A father.

So much has changed. None of this seems real. I feel like I'm going to wake up any minute now and find out it's all been a dream.

When I first saw Garret, I was overwhelmed with so much emotion I almost couldn't speak. He looks just like Pearce did at that age. Tall and muscular. Even his face looks just like his Pearce's, except Garret has my eyes. The exact same bright blue color.

He's very handsome. Just like his father. Even looking at him now as he drives, he reminds me of Pearce. He has the same profile. He sits tall, with confidence. He even holds the steering wheel like Pearce does. Is that genetic, or did he just learn that from his dad? I wonder who taught him how to drive.

I have so many questions, but I don't want to ask them all at once. And it seems like Garret doesn't want to tell me much about what went on while I was gone. That concerns me. It makes me think there's something he doesn't want me to know. Is it about Katherine? Did she not treat him well when she was his stepmother? I cringe just thinking about that woman trying to act as his mother. I can't imagine her as a mother. She always seemed so childish and self-centered.

"We're almost there," Garret says. "I'm going to call Jade." He presses something on the dashboard and the phone rings. I'm not used to all this new technology. I don't even have a cell phone.

"Hello?" a soft voice answers.

"Hey, it's me. Were you sleeping?"

"Yeah. I was taking a quick nap."

"I just wanted to let you know I'll be home in a few minutes."

"You're already done at Grace's house? How'd you get done so fast?"

"It didn't take long. She decided to stay there the rest of the weekend. Hang out with her flowers."

Jade laughs. "She has flowers *here*."

"Well, maybe she missed her house. I don't know. I'll see you soon."

"Okay. Bye."

He presses a button that ends the call.

"She sounds nice," I say.

"Yeah, she's great. She's really tired right now because of the baby. It was like this with her last pregnancy too. The first trimester she was really tired, and then after that she was fine."

He's so excited about this baby. His whole face is lit up. I'm so happy for him.

"Do you two plan on having more children after this one?"

"Probably not. I told Jade I'd like to have three, but she only wants two, which is fine. Back when I met her, she didn't want *any*, so two kids is a lot for her."

"How does she like being a mom?"

"She loves it. But she was worried about it before we had Abi. Jade had a really tough childhood and basically had to raise herself. Her mom was hooked on drugs and alcohol so Jade had no example of how to be a mom. She was scared she'd abuse our child like her mom abused her. That's why Jade didn't want kids. But she went to counseling and worked through all that stuff and now she's a great mom." He smiles at me. "Just like you. You were the greatest mom ever."

My eyes tear up. "Oh, honey."

"Remember when we used to go to the pool every week?"

I smile, thinking back. "When you were a baby, we went every day."

"Really?"

"Yes. I'd take you to the pool at that gym we used to go to. I used to give swimming lessons there."

"Yeah, I remember. I used to go with you. I'd pick up the towels after class."

In my mind, it seems like that happened just yesterday. Probably because that's how I remember him. As a young boy. And now, he's a grown man.

"This is it." He points to a large, single-level house. "We built it a few years ago. Grace gave us the land."

"It's a gorgeous location. Right on the water?"

"Yeah. We have a private beach but you have to go down some steps to get to it. The house sits higher up, which gives us a great view of the ocean."

He parks in the driveway. "I'll get your suitcase later."

He shows me to the front door, which is a wide wooden door. He unlocks it and opens it halfway.

"Jade?" he calls out.

"I'm in the kitchen," she says.

He motions me inside. We walk into the living room. It's a large open area with high ceilings and a big stone fireplace and wood floors. In the middle of the room there's an oversized couch layered with throw pillows. A cable-knit red blanket is draped over the side. Two brown leather chairs are situated across from the couch, and between them is a square coffee table made of light wood with a distressed finish that's similar to driftwood you see on the beach. Both the house and the furnishings have a comfortable, casual feel that reminds me of our house in Connecticut.

"Wait here," Garret says. "I'll go get her."

He walks toward the back of the house. I hear him talking in the other room. "Hey. I need to tell you something."

"Is something wrong?"

Their voices get quieter so I can't hear what they're saying.

Then his wife's voice rings out. "Are you serious? She's really here? Where is she?" I can't hear Garret's response, but I hear his wife again. "I'm meeting your mom? Right now? This is crazy! And I'm a mess. Let me go clean up."

"Jade, you look great," I hear Garret say. "And my mom really wants to meet you. Come on."

Garret appears first, then his wife. She looks like the type of girl I would pick for him. She has a natural, girl-next-door look, like someone you could instantly be friends with. She has dark brown hair that's pulled up in a ponytail with some strands hanging loose around her face. I notice her green eyes. Garret loves green eyes, so I'm sure those green eyes caught his attention when they first met. She's petite; maybe five-five with a small frame. She's wearing red cotton shorts and a white sleeveless button-up shirt that shows off her tan and toned arms. She seems athletic. Maybe she swims, like me.

We're both staring at each other, the room silent. She's about as shocked as Garret was when he saw me.

"Mom, this is Jade." Garret walks her toward me. "Jade, this is my mom."

"Hi," Jade says, then breaks down crying.

Garret smiles at me. "Happy tears."

I hug her. "Jade, it's so nice to meet you."

I don't think she was expecting the hug because at first she didn't hug me back, but now she is.

She lets me go and wipes her tears. "Sorry. I'm just so shocked."

"Don't apologize. I've been crying since the moment I saw Garret. I'm trying not to, but I can't seem to stop." I smile as my own tears trickle down my cheeks.

"I'll be right back." Garret leaves, then appears moments later with a box of tissues. "I think we'll be needing a lot of these." He holds the box up and Jade and I both take a tissue. "Let's sit down."

Garret sits on the couch and puts his arm up and Jade snuggles up beside him. I can already see how much they love each other. I could feel it when they walked in the room together.

I sit across from them on one of the chairs.

151

"Garret's told me so much about you," Jade says, sniffling. "And now you're here. Sitting in our house. This is so amazing. I don't even know what to say." She starts crying again.

"Jade, honey." I reach out for her hand. "It's okay." I already feel a motherly instinct toward her. Maybe because I know she never really had a mother. I'm not sure if that's it, but I feel this need to comfort her.

Garret kisses her head, then says to me, "She gets really emotional during pregnancy."

"Garret," she whispers, her eyes darting over to him.

"Oh. Yeah. I told her. Sorry."

"I won't tell anyone." I wink at Jade.

Jade grabs another tissue, smiling at me. "It's okay. It's just that we haven't told anyone yet so I was surprised you knew."

"I kind of told Dad as well," Garret says to her.

"Garret!" She laughs. "We were supposed to tell him together."

"I didn't actually tell him. He guessed. When I told him he had to get out here, he asked if we were having another baby. I couldn't lie to him."

"Okay, but I get to tell Frank and Ryan."

"Yes, I won't say a word to them." He kisses her again.

They are so sweet together. And they both look so happy.

"So Pearce doesn't know you're here?" Jade asks me.

"Not yet. I think it's best if he finds out in person."

She nods, sniffling. "So how did you find Garret?"

"She ran into Grace at the grocery store," Garret answers. "It's a long story. I'll tell you later."

I notice some stuffed toys in a basket near the couch and realize I haven't seen their daughter.

"Is the baby sleeping?" I ask Jade.

"Yeah, she's taking a nap."

As if on cue, the baby cries out through the baby monitor sitting on the table.

Garret jumps up. "I'll get her."

While he's gone, Jade says, "This is so incredible. I can't even tell you how happy I am right now. This is like a dream come true for Garret. When I first met him, he had a hard time talking about you. He missed you so much that….well, anyway, he started to talk about you more as I got to know him. He told me how you taught him to swim and how you used to have movie nights." She smiles. "Garret and I have movie nights too. He even makes a concession stand. He wanted to keep the tradition going."

Garret walks in with the baby. She's in tiny pink shorts and a white t-shirt, her dark brown hair messed up a little from her nap. "Abigail, meet your grandmother."

"Hello, Abigail." I take her from him and set her on my lap. Her bright blue eyes look back at me. I smile at her, tears falling again. "You are the most adorable little girl I've ever seen." She smiles and holds her arms out to me and I hold her against my chest.

"She likes to give hugs," Jade says. "Garret taught her that."

Jade's crying again and so am I. We're a mess. A mess of happy tears.

Garret hugs Jade into his side. "I think we might need more boxes of tissues."

Abigail tugs at my necklace, then pushes herself back to inspect it.

"Do you want to see a picture?" I open the tiny heart locket, her eyes watching me the whole time. "That's your daddy when he was a tiny infant."

"Really?" Jade jumps up and comes over to me. "Can I see it?"

I hold it out for her to look at.

"He's so cute," she says. "It's hard to believe he was ever that small."

I laugh. "Yes. He's grown a lot since then. He was such a cute baby. He made the cutest faces. Have you seen some of the photos?"

Jade sits next to Garret again. "Um, no. I haven't."

"Garret, you should show her the photos of you when you were little. Does your father have them?"

He shrugs. "I'm sure he does, but I don't know where he keeps them."

He seems uncomfortable. Jade does too. Why are they acting this way? Did something happen to the photos?

Abigail squirms on my lap, turning and pointing at Garret. "Dada."

I kiss her cheek. "You want to go back to your daddy?"

Jade smiles. "She always does that. You have to distract her or she'll keep asking to go back to Garret."

"You used to do the same thing when you were her age," I tell him. "If your father was around, it was like I wasn't even there. You wanted to be with your dad. But he was always at work, so I think you just missed him and wanted to be with him when he was home."

"I didn't know Dad worked so much back then," Garret says.

That was a bad year for Pearce and me. I probably shouldn't have brought it up, but I said it without thinking.

"A few months after you were born, your father had to take over the company for Holton. It was when your grandfather was going through cancer treatments."

"Yeah, that's right," he says. "So Dad wasn't around much my first year?"

I don't want Garret thinking poorly of his father, so I say, "He tried to make it home for dinner, then he'd go back to the office after you went to bed. And once Holton came back to work, your father returned to working more normal hours."

Abigail's now leaning forward on my lap, reaching for Garret. "Dada!"

He laughs and gets up and takes her from me. "Okay, but you need to spend time with Grandma later."

"I could hold her all day," I say. "She's so sweet."

"I'm already teaching her how to swim." Garret sits down with her and she puts her head on his shoulder, gripping his shirt. It's so cute. I wish I had a camera to take a photo of them. "She's already able to swim on her own."

"That's great, honey," I say, smiling at the two of them.

Just as I'm about to ask him about his swimming, his phone rings. He reaches in his pocket to get it. Abigail won't let him go, gripping his shirt even tighter. It reminds me so much of when Garret was that age, the way he'd hold on to Pearce.

154

Garret answers the phone. "Yeah, Dad...okay...what time?...yeah, we'll be here..."

A nervous flutter ignites in my stomach as I listen to Garret talking to his dad. Pearce is right there, on the other end of the line. I still can't believe this is happening. That it's real. That I'm actually here. Back with my son. And will soon be reunited with Pearce.

CHAPTER SEVENTEEN

RACHEL

"Is he still coming?" Jade asks Garret as he sets his phone down.

"Yeah, but it's getting late out there so he's going to fly out in the morning. He should be here around noon."

Jade checks her watch. "It's almost dinner time. Are you hungry?" she asks me.

"I am, but we can eat whenever you normally eat. There's no rush."

"Why don't we order something?" Garret says to Jade. "I don't want to waste time making dinner."

She gets up. "I'll go get the take-out menus."

She leaves and I gaze over at Garret holding his daughter.

"I know I said this before," I tell him, "but I'm so happy for you. You have that beautiful little girl. And you and Jade seem so in love. It reminds me of the type of love your father and I used to have."

"Mom, you can have that again. Dad's not seeing anyone." He rubs Abigail's back as she lies against his chest.

"I know you'd like your father and me to be together, but we can't just go back to how things were. I'm not even sure if I'm stay—" I stop, not wanting to say it. More than anything I want to remain with my family, but now that I'm here, I'm panicking, thinking I'm putting them in danger. I don't want the organization finding out I'm alive and then punishing Pearce or harming Garret or his family.

"Mom, you're not leaving us again. You can't do that to me. Or to Dad."

I go over and sit next to him on the couch. "Honey, believe me, it's not what I want, but I can't have people see me and find out who I am. Your father is well-known. Having me appear after people assumed I was dead could cause an investigation. And if reporters dug deep enough, they might find out about the organization. If they did, the members would blame me for that. And then they'd kill me, or do something to you or your father, and all those years of us being apart would've been for nothing."

"It will have been for nothing if you leave again. You went away so that someday we could all be a family again. And now that you're back, you can't go."

"I don't know if I'll have a choice. I would never do anything that would put you or your father in any kind of danger. And seeing your beautiful wife and daughter, I'm panicking even more. I don't want anything to happen to them."

"Nothing's going to happen. I told you, William will protect us. He's at the highest level you can go. He's changed how things are run there. Yes, they still do bad things, but they're not nearly as bad as they used to be. The older members are dying off and the younger members are doing things differently. And they aren't allowed to hurt a member's family. It's against the rules."

"Technically I'm no longer married to your father, so I'm not family. I'm not protected."

"Dad will protect you. If the members threatened to hurt you, Dad would go after them. And William would destroy them. William is very protective of our family. He'd never let anything happen to us."

"But that doesn't mean he'd do the same for *me*. I've only met him a few times, but I'm sure he's not going to put himself at risk to protect me."

"He's not putting himself at risk. He's at the top. Nobody can hurt him. He has power. A lot of power. And if he says you're not to be harmed, you will not be harmed. I promise you."

I gaze down at the table.

"Mom." He nudges my arm and I look back at him. "Promise me you won't leave again."

"I can't promise you that, honey. But if I have to hide out somewhere, this time you'll know where I am. You can come visit me."

"That's not good enough. I want to see you more than a few times a year. I want you back in my life and I want my kids to grow up around their grandmother."

"I know you do. I want that too. Let's just wait and see how things go with your father. We'll figure this out. I want more than anything to be back in your life." I put my hand on Abigail's head, which is still on Garret's shoulder. "I want to be around to see this precious little baby grow up. She's so beautiful, Garret. And so is your wife."

He smiles. "So you like Jade?"

"I do. I know I just met her, but she's exactly the type of girl I wanted for you. I never wanted you to marry one of those wealthy girls you grew up around. I knew they'd never love you for you. I saw the women Pearce's friends married. Women like Victoria, Royce's wife. Those women didn't even like their husbands. They married for money and the right last name. I hoped you wouldn't end up with someone like that. And thank goodness you didn't. Jade seems like the perfect girl for you."

"She is. I love her more than anything."

"I know you do. And I can tell she loves you just as much."

Jade returns with a stack of take-out menus and we pick out what we want for dinner.

This is so strange. Last night at this time, I was on a plane, heading to the U.S., not sure when, or if, I'd see my son. And now, I'm here with him and his family at his house.

We have dinner outside on their back patio that overlooks the ocean and the pool. They have a large in-ground pool. Next to the house is a smaller house, which is where Grace lives. They said they built her that house so she could live right next door. It's nice that they look after her the way they do. Garret was always very caring and concerned about others, and Jade is the same way.

158

They used Jade's money to build this house. Apparently Grace set up a very large trust fund for Jade when she found out Jade was her granddaughter. Garret's trust fund was taken from him. He said it was part of the deal when he was released from his obligation to be a member of the organization. He didn't want to tell me the whole story about that.

During dinner, Jade and Garret tell me they own a sporting goods company. Garret runs it and Pearce is a silent partner and part owner. Garret always loved sports so it's the perfect job for him. Jade also has a business, giving speeches to young women who are struggling in life, like she used to be. I'm amazed that both Jade and Garret have accomplished so much at such a young age.

Then they tell me about the colleges they went to. They started out at Moorhurst in Connecticut, and finished their last three years at Camsburg, which is just an hour north of here. Garret didn't give me the whole story, but he did say that he switched colleges to get far away from the members of the organization, who mostly live on the East Coast.

For dessert, Garret makes everyone a sundae with ice cream and crushed cookies. He knows it's my favorite dessert. I'm sharing mine with Abigail. She's sitting on my lap and picking the cookies out of the ice cream with her fingers. She's now a sticky mess, but so adorable. I love her to pieces.

"We have some charities," Jade says as we're finishing our sundaes. "One of them is the Taylor Foundation. Taylor was my maiden name so it's in honor of my mom and her parents. The foundation helps out people who are struggling to pay their bills and just need a little help."

"That's very generous of you," I say.

Jade shrugs. "Garret and I don't need all that money. We'd rather give it away."

This girl is so sweet. I'm so glad Garret found her. And to think she grew up with nothing and now finally has money but wants to give it away. It shows what a big heart she has.

She sits back and smiles at Garret. "Tell her about our other charity."

Garret sets his spoon down. "We started an organization that gives free swim lessons to kids. It's nationwide." He smiles. "It's called Rachel's Swim Club."

I tear up for about the hundredth time today. "You really named it that?"

"Yeah," he says softly. "You always said you wished every kid could learn to swim so we're trying to make that happen."

"Thank you." I reach over and take his hand and squeeze it. "I'm so proud of you, honey." I look at Jade. "Both of you."

Abigail yawns and drops her head back on my chest. We all look at her and laugh because she's covered in ice cream and looks knocked out from all the sugar.

"I'll go clean her up," Jade says, rising from her chair. "She needs to get to bed."

"Could I help?" I ask.

"Sure." She leans down and kisses Garret's cheek. "That means you're in charge of cleaning the dishes."

"I already assumed that," he says, kissing her back.

Jade and I take Abigail inside. I talk to Jade as she gives the baby a bath and puts her pajamas on. Then she puts Abigail in her crib and we wait until she falls asleep and then watch her for a few minutes.

As we walk back to the kitchen, Garret is coming toward us down the hall.

"Did you guys stand there and watch her sleep?" he asks Jade.

"We had to. She's adorable when she sleeps."

"I used to watch Garret sleep too," I say to Jade. "But he rarely slept so I didn't get to watch him very often."

"He didn't sleep?"

"No, he didn't like sleeping. I'd go check on him in the night and he'd be up, not crying, but just staring up at the mobile above his crib or moving around."

Garret shrugs. "I didn't need to sleep. I had things to do."

Jade laughs. "What exactly did you have to do as a baby?"

"I don't remember, but I know I had better things to do than sleep." He puts his arm around Jade. "How are you feeling?"

"I'm fine. You don't have to keep asking me that."

160

"You're pregnant. It's my job to ask you that. I have to make sure you're okay. I don't have much of a role here, Jade, so you've gotta give me something."

I like that Garret worries about her like that, and takes care of her. Pearce was the same way with me, even when we first met. It's one of the reasons I fell in love with him.

Jade yawns and Garret notices. "Why don't you go to bed?" he asks her. "I know how tired you've been with the pregnancy."

"But it's still early. I want to talk to your mom some more."

He hugs her to his side and kisses her head. "You can talk to her tomorrow. You need to sleep."

"Actually, I should probably go to sleep too," I say. "I haven't slept much the past couple nights."

"Then I guess we'll all go to bed," Garret says. "It's been a long day. I'll go get your suitcase from the car."

"I'll show you the guest rooms," Jade says, walking back down the hall. "You can pick whichever one you want. Pearce always takes the one at the end. You want that one?"

"Sure, that's fine." I follow her down there.

"If you open the window," Jade says, "you can hear the ocean. It's really relaxing. There are extra blankets in the closet, and the bathroom is just through there." She points to a door on the side of the room. "Towels are in the cabinet."

"Thank you." I give her a hug. "I know my showing up here came as a total surprise and you weren't expecting to have a guest tonight, so thank you for being so kind to me."

"You're not a guest," she says. "You're family. You can stay here as long as you want."

"I want you to know that if my being back in Garret's life puts your family in any kind of danger, I'll leave. I would never—"

"You're taking Dad's room, huh?" Garret walks in with my suitcase.

"Yes." I smile. "Jade picked it for me."

"I should get to bed," she says as she walks to the door. "I'll see you tomorrow."

"Did she go over where everything is?" Garret asks.

"Yes. I think I'm all set."

161

"Then I'll let you get some sleep. Goodnight." He turns to leave.

"Garret?"

He turns back. "Yeah?"

"I'm so proud of you. You were always a good son, but now you're a good husband and a good father. And the fact that you run a business and have charities? I couldn't be more proud of you and the man you've become."

He smiles. "Thanks, Mom."

I step up to him and hug him. "I love you, honey."

"I love you too."

After he leaves, I change into pajamas and get into bed. The queen bed feels big and luxurious compared to the twin bed with the thin mattress I'm used to sleeping on.

As I lie here, I think about what Jade and Garret said about this being Pearce's room. This is where he stays when he's here. In this room. In this same bed. It stirs something in me just knowing that. When I see him, I wonder if I'll still feel the same way about him as I did before. I love him, and I always will, but will we still be attracted to each other? And if we are, we will allow ourselves to be together that way? Or do we need to get to know each other again before we do?

I'm not sure how I feel about that. I'm still attracted to the Pearce that I remember, but he's different now. He's older and he's been married and divorced and has probably been with more women than just Katherine. Maybe he won't be attracted to me anymore.

Why am I thinking about this? Sex should be the last thing on my mind. I need to focus on figuring out what to say to Pearce. I'm nervous, but also excited. He'll be here tomorrow. I'll see him in just a few short hours.

And with that thought, I fall asleep.

CHAPTER EIGHTEEN

GARRET

After I say goodnight to my mom, I go to Abi's room. She's sound asleep. There's a white rocking chair next to her crib and I sit there and watch her and think about all that happened today.

When I woke up this morning, I thought my mom was dead. And hours later, I found out she's alive. She's been alive all this time and my dad and I never knew. My life would've been so much different if we'd only known about this. If she'd never left, I wouldn't have been so out of control during my teen years, which means my dad wouldn't have forced me to go to college close to home. So I wouldn't have gone to Moorhurst, and if I hadn't gone to Moorhurst, I wouldn't have met Jade. And if I hadn't met Jade, I wouldn't have Abigail.

It's strange how one incident can completely change your life and send you down a different path. When my dad and I thought my mom died in that plane crash, we were devastated to the point that it nearly destroyed us. But that horrible tragedy set me on a path to meet Jade. And if my dad had never married Katherine, he wouldn't have Lilly. Maybe that's how life works. You have to suffer through the bad to get to the good. I hated losing my mom, but I can't imagine my life without Jade and Abigail.

I get up and go over to her crib and gently touch her head. "Goodnight, Abi."

After I leave her room, I go down the hall to the master bedroom. Jade's in bed and the lights are off. I change into pajamas and slip under the covers. Jade scoots back into my arms.

"I thought you were asleep," I say, kissing her cheek.

"I heard you come in. Where were you?"

"Checking on Abi."

"Did she wake up?"

"No, she was sound asleep."

Jade flips over to face me. "You were watching her sleep, weren't you?"

"Yeah." I kiss her. "I needed to. Seeing her asleep in her crib just reminded me how I'd do anything to keep her safe. If I thought I was putting her in any kind of danger, I'd leave, just like my mom did. At first I couldn't understand why she left like that. But I get it. She had no choice. She had to keep me safe. After she found out about the plane, she could've come home and told my dad, but she didn't because she knew they would still try to kill her. She knew they'd find another way. And what if I was with her when they did it? What if I got in the way or did something stupid and ended up getting hurt? Or killed? She'd never put me at risk like that, just like I wouldn't put Abi at risk. Or you."

Jade hugs my chest. "Garret, if something like that ever happens and you have to make a choice like that, please don't leave without telling me. Don't go missing and leave me wondering what happened to you."

"I'll never have to make a choice like that. We're out of that world. And we're never going back."

We both get quiet, which is what always happens when we bring up the organization. It's like we have to take a moment to remind ourselves that it's over and they'll leave us alone.

"What about your mom?" Jade asks. "If they find out she's back, would they try to come after her?"

"If they did, my dad would kill every fucking one of them. And I am not joking."

Jade knows the world my dad lives in. She knows he's killed people. She watched him kill her father. She knows he'd do anything to protect our family.

"We have to tell William," she says. "He'll make sure nothing happens to her."

"Yeah, I told her I'd talk to him, but it's probably better if my dad did."

"Is she worried they'll do something to her? Is that why she was talking about leaving again?"

I sit up a little. "She told you she's leaving again?"

"She said she'd leave if being back in your life would put us at risk."

"Fuck. I wish she would stop thinking that way. She's not putting us at risk. They wouldn't do anything to us." I sigh. "She can't leave again. She can't do that to me."

"Did you tell her that?"

"Yes." I lie back down on the bed. "And she said that if she *did* leave, she'd tell me where she is so I could go see her. But I told her that's not good enough. I want to see her all the time, not just once or twice a year. There's no need for her to go into hiding. William will deal with the organization. And my dad will protect her. He'd never leave her side if that's what it took to make sure she's safe."

"How do you think your dad's going to react when he sees her tomorrow?"

"He'll be shocked, like I was, and then...I don't know."

"You don't think he'll be happy?"

"He'll definitely be happy. I just hope he doesn't get mad at her for leaving."

"Why would he get mad at her for that? She didn't have a choice."

"Yeah, but you know my dad. He thinks he can fix every problem. He might be mad that she didn't tell him what was going on so that he could try to fix it so she wouldn't have had to leave."

"But I thought you said some guy was supposed to tell your dad what happened."

"Yeah. Jack was supposed to tell him, but he died before he could."

"That sounds suspicious."

"I know. I'm sure his death wasn't an accident."

"So when your dad never showed up in Italy, why didn't your mom try to come back?"

"My grandfather kept her prisoner there." I hear Jade gasp, but I continue. "He found out she was alive and he hired some men to keep watch on her so she couldn't leave."

"Oh my God," Jade whispers. "He knew she was alive? And he didn't tell your dad?"

"Yeah. My dad's gonna be so pissed when he finds out."

"Did Holton go over there, or what—"

"Jade, let's not talk about it. You need to get to sleep." I kiss her. "You're growing a baby. That's gotta be tiring."

She smiles. "You wouldn't believe how tiring it is. But can I ask you one more thing?"

"Go ahead."

"How does it feel? To have her back?"

"Like a freaking dream come true. Part of me still doesn't even believe it. When I saw her at Grace's house, I thought it was someone else. I kept telling myself it couldn't possibly be her. I was yelling at her, telling her to stop pretending to be my mom. Now I feel like an ass for doing that."

"Garret, you were in shock. You thought she was dead, and then this woman shows up claiming to be your mom. I would've reacted the same way."

I kiss her cheek. "Enough talking for tonight. Go to sleep."

"Okay." She yawns and turns back around. "Goodnight. I love you."

"I love you too." I hold her against me, my hand over her stomach where our new baby is growing.

We just found out last week. Jade had been really tired lately so I kind of wondered if maybe she was pregnant. We weren't really trying to have a baby. We said we'd wait a year before trying again, but we also weren't using birth control so we both knew it was a possibility.

Jade told me the news when I got home from work last week. But instead of telling me, she made up a letter from the stork, since I always tell her we have a standing order with the stork. He brought us Abigail and now we're waiting for him to bring us baby number two. But according to our original plan, or order, he's not supposed to drop off this baby for a couple years.

166

Jade put the letter in an envelope and stamped and addressed it, then left it in our stack of mail. As I was sorting through the bills and the junk mail, I stopped when I saw the plain white envelope with a return address of '801 Birdland Drive, Some Beach in Florida.'

"What's this?" I asked, holding it up.

Jade shrugged. "I don't know. Open it and find out."

We'd just had dinner and Jade was cleaning up the kitchen. I was sitting at the kitchen table. Abi was asleep in her room.

I opened the envelope and pulled out the letter. Jade even made official letterhead with Stork, Inc. at the top. The letter read as follows.

This is to inform you that the baby you requested to arrive at your house approximately two years from now will not be arriving as planned. There was a mix-up with your order due to an error made by my senile frog assistant who misread the dates you originally asked for. Because of this, your delivery will be arriving in approximately seven and a half months. We apologize for this mix-up, and since it's our fault, we won't charge you our usual delivery fee. We hope you continue to use our services in the future -Sincerely, Mr. Stork

I laughed when I read it, then realized what it said and got this huge grin on my face.

Jade stood in front of me and said, "So what do you think?"

"I think the frog should get a raise." Then I got up from my seat and wrapped my arms around her waist and kissed her.

"So you're okay with this?" she asked. "You're not going to yell at the stork for this?"

I kissed her again and said, "He can make a delivery whenever the hell he wants."

"But this isn't what we planned."

"Yeah, well, plans change." And then I asked her, just to make sure. "We're really having another baby? You went to the doctor?"

She smiled. "Yeah. It's confirmed."

"Holy shit! We're having another baby!" I kissed her again, then told her how much I love her.

We heard Abi crying on the baby monitor and Jade said, "I think she heard the news."

"Go get her. She can celebrate with us."

And she did. The three of us had ice cream, then watched a movie on the couch. Well, I watched the movie. Abi fell asleep in my arms and Jade fell asleep on my shoulder. That was a great night. I'll never forget it. I was so freaking happy. And now, a week later, I've got my mom back. No wonder I can't stop smiling.

The next morning I go to the small private airport to pick up my dad. He arrived a little after noon.

My mom stayed home with Jade. When I left the house, my mom seemed nervous. She kept asking me if she looked okay. I told her she looked beautiful, because she does. She's wearing a light blue dress, which was always my dad's favorite color on her. The blue brings out the blue in her eyes. It's a sleeveless dress and shows off her toned arms. She's in good shape for someone her age. She said in Italy she spent a lot of time walking and biking, so she stayed active and it shows. She doesn't wear much makeup, but she never did. She doesn't need to. Her face is pretty without it.

I don't know how my dad's going to react when he sees her. During the night, I was up thinking about what I told Jade. About how my dad thinks he can fix every problem, and how he might get mad at my mom for not calling him and telling him what was going on the minute she found out.

Shit, now I'm getting worried. I don't want him to reject her or start fighting with her.

"How was the trip?" I ask my dad as we're driving to the house.

"It was fine. It was a smooth flight. No problems."

"Good."

"Garret, are you going to tell me why I'm here?"

"You'll understand when you get to the house."

"I'm not liking the sound of this. You know I don't like surprises."

"I can't tell you this. It's something you just need to see for yourself. And please, whatever you do, don't freak out. Just stay calm and don't get mad."

"Why would I get mad?"

"I don't know. I don't know how you're going to react."

168

"Garret, just tell me what this is about."

"You'll see when we get inside."

We're at the house now and I park the car in the driveway instead of the garage. I want to go in the front door because it leads right into the living room, where Jade and my mom are waiting. I texted Jade just now and told her we're here.

My dad gets out of the car and goes around to the trunk to get his luggage.

"Just leave it, Dad. I'll get it later."

He follows me to the door and I open it and step inside to the living room. My mom isn't there, but Jade is. She glances back at the hallway. My mom must be waiting back there.

My dad walks in and sees Jade. "Hello, Jade." He gives her a hug. "Congratulations! I hear I'm getting another grandchild."

"Yeah, it's a ways off but we're really excited."

"How are you feeling?"

"Good. Just tired." Jade steps back and stands beside me.

I see my mom peeking out the side hallway.

"Dad," I say, getting his attention. "This is why I had you come out here." I look over at my mom.

She slowly walks into the room, stopping a few feet in front of him, tears falling down her face. "Pearce."

He stands there, frozen in place, staring at her in disbelief.

"Pearce," she says softly. "It's me."

He doesn't respond. He's in total shock. Speechless.

"Dad, it's her," I tell him. "She was never on the plane. She's been hiding out in Europe until she knew it was safe to come back."

I don't know if he's listening. He's just standing there, his eyes on her.

"Pearce, I'm so sorry." She steps closer to him. "I didn't think I had a choice. I knew they were going to kill me and I was afraid to go back. I didn't want them to hurt Garret. Or you."

She's now right in front of him and he's still not saying anything. This isn't going well. Why isn't he saying anything? Is he mad? Really? Shit, get over it. This is your wife back from the

169

dead. Do something. Say something. I'm about to intervene, but then he finally wakes up.

He steps up to her and wraps his arms around her and hugs her into his chest.

"Rachel." He breaks into tears. Big tears, streaming down his face.

I've only seen my dad cry once that I can remember. It was when he told me about the plane crash. He's always so strong. He rarely shows emotion. But right now? He's full-out crying. They both are. He's hugging her so tightly she probably can't even breathe.

I look over at Jade, who's also crying. Jade cries all the time now because of the pregnancy hormones. She even cries over commercials. But I think she'd be crying even if it weren't for the pregnancy hormones. I've got tears going as well. Seeing my dad cry really got to me. And seeing my parents reunited is overwhelming. It's something I never thought I'd see, and here it is, right in front of me.

My dad pulls back just enough to see my mom's face. "It's really you."

"Pearce." She looks up at him. "Please don't be mad at me. I didn't know what else to do. I swear to you if I—"

"Rachel, don't. I know you'd never leave us by choice. I understand why you did it."

"You do?"

"We'll talk about it later. Right now I just want to look at you." He holds her face, smiling, the tears continuing to fall. "God, I've missed you so much. I can't even tell you."

"I've missed you too. I haven't stopped thinking about you since the day I left. The only thing keeping me going was knowing that someday I'd see you and Garret again."

The baby monitor goes off. Abi's awake.

"I'll get her," Jade whispers to me. "I'll take her out on the patio so you guys can talk."

She leaves, and I look back at my parents who are still staring at each other. They're not crying anymore, but this seems like an intimate moment and I'm feeling awkward.

"I'll just leave you guys alone," I say.

My mom stops me. "Garret, wait. Come over here. I want to hug both of you, like we used to."

When I was little, my dad would pick me up and then my mom would hug him, making kind of a hug sandwich. She was really into hugs. All kinds. Which is why I'm into hugs as well.

"Mom, I don't think that'll work anymore. I'm a little bigger now."

She laughs. "We'll make it work."

She lets go of my dad and the two of them put their arms around me and we hug. It's an awkward three-way hug but my mom doesn't care. She's crying again, a big smile on her face.

"I've been waiting for this for so long. I love you both so much."

"We love you too, Mom."

"Garret, could you give us some time?" my dad asks.

I step back. "Yeah. Of course. I'll be out on the patio with Jade."

As I leave, I turn back and see my dad leading my mom to the couch to sit down. He can't take his eyes off her.

When I get outside, Jade's sitting on one of the patio chairs, quietly singing a song to Abi, who's on Jade's lap.

"Hey." I sit next to her.

"Garret, don't sneak up on me like that. You know how embarrassed I get when you hear me sing."

"You shouldn't be embarrassed." I put my arm around the back of her chair.

"Well, I am. I'm a horrible singer." She kisses Abi's cheek. "But Abi doesn't mind. She likes my singing." She kisses her again and Abi smiles and tilts her head toward Jade. It's freaking adorable. It's these little moments that make me love being a dad. And a husband. I love seeing Jade and Abi together. I keep trying to store these little moments away in my brain because I don't want to forget them.

Abi notices me and holds her arms out.

"You want to go to Daddy?" Jade lifts her up and I take her.

I set her on my leg but she reaches up, which means she wants to lie against my chest. It's her favorite spot. It's her mom's favorite spot too. I hold her against me and she lays her head on my shoulder, her tiny hands gripping my shirt.

"Did they want to be alone?" Jade asks.

"Yeah. They have a lot to talk about."

"What do you think is going to happen? Do you think they'll get back together?"

"I don't know."

"Maybe she'll go live in Connecticut so she can be by your dad."

"She can't be seen with him, at least not yet, and not in an area where he's surrounded by people he knows. They need to go somewhere private and figure out what they're going to do. Everyone thinks Rachel Kensington is dead, so if she shows up alive, the media will be all over that and reporters might link her disappearance back to the organization."

"What does that mean? She can't live here in the U.S. anymore?"

"She can, but they'll have to make up a story about what happened to her. Something that explains why she was gone for so long."

Jade nudges my arm. "Look." She nods toward Abi, who's sound asleep.

"She's asleep again? She just got up from her nap."

Jade leans over and kisses me. "She always falls asleep on your chest. You have a comfy chest. And she didn't sleep well last night. She's tired."

The three of us remain on the patio so my parents can have privacy.

My parents. Even just thinking those words seems strange. Like it's not real. For so long, it was just my dad and me. But now, my dad and mom are together. I just hope they *stay* together.

CHAPTER NINETEEN

PEARCE

I'm sitting here, looking at Rachel. She's not dead. She's here, right in front of me. And all the feelings I had for her are flooding back, like she was never gone.

These past fifteen years, my love for her has never waned. But I've had to hide it. Bury it deep within my soul. Because it's too painful to feel that kind of love for someone who's no longer here.

But now she's back and that love is rising to the surface again. And the memories I tried to forget are racing to the front of my mind. I never wanted to forget her, or the life we shared, but it was too painful to remember that part of my life. So I buried those memories and tried not to think about them. But now, as I look at her, those memories are flashing through my head. They're all there. From the day we met to the day she left, I haven't forgotten a single moment of my life with her.

It's almost too much. Too much emotion all at once. The love I feel for her is so strong, it's overpowering. But I also feel anger. Why am I angry? I can't be angry. She's back and I love her and I can't be angry. I'm fighting the anger. Trying not to show it, but it's still there. I need answers. Why did she leave? Where has she been? And why has she not contacted me all these years? I need her to explain. She has so much to explain.

"Rachel, I don't understand this." I place my hand along the side of her face, my thumb grazing her cheek. I feel like I have to touch her or she'll disappear.

Her hand covers mine and she shuts her eyes and breathes, like she's savoring my touch. I'm savoring hers too. The feel of her hand on mine. Warm. Gentle. God, I want to touch her. All of her. She's just as beautiful as she was years ago. I still feel that spark. That intense attraction. I've never felt that with anyone but her.

I can't think about that right now. I need to get answers.

"Rachel, please tell me where you've been."

She opens her eyes and takes my hand from her face and holds it, setting it on her lap. "I was in Italy, in that tiny village where we went on our honeymoon. We were there on Christmas. Do you remember?"

"Of course I do." I look into her eyes. Those stunning bright blue eyes that mesmerized me on that first day we met. "You've been there this whole time? The past fifteen years?"

"Yes. Jack told me to pick someplace—"

"Wait." I hold her arm. "Jack? What does Jack have to do with this?"

"Jack is the one who told me. He stopped me from getting on the plane. He picked me up at the hotel after Senator Wingate's speech and took me to an underground room and told me what was going on. By the time we got to the room, the plane had already crashed. Jack showed me the video. And he showed me their order to kill me."

So she knows. Rachel knows about the organization. Does she know I'm part of it? I hope not. But I'm sure she does. I'm sure Jack told her.

I rub my hand over my jaw, my other hand still holding hers. "Rachel," I say, not sure how to explain this.

"I already know. I know about the organization. I know what they do. I know that you're a member."

Shit. She'll never want to be with me now. She knows who I am. She knows I lied to her. She'll never forgive me.

I immediately withdraw my hand from hers, but she takes it right back.

"No," she says, softly, as she rubs her thumb over mine.

I look at our hands, our fingers now woven together. What does this mean? That she forgives me? How could she forgive me? How could she accept me, knowing what I've done?

"Pearce." I look up at her again. "We need to talk about that, but not right now. For now, I need to finish telling you what happened."

I nod. "Go ahead."

"Jack told me to leave the country and hide out in a small town where no one would find me. The plan was for him to tell you what happened and tell you where I was so you could come get me once you figured out a way to keep me safe. But then..."

"Jack died," I say, remembering the scene. "The night of the plane crash, Jack said he had to talk to me right away. He was in Connecticut and he wanted us to meet somewhere but I didn't want to. I was too upset. I had spent that night trying to calm Garret down. We were both in shock over what had happened."

Rachel is quietly crying now, and her pained expression causes an ache in my chest. I can see how much it hurt her to leave Garret and me, knowing what it would do to us. I can feel the guilt and regret she still carries with her, wondering if she made the wrong decision.

"So you didn't go to meet him," she says.

"I DID go. I met Jack at a scenic turnoff point just a few miles from the house. We were in his car, and he was talking to me, and then he suddenly collapsed forward onto the steering wheel. Someone was hiding in the woods and shot him in the head. Jack never told me about you. I never knew. If I had—"

"I know," she says, grabbing a tissue from the box on the table. "After a few months, when you never showed up, I assumed something had happened. But I still had hope. I thought maybe you just hadn't figured out a way to get me back. I didn't know about Jack until three years later. That small village didn't have Internet access so I had a friend of mine take me to Naples and I found a place where I could go online and look up information about you and Garret and Jack. That's when I found out Jack died the night of the crash." She looks down. "I knew then that you were never coming for me. You thought I was dead, and you'd moved on." She shuts her eyes, tears spilling out.

So she knows about Katherine. And it still hurts her.

"Rachel, no." I squeeze her hand. "I hadn't moved on. I was forced to marry her."

She nods. "I assumed that's what happened. They're supposed to choose who you marry. And it needs to be a daughter of a member. That's why they wanted to kill me. They didn't want you to be with me."

How does she know all this? Did Jack tell her everything? Even our rules about marriage? Or did she just figure this out on her own?

"Pearce? Please answer me."

"Yes. I was never supposed to marry you. It's against the rules."

"And yet you did it anyway, knowing what could happen to me."

I am not prepared to have this conversation. I never thought I'd be having it. But now here we are. Everything's out on the table. And I have to tell her the truth. Except I don't have an explanation for what I did, at least not one that makes logical sense. My decision back then was driven solely by my heart, not my head.

"I was selfish," I admit. "I fell so deeply in love with you that I couldn't give you up. You made me feel something real for the first time in my life. I felt like my life finally had meaning. Purpose. I wanted to have a life with you. I wanted to make you happy. And I thought that you were." My voice drifts off.

"I was," she says gently. "I'm not saying that us being together was a mistake. I've never let myself even think that. Those twelve years with you were the best years of my life, and if I hadn't married you we wouldn't have Garret. I only made that comment just now because I had to know what you were thinking. Why you pursued me, knowing what could happen."

"When I married you, there was no rule saying I couldn't. It was supposed to just be a given. Nobody else had ever tried to marry someone who wasn't approved. But the week after we

176

eloped, they made it an official rule. That's why I wanted to get married that weekend. But Rachel, I would've married you even sooner than that if you'd agreed to it. I knew I wanted to marry you long before I asked you."

"What about Katherine? Did you know she was the woman they picked for you?"

"No. I had no idea. About a year after the plane crash, they told me I had to get married again, and that Katherine would be my wife. I fought their decision, but then they threatened me so I agreed to it."

"How did they threaten you?"

I don't want her knowing they threatened to harm Garret. It was a long time ago, and he's safe now.

"It doesn't matter. The end result is that I was forced to marry her. But Katherine and I are divorced now. We have been for years."

"You had a child." She looks down as she says it.

"Yes. Lilly. She's 12."

Rachel takes another tissue and wipes her eyes, then sits there quietly. It hurts her to know I was married to Katherine and had a child with her, but I can't change that. And I don't regret having Lilly. I love my daughter and can't imagine not having her in my life.

"Rachel." I wait until she looks at me. "Say something."

She takes a breath. "Out of all the women they could've chosen for you to marry, I just wish it hadn't been Katherine. It makes me sick thinking of you and Garret living with her. Having dinners and holidays with her parents, with Leland knowing what he'd done."

With Leland knowing what he'd done. What does she mean?

"What did he do?" I ask, my jaw clenched.

"He rigged the plane to go down."

I pinch the bridge of my nose, close my eyes, and try to breathe. I'm so furious right now, I feel like I can't control it. "How do you know this?"

"Jack told me. He saw Leland at Wingate's fundraiser, the night before the crash. Jack said Leland wasn't supposed to be there, so

177

when he saw him, he became suspicious. Jack confronted Leland and he admitted he was in on the plan to kill me. Jack recorded their conversation. I saw the video. I saw Leland telling Jack they were going to kill me. He showed Jack the order to do it. Leland was the person put in charge of bringing down the plane."

I can't fucking believe this. Leland killed my wife, or thought he did, and yet he came to my house, ate dinner with my family, had holidays with us. All the while knowing what he'd done. Gloating over it, right in front of me. All those condescending looks. Odd comments that never made sense. He was playing me. Playing me like a fool under my own roof.

"I'll kill him," I say, then realize I said it out loud.

"Pearce, no."

I look up and see Rachel watching me, concerned about what I might do. I don't care. She knows who I am now. She knows what I've done. She knows what I'm capable of. And if anyone's worthy of being killed, it's Leland. An eye for an eye. He killed my wife, or at least tried to. And now he will die.

"That man will not live to see another day." I try to get up but she takes hold of my hand.

"Pearce, don't do it. It's over now. He didn't succeed."

"And you think he won't come after you after he finds out you're alive?"

"He has no need to. Why would he care about me? You're no longer married to Katherine and…you and I are no longer married."

I can't tell if she's saddened by that or not. I'm unable to tell how she feels about me. She's holding my hand and sitting close to me, but that doesn't mean she wants me back. So much time has gone by. So much has happened. Did she ever remarry? Or did she date other men? If so, how many? I can't think about that right now.

I return to the topic that has me so enraged I want to fly to New York this instant and shoot Leland and watch him die.

"Leland would kill you just to spite me," I tell her, being completely honest. "He has to die, and I will be more than happy to do the job."

178

She covers her mouth with her hand, her eyes on me, her expression fearful. She's fearful. Of me. Dammit. I shouldn't have said that to her. She knows I've done bad things, but I don't need to remind her of it. Then again, she needs to know the world I live in, and that in order to survive in that world, you do what you have to do.

"Rachel, he tried to kill you. And he'll try again."

"I don't want you killing someone." She lowers her hand from her mouth. "There has to be another way."

I put my hand firmly on her shoulder. "If Leland were trying to kill Garret, would you kill him?"

She swallows. "Yes."

"I would as well. I would do anything to protect my family. You're my family, Rachel. And I will not let any harm come to you." I gaze at her and see her fear turn to understanding. Putting this in terms of Garret made her realize I don't have a choice. Leland has to be killed. "We will not speak of this again. I will take care of it."

We hold gazes for a moment, and then she looks away.

"What is it?"

"I need to finish telling you what happened."

"Go ahead." I let go of her shoulder and sit back, still holding her hand.

"After I found out about Jack and realized you never got the message, I tried to leave. I was going to fly home that week. But before I could, these men came to my room in the middle of the night and tied me up and showed me a video."

I'm tensing up again, my muscles clenched. "A video of what?"

"Your father."

My blood is boiling, my temper rising. "Are you saying my father knew you were alive?"

"Yes. He knew Jack had gone to speak with you the night of the crash." She pauses. "Holton is the one who killed Jack."

Rage surges through my veins. "He said that? My father admitted to killing Jack?"

She nods. "Yes. I'm sorry, Pearce. I know how much you loved Jack."

"What else did my father say?" I ask through gritted teeth.

"When Holton saw Jack going to meet you that night, he suspected he was there to tell you that I was alive. He assumed Jack had saved me. Holton didn't know where I was, but he was looking for me. And he found me when I went to Naples. The street cameras captured an image of my face and it was fed into a database and linked back to me. Your father was alerted and he sent those two men after me."

My father knew she was alive. He knew, and he didn't tell me. And he killed Jack, the man who was like a father to me.

The rage inside me is so intense I'm about ready to explode. I'm trying to control my temper, for Rachel's sake, but I need to at least move. I need to stand up and pace the floor, but Rachel's holding both my hands and looking at me so intently that I remain where I am.

"I thought for sure Holton sent those men there to kill me," she says. "But then on the video, he said instead of killing me, he wanted me to be stuck in that town forever, unable to get back to you. He called it my own personal hell. He threatened me. And he threatened Garret. He said something would happen to Garret if I ever tried to leave or tried to contact you or anyone else from my old life. When the video ended, the men in my room drugged me, and when I woke up, my passport and all my money were gone. But they left me this." I take the necklace out from underneath the neckline of my dress and hold up the small heart locket. "He wanted me to see Garret in this photo every day, knowing how much it would hurt me to know I would never see him again."

I force myself to set aside the fury I feel at my father and put my focus on Rachel. My father is gone. And in the end, he got what he deserved. I don't want to waste more precious time and energy being angry at him. That's what he would've wanted. So instead of giving him that, I calm down and focus on Rachel and what she went through. It was all because of me. Because I exposed her to this world she never should've been part of. Because I didn't see my father for who he was. I wanted to believe he'd never harm her, and even though the signs were there, I ignored them. I lived in denial. He kept her there for all those years and I never even suspected it.

I pull her into my arms. "Rachel, I'm so sorry. If I'd only known."

"I was so scared." She's shaking just thinking about it. "I didn't know what to do."

I hold her tighter. "He lied. My father lied. He never would have hurt Garret." I don't want to tell her why. How he had plans for Garret. That story will have to wait for another day.

"That's what I thought. I couldn't imagine him hurting his own grandson. So I decided to try to leave. But I couldn't. Holton had those masked men watching my every move. When I tried to leave, they kept stopping me. They wouldn't let me get beyond the outskirts of town. Then I tried getting a message to you. I worked at a restaurant and whenever American tourists came in, I tried to get them to give you a message. But none of them did."

My arms relax around her and my shoulders slump. "Shit."

CHAPTER TWENTY

PEARCE

"What?" Rachel asks. "What is it, Pearce?"

"There was a man." I rub my forehead, remembering him. "A banker from Wall Street. He came up to me after a speech I gave at a conference a few years ago."

"Was his name Michael?"

"Yes. I believe it was." I look at her and sigh. "I'm sorry, Rachel. He told me about you, but I thought it was some kind of hoax. The things he knew about you were all things anyone could obtain from the Internet."

"Did he mention the town in Italy?"

"Yes. And when he said it, I assumed someone from the organization was playing some kind of sick joke on me. When we were at parties, we told people about that town and how we'd been there. Those parties we used to go to were all attended by my fellow members. So when I heard this man mention that town, I assumed he was hired by one of the members."

"They'd really do something that cruel?"

"Yes. But if this man had said just one thing that was personal, something only you and I knew, I would've looked into what he was saying. But he didn't, so I didn't believe him."

She has that pained expression again. "I told him to thank you for the Christmas ornament. The angel. I told him to tell you that I put it on the fireplace mantel."

"Rachel, if he'd told me that, I would've been on the first flight out. That would've been enough for me to at least have hope that maybe he was telling me the truth. I would've looked for you."

"I guess it wasn't meant to be," she says softly.

Why didn't I listen to that man? Why didn't I look for her? If I had, I would've found her years ago.

"So how did you get here?" I ask. "How were you finally able to leave?"

"An American family came into the restaurant earlier this week and the two daughters were talking about Garret. They said he was on some TV show. I forget to ask Garret about that. Was that true? Was he on TV?"

"It's a long story. I'll tell you later. Just continue."

"I was talking to the father and asking about you and Holton and that's when he said Holton had a stroke and died five years ago." She sighs. "I'd gone five years without knowing. I could've left five years ago."

"If I'd known what he'd done to you, I would've killed him long before that."

Maybe I shouldn't have said that. Then again, maybe she needs to know. If I want a future with her, I can't continue to keep secrets from her.

"What are you saying, Pearce? Did you do something to your father? He didn't die from a stroke?"

I fix my eyes on hers. "Protect your family above all else. Do you agree with that statement?"

"Yes. But what does that have to do with—"

"I killed him. I had to in order to protect my family. By that point, I no longer considered my father to be my family. He had become the enemy. So I killed him. I didn't do it myself. I had someone else do it."

She looks fearful again. Perhaps because I talk about his death so casually. So nonchalantly. But I attach no emotion to that event. I had just cause for his demise. He backed me into a corner. Made threats against my family. I'd kill him again in a heartbeat, especially knowing what I know now.

"Before he died, my father told me that the plane crash was his idea," I explain. "He told me he was the one who asked the organization to kill you. They wanted to punish me for marrying you, but they were going to harm me professionally. Do something to hinder my career, thus making me have to work even harder. But instead, my father insisted they kill you, and that he be allowed to pick when it would happen."

Rachel's eyes haven't left mine as she listens carefully to my every word.

"It's another very long story and I don't want to get into it today. The bottom line is that my father saw my life repeating with Garret. When Garret married Jade, it was like you and me all over again. Another Kensington marrying an outsider. My father wouldn't stand for it. He threatened to kill Jade."

Rachel inhales sharply, covering her mouth with her hand.

"The only reason he admitted to being responsible for your death was simply to prove that he was capable of doing the same thing to Jade. That he would have no problem killing her. So I had to make a decision. It was either him or Jade. And without hesitation," I pause, "I chose Jade."

She glances toward the back of the house. "Does she know this? Does Garret know?"

"Yes. They both know what my father was planning and they know I took care of him. Jade is aware of the organization. She has been for years."

"And they've left her alone? They haven't tried to harm her? I mean, besides Holton."

"She's been threatened in the past, by more than just my father. And she was shot at and almost killed."

She gasps. "By who?"

"Her father. Royce is Jade's father. He met Jade's mother while on a campaign event for one of our politicians. Royce never wanted anyone to find out he had a child with this woman so he kept it hidden. Years later, Royce was running for president and suspected Jade knew he was her father and feared she might tell the media. So he tried to kill her."

"Who stopped him?"

"I did. I shot him. But very few people know that. Rachel, everything I've told you today must remain confidential."

"You killed Royce." She says it to herself, like she's thinking aloud.

184

"I didn't have a choice. Jade was just an innocent girl. She did nothing wrong. I wasn't going to let Royce kill her. And…"

"And what?"

She'll find this out eventually. If she sees Garret without a shirt, she'll see the scar and then be angry that I didn't tell her.

"Garret was there that day," I say. "Royce had a gun pointed at Jade and when it went off, Garret threw her to the ground and…he ended up getting shot."

"No." She's crying again.

I reach over and hold her in my arms. "He's okay now. He's healthy. He's safe. Jade is safe. Now we just need to make sure that you're safe."

She knows what that means. She knows I'll kill Leland, and this time, she's not trying to talk me out of it. I think she's starting to understand that in my world, there is no gray. It's black and white. Good and evil. The lines are clear. There are rules. And although there's a rule saying I can't kill Leland, he will be killed. I will find a way.

"Hey." I hear Garret behind me and Rachel and I break apart. "I was just checking in. Do you need anything?"

Rachel stands up as Garret approaches us.

He sees her tears. "Is everything all right?"

She hugs him tightly. "I'm just so thankful you're okay."

Garret glances at me. "I'm fine, Mom."

She lets him go. "I need to go in the bathroom and clean up my face. I've been crying so much I must look like a mess. I'll be right back." She walks away.

Garret sits down across from me. "Why was she acting that way? What did you say to her?"

"I told her you were shot. I wasn't planning to, but it came up when we were talking about Jade."

"What else did you tell her?"

"Let's talk about it later. She'll be back in a minute."

He checks that she's still gone, then asks, "So what do you think?"

I lean back on the couch. "I can't believe she's actually here."

"Yeah, I know. I thought I was hallucinating when I first saw her. How are you feeling right now?"

"I'm elated to see her, but I'm still in shock."

"Are you mad at her for leaving?"

"No. I understand why she did it. She had to save herself and she didn't want to put either of us in danger by staying. She thought I knew she was there. She was waiting for me to come get her."

"Yeah. She told me. And she told me about Grandfather."

"And Leland?"

"No." He moves to the edge of his chair. "What about Leland?"

"He's the one who arranged for the plane to go down."

"You've gotta be fucking kidding me."

I shake my head. "No. All these years, Leland thinks he killed her in that plane crash. He came to our house all those times. Had dinner with us. Holidays. And the whole time...he knew what he'd done."

"Fuck." Garret clenches his fists. "Can I be the one to kill him?"

"That's not funny, Garret. Don't even joke about that."

"Well, *you* can't do it. It's against the rules."

"There are ways around the rules. I will find a way."

"So what are you going to do now?" Garret asks. "I mean, with Mom?"

"Are you referring to our relationship?"

"Yeah. Did you guys talk about it?"

"No. We've just talked about what's gone on since she left."

"But you want to be with her again, right?"

"More than anything. Seeing her again, it's like nothing's changed. I feel the same way about her now as I did before she left." He sighs. "But I don't know if she feels the same way."

"She wants you back, Dad. I know she does. She told me she still loves you."

"When did she tell you that?"

"Last night. And this morning. And she said how much she's missed you. Last night, she was asking me all these questions

186

about you. And you should've seen how nervous she was before you got here. She kept asking me if she looked okay."

I smile. "She looks beautiful. She always has."

"So tell her that. Tell her how you feel. This isn't the time to hold back. You need to let her know what you're thinking and how you feel. She needs to hear that. And she needs to know that she's safe. That you'll protect her. And our family. She's afraid, Dad. She wants to be with you but she thinks if the members find out she's back, they'll do something to you, or to me. Or to Jade and Abigail."

He's right. I can tell how afraid Rachel is, more for the rest of us than for herself. And if she's afraid we'll be harmed, she'll leave again. She'll go into hiding to protect us. I can't let her do that.

"Why don't you go somewhere?" Garret says. "Get a hotel room where you two can be alone and not have Jade and me around. You have so much to talk about and I don't want to get in the way or make you guys feel like you have to spend time with us."

"I suppose we could do that. Are there some decent hotels nearby that would have two open rooms on such late notice?"

"Yeah. There's a really nice place on the ocean, like ten minutes from here. But, um, Dad, you only need one room. You guys are married."

"We're not married. Not legally anyway. Not anymore. And I don't think your mother would be comfortable sharing a room."

He laughs a little. "I'm pretty sure she would be okay with it. Why don't you just go with one room? She'll tell you if she wants her own."

I would prefer we share a room, not for the reason Garret is referring to, but because I don't like the idea of Rachel being alone. I know my father is no longer a threat and Leland is unaware she's alive, but I would still feel better if I were with her. If she's in another room, I won't sleep. I'll be up worrying about her.

As for the other reason I'd want her in my room? The one Garret hinted at? Of course I want that. But it's too soon. She's not ready for that. And I don't want to rush her into anything. We

187

need to gradually become a couple again. I just hope she wants that.

"I'll let you guys talk," Garret says, getting up as Rachel comes back in the room.

She's smiling. That beautiful smile that lights up a room.

"Where are you going, honey?" she asks Garret.

"Jade needed help with something. I'll come back when I'm done." He leaves the room.

"Rachel, come sit down," I tell her, then wait until she's seated next to me. "I was thinking we should go somewhere. Someplace we could talk."

"We can't talk here?"

"We have a lot to talk about. And I don't want Jade and Garret to overhear us or interrupt us. We need time alone to discuss some things."

"Where do you want to go?"

"Garret said there's a hotel not far from here along the coast. I think we should stay there tonight."

She nods. "Okay."

I was expecting more of a reaction. I just invited her to stay at a hotel with me. Does she assume we'll be staying in separate rooms? I'm sure she does.

"When do you want to leave?" she asks.

"I think we should go right now."

She smiles slightly. I don't know what that means. Is she as eager to be alone with me as I am to be with her? Maybe she doesn't want her own room. Maybe she wants to stay with me.

I stand up and offer her my hand. "Let's go say goodbye."

We go into the kitchen. Off to the side is a small sitting area with some chairs. Jade and Garret are in there watching TV. Abigail's playing with her toys on the floor.

Garret sees us and turns the TV down. "Hey."

"We're going to the place you suggested," I tell him.

"When are you leaving?"

"We're going to head over there now."

"Do you want to eat something before you go?" Jade asks, getting up from her chair. "I can make some lunch."

"We'll just order something," I say. "But thank you."

Abigail sees me and crawls over to my legs. I pick her up and kiss her. "Did you miss your grandpa?"

"Papa!" She hugs me. I miss seeing her. And her parents. I wish I lived closer to them.

Rachel stands beside me, smiling. "Look how she holds onto you. Like she doesn't want to let go."

"She loves Grandpa," Jade says. She holds Abigail's hand, talking to her. "You miss your grandpa, don't you?"

"Papa!" she squeals.

Jade laughs. "We're working on the grandpa word. For now, you're papa."

"That's fine." I kiss Abigail's cheek. "She can call me whatever she'd like." I try to peel her off me. "I'm sorry, honey, but Grandpa has to go."

She shakes her head. "No."

"She's got that word down," Garret says, laughing. "She says it all the time."

"You better take her," I say to Jade as Abigail clings to me.

"Can I have her?" Rachel asks.

I kiss Abigail again. "I guess you're going to Grandma."

That's the first time I've called her that. Rachel is a grandmother. It's strange to think of her as a grandmother. Maybe because she still looks so young to me. She's in great shape. I've been trying to keep my eyes on her face, but now that she's preoccupied with the baby, I take a moment to discreetly look at her.

She has a light blue cotton dress on. My favorite color is blue and I always loved it when she wore that color. It's a sleeveless dress and her arms are lean and toned, like they were when she was younger. I wonder if she's been swimming all these years or if she stayed in shape some other way. She's maintained her hourglass figure, the dress hugging her curves.

"You are so sweet," Rachel says to Abi, kissing her cheek. "I can't get enough of you." She hands her to Jade, then gives Jade a hug. "Bye, Jade. Get some rest. I'm sure you're tired. I slept through most of my first trimester."

Jade smiles at Rachel. "I'm glad I'm not the only one."

"We'll see you guys tomorrow," Garret says. "Are you coming over in the morning?"

"We'll call you and let you know," I say.

Garret smiles, as if my answer means something. I know he wants his mother and me to get back together, but I don't know if that's going to happen.

Rachel hugs Garret. "Bye, honey. I love you."

"I love you too. Oh, let me get your suitcase."

Jade walks us to the door and Garret meets us there with the suitcase. It's just one small suitcase. Is that all Rachel has? Everything she owns fits in one suitcase?

"See you guys later," Garret says.

I look out at the driveway. "I forgot, I don't have a car."

Garret takes his keys from his pocket and hands them to me. "It's all yours. Your suitcase is still in the trunk. I never took it out."

Rachel and I go out to Garret's BMW. I open the door for her, then put her suitcase in the trunk next to mine, and go around to the other side. Then we head to the hotel.

I'm going to a hotel with the love of my life who I thought was dead. And I have no idea if she wants me back.

This should be interesting.

CHAPTER TWENTY-ONE

RACHEL

Pearce and I are driving along the coast to the hotel that Garret suggested. Pearce thinks we need time alone. I don't know if he means to just talk or do more than that. We probably shouldn't do more than talk. After all this time apart, it's probably not appropriate. And maybe Pearce doesn't want that. I can't really tell if he still feels that way about me. If he's still attracted to me.

I'm definitely still attracted to him. As soon as I saw him, my heart took off, racing in my chest. He's still so incredibly handsome. Extremely handsome. Even more handsome than I remember.

He's wearing a dark gray suit with a crisp white shirt and a gray and black striped tie. And he smells amazing. It must be a new cologne. It wasn't one he used to wear.

When he hugged me, I felt like I was home again. Where I belonged. I didn't want him to let me go. And I almost kissed him. I used to always kiss him after a hug so it felt natural. Like what I normally do, but then I stopped myself before I did it.

I have to keep reminding myself that things are different now. We're not married anymore. And we've both changed. Pearce has a different life now. He has a daughter and has custody of her. And I've spent the last fifteen years being someone else. I'm not even sure the old Rachel exists anymore. After what I've been through, and what I've seen, and what I know, I feel like a whole different person.

"I think this is it." Pearce pulls up to the hotel entrance.

It's a beautiful hotel. The exterior is a mix of dark wood and stacked stone, like an upscale lodge. Colorful flowers surround the building and line the road that leads to the entrance.

A valet opens my door. "Welcome."

"Thank you." I get out of the car and see another valet taking our luggage from the trunk.

Pearce appears next to me.

The valet approaches him. "May I show you to the registration desk?"

"Not just yet. We'd like to look at the gardens first."

He smiles. "Of course. Take your time. Your luggage will be waiting inside."

Pearce holds his arm out for me, in true gentleman form, and I take it. He walks us toward a stone path that's nestled among the flowers. I can hear the roar of the ocean in the distance.

I stop him before we reach the path. "Pearce, what are we doing?"

"We need to discuss this before we check in."

"I agree. So how are we going to do this? I don't have a credit card."

His brows furrow. "Why is that a concern?"

"I need it to check in. I have cash, but they require a credit card."

"Rachel, you are not paying for the room. I will take care of it. What I wanted to discuss is…whether you would like your own room or if you would be okay staying with me. I am not trying to imply anything here, so please, do not take it that way. I would simply feel better having you with me than in a different room. Until I know for sure that you're safe, I would prefer that you stay with me."

So he wants me to stay with him to make sure I'm safe. Nothing more. He's being a gentleman, just like he was when we met. In a way, I feel like we're going back to that time. Starting over. Getting to know each other again.

"Rachel, what would you prefer? One room or two?"

"One." I say it a little too quickly and see a hint of a smile on Pearce's face.

"One it is. Shall we go check in?"

"Yes." I smile at his formality. Again, it's like when we met. He was always so formal. As we walk back to the entrance, I say, "What if someone sees us together? Should I go wait off to the side while you check in?"

"No. Just stay with me." He takes my hand and we walk inside and up to the woman waiting at the check-in desk.

"How can I help you?" she asks. She's beautiful and exotic-looking with dark skin and jet black hair. She's in her twenties, but smiling at Pearce like she'd go out with him in a heartbeat. Any woman would. He's hot. Hotter than most guys half his age.

"I need a room for tonight," he says.

"You don't have a reservation?"

"No. What do you have available?"

She clicks on her computer, glancing up at me, then back at her screen. "The only room I have open tonight is our suite. It has a master bedroom with a separate guest room and a large living room with a bar."

"Excellent. I'll take it." He reaches in his suit jacket for his wallet.

"Sir, it's $1500 a night," she says cautiously.

"That's fine." He gives her his information and hands her his credit card.

She swipes his card, then hands it back to him along with the room key. "The suite is on the top floor. You'll need to use your key to access the floor. Your luggage is already being brought up to your room. Enjoy your stay, Mr. Kensington." She smiles again, flirtatiously this time.

It makes me wonder how many women Pearce has been with since I left. Did he cheat on Katherine? It wasn't a real marriage so maybe he did. Even if he didn't, he's been divorced for five years. He could've been with a lot of women in those five years.

"Shall we go?" Pearce puts his arm around my waist and leads me away from the desk and to the elevator.

I don't know if he did it on purpose, but his hand placement is causing heat to build inside me. His hand remains there as we go in the elevator. He slides his room card in the slot and pushes the button for the top floor.

"Is something wrong?" he asks as the elevator moves. His arm is still around me and he has that hint of a smile again.

"Nothing's wrong. Why do you ask?"

"You seem tense, but perhaps I'm imagining it."

He's right. My body tensed up when he touched me, not because I don't like it, but because I like it too much. Every time he touches me, heat surges inside me. Desire. Want.

Pearce has always had that effect on me. Even after we were married for years, his touch still affected me this way. I wasn't sure if I'd still feel that way when I saw him again, but I do. I definitely do. My desire for him is intense.

I need to focus on other things. We're not here to do that. We need to talk. We're supposed to spend tonight talking. Just talking.

The elevator opens to a hallway that has just one door. The suite must take up the entire floor.

Pearce unlocks the door and holds it open for me. "After you," he says.

I step inside the suite and enter the living room. The two bedrooms are off to the left. The living room has a dark brown leather couch that faces a stone fireplace. On each side of the fireplace are expansive windows that look out at the ocean. My apartment in Italy had magnificent views, but this is so much better. Because this is home. Where my family is.

"It's a nice view." Pearce comes up behind me, placing his hands on my shoulders.

"Yes. It's gorgeous." Standing this close to him, I smell his cologne again. It's excellent cologne.

"Can I get you something to drink?" he asks.

I glance over and see the bar off to the side. "Maybe later." I turn around and his hands drop from my shoulders, but I want them back. I already miss his touch. "I think I'll take a quick tour of the room first."

"They brought the luggage up." He walks over to where it's sitting and picks up my suitcase. "Where would you like it?"

I feel like it's a trick question. Like he's asking if I want to sleep with him. I *do* want to sleep with him, but I think it's too soon.

"The guest room is fine."

"The master bedroom is yours. I'll take the guest room." He brings my suitcase into the oversized room with the king-size bed.

I follow him. "Pearce, no. You should take this one. You paid for the room."

"Rachel, stop talking about the cost. You're my wife and—" He stops and clears his throat. "The room is yours."

He still considers me his wife. And I still consider him my husband. So why are we acting so formal with each other? Is it because we've been apart for so long? We're not sure how to act?

"Thank you." I go up and hug him.

"Don't thank me." He hugs me back. "What's mine is yours. It always has been and always will be. Anything you need, just ask and I will get it for you."

"I already have everything I need." I hope he knows I wasn't just referring to Garret when I said that, but to him too. The two of them are all I need.

His cell phone rings and I step back so he can answer it.

"It's Garret," he says, then talks into the phone. "Hello, Garret....yes, we found it...they had a room available...I'll call you tomorrow." He ends the call and his phone rings again. "It's the office." He ignores the call and puts his phone away.

I smile at him. "So you're the CEO?"

"Yes. I have been for years. Ever since....well, it's been a long time."

"Do you like it?"

"I'm not particularly fond of the chemical industry and manufacturing, but as for running a corporation, yes. I find it challenging, yet also rewarding."

"That's good." I smile a little. "My job wasn't quite as challenging."

"You said you worked at a restaurant?"

"Yes. I didn't have many options. When I first arrived in Italy, I moved into a studio apartment above the restaurant and my landlady, Celia, who also owns the restaurant, offered me a job there. Celia was very good to me. She treated me like a daughter. She helped me get out of Italy and gave me some money. I need to write her and tell her I made it. And pay her back the money."

"Tell me where to send it and I'll have it sent to her right away."

I nod in agreement. "I also taught English to children."

He smiles. "Did you enjoy that?"

"I did. Very much. The children were all very sweet but..." I take a breath, trying to fight back tears. "They reminded me of Garret." A tear trickles down my cheek.

Pearce runs his hand down my arm. "Rachel."

I squeeze my eyes shut, then open them again. "I need you to tell me, Pearce. I need you to tell me about Garret and everything I missed when I was gone. Birthdays. School events. Baseball games. Football games. His swim meets." I wipe my eyes and smile. "He was always so into sports, even as a toddler."

"Yes," Pearce says quietly. "That's never changed."

"I want to hear every detail about his life. Everything that I missed. Can you do that for me?"

"Of course." He glances down as he says it. He seems uncomfortable.

"Pearce, is something wrong?"

He looks up again. "No. Sorry. I was just thinking about Garret. There's so much to tell you I'm not sure where to start."

"You don't need to tell me right now. In fact, I don't think I'm quite ready to hear it."

He nods. "We'll do it later. There's no rush. We have plenty of time."

I glance down at my suitcase. "Well, I think I'll unpack my clothes."

He points to the suitcase. "Is that all you have?"

"Yes. Why?"

"Did you leave the rest in Italy?"

"No. That's everything."

Now *he's* the one who looks like he's fighting back tears. He draws me into his arms. "Rachel, I'm so sorry. This never

196

should've happened. I wish I could go back in time and change it all. I have so many regrets. So much guilt."

I pull back enough to look at him. "Guilt over what?"

"Everything. Not knowing this was being planned. Trusting that my father wouldn't hurt you. Making you go to that fundraiser. Making you stay behind to attend Wingate's speech. Encouraging you to get on that plane."

"Pearce, don't. Don't feel guilty about any of that. You weren't aware of what was going on. You couldn't have stopped it. And now it's over. It's time to move on."

His phone rings again and he checks it. "It's the office. I'll just turn my phone off. I shouldn't be answering calls right now."

"Go ahead and deal with work. It'll give me time to unpack."

"All right." He pauses, his eyes on mine. He lifts his hand up, smoothing my hair. "I still can't believe you're here."

I smile at him. "I can't either."

He pauses again, his eyes lingering on my face, then he says, "Come out when you're done. I just need to make a few phone calls. It shouldn't take long."

"Okay."

He walks out of the room and I panic for a moment. After being apart from him for so long, I want him beside me, right next to me, where I can see him, and touch him, and make sure he's really there. But I can't be that way. I can't be with him every second of every day. He has other people in his life now. People who depend on him, like his daughter.

I close the door and open my suitcase and hang up some of my clothes. I'm so used to not having much that Pearce's reaction surprised me. He looked so sad when I told him this suitcase holds everything I own. When we were married, I had way more than I needed, but now I'm used to having almost nothing. And the past fifteen years, that never bothered me. I never even gave it a thought. I didn't miss my designer dresses or my expensive car or my diamond jewelry. I didn't care if I never had those things again. I only wanted my family back. That's all that mattered. It's all I wanted.

After I unpack, I lie down on the bed for a few minutes. I'm so tired. I didn't sleep much last night. I kept having nightmares that Holton's men were following me and then found me and took me back to Italy. I woke up sweating and out of breath and couldn't get back to sleep.

When I return to the living room, Pearce is on the phone, facing the windows, his back to me.

"No, absolutely not. We already agreed to the terms. They can't go back and change them." His voice is forceful. Commanding. I find it very sexy.

He has his suit jacket off and I check out the back of him. I always loved how well his clothes fit him, perfectly tailored to his body. His dress shirt wraps over his broad shoulders with no gaps or wrinkles. My gaze wanders lower, to his gray dress pants, which fit his backside in a way that makes me stare for a moment.

The room is quiet and I look up and see Pearce swiping through his phone. He still hasn't noticed I'm here. He puts his phone to his ear. "Hi, honey. How's everything going?"

I assume he's talking to his daughter.

"What does your mother have planned for the rest of the week?" He listens. "I don't know yet. Something came up, so I won't be back tomorrow...No, I don't need to talk to her...Yes, I'll call you tomorrow...Love you too...Goodbye."

It sounds like he has a good relationship with her. I wonder how often she sees her mother. Does Katherine live next to Pearce? Or did she get the house in the divorce?

Pearce is on his phone again. "Lisa, I need you to cancel my meetings for the rest of the week, including any conference calls...no, not just today, I need you to clear my calendar for the entire week...I know they've been waiting, but something came up...just tell everyone we'll reschedule...thank you."

He ends the call and turns around and sees me there. "Rachel. You should've said something. I didn't know you were there." He turns his phone off.

"Pearce, you didn't have to cancel everything. If you need to work, I can spend time with Jade and Garret."

198

He walks over to me. "You've been gone for years. I want to spend every moment I can with you. I don't care about work. It'll go on without me. Now should we order some food? I haven't eaten yet today."

"Then yes. Let's order something."

We find the room service menus and he says, "Order whatever you'd like. Don't worry about the cost." He smiles. "You always had trouble spending money."

I smile back. "No, I didn't. I just didn't like buying things I didn't need."

"Well, you arrived here with one suitcase. I think it's safe to say you need some things. Make a list and I'll have someone go and get you whatever you need."

"I'm assuming I can't be seen in public. That's why you're having someone go shopping for me?"

He brings me over to the couch to sit down. "I don't think anyone would know it's you unless you're seen with me, and even then I don't think they would believe it's you. Only our friends and family would know. That's why I wasn't concerned about you being seen here at the hotel. But we do need to figure out a way to bring you back."

"You mean, as myself? I was thinking I would have to pretend to be someone else."

"No. That's not a good idea. We used to be in the media a lot and those photos and articles are still out there. It wouldn't take long for someone to discover it's you and not whoever you're pretending to be. I need to give this some thought. For now, let's not worry about it." He holds up his menu. "Let's find something to eat."

We order our meals and Pearce orders a bottle of champagne. A half hour later, the waiter arrives and sets up a table in our room, complete with a white linen tablecloth. He sets out our meals and as he leaves, Pearce follows him out into the hall. I assume he's giving him a tip.

Pearce returns and opens the champagne and pours it into our glasses. He hands me a glass and holds up his for a toast. "To having you back. And to new beginnings."

I smile and clink his glass and sip the champagne. He sets his glass down and comes around and pulls out my chair for me. Once he's seated in his own chair, he reaches over for my hand. "I meant to say this earlier. You look beautiful, Rachel."

"Thank you. You look good too. Don't you ever age?"

He laughs and lets go of my hand. "I'm quite certain I've aged. Perhaps you don't remember what I used to look like."

I set my napkin on my lap. "I remember. I pictured you every day in my head. I used to imagine you walking in the restaurant. In fact, every time the door opened, I'd check to see if it was you."

Guilt covers Pearce's face and I quickly regret telling him that. It's not his fault he never showed up. He didn't know. He never got the message.

"Garret looks just like you," I say, changing topics. "Don't you think?"

"Yes, we look very similar." He cuts into his steak.

"What does your daughter look like?"

"Lilly looks more like Katherine. Blond hair. Blue eyes. She's tall for her age, like Garret was."

"Does she see her mother much?"

"No. Katherine is remarried and has a son. She lives in Manhattan and goes to see her sister in Paris several times a year. She doesn't have much interest in being a mother. She never has."

"So you and Lilly live in Connecticut?"

"Yes. I kept the house after the divorce."

"Is it the same house that Garret lived in?"

"Yes, I built it a couple years after..." He pauses. "After you were gone. It's a large house. Much larger than we need. I've considered selling it and getting something smaller."

"Do you have any other houses?" I ask because Katherine seems like someone who would've wanted more than one.

"I own several homes and I have apartments in LA, New York, and London."

"Where are your other houses?"

"I have one outside San Francisco, close to wine country. It's a smaller home. Then there's one in Arizona that I bought when the company was expanding in the Southwest. I was there so often for business that it made sense to buy the house, but I haven't used it in years so it needs to be sold. I have another house in Aspen, which Katherine insisted we buy. She doesn't ski but her friends had houses there so she wanted one there as well. And then I have one at Hilton Head, which I only go to when I want to get away and do some golfing."

"Wow, that's a lot of houses."

"Yes, I need to sell some of them."

We eat in silence for a few minutes, and as we do, I think about how much Pearce's life has changed. If I hadn't left, would we have all those homes? It seems so extravagant and unnecessary. Who needs that many houses and three apartments? He has so much money that maybe it doesn't seem like a lot to him, but to me it does.

"I have one more," I hear Pearce say.

I look up and see that he's put his fork down. "One more what?"

"One more house." His face is serious and I'm almost afraid of what he's going to say.

"Where is it?" I set my fork on my plate.

His gaze meets mine across the table. "Indiana."

My eyes immediately tear up, but I'm smiling. "You kept it?"

"Yes." His face has a hint of a smile now. "I wasn't sure how'd you feel about that, but from your reaction, I think you're okay with it."

"I'm more than okay with it." I shove my chair back and go around the table and hug him.

He stands up and hugs me back.

"Thank you," I say, hugging him tighter. "For keeping it all these years."

"I couldn't bring myself to sell it. That was your childhood home. And even though I thought you were gone, I couldn't sell it. It was one of the few remaining pieces of you I had left."

I let go of Pearce but hold onto his hand. "It means so much to me that you kept it. I thought for sure you would've sold it."

"I had no intentions of selling it." He smiles. "Would you like to go see it? We could even stay there if you'd like."

201

"Doesn't someone live there?"

"No. It hasn't been rented out for years. But I pay someone to take care of it. A retired farmer. I've never met him but we've talked on the phone. He knew your family."

"What's his name?"

"Gerald Henderson."

I smile. "Yes. I know him. His wife was my teacher back in third grade. So what about the land? Did you keep it too?"

"Yes. I rent it out to a man who has the farm adjacent to yours."

"Have you taken Garret there? To see the house?"

"No. And he doesn't know I still own it. I suppose I should've taken him there at some point, but it just didn't seem right to go there without you. We always said we'd take him there together and…"

"We never had a chance to," I say, finishing his thought. "It was too hard for me to go back. But I should've just done it. I think Garret would've liked seeing where I grew up, and where his grandparents lived."

"We can still go there, Rachel. We'll plan a trip. We'll take the whole family."

Family. My heart warms hearing him say that. Talking as if nothing has changed. As if we're all still a family. I was so afraid he wouldn't see it that way anymore. That I'd be an outsider after being gone for so long.

"I would love that," I tell him.

He nods. "Then we'll bring up the idea to Garret." He glances at the table. "Shall we finish our dinner?"

I go back to my chair, and as we continue eating, my mind fills with questions, about Pearce and me and where we go from here. I get the feeling Pearce wants to continue where we left off, but that's not really possible anymore. For fifteen years, he's had a different life. A life without me, and that's not just going to go away or change because I'm back.

"So do you think you'll stay in Connecticut?" I ask, then realize he doesn't really have a choice. "I guess you have to for Lilly's sake."

"It's more for work than for Lilly. She has some friends there, but she wouldn't be opposed to moving." He chuckles. "She used to beg me to move out here next to Jade and Garret. But we've remained in Connecticut because the company headquarters is still there."

I've only finished half my meal but I'm done eating and set my fork down. Pearce does as well.

"We should talk about this," he says.

"About what?"

"About where you want to live."

"I haven't really thought about it."

"I'm getting the feeling you don't want to live in Connecticut."

I'm not sure what his comment means. Does he want to know where I'll be living so he can come visit me? Or does he want us to live together?

"I'd rather not live on the East Coast," I say. "I feel like I'd be surrounded by enemies there."

He nods. "I understand. So where would you like to live?"

"Probably out here. I want to be close to Garret and his family."

"I see." He glances down at the table and slides his plate aside.

He seems disappointed and a little sad, and I realize my comment just implied I don't want to be with him. That's not what I meant. But I don't know what he wants me to say. He has a new life and a daughter and I don't know how I fit in that. I have to ask. I can't keep guessing.

"Pearce. What are we doing here?"

"What do you mean?"

"I don't know why you're asking these questions. I don't know why we're here at this hotel. I don't know what you want. You have this whole new life that I'm not part of and I don't know where we go from here."

"Let's go sit somewhere else." He gets up from the table and comes around to pull out my chair. We both go sit on the couch, turning to face each other.

"You asked me what I want," he says. "So here's my answer."

CHAPTER TWENTY-TWO

RACHEL

Pearce takes my hand, gazing into my eyes. "What I want is to have you back in my life. I don't want to rush you or pressure you in any way. I know you've been through a lot and learned things about me that you didn't know before. But my hope is that we can get past that and be together again, as husband and wife." His hand moves to the side of my face. "I love you, Rachel. I've never stopped loving you. You're the only woman I've ever loved." He pauses. "I asked you where you'd like to live because I want to be wherever you are. Now that I finally have you back, I don't want us to be apart. If you want to live in California, then I'll move here."

"But you said you need to live in Connecticut because of the company."

"I own the company. I can live wherever I choose. No one is telling me what to do. I'll make it work. I want to be with you. And whatever I have to do to make that happen, I will do it." He waits for me to say something and when I don't, he says, "But if that's not what you want, I understand."

"Pearce, I *do* want that. But you have a new life now and I don't expect you to change everything now that I'm back."

"That's not for you to worry about. Any inconveniences that come from whatever changes I need to make are nothing compared to what you've gone through. You were nearly killed and had to go into hiding and then were held hostage in that town. And that was all because of me. Because I exposed you to this world that you weren't even aware existed. And I can't apologize enough for that. Truthfully, when you told me you knew about the organization, I assumed you'd want nothing to do with me."

"I've had a lot of time to think about that. And it's that part of your life that concerns me the most when I think about our future together. I don't like that you're part of that group, or that you hid it from me for all those years. Jack explained why you had to keep it a secret, but by doing so, I feel like I didn't really know you. Part of me still feels that way. I don't know who this man is that does these terrible things. That's not the Pearce I know."

He sighs. "I never wanted to do those things. I was forced to be a member and forced to do what they told me to do. But I'm no longer part of it."

"You're not?"

"I'm still a member, but I'm no longer involved in their activities. I don't even go to the meetings."

"Why are they allowing that?"

"It's another long story, but basically there were some reporters who suspected I belonged to a secret group and they were following me around, watching my every move. The organization felt it was too risky to have me involved in their activities so I haven't been for several years now."

"But eventually, they'll involve you again."

"It's possible, but Rachel, the organization has changed how it operates. It's significantly different than when I was first a member. They aren't doing the things they used to do."

"Are they still rigging elections? Killing people?"

He hesitates. "I'm not allowed to tell you that."

"This is what I mean, Pearce. You'll always be living this secret life."

"It's not a secret life. You're now aware that I'm part of it. You just don't know everything about it. And it's better if you don't. I don't share this information with Jade or Garret either. They know the group exists and that's all they need to know. I'm so far removed from the organization that even *I* don't know everything that's going on there."

"So you're not still doing things for them?"

"No, I haven't had an assignment in years."

"You talked about killing Leland as if it wasn't a big deal. Killing someone is a big deal, Pearce. It's murder. People go to prison for that."

"In my world, they don't. Rich and powerful people can get away with things. It may be wrong, but it's the way it is and always has been. Did anyone go to prison for taking down that plane?"

"No," I say quietly, remembering the articles I read about the crash when I was looking things up on the Internet that day I went to Naples years ago.

"When Leland rigged that plane," Pearce says, "he killed five people, and it would've been six if you'd been on board. And yet he was never punished. There was never an investigation. No jail time. No bond to pay. Nothing. He just continued on with his life. And if he found out you were alive and then killed you, he wouldn't go to prison. He'd go on living as if nothing had happened. Do you understand what I'm saying?"

"That you feel you have no choice but to kill Leland. But I still don't like it."

"I don't either. If there were some other way to deal with him, I would. I promise you I would." He lightly rubs my hand. "Rachel, I am not some evil monster. I spent years thinking I was, and I hated myself for it. But then Jack told me that I cannot define myself by the things they force me to do. It took me years to accept that, but doing so freed me from the guilt that used to consume me. So please, don't define me that way."

"I don't think you're evil, Pearce. I understand that you didn't want to do those things. But I *am* worried about what they'll make you do in the future and whether I can be okay with the fact that you're doing those things again."

"Rachel, I'm telling you, they've changed. It's not like it was before."

I nod. "I think I just need some time to think about this."

"What does that mean for *us*? How much time do you need? Weeks? Months? Longer than that?"

"I don't know."

"So while you think about this, you don't want us living together?"

I'm not sure how to answer him. The truth is I *do* want to live with him. I don't want us to be apart. But I also don't want to live in fear, knowing he's still part of this group that tried to kill me.

"Can I answer that question later?" I ask.

"Of course."

Someone knocks on the door. "Room service."

Pearce goes over and opens the door. The waiter who set up our dinner is standing there.

"Are you finished with your meal?" he asks Pearce.

"Yes. You can clean it up."

The waiter comes in and clears the dishes but doesn't take the table down. Instead he brings in a big bowl of something with two spoons. Pearce follows him out to the hall and I hear him thank the man.

Pearce returns with a bouquet of yellow tulips in a vase. He used to always bring me tulips when we were dating. I stand up and smile as he hands me the flowers.

"For you," he says and kisses my cheek.

"Thank you. That's very sweet."

"Come have dessert." He leads me back to the table. "I hope you don't mind sharing."

I smile even more when I see the dessert. "Did you special order this for me?"

"I did. I think the waiter found it to be a rather odd request, especially since I asked for a specific brand of cookie."

The dessert is a cookie sundae. I don't tell him that Garret made me one last night. Besides, this one is more like the one I used to make; chocolate and vanilla ice cream layered with my favorite chocolate chip cookies. The cookies are crumbled up and soaking up the ice cream. The bowl is in the middle of the table so we can share.

"This is so good," I say, as I savor a chunk of cookie. "I could've just had this for dinner."

He chuckles. "I'm glad you like it."

"Do you still not eat dessert?"

"I eat ice cream." He peers up at me and smiles. "Someone got me hooked on it years ago."

I smile back. "That's it for desserts? Just ice cream?"

"I also eat carrot cake. The same person who got me hooked on ice cream got me hooked on carrot cake. And I seem to remember her making an apple dessert that was quite good. But I haven't had it for years."

"I think you could persuade that person who got you hooked on ice cream to make you that apple dessert."

"And what would I have to do to persuade her?"

"I'm sure you'll think of something. You seem like someone who's very persuasive."

"I *am* quite persuasive. Challenge accepted."

His tone is very flirtatious and it's making my stomach all fluttery like we're on a first date. The chemistry between us is still there. The second I saw him, I felt it again. That spark. That energy. That intense attraction.

I dip my spoon deep into the bowl to find the cookies. "So do you cook? Or do you and Lilly eat out a lot?"

"We have a live-in chef." He takes a drink of his water. "A friend of yours, actually."

"A friend of mine?" I try to think of who I used to know who cooks. "You don't mean Charles, do you?"

He nods. "Yes. He came to work for me right after you left. And when we moved to the new house, I asked him to continue working for us. He lives in the guest house. We've become good friends. He's like a brother to me."

"I always liked Charles. I'd love to see him again."

"He'd love to see you as well." He pauses. "Rachel, I want you to come back to Connecticut with me. As long as you stay at the house, you won't run into anyone we know."

"When are you leaving?"

"I was planning to fly home in a week."

"That's a long time to be away from work."

He reaches across the table and slips his hand around mine. "You don't seem to be getting the fact that I don't want to be apart from you."

The touch of his hand sends a ripple of heat through my core and causes my pulse to quicken. How does he do that? No other man has ever had such a strong effect on me. So strong that I drop my spoon in the bowl.

"Are you done?" he asks, assuming that's what the spoon drop meant.

Half the sundae remains but it was a huge sundae. There was no way the two of us could eat it all.

"Yes, I'm done."

"We should take a walk. The sun is setting. We could go on the path along the beach."

Out the window, I notice the pink and orange sky. "That would be nice."

We get up from the table and Pearce asks, "Would you like to get a sweater? It can get chilly at night."

"I think I'll be fine." I could use some cool air. I'm burning up from all the sexual tension between us.

His arm goes around my waist as we leave the room, and he keeps it there as we go in the elevator and out to the beach. We walk along the path, taking in the gorgeous sunset, the ocean roaring off in the distance. It's very romantic. This whole evening has been romantic. The hotel suite. The flowers. The champagne. And now a walk along the beach.

Pearce has made it clear he wants me back, and I'm happy about that. Beyond happy. So why aren't I telling him I want the same thing?

I know why, but I'm trying to ignore it. The truth is that I'm scared of that group. The organization. I'm terrified they'll come after me or my family once they find out I'm alive and back with Pearce. What if they punish Pearce for being with me? Or threaten to hurt Garret unless I leave Pearce alone?

"Rachel." Pearce stops and turns me toward him. "Why are you so quiet?"

"No reason. I'm just listening to the waves."

We're in a secluded area on the stone path that goes from the hotel to the beach. There are flowering bushes all around us and the ocean is off in the distance.

Pearce runs his warm hands down my arms and my heart beats faster. "Are you sure you're not cold?"

I smile at him. "I'm fine."

The ocean breeze blows my hair in my face and before I can get it, Pearce does, tucking the strands behind my ear. He keeps his hand there and our eyes meet, that fiery hot sexual tension burning up the air between us.

It seems like minutes go by, but I'm sure it's only seconds before he slowly leans in and puts his lips to mine. It's a soft gentle kiss, but it's followed by another, and another after that. Gentle, sweet kisses. He's being cautious. Trying not to push me. But now that he's started this, I want more.

I kiss him back, holding onto his shirt. His hand remains on my face, while his other hand wraps around my waist, drawing me into him. I part my lips and his tongue sweeps over mine.

The sparks I felt earlier have now become fireworks, and my heart beats wildly at his touch. Pearce tightens his hold on me as his kiss goes deeper. Sensations are firing off all up and down my body, a feeling I haven't experienced in fifteen years, not since I was last with Pearce in that hotel room in DC. Words can't describe how good it feels to kiss him again, to be in his arms, to feel my body come alive after years of feeling nothing.

Minutes go by. I don't know how many and I don't care. I don't want him to stop. Or let me go.

The sound of loud talking from one of the hotel balconies startles us both and our lips part. But we don't back away. Pearce has me in a such a solid grasp, I couldn't move if I tried. We're both breathing hard, and he's gazing down at me with dark, heated eyes.

I'm clutching the back of his dress shirt. Our bodies are pressed together and I feel his arousal against me. But he's not backing away. He wants me to feel it.

"Let's go inside," he says, low and deep.

It's dark out now and he keeps his arm around me as we make our way back down the path to the hotel. We go straight to the elevator, but when we get to our room, the waiter is there, taking the table away.

He sees us walk in. "Sorry. I was just leaving." He wheels the table out and Pearce shuts the door behind him.

That short interruption was enough for me to rethink what we were about to do. I feel like we should wait. We still have so much to talk about.

"Do you want to watch TV?" I ask.

"No." His eyes still have that look of desire. Need. Want.

"Maybe we should talk some more."

He's quiet for a moment, his eyes on me, and then he says, "If that's what you'd like to do, then yes, we can talk."

"Or maybe we could just watch TV. I feel like I'm all talked out for tonight."

"Whatever you'd like."

We sit on the couch, right next to each other. Pearce puts his arm out and I immediately snuggle up against his side. He smiles at how quickly I moved into my spot. He knows how much l used to love being next to him like this when we'd watch TV. I still love it.

A couple hours go by and I don't even know what we watched. It doesn't matter. What matters is being together like this again. It feels so natural. So right.

Around eleven, I sit up a little. "I think I'll go to sleep."

He turns the TV off. "I think I will too."

We walk to the bedrooms. I go in mine and stand at the door. "Goodnight."

He leans down and kisses my cheek. "Goodnight, Rachel."

I close the door, then change into my lightweight nightshirt because I'm warm from lying next to Pearce on the couch. He's probably wondering why I cut him off like that after the kiss. Actually, I'm starting to wonder that too.

CHAPTER TWENTY-THREE

RACHEL

I climb into the massive bed which sits high up off the floor. I hear the water running in the bathroom and then it shuts off and I hear Pearce walk into his room. But I don't hear the door close. Maybe he's leaving it open as an invitation for me to come in. Should I? No. I should go to sleep. I need to sleep.

A few minutes later, I drift off.

"Tie her hands," the voice says. It's Holton's men. Except there aren't just two. There are ten. Or more than that. They're all around me, surrounding my bed.

"No!" I scream. "Let me go!"

I try to move my feet but I can't. They're tied.

"Put her in the car," the man says. "And if she escapes again, she's dead."

"No! Don't take me back there! No!"

I feel his hands on my shoulders and scream even louder. "Stop! I won't go back there! No!"

"Rachel."

I'm startled awake by a different voice. A voice I recognize.

"Rachel, wake up."

I open my eyes and see Pearce sitting next to me on the bed. The light in the hallway is on and shining into my room. I can see Pearce's face, the concern in his eyes.

I sit up. "I'm sorry. I didn't mean to wake you." I'm gasping for breath, my heart pounding.

"Rachel, you're shaking. What happened?"

"It was just a dream."

212

"You were screaming. Telling someone to let you go. Who were you talking to?"

"Holton's men. The ones he had watching me." My voice is shaky, my breaths uneven. "I had this dream where they found me and took me away."

Pearce pulls me into his arms. "Nobody is going to take you." He holds me tightly against him. "I won't let them."

"It seemed so real."

He strokes my hair and kisses my head. "It's not real. You're safe. You're here with me and you're safe."

"What if they're looking for me? What if they find me?"

"Nobody is going to hurt you. I will not let anyone hurt you or take you away from me. I promise you."

I hold onto him and we sit there quietly on the bed. After a few minutes, I let go of him and sit back.

"Are you okay?" he asks.

"Yes."

"Then I'll let you get back to sleep."

As he's leaving my room, I say, "Would you stay?"

He turns around. "You want me to stay?"

"Yes. If you don't mind."

His lips rise just slightly. "Of course I don't mind. Let me just get the light."

He turns off the hall light and joins me in bed, lying on his back. He puts his arm up and I press myself against his side, my arm draped over his bare chest. He's only wearing pajama pants, no shirt. His chest is warm, solid, muscular. His arm goes around me, making me feel safe and protected.

I love this. I love being here like this. With him. It feels right. It felt right even when I'd only known him a few weeks. It was one of the signs that told me we were meant to be together. And now I feel it again. That feeling deep inside that tells me Pearce and I belong together. That despite everything that's happened, everything we've gone through, we were meant to find each other and spend our lives together.

So why am I even questioning this? Us? The love I have with Pearce is a once-in-a-lifetime love. He's my soulmate. My one and only. My true love. The man who stirs up passion in me just by walking in the room. The man who excites me and whose simple touch sparks a desire in me that I've never felt with anyone else. My heart aches when I'm not with him. When he said he didn't want to be apart from me, I felt the exact same way. All I want is to be with him. And now I am. We're finally reunited, and despite whatever challenges we'll face by being together, I don't want to be apart from him ever again.

If I let my head make this decision, it would tell me to wait. To take it slow and wait until all our issues are resolved before being together again. But my heart wins out when it comes to Pearce. It always has.

I don't need time to think about this. I still have worries and fears about being with him, but Pearce and I will talk them out and find a way to deal with those worries and fears. But as for this? Pearce and me? I don't need to think about it. Being with him tonight just confirms how much I love him. How much I can't see a future without him.

"Pearce?" I lift my head to look at him in the dim light of the room.

"Yes?"

"I love you."

His hand brushes over my cheek. "I love you too."

I slide up so that our faces are aligned, and softly kiss him. He kisses me back, sitting up slightly, his hand moving to the back of my head. He deepens the kiss and my hand slides down his chest, then his abs, then under the waistband of his pants.

"Rachel," he whispers.

He's already aroused and I stroke him, my breaths becoming ragged, my body coming alive again, sparking with sensations.

The heat in the room has just jumped a million degrees. Pearce tugs my nightshirt up and takes it off. Then he lies on his side, skimming his hand along my skin, over my breast, my hip, my stomach, and along the inside of my thigh. He leans down and kisses my neck, sending a shiver through me. His mouth makes its way to my breast I arch up, desperate for more. When his hand slips under my panties, I suck in a breath. I haven't been touched like this in fifteen years. I haven't been touched at all. Or kissed. Every part of me is so sensitive to his touch, reacting, and relishing the feel of it.

"I want to be with you," I whisper, raking my fingers through his hair.

He doesn't question my request. He wants this as much as I do. He shoves his pants off, then slides my panties down my legs, making me shiver with anticipation. He shifts his body over mine and I feel him enter me, excruciatingly slow. He lets out a low sexy groan as I grip his backside, urging him to go deeper. He does, and I breathe out his name as sensations flood my core. He pauses a moment, buried inside me, as though savoring the feel of being united like this again.

"I love you, Rachel," he whispers against my ear, his lips grazing my skin.

"I love you too," I whisper back.

He pulls out, then sinks into me again, flooding me with more pleasurable sensations that reach all the way down to my toes. And then he does it again, and again.

He thrusts slowly, deeply, in a steady rhythm I find intoxicating. Addicting. I want more. I never want this to end. His lips cover mine, giving me those slow sensual kisses of his that I've always loved. The kind that got me all fired up on the beach earlier.

"Pearce." His name escapes my lips as his pace quickens. He can tell I'm close. He always could. He keeps going and going until I'm free-falling down waves of mind-blowing pleasure. Deep, intense, and better than I've ever felt. I feel his body quaking above me, then gradually come to rest. He holds himself up on his forearms, catching his breath.

"Pearce. That was..."

"Yes." He kisses me. "I agree."

"We're definitely still compatible that way."

"Were you thinking that would change?" He softly kisses my shoulder.

"No. Not really. I just forgot how good that feels. It's been so long since I've done that."

He looks at me. "You mean with me? Or with anyone?" He pauses. "Sorry. I shouldn't have asked. It's not appropriate and...well, I'd rather not know."

"Pearce." I look at him. "I haven't been with anyone since you."

He's quiet, but then says, "No one? In fifteen years?"

"There weren't many single men in that town, and even if there were, I couldn't have done it. I would've felt like I was cheating on you."

"Rachel, I would've understood. I wouldn't have expected you to—"

"I know. It just wouldn't have felt right to me. In my mind, you were still my husband." I shouldn't ask this, but then I do. "So um, I'm assuming you've been with other women...besides Katherine?"

"Katherine and I didn't have much of a marriage, so there wasn't much intimacy between us."

"So you went outside the marriage?"

"We both did. I'd rather not talk about it."

"But you're not seeing anyone now?"

"No. I haven't in years. I've put all my focus on work and taking care of Lilly. I haven't had time to date."

"So it's been a while for you too."

"Yes, but not fifteen years. That's a long time. We're going to have to make up for all that time. I'd do it right now but I'm older now and need a little longer before...."

I kiss him. "We can do it later. Right now, I just want to lie here with you."

He moves off me to the side. "Come here."

I turn and lay on his chest, looking up at him. "I love you, Pearce."

"I love you too, sweetheart."

It's the first time he's called me that since I got back. Hearing him say it makes me feel like we're married again. Just like snuggling on the couch did. And kissing him. And being intimate again. I didn't expect us to go back to being a couple this fast. I thought it would take some readjustment. But I feel like we're already back to the place we left off. We're just older now and have spent time apart. We both wish that hadn't happened but at least I made it back to him. Back to us.

"I don't need time to think about it," I tell him.

"Think about what?"

"About being with you. Living with you. Being part of your life again. I don't need to think about it. I already know that's what I want. That's all I've wanted this whole time we've been apart."

He lets out a sigh of relief. "I'm glad that's your answer, because I don't think I could've survived knowing you were back, but unable to be with you. I love you too much to let you go."

"I feel the same way about you. But I'm still afraid of what they might do to you or Garret when they find out about me."

"I'll call William tomorrow. I'll ask him to come out here so we can discuss how to handle this."

"Do you really think he'll help me?"

"William and I are close friends. And our families are connected through Jade and Garret. He wouldn't think twice about helping me. Or my wife."

I smile. "You called me your wife."

He kisses me. "Because that's what you are."

"Not legally. Right? We're not really married anymore given that I'm dead and you married someone else."

"I don't know all the legalities yet, but I'm assuming we're no longer married. So I will marry you again."

"You will?" I laugh. "You haven't even asked me."

"I will ask you once we have courted for an appropriate length of time."

I laugh again. "Are you saying I have to date you again?"

"Do you have a problem with that?"

"It depends on how long I have to date you for."

"Well, the last time you married me after three months. Given that we already know each other, I think the courtship time could shrink significantly."

"And I'm going to live with you during this courtship? Because that doesn't seem right."

"There are no rules to this arrangement. It's very unconventional. It's probably never been done before. Dating your wife after she's been in hiding for fifteen years? I am most certain this is a first."

I rub my hand over his abs and leave kisses along his chest. "Is sex allowed during this courtship?"

"It's not only allowed. It's encouraged."

"Hmm. I like this arrangement." I continue softly kissing his chest, my hand slowly making its way down until I feel the length of him, ready to go again. "I thought you needed more time."

"Apparently with you, I don't." He flips me on my back and kisses me and we do it again. It's just as good. Maybe even better. We are definitely back to where we were. Physically. And emotionally. And I couldn't be happier.

We fall asleep, and when I wake up it's morning and I realize I didn't have that nightmare. Probably because I felt so safe in Pearce's arms.

I turn over and find Pearce is no longer in bed. The door is open and I hear noise in the other room.

"Pearce?"

"I'm right here." He walks in, shirtless, but wearing his pajama pants. My eyes focus on his muscular arms and chest. How is he able to still look that good?

I smile as he comes over to the bed.

"Good morning." He kisses me as he lies beside me. He tastes minty and still smells of that great cologne.

"Good morning." My hand wanders over his abs. "How do you stay in such good shape?"

"I have a trainer. I work out with him several times a week."

"How do you have time for that?"

"I make time for things that are important." His lips skim over my neck. "Like you." My eyes shut as I feel his warm breath next to my ear. "How did you sleep?"

"Better than I have in years. At least I did after a certain someone joined me in bed."

"That certain someone is going to join you in bed again right now." His hand slips under the sheet and over my naked body.

My lips curl up. "I'd love that, but I think I want to brush my teeth first. And take a shower."

"How about a bath? I'll draw you one."

"Will you join me?"

"I will do more than join you." He kisses me. "We're making up for fifteen years, remember?"

He's got me burning up with desire again. "I'm looking forward to this bath. Let's go."

He gets up from the bed and my eyes follow him. I can't stop staring at his muscular chest and arms and back.

I sit up. "Did you already shower? Is that where you were before you came in?"

"No. I was checking in with the office." He walks out the door and disappears into the hall.

"Pearce," I call out. "If you need to work, go ahead. I don't mind."

He comes back, holding one of the hotel robes. "What I need…" he leans down and kisses me, "is to be here with you." He hands me the robe. "I'll get the bath ready."

"Did you call Garret?"

"No, but I suppose I should. It's after nine."

I move the covers back and step out of bed. "Maybe we should go over there."

He eyes my naked body. "We will later. There's no rush."

"Do you have plans for us this morning?" I slip my robe on.

"I do." He takes me in his arms. "Very important plans."

I look up at him. "Can we call our son before these plans begin?"

"Yes." He lets me go. "I'll get my phone."

He goes in the bathroom to start filling the tub, then returns with the phone. He calls Garret and puts it on speaker.

"Hey, Dad," Garret answers. "You guys coming over soon?"

"We thought we'd stay here a little longer."

"Oh, yeah?" I can hear the smile in his voice. I don't want my son knowing what his father and I are doing, but I think he's already figured it out.

"How about if we come over there around noon?" Pearce asks him.

"Sure, that works. Grace is on her way back. Maybe we could all have lunch on the patio."

"Sounds good. We'll see you then."

I reach for the phone and Pearce nods. "Garret, your mother wants to talk to you." He hands me the phone.

"Hi, honey. It's Mom." It feels strange to say that. It's been so long since I've been able to.

"Hey, Mom. How's the hotel?"

"It's very nice. It's right on the ocean and there's a walking path that's surrounded by flowers. Your father and I took a walk last night at sunset."

"Sunset, huh?" He laughs a little. "Sounds romantic."

I look at Pearce. "Yes, it was. I'll let you go. We'll see you soon."

Pearce takes his phone back and sets it on the dresser. Then he comes back and undoes my robe. "Now where were we?"

"Hey, I just put that on," I say, as he slips the robe off.

"You don't need it. The bath is ready."

He takes me into the huge bathroom and over to the oversized whirlpool tub.

Pearce helps me into the water, then slips in behind me and I lay back against his chest.

"Is it too hot?" he asks.

"No." I inhale the steam as the bubbles surround me. "This feels heavenly. I haven't taken a bath since I left. My apartment in Italy only had a shower and it wasn't a very good shower. Half the time the water wasn't even warm."

I hear him mumble a curse word behind me.

"Pearce, what's wrong?"

"I am beyond angry you had to live that way. If you were here, you would have had everything you could possibly need. But instead, you were living in a one room apartment without even the simplest of necessities."

"Don't be angry. It was fine. It wasn't luxurious, like this, but it had the basics."

"The basics aren't good enough. From here on out, you will have luxury. In everything." He still sounds angry.

"Pearce." I reach behind me and run my fingers over his lips. "Relax. That's the point of this bath, isn't it? To relax?"

"Yes." He kisses my fingers. "Among other things." His hands massage my shoulders and I sink deeper into the tub.

"Mmm. That's nice." I close my eyes as he massages me. After a few minutes, I say, "What exactly are these other things you were referring to?"

He kisses the side of my neck as his hand slides down to my breast. "When you're ready you'll find out."

I feel his arousal against my backside and it turns me on. I press into him to feel it even more.

"I think I'm ready to find out," I say.

And so he shows me, and the tub heats up even more.

CHAPTER TWENTY-FOUR

GARRET

"What time are they coming over?" Jade asks. We're in the kitchen and she hands me the orange juice from the fridge.

"They said they'll be here around noon. I told them we'd have lunch on the patio." I take some glasses from the cupboard and pour the juice.

"Why are they getting here so late?"

"They're busy." I try not to laugh. My sweet, innocent Jade doesn't get it. "They seemed kind of preoccupied when they called."

"Are they staying with us tonight?"

"Probably not." I grab some cereal from the pantry.

"Why aren't they staying with us?"

"Jade, really?" I smile at her. "They haven't seen each other in fifteen years."

"Oh." Now she gets it. "I guess I just didn't think they'd get back together that fast. I thought they'd want to get reacquainted first."

I laugh. "Yeah, I'm pretty sure that's what they did last night. And this morning. I don't want to think about it. They can do what they want. They're married."

"Not really. I mean, they're not legally married anymore, right?"

"I'm not sure how that works. Even if they're not legally married, in their heads they are. When they were together yesterday, they were already acting like they used to when I was a kid."

"What do you mean?" She hands me a cereal bowl.

"I don't know. I just felt like I was watching my parents again. Like how they used to be. My dad was looking at her the same way he used to look at her. And my mom kept touching his hand and his arm and smiling at him. They were always really affectionate with each other."

Jade steps up to me and whispers, "So you really think they did it last night?"

I smile. "Why are you whispering?"

"I don't want anyone to hear us."

I glance left and right. "There's nobody here, Jade."

"Abi's here." She points to Abigail, who's in her high chair, munching on some dry cereal and concentrating on picking up each little round circle. She's into finger foods right now. Mastering fine motor skills, according to the parenting books.

"Abi has no clue what we're talking about." I give Jade a kiss, then turn around to pour my cereal. "And to answer your question, yes, I'm pretty sure they did it. Probably more than once."

Jade grabs my arm. "Garret! What if she gets pregnant?"

"Who?"

"Your mom!"

I laugh again as I pour my cereal. "My mom is not going to get pregnant."

"How do you know? I bet your dad didn't bring any condoms."

"Jade, they don't need condoms. My mom isn't in her childbearing years anymore. Now what do you want for breakfast? I'm just having cereal but if you want some eggs or pancakes, I'll make some."

"Your mom's not that old, Garret. I bet she hasn't even hit menopause. I saw this story on TV where this woman was like 50 years old and she thought she couldn't get pregnant, but she did. She had a baby boy. It's not that unusual. I've heard other stories like that."

I shrug. "Then maybe I'll get a baby brother or sister out of this. I'd be okay with that."

223

She rolls her eyes. "You are not taking this seriously. You should've sat those two down before they left and had a talk with them."

I raise my brows. "About sex?"

"Shh. Don't say that word." She points to Abi, who has absolutely no interest in us. She's pushing her cereal around the tray of her high chair, babbling to herself.

"She's not listening," I say to Jade, turning her toward Abi. "Look. She seems to be concocting some kind of scheme over there. Maybe she's playing war games and the cereal pieces represent tanks and she's mumbling her strategy so we can't hear. We should be worried, Jade. Very worried."

She flips around and swats at me. "Fine. Don't believe me. But when your mom gets pregnant—"

I kiss her mid-sentence. "She won't get pregnant. Now as for the person standing in front of me who actually *is* pregnant, tell me what you want for breakfast."

"I'm not hungry. I'll just have juice."

"You need to eat." I put my hand over her stomach. "You're growing a baby in there and she needs to eat."

Jade smiles. "*She?* Did you decide we're having a girl?"

"I was just throwing it out there to see how you'd react. And you smiled, so does that mean you want another girl?"

"I'd take either one. It doesn't matter to me. Are you hoping for a boy?"

"I just want a healthy baby, which means you need to eat." I kiss her again.

"Then I'll have some cereal." She gets another bowl and pours herself some. I grab the milk and some spoons.

We go to the table and I sit next to Abi, who's still moving her cereal pieces around. She seems very focused.

"What do you got going on over there?" I ask her. "Are you gonna let me in on your strategy?"

Jade's sitting across from me, laughing. "She's not playing war games, Garret."

"She's planning something over there." I point to the cereal that's scattered across Abi's tray. "That's not random, Jade. She's

224

deliberately placed them that way. She has a definite strategy going on there. The question is…" I hold my spoon up. "What is it a strategy for?"

Jade scoops up her cereal. "You're crazy,"

"No crazier than you, thinking my mom's going to get pregnant." I smile at her.

"So why didn't your parents ever have more kids?"

"I don't know. They never said. I'm guessing it's because of the organization. My dad didn't want his kids to be part of it."

"But he had you."

"Probably to make my mom happy. I'm sure she wanted more than one. She loves kids. But my dad must've only agreed to one."

"I don't know how he kept the organization a secret from her all those years."

"He didn't have a choice. He couldn't tell her. She's not allowed to know."

"What happens now? You think your dad will get in trouble because she knows?"

"No. He'll talk to William and they'll figure it out."

"Gah!" Abi yells as she shoves all her cereal on the floor in one big swoop of her hand.

I look at Jade. "Apparently that particular strategy wasn't working for her. Or maybe it wasn't a strategy at all. Maybe it was some type of artwork. What she did just now? That was the move of a temperamental artist."

Jade's laughing so hard she spits some of her cereal out.

"Mama." Abi points to Jade and giggles.

I've found it's best to laugh it off when Abi throws food on the floor or spills her juice or does other stuff kids her age do. Jade tends to overreact to that stuff, which she did when Abi was younger. She didn't yell at her, but I could see Jade tensing up, like she was trying to hold in her anger. Her own mother would've hit her for tossing food on the floor, so Jade isn't always sure how to react. So it's my job to keep her calm and remind her that it's not the end of the world if Abi dumps her bowl of milk over her head, which she has done several times. Jade is much better now than even just a couple months ago, which is why she didn't even react when the cereal went all over the floor, other than to laugh at my joke.

The back door opens and Grace walks in.

"Hey, Grace," I say. "Do you want breakfast?"

"No, thank you. I already ate." She goes over and kisses Abi's head. "How's my little Abigail Grace today?"

"We're not sure," I say. "We're keeping a close eye on her. We think she's up to something."

"What?" Grace asks, confused.

"Don't listen to him." Jade gets up from her chair. "He has an active imagination this morning." She starts to pick the cereal off the floor.

"Jade, I got it. You shouldn't be doing that."

"Garret, I can clean up cereal from the floor. I'm barely pregnant."

"You're pregnant?" Grace asks.

Jade sighs as she stands up. "Yes. I wasn't supposed to tell you that. I was going to wait."

I laugh. "Jade, you might as well tell everyone. We already told my mom and dad, and now Grace knows."

Grace hugs Jade. "Congratulations, honey. That's wonderful. When did you find out?"

"Last week. I'm not very far along, which is why I was going to wait to tell people. But I guess I don't need to wait anymore."

Abi starts banging her fists on the high chair and kicking her feet, which is her not-so-subtle way of telling us she wants out of the chair. A few months ago, that would've driven Jade crazy, but now it doesn't bother her at all.

Jade lifts Abi out of the high chair. "Looks like she's done with breakfast."

"So Garret, where are your parents?" Grace asks. "I wanted to say hello."

"They're not here right now, but they'll be here at noon. We're going to have lunch outside. I was hoping you could join us."

"I'd love to. How did everything go with your father? He must've been thrilled to see her again."

"He was. They both looked really happy."

She smiles at me. "You look happy too."

"Yeah, I am."

"Well, I'm going to go tend to my garden. I'll cut some flowers for the table and bring them over when I come by for lunch."

"Bye, Grace." Jade's at the sink now, washing off Abi's hands.

"Bye, honey. Bye, Abigail." She waves at her as she leaves.

Around noon, my parents arrive. My dad has his arm around my mom and they're both smiling. They obviously did not get two rooms last night. I don't know what my dad was thinking. I knew my mom would want to be with him. I saw how she looked at him when he got here yesterday.

I *am* surprised that she didn't need more time to get over the fact that he's a member. I thought that would be the one factor that would keep them apart. But she seems to have accepted it. Then again, she's had years to think about it so maybe she's accepted it over time.

"Hi, honey." My mom gives me a hug. "I missed you."

"Yeah, we didn't get much time together yesterday."

My dad gives me a look to keep quiet. He wants more time alone with her, which he won't get if she's spending time with me.

I just smile at him. "Hey, Dad."

"Hello, Garret. Were you working this morning?"

"No, I took the day off and so did Jade."

Jade walks in, holding Abi.

"Hello, Jade. Hi, Abigail." My mom goes up and hugs them both.

"I see where you learned to hug, Garret," Jade says. "Your mom's really good at it."

She laughs. "Did Garret tell you how I hug everyone? It's kind of a problem since not everyone likes to be hugged."

"Jade was one of those people." I come up behind her and hug her. "I had to teach her how to hug. She was an extremely difficult student."

"I was," she admits. "And it took me forever to get it right."

"Rachel had to teach me as well." My dad puts his arm around her again.

"You did?" I ask her.

"Yes. Your father was not a very good hugger when I met him. His technique was all off. But he improved over time."

"Over time?" He acts offended. "After you corrected me, I had it down after one hug."

We all laugh.

"Lunch is almost ready if you guys want to go outside," Jade says.

"Rachel, go ahead," my dad says. "I want to talk to Garret."

"Just follow me," Jade says, and the two of them go out to the patio.

"So I'm guessing you went with one room?" I laugh as I say it.

He tries to hide his smile. "Yes. But I let your mother make that decision."

"So are you two back together now?"

"We're getting there. She's agreed to move in with me."

"In Connecticut?"

"No, she doesn't want to go back there. She wants to live out here."

"Really?" I smile. "And you agreed to that?"

"I want to be with her, so if she wants to live here, then that's where we'll live."

"What about the company? And Lilly?"

"I'll find a way to work from here. As for Lilly, she'll be thrilled. You know she's always wanted to live closer to you and Jade."

"Katherine will fight you over it."

"Let her try. She knows doing so will get her nowhere."

"Shit, this is awesome. I can't believe you guys are going to live out here. Jade's going to be so excited."

"Don't tell her just yet. And don't tell Lilly. I don't want anyone to know about this until things are more settled. Your mother and I have a lot to work out before we move here."

"How do you think Lilly will take the news about Mom?"

"I'm not sure. I'll tell her about Rachel when I get back. I don't want to tell her over the phone."

"When are you going back?"

"In a week. I asked your mother to go with me, but she hasn't agreed to it yet."

"She could stay here with us."

"She would love that, but right now, I'd feel better if she were with me."

He says that because he would kill anyone who tried to hurt her. I would too, but I don't have his level of experience and training. I haven't shot a gun in over a year. I have one, locked away, but I haven't ever used it, other than for target practice. My dad is an expert with guns. I've gone to the shooting range with him and he has perfect aim. And he's killed people before. I haven't. I'd hesitate. He wouldn't.

"Have you called William yet?" I ask.

"No. I was going to do that now. I don't want to discuss this over the phone so I'm going to ask him to meet me here, if that's okay."

"Yeah, it's fine. I'll let you make the call. I'll be out on the patio." I go to leave but hear him behind me.

"Garret?"

"Yeah." I turn back and see him holding his phone.

"I would prefer that your mother not know what went on with us during your teen years. If you decide to tell her, I understand, but I don't think it's something she needs to know, at least not now. Not when she's dealing with so many other issues."

"Yeah, I agree. I won't tell her." I point to his phone. "Call William. He needs to get out here."

I walk out to the patio. Grace is there, along with Jade and my mom. My mom is holding Abi. I instantly smile seeing them together. I always wished my mom could've met my daughter. I never thought she actually would.

"Lunch is ready," Jade says as I sit next to her. She has all the food set out on the table. It's nothing fancy, just some sandwich meats and salads we picked up at the deli. "Is your dad coming?"

"Yeah. He just had to make some phone calls."

My mom is sitting on my other side, trying to hold onto Abi as she reaches for me.

I lean over and kiss her. "You stay with Grandma. She wants to spend time with you." Abi fusses and tries to climb off my mom and over to me. "I think I better move." I get up and go to Jade's other side just as my dad comes out of the house.

"You ready to eat?" I ask him.

"Yes." He eyes the food. "It looks good."

He sits next to my mom and they smile at each other, in a flirtatious way. My dad lays his arm along the back of her chair and she scoots closer to him.

Grace, Jade, and I are all staring at them. We shouldn't stare but we can't help it. It's so shocking to see my parents back together. They don't even notice us staring. It's like they're in their own little world. They can't stop smiling and looking at each other.

"Papa!" Abi squeals, holding her arms out toward him. She loves my dad. Whenever he's here, she gets all excited and begs for him to hold her.

My mom frowns. "She doesn't want to stay with me."

"She's just not used to you yet," Jade says. "Once she knows you, she won't let you put her down." She smiles at my dad. "Right, Pearce?"

"Yes, that's true." He takes Abi from my mom. Abi hugs him, her little arms around his neck and her head on his shoulder. "She's just like Garret that way."

"What are you talking about?" I ask him.

"You used to get mad when I'd put you down. You wanted me to hold you all the time."

"I did?" I laugh. "I don't remember that."

"You wouldn't. You were too young. This is when you were Abigail's age. And when you were just an infant, you hated being in your crib. You'd cry until we picked you up."

"But you were better after a couple months," my mom says.

"You must not have got much sleep," I say to her.

"Actually, it wasn't too bad. Your father got up a lot and took care of you so I could sleep." She smiles at him. "It was very sweet of him."

My dad used to take care of me as an infant? I never knew that. My dad's never told me anything about when I was a baby. I

230

didn't think he was that involved during that stage of my life. I assumed my mom did all the work.

A phone rings. It's my dad's cell phone and he has to maneuver around Abi to retrieve it from his pocket. She won't let go of him.

"Yes, William," he says as he answers the phone. "Tomorrow would be perfect. Thank you. We'll see you then." He hangs up and sets his phone on the table.

"William is coming?" Grace asks.

"Yes. We have some things to discuss."

"Good." She sips her iced tea. "It will be nice to see him again."

She knows he's not coming for a family visit. She knows it has to do with my mom and the organization, but she doesn't mention it. None of us do. The organization is a taboo topic that is never discussed openly.

"Should we eat?" Jade stands up and picks up the stack of plates sitting in front of her. She passes them out to everyone. "Feel free to start serving yourselves."

My dad tries to pull Abi off him but she won't budge.

"No, Papa!" She holds onto him even tighter.

"I'll get her." Jade attempts to peel Abi off him but Abi starts crying. "Sorry. She just misses you."

"It's fine," my dad says. "She can sit on my lap."

"Are you sure?"

"Yes. I don't mind." He kisses Abi's cheek. "I guess Grandpa needs to see you more often."

"She would love that," Jade says as she sits down again. "We all would."

As soon as she says it, I almost let it slip that my parents are moving here, but then catch myself before I do. I'm not confident they'll move here, or if they do, I'm guessing it won't be for a while. Like my dad said, they have a lot to figure out before they can settle back into a regular life.

We all serve ourselves, except for my dad. He's unable to reach the food with Abi on his lap, so my mom dishes up a plate for him. She didn't even ask. She just did it and he didn't act surprised. It's like they're a married couple again.

231

"Those flowers are gorgeous." My mom points to the vase in the center of the table.

"Thank you," Grace says. "Those yellow ones are a new variety I'm trying. You'll have to stop over and see my flower gardens."

"I'd love to. And I'd love to see the ones at your house in Santa Barbara. That house is beautiful. It reminds of an English cottage with the stonework and the flowers all around it."

Grace smiles. "You're welcome to stay there anytime you'd like. Garret has a key if I'm not around and you want to use it."

"That's very generous of you. Thank you for offering."

"Are you guys staying at the hotel again tonight?" I ask.

My dad looks at my mom. "It's up to you, sweetheart."

Sweetheart. He always used to call her that.

"Yes, we'll be staying there another night." She smiles at my dad as she says it.

He smiles back. "Just plan on us staying there the rest of the week."

Jade nudges my foot under the table. I almost laugh. I think she actually believes my mom's going to get pregnant.

"Mama." Abi's pointing to Jade's plate. She has watermelon on there and Abi loves watermelon.

"You can have some but I have to make sure there aren't any seeds." Jade starts cutting through a piece, searching for seeds. We buy seedless but sometimes you still find a few.

Abi goes back to picking food off my dad's plate. They're sharing a plate but he's mostly just eating the sandwich my mom made him while Abi eats whatever she can pick up with her fingers.

Watching her sitting on my dad's lap eating her lunch makes me think how great it would be if my parents really did live close by. I'd love to have my kids grow up seeing their grandparents all the time.

"When do I get to see Abigail swim?" my mom asks me.

"We can take her in the pool after her nap. Did you bring a suit?"

"No, I don't have one." My mom sips her iced tea.

My dad looks at her. "That reminds me. I need to call someone about getting you more clothes. Did you want to make a list of items or should I just have the shopper send things over?"

My mom glances around the table at us. I think she's embarrassed that he's bringing this up now. "It's fine. I don't need anything."

"I'll have some items delivered to the hotel," he says, then goes back to eating his meal. My dad is a take-charge person. If he thinks she needs clothes, he'll get her clothes. It doesn't matter if she wears them or not. He'll still get them.

"So when did you teach Garret how to swim?" Jade asks my mom.

"I had him in the water when he was just an infant. By the time he was a year old, he was swimming on his own. And when he was five, they had a swimming competition at the Y and Garret won for his age division. It was his first competition."

"I don't know how I won," I say. "I wasn't very good back then. But I did really well in high school," I tell my mom. "Jade made me a scrapbook of all my wins. I can show it to you later."

"Garret was the best swimmer at the school," my dad says. "He was the fastest one there. Even set some records."

My mom's smile drops to a frown. "And I missed it. I know your father was there, but I wish I could've been there too."

My dad glances at me, reminding me not to tell her what a shitty father he used to be and how he never went to my swim meets.

"I was also on the football team," I say. "Dad can show you some pictures."

My dad didn't go to my football games either, but I want to make it sound like he did. He doesn't actually have photos from the games, but I can give him some if she asks to see them.

"What position did you play?"

"I was quarterback. I also played baseball, basketball, soccer, lacrosse. Pretty much every sport."

"He was quite the athlete," my dad says. "He swam in college too."

233

"Yes, he told me." My mom's beaming. If only she'd been able to see me compete. She would've been at every swim meet, cheering me on. Jade went to my meets in college, but in high school, I had no one there, except sometimes Charles, but Katherine used to yell at him for leaving during work hours so he wasn't able to go to many of my meets.

We finish lunch and Jade brings out a plate of cookies and brownies for dessert. Abi has made herself comfortable, cradled in my dad's arm, lying on her side and hugging his chest and looking like she's about to fall asleep. My dad's other arm is around my mom's chair and the two of them keep glancing at each other like they can't wait to be alone.

I try not to think about that, but it's good they're together like that again. It proves they're still in love after all these years. They're happy. And so am I.

CHAPTER TWENTY-FIVE

RACHEL

"Can I hold her?" I ask Pearce.

"She's all yours." He goes to hand her to me but she grips his shirt and fusses in protest. He kisses her head. "I'm not going anywhere. I'll be right here."

She still fusses as I take her from him. She loves her grandpa, probably because he looks just like Garret.

"I should put her down for her nap," Jade says as Abigail yawns.

"Can I do it?" I ask.

"You don't have to."

"I want to. I love babies, and I especially love this one." I kiss Abi's cheek.

"Okay. I'll go with you."

We get up and go inside and down to Abi's room. It's pink and white. Very girly and sweet. If I'd had more children, I would've loved to have a girl. But now I have a granddaughter, which is just as good.

"I think she needs to be changed," I say. "Do you mind if I do it?"

"No, go ahead. Everything's on the changing table. Thanks for helping out like this."

"I love doing it. If anything, I need to thank *you* for taking such good care of my son. I can see how happy he is and how much he loves you." I set Abigail down on the changing table and get to work on her diaper. "After I left, I worried about Garret being raised by his father. When I first met Pearce, he wasn't in a good place. He worked all the time and was very detached and had a hard time showing emotion. Part of me feared he'd go back to being like that after I left."

Jade's quiet as she watches me take care of Abi, who's now smiling and giggling as I tickle her tummy.

"We're all done." I pick her up and kiss her. "You're such a happy baby."

"So, um, what happens now?" Jade asks.

I turn to her, holding Abigail on my hip. "What do you mean?"

She hesitates. "I mean, are you going to stay here in California?"

Jade has a worried look on her face. But why? Is she worried I'm putting her family at risk by being here? Because I hope she knows I would never do that. I feel like I need to make that clear.

"I'm not sure yet, but Jade, whatever I do, I promise you I won't put you or your family at risk. If I even think that's a possibility, I'll leave. I'll go—"

"No," she interrupts, her voice urgent. "You can't do that." She takes Abi from me and storms out of the room.

What just happened here? Why is she so upset?

"Jade, wait." I follow her down the hall. "Is something wrong? Did I do something?"

She whips around, tears running down her face. "You can't do that again! I know you felt like you had to before, but this time is different and you can't do that to Garret again. Or to Pearce."

"No, that's not what I—"

"Do you have any idea what they went through after you left?" She holds Abi closer, pressing her head against her shoulder as she continues. "Pearce completely shut down. He stopped being a father. He ignored Garret and barely talked to him. And Pearce refused to talk about you. He told Garret he destroyed all the photos of you. He wouldn't even let Garret say your name. Then he married Katherine and it got even worse. He sent Garret to boarding school in England, but Garret hated it and ended up getting sent home. Pearce never went to his swim meets or his football games. He didn't do anything with Garret. And Katherine was horrible to him. So Garret drank. He drank almost every night. It was the only way he could deal with losing you and losing his dad. And that's all because you left."

She's still crying and now so am I. "Why didn't Garret tell me this?"

"Because he didn't want you to know. He says it's the past and it doesn't matter. But it DOES matter. You need to know what he went through." She wipes her cheek. "I know you said you had no choice but to leave years ago, but now you *do* have a choice. You don't have to leave." She sniffles. "You can't. Garret can't handle losing you again. Pearce can't either. And I can't handle seeing both of them hurt that way."

"Jade, you don't understand."

"Then tell me so I do understand. Why would you even think about leaving again? Pearce will take care of anyone who threatens you or tries to come after you. I promise you, he will. And William will protect you. He'll protect all of us. So please, don't leave again. You'll ruin everything if you do."

She turns and hurries down the hall toward the master bedroom.

"Jade," I call after her, but she's already in the room, the door closed behind her.

She didn't let me explain what I meant. I wasn't telling her I was leaving. I was just trying to reassure her that her family would be safe. That I would hide out somewhere if I needed to in order to protect her family from being harmed. But I'd tell Garret where I was staying. I wouldn't just leave. I should go talk to Jade and explain what I meant, but I think she's too upset right now. And so am I, not with Jade, but with what she told me about Pearce.

Did he really abandon Garret like that after I left? Did he really send him to boarding school? Not go to his swim meets? His football games? Jade wouldn't just say that, which means it must be true.

My anger swells and rises to the surface as I storm out to the patio. Grace has gone back to her house and Pearce and Garret are at the table, talking.

Pearce stands up. "Hello, sweetheart. Did you get Abigail to sleep?"

237

I go over and stand right in front of him. "How could you do that to him?"

"Do what?" Pearce notices my tears. "Rachel, what's wrong?"

"How could you just abandon our son when he needed you? How could you do that to him?"

Garret gets up from his chair. "Mom, it's not—"

"Who told you this?" Pearce holds my shoulders.

"Jade. She said you ignored Garret all those years. That you wouldn't let him even talk about me. That you sent him away to boarding school. That you weren't even involved in his life. And that he drank because he didn't know how else to deal with the fact that you just abandoned him like that."

"Rachel, please let me explain."

I shove his hands off me. "Did you do that or not? Tell me!"

Pearce looks at Garret, then back at me. He sighs. "Yes."

"How *could* you! He's your son! I trusted you to take care of him! And you didn't! Instead you became just like your father. Is that what you wanted for Garret? For him to grow up like *you* did? With a father like Holton? Is that what you wanted for our son?"

He's quiet, his eyes on the ground.

"Answer me!"

His eyes jump back to mine. "No! Of course not! It's not at all what I wanted. It was wrong of me to act that way. I just didn't know how else to act. When you died I—"

"That's not an excuse! You don't get to use my death as a reason to treat our son that way!"

Garret comes over to us. "Mom, it's okay. It was a long time ago and I'm fine now. I don't drink anymore and Dad and I get along great. He's a good father now."

"It's not okay." I hug him. "I'm so sorry, Garret. I'm sorry he did that to you. I'm sorry I left. I never should've done it. If I'd known your father was going to treat you that way, I would've found another way."

"Mom, that wasn't the answer. You had to leave to protect yourself, and to protect us. Don't feel guilty about that. And don't blame Dad for what he did. He was grieving and it took him a long time to get over what happened."

238

Pearce takes a step back, putting some distance between us. "She's right, Garret. There's no excuse for how I treated you. I never wanted to be like my father, and yet for some reason, I became him. I treated you like he treated me, and it was wrong. Rachel, I can't go back and change the past. If I could, I would do it all differently."

I swallow hard and wipe the tears from my face.

"Garret." Pearce nudges him, his eyes on me.

Garret nods and goes back inside so Pearce and I can talk. But I don't know if I want to talk to him right now. I'm so angry. Beyond furious.

"I don't even know what to say to you," I tell him. "Other than how disappointed I am."

He collapses into one of the patio chairs and leans over, his forearms on his knees, his head dropped down. "I'm sorry, Rachel. I know that doesn't change anything or make this any better, but I truly am sorry. I beat myself up every day for how I treated Garret and I've apologized to him repeatedly. He says he's forgiven me, but it doesn't take away the pain and the guilt I feel over not being there for him after you left."

"Why did you do it?" I sit next to him. "Explain to me why you did that to him."

"I can't give you a reason that will justify my actions or make this any easier for you to accept. I shouldn't have done it. It was a mistake and it was wrong and I know that. I take full responsibility. I'm not going to make excuses for my behavior. I'm his father and he needed me and I wasn't there for him." Pearce rubs his hand over his face. "And I can't even begin to tell you how much I regret that."

"Did you really send our son to boarding school? In a different country?"

"Yes." He keeps his eyes on the ground. "It was Katherine's idea. She wouldn't stop fighting with Garret so I agreed to send him to boarding school because I thought it might be better if he were far away from her. But it was a mistake. I never should've agreed to it."

"How old was he and how long was he there?"

239

"He was 13 and he was there for just a few weeks. He set his room on fire and they sent him home. After that, he went to Tolshire Academy, which he's already told you about. It's an excellent school and they have a very good swimming program."

"But you didn't go to his swim meets."

"I went to a few."

"How many?"

He sits up. "Rachel, I think it's best if we don't relive all of this. It'll just upset you and you're already very upset."

"Tell me. How many of his meets did you go to?"

He sighs. "I don't remember the exact number. I'm guessing maybe four or five."

"Four or five? That's it?" Tears fall as I think of my son swimming his heart out with no one in the stands, cheering him on. No one supporting him. "And you didn't go to his football games? His baseball games? Basketball games?"

"Rachel." He reaches for me.

I push him away. "Answer me."

"I went to some of his football games. Garret was very good at football. And basketball. He was good at all the sports he played."

"How would you know? You didn't even see him play."

"I went to a few games, just not all of them."

"Why? Where were you? What were you doing all that time?"

"I was at the office. Or traveling for work. I didn't spend much time at home. Part of the reason for that was Katherine. She and I fought constantly. The second I got home, she'd start a fight, usually about Garret and how he did something she didn't approve of and how she wanted me to punish him."

My blood boils as I think of that horrible woman living with my son, trying to pretend she's his mother.

"You didn't do what she said, did you?"

"No, which made us fight even more. It got to the point that I avoided coming home. I didn't want to be around her."

"But you left Garret there with her."

"Garret wasn't home much either. He was out with his friends or he'd go to the gym at his school and lift weights or play

240

basketball. And he spent a lot of time at the pool. I built him both an indoor and an outdoor pool at the house but he didn't use them much. He didn't want to be home with Katherine there."

"When did he start drinking?"

Pearce sighs. "I'm not sure. Maybe 14."

"You don't know? How could you not know this?"

"He hid it from me. He'd go out with his friends and drink and come home late and I just didn't know."

"As his father, it's your job to know. He should've had a curfew. At 14, you should've known where he was and what he was doing."

Pearce doesn't respond. I can tell he feels terrible about this, but it doesn't make me any less angry. He still did it, and Garret suffered because of it.

"Pearce, how could you do that to him? How could you just abandon our son like that? You were such a good father before. What happened?"

"Like Garret said, I couldn't handle the grief I felt over losing you. And the guilt I felt, thinking what happened to you was all my fault. I tried to be a father to him. I really did. A few months after you left, I had Garret go to counseling and I started spending more time with him, and things were getting better for both of us. But then I was forced to marry Katherine and it all went to hell. Years went by and things kept getting worse. I wasn't just a bad father to Garret. I was a bad father to Lilly too. Both my children suffered and I deeply regret it."

"Why didn't you tell me this, Pearce? We spent yesterday and last night together. You had plenty of opportunities to tell me this."

"I didn't want to tell you. It's the past and it's over and I'm not the same man anymore. When Garret was a freshman in college, I went to counseling to try to figure out what had happened to me and how I could repair my relationship with Garret. And I've done that, Rachel. Garret and I have a good relationship now. We're closer now than we've ever been."

We sit there in silence. I'm not sure what else to say to him. I'm confused about how I feel right now. I love Pearce, but I also love our son, and to think that Pearce wasn't a father to him for almost ten years hurts me and makes me so angry that I feel it's probably best if I don't talk to Pearce until I've calmed down. So we remain there, sitting in silence.

CHAPTER TWENTY-SIX

GARRET

Jade is in Abi's room, so I wait for her to come out. I don't know why she told my mom all that stuff. She had to have known how upset it would make her.

"She's asleep," Jade whispers as she closes the door. "I was just checking on her."

"I need to talk to you." I take her hand and lead her down to our bedroom and shut the door. "Jade, what the hell were you thinking telling my mom all that shit about my dad and me?"

"I had to. She had to know what you went through."

"No. She didn't. She didn't need to know any of that. Now she's out there crying and upset and yelling at my dad for acting that way all those years. Why the hell did you tell her that?"

"Because I'm worried she might leave again. She said if she thinks we're at risk, she'll leave. She can't do that, Garret. After what you and your dad went through the last time she left, I can't let her do it again. So I told her what happened because she needs to know the damage she'll cause when she leaves again."

"She's not leaving! She never said that!"

"Why are you yelling at me? I was just trying to help." Jade's crying. She normally wouldn't cry over something like this, but she's been an emotional mess for weeks now because of the pregnancy hormones and every little thing makes her cry. Now I feel bad for raising my voice.

"I'm sorry, Jade." I take her in my arms. "I didn't mean to yell at you. I just didn't want my mom to know all that stuff. It'll just make her feel bad and make her angry at my dad."

"You're right. I shouldn't have told her. I guess I just panicked. I'm so worried about you and your dad. I don't want you getting hurt again."

"You don't need to worry about that. My mom isn't leaving, and if she had to go into hiding for a short time, she'd tell us where she's going."

"You should go talk to her. Or I can. I need to apologize to her. I was yelling at her and then I ran off." She sniffles and her shoulders slump. "I'm such a mess right now. You should keep me away from people until this baby comes."

I smile. "I think that's a little extreme." I wipe her wet cheek with my thumb. "I know you were just trying to help. But next time, maybe just talk to me first."

She nods.

"I love you." I kiss her. "I'm gonna go talk to my mom."

When I get out to the patio, I see my parents sitting next to each other, both looking down and not talking. That can't be good.

"Hey," I say, making them both look up. "Can I talk to Mom for a minute?" I ask my dad. His face is filled with pain and regret. He didn't want my mom to know this, and I didn't either, but now it's too late.

He gets up. "I'll be inside."

I wait until he's gone, then sit down, turning my chair so that I'm facing my mom. She still looks angry and hurt and confused.

"Mom, don't be mad at Dad. He didn't mean to be that way. He just couldn't handle losing you. He did the best he could given the circumstances."

"That's the best he could do? Pretend you didn't exist?"

"He didn't exactly have the best example of how a parent should act. And after you left, Grandfather was even worse to Dad. He made him take over the company. He made him marry Katherine. His life pretty much sucked. And he missed you. He missed you so bad, Mom. I was the only thing left from his old life and I was a constant reminder of you and he couldn't handle it."

"Don't make excuses for him, Garret. He's a grown man. He knew what he was doing."

"I don't know that he did. I seriously don't. He was so out of it. It was like he was walking around in a fog. Those months after you left, he didn't eat, he didn't sleep, and sometimes I'd hear him crying in his room."

She closes her eyes and takes a shaky breath. I know it hurts her to hear this, but she needs to know what my dad went through, not just what I went through. My dad suffered just as much, if not more, than I did.

"He tried to be there for me. He'd come home after work and we'd have dinner, but it's like we were both in our own worlds. We didn't know what to say to each other. We couldn't connect. We were both lost, struggling to go on without you."

"Your father needed to be strong for you. That's his job as your parent."

"Yes, but it's hard to be strong when you're drowning in grief. I didn't understand it when I was younger, but now that I'm older, and married, I understand where Dad was coming from. He lost his wife. His best friend. His soulmate. That's not something you can just get over. I can't imagine what a mess I would be if I lost Jade."

"Was he ever a father to you during those years?"

"He was always a father to me. Just because he was gone a lot didn't mean he wasn't a father. And honestly, I think he would've been a great father if he hadn't been forced to marry Katherine. Before that happened, Dad and I were getting along better. Things were starting to improve, but then Katherine came along and ruined everything. She made our lives hell. But Dad always stood up for me whenever Katherine would try to turn him against me."

She's quiet and I give her a moment to think about what I said.

After a while, she softly asks, "When did you start drinking?"

"When I was 14, but don't blame Dad for that. That was my fault, not his. Dad would always ask where I'm going and when I'd be home, like any parent would. He just thought I was out with my friends. He didn't know I was drinking. I hid it from him."

"But you kept drinking."

I didn't want her to know this. Dammit. How much did Jade tell her?

"Yeah. I kept drinking. As I got older it got worse. Dad caught me a few times and I got in trouble for it, so it's not like he didn't try to stop me." It's not entirely true. Sometimes he ignored my drinking, but my mom doesn't need to know that. "Mom, I wasn't a perfect kid. I was kind of out-of-control in high school and nothing Dad could've done would've changed that."

"You wouldn't have been that way if your father had been there for you after I left."

"No, that's not true. Dad was only part of the problem. Katherine was a bigger problem. Living with her was hell, so I tried to never be home, which meant I was always at someone else's house and we usually ended up drinking."

She reaches for my hand. "Honey, why were you drinking so much? Just because you could? Or because you thought it was fun?"

"That was part of it, but I also drank because I didn't want to feel anything. Back then I was always so angry and…sad."

"Because of how your father was treating you?"

"That was part of it, but I was also angry about how my life had turned out. I was angry about the plane crash. I was angry that it changed our lives. And I was sad that you were gone. I never really got over your death. I went to counseling, and it helped, but there was still this part of me that couldn't get past it."

She squeezes my hand, tears running down her face. "Honey, I'm so sorry. I never wanted to put you through that."

"I'm not blaming you. I'm just saying you can't put all the blame on Dad. He wasn't that bad of a father. In fact, when I look back at those years, and consider what he was going through, I'm surprised Dad did as well as he did. I mean, he had just lost his wife and then was forced to take over the company. A company he didn't even want. Then he had to marry a woman he didn't like, or more like hated. And he had to deal with Grandfather, who treated him horribly. And if that wasn't enough, he had the organization ordering him to do things he didn't want to do."

She nods, tears now pouring from her eyes.

I rub her arm. "Mom, what is it? What's wrong?"

"You're right. I can't put all the blame on your father. So much of this was my fault. If I hadn't left…if I'd gone back to your father after the crash…things would've been different. He wouldn't have married Katherine and—"

"Mom, don't. Don't try to go back and imagine how things might have been different if you'd made a different choice. Believe me, I've done that and it doesn't help. What's important is the here and now, and right now, you're back with us and back with Dad and he loves you more than anything. And I know you love him."

She nods and wipes her eyes.

"I don't know if Dad told you, but he went to counseling back when I was a freshman in college. I was shocked when he told me he did that. You know Dad. He's all about being in control and being strong and doing things without any help, so for him to seek out a counselor and actually go to the sessions is a huge deal. It just shows how committed he was to being a better father. And ever since then, he's been a great dad. He's done a lot for me. He kept me out of the organization. He's the reason I'm not a member. He put himself at risk to do that, but he saved me. They had plans for me. Big plans. But Dad got me out of it. If he hadn't, my life would be totally different. I wouldn't be with Jade. I wouldn't have Abigail." I put my hand over hers. "So, please, Mom. Don't be mad at him about the past. It's over. And I swear to you, he's changed. I couldn't ask for a better dad."

"I'm sorry to interrupt." It's Jade. She's standing at the door to the patio. "Can I come out for a minute?"

"Yeah." I pull a chair over so she can sit.

But she stands instead. "I won't stay long. I just wanted to say I'm really sorry, Rachel. I didn't mean to yell at you and I'm really sorry for saying those things to you. I overreacted and butted in when I shouldn't have, so again, I'm really sorry."

"It's okay," my mom says. "I think it's good we got all this out in the open."

"I hope you're not mad at Pearce. If you are, please don't be. I'm sure Garret already told you this, but I need to say it too. Pearce is a great dad, to both Garret and me. Even though I'm not his real daughter, he treats me like I am. He's done so much for

247

me. And if he'd never given me that scholarship years ago, I never would've met Garret. I might not have even gone to college. Anyway, I just want you to know that Pearce is a really good person and I hope that what I said doesn't change how you feel about him."

My mom looks down. I can't tell if she's sad or confused or what she's feeling.

"Where'd he go?" I ask Jade. "Have you seen him?"

"He's in the living room with Abi. She just woke up. He's going to leave soon to go back to the hotel."

My mom looks up at Jade. "Why is he leaving?"

"He thinks you'd be more comfortable if he wasn't around. He said he'd bring your suitcase over later."

"Oh. Okay."

"Mom." I wait for her to look at me. "He doesn't want this. He doesn't want to be apart from you. He's only doing this because he thinks it's what you want. If it's not, then go tell him that."

Her eyes go back to Jade. "Did you say he's in the living room?"

"Yeah. With Abi. I can go get her if—"

"No, she's fine." My mom stands up. "I'll go talk to him."

She leaves, and Jade sits in the chair next to me. "I'm sorry, Garret. I messed everything up."

I hold her hand. "Don't worry about it. It'll work out."

"Do you really think so?"

"Yeah." But the truth is, I don't know. My mom is really upset and really mad at my dad.

I hope she can get past this. I really want my parents to be together again.

CHAPTER TWENTY-SEVEN

RACHEL

I walk in the living room, but stop when I hear Pearce talking to Abigail. He's on the couch with his back to me so didn't see me walk in. Abigail is on his lap and he's reading her a book.

"And then the little dog, who finally had a home, went up to the little girl and said 'woof!'" He says 'woof' like a dog and Abigail laughs and claps her hands. "Show Grandpa where the dog is." She points to a spot on the book. "Very good." He kisses the top of her head.

He closes the book, but she opens it again. "Papa." She points to a page.

"We'll read it again later. Your mother will be back soon and then I need to go."

He sets the book down and she turns around and hugs him. He hugs her back. Watching them together is so sweet it almost makes me cry. He's a good grandpa. And a good father. I may always be angry about how Pearce treated Garret when I was away, but like Garret said, that's the past and what matters is now.

I walk up behind Pearce. "Pearce, can we talk?"

He turns back and sees me. "Yes, of course. I didn't hear you come in."

I go around the couch and sit next to him. Abigail is resting on his shoulder.

"You don't need to leave," I tell him.

"I just assumed you'd be more comfortable if—"

"No. I don't want to argue about this anymore, or even talk about it. Although I'm not happy about what happened, it's the past and I can see what a good father you are now." I hold Abi's tiny hand. "And a good grandfather."

"Rachel, I need you to know that I deeply regret how I acted all those years. If I could go back and change it, I would. Believe me, I would do anything to change it. I love Garret, and I never wanted to treat him that way. I was just at a bad place back then. I know that's not an excuse but—"

"You don't have to explain." I put my hand on his arm. "Let's just put this behind us."

Abigail babbles to herself and he glances down at her. "Would you like to hold your granddaughter?"

"I would, but I don't think she'll let you go."

"Abigail," he says very seriously. She pops her head up and looks at him. "I would like for you to sit with your grandmother." He points to me and her eyes follow his hand. "Can you do that for Grandpa?"

Her eyes dart from him to me, like she's not sure. But then she reaches for me. I take her and she hugs me.

"You're so sweet," I tell her, "and you give the nicest hugs."

Pearce smiles. "She's getting used to you. Give her another day and she'll lose all interest in me."

"I don't think so. She seems to have a special bond with you."

"Oh, I heard from the shopper. Some clothes were delivered for you. They're at the hotel. Would you like me to go get them?"

"But we're staying at the hotel. Why would you bring them here?"

He smiles even wider. "Yes. You're right. I don't know what I was thinking. I guess I'm just tired. Someone didn't let me get much sleep last night."

"Hey!" I laugh. "I think that was a mutual decision. But I'll be sure and let you sleep tonight."

"I have no interest in sleeping." He leans over and gives me a kiss.

I hear someone clearing their throat. I look back and see Jade and Garret standing there.

"Sorry to interrupt," Garret says, "but um...you guys probably shouldn't do that in front of an innocent child."

"Garret!" Jade elbows him, then says to me, "Ignore him."

He laughs. "I'm just kidding. Feel free to continue."

I turn more so I can see him. "Remember when you were little and your father and I would kiss? You'd always cover your eyes and tell us to stop."

"Yeah, I remember. But it didn't stop you. You guys used to kiss all the time."

I smile at Pearce. "I couldn't help myself. It's what you do when you're in love. You kiss."

He smiles back. "Which is why we're still doing it."

From the side of my eye, I see Jade and Garret smiling at each other.

"Maybe we could take Abigail out in the pool now," I say. "It's such a nice day."

"Yeah, we could do that," Garret says. "You're not going back to the hotel, are you Dad?"

Pearce looks at me. "Maybe we should. There's a swimsuit in the clothes that were delivered, if you'd like to go get it so you could go in the pool."

"Yes, let's get it." I kiss Abigail. "Grandma will be back soon and then we'll go swimming." I hand her to Garret.

"Shall we go?" Pearce is standing up, offering me his hand.

Is it wrong that I secretly want to go back to the hotel to be alone with him and not just to get my swimsuit? An hour ago I was furious with him, but I've always had a hard time staying mad at him. And hearing Jade and Garret say how much they love Pearce, and seeing him with Abigail, diminished my anger. I know in my heart he would never intentionally treat Garret poorly. Those ten years when I was away were difficult on all of us and now it's time to move past that and focus on the future.

I take Pearce's hand and he keeps hold of it as we walk to the door. As we're driving to the hotel, he takes my hand again. It's like he doesn't want to let me go, and I don't want him to. I love feeling his hand around mine again.

"We'd like to book the suite for the remainder of the week," Pearce says to the desk clerk. We're back at the hotel and the same girl is working at the front desk.

251

She smiles at him, flirtatiously again. Does she not notice I'm here? Or does she think he'll trade me in for a younger woman, specifically her?

"It's all yours," she says. "Just so you know, the rate goes up to $2000 a night on the weekend."

"Just charge it to my card." He turns away from her, his arm going around my waist.

"Enjoy the rest of your stay," she says, but Pearce is already walking us to the elevator. He has no interest in the young exotic beauty who was definitely flirting with him.

When we reach the room, he shuts the door, then holds my face in his hands and presses his lips to mine. I wasn't expecting the kiss. After having that argument at the house, I thought he'd hold back, unsure if I would let him kiss me. But Pearce isn't one to hold back. When he wants something, he goes for it, which I've always found to be very sexy.

He talks over my lips. "I've wanted to do that since we left here this morning."

I kiss him back, and feel him smile slightly at my response. I'm sure he thought I'd tell him I wasn't in the mood or that we needed to talk some more before we did this. But instead my response is begging him to continue. My body is already aching to be with him. We did it this morning, twice, and yet I still crave more. Maybe it's because I haven't done it in fifteen years. Or maybe it's just Pearce.

Yes, it's definitely Pearce. He's now kissing his way down my neck, awakening sensations along every inch of my body. I don't know how he does it. How he makes me feel this way from just his kisses, but I don't want him to stop.

I close my eyes and tilt my head, wanting to feel more of his soft lips along my neck.

"Pearce," I whisper.

"Yes, sweetheart," he whispers back, his warm breath by my ear causing bumps to rise up on my skin.

"Don't stop."

"I had no intentions of doing so." His lips return to mine as he slips my dress off my shoulders, letting it fall to the ground. I hadn't even realized he'd unzipped it.

I start undoing his belt, gently tugging on it as I walk backwards toward the bedroom. It seems to take forever to get there, and when we do, I quickly undress the rest of myself while he takes off his suit. I don't know why he wore a suit today, but the sight of him in a suit is extremely hot. Maybe that's why he wore it. He knows I love seeing him in a suit. Then again, he looks good in everything he wears.

Before I can even get a glimpse of his naked body, he's over me, inside me, filling me completely. I close my eyes, savoring the feel of him. The feel of his body over mine. The feel of him inside me. The feel of his hands sliding over my skin, his lips covering mine.

"Open your eyes," I hear him say.

I open them and see him looking at me. "I love you."

I smile. "I love you too."

Our eyes remain open as he continues, my body responding to his every move, the tension building, rising, waiting for the release. When it comes, I can no longer hold his gaze. My eyes fall shut as it washes over me, overwhelming me with pleasure, leaving me breathless. I hear Pearce's deep, husky groan and feel his body respond as well as he releases.

He stays there a moment, then moves off me, and we both lie there, arms and legs entwined, my head on his chest.

"That's the third time today," I say, still breathless.

"I didn't know you were keeping track." He kisses my head.

I look up at him. "Don't you think that's a lot?"

"I'd do it again if the kids weren't waiting for us back at the house."

"We should probably get going."

He sighs. "If we must."

I laugh. "Pearce, I want to spend time with them."

He kisses me. "I know you do, but you're coming back with me next week, right?"

"I haven't decided yet."

He sits up a little. "Rachel, I don't want you out here all alone."

"I wouldn't be alone. I'd stay with Jade and Garret."

"My house in Connecticut is much more secure than Garret's house. A gate surrounds it and there are cameras and motion sensors and I have security guards working round the clock." He rubs his hand softly over my cheek. "Plus...I don't want to be apart from you. Not even for a day."

I smile at him. "Then yes. I'll go back with you. But how long are we going to stay?"

"We'll decide that once we figure out what we're going to tell the media about you." He glances at the side of the room. "It looks like they put your clothes over there. Let's get dressed and head back to the house. The sooner we get there, the sooner we can leave."

I laugh. "Pearce, stop it. You want to spend time with the kids as much as I do."

"That may be true." He kisses me and runs his hand over my hip. "But I also want to be alone with you."

"We'll be back here tonight. Like you said, we don't need to sleep. We have better things to do." I give him a sexy smile as I step out of the bed. I turn and go over to the clothing rack set up next to the closet. It has some dresses, a pair of jeans, some shorts, a few t-shirts, and some button-up shirts. The shopper did a great job. The styles are cute and modern and look like stuff I would wear.

"What do you think?" I ask Pearce. "Shorts and a t-shirt?"

I turn around and see him eyeing my body.

"Maybe you could just stay like that a little longer."

I smile. "Pearce, come on. Get dressed so we can go."

"You do not look your age. You have the body of a 20-year-old."

"That's very sweet of you to say, but it's not at all true." I turn back to the rack of clothes and pick out a white t-shirt and tan shorts, then grab the swimsuit that's hanging on the end of the rack.

"It's true." I feel Pearce behind me, pressing his naked body against mine. "You're gorgeous."

254

"Pearce, we don't have time to do this again. They're waiting for us at the house."

He sweeps my hair aside and kisses my shoulder. "I'm quite certain our son wouldn't mind if we stayed here just a little longer. In fact, he'd probably encourage it. He's elated that we're together again. As am I." Pearce remains behind me, his hand cupping my breast, his other hand moving slowly down my stomach, landing between my legs.

I drop the clothes, my head falling back on his chest. And before I know it, we're back in bed. We haven't done it this much since our anniversary trip to DC, which was the last time I saw Pearce before I left. It was a great trip, but I try not to remember it because of the way it ended.

Now we're making new memories. Better memories. Ones I'll want to remember. Like today. Right now. I'll definitely want to remember this.

CHAPTER TWENTY-EIGHT

PEARCE

These past couple days have been like a second honeymoon for Rachel and me. We can't get enough of each other. Yesterday, we came back here to get Rachel's swimsuit and ended up doing it twice in one hour. The chemistry between us is as strong as ever. I've never felt anything like it with anyone but her.

This morning, we woke up early but stayed in bed, enjoying each other once again before having to leave to go to Garret's house. We're on our way over there now.

William Sinclair is arriving today. He may already be here. Garret was going to pick him up at the private airport. I offered to do it, but Garret insisted on doing it. He wants his mother and me to spend as much time together as possible, in the hopes that we'll remain a couple beyond just this week. He's concerned it won't last, but I've assured him that's not the case. Rachel and I are committed to making this work, but in order to do that, I need to make sure she'll be safe being with me. That's where William comes in. As a high-ranking member of the organization, we need his help to convince our fellow members to leave Rachel alone.

"I don't remember much about William," Rachel says as we're driving to the house. She's wearing a sleeveless yellow dress and sunglasses, her long brown hair falling over her shoulders. The dress reminds me of the one she wore when I first saw her at Yale. The yellow color caught my attention, and when I saw who was wearing it, I couldn't take my eyes off her. She was so incredibly beautiful. She still is. She's barely aged.

"Pearce? Did you hear me?"

256

"Yes." I lift her hand up and kiss it, then set it back between us, my other hand on the wheel. "We'd talk to William at the parties we used to go to, but never for very long, so it's not surprising you don't remember him."

"He's not like Royce, is he?"

"No, not at all. He's more like Arlin, his father."

"But he's the head of the organization? That worries me, Pearce."

"He's not the head of it. He's just at the highest level. There isn't one person in charge. It's a group of men, and William is one of them. But he's a natural-born leader and has, by default, taken on a leadership role among the other men at his level. He's changed the way we do things. Made the members more accountable for their actions."

"I don't like it when you include yourself as one of them," she says quietly.

I glance at her. "Rachel. I'm trying to be honest with you. You know this group is part of my life. I can't change that."

"Yes, I know. I just wish there was a way for you to get out of it."

"For the most part, I am. As I told you, I'm no longer involved in their activities."

She gazes out the side window. It's going to take time for her to accept this other side of my life. And that's fine. As long as she accepts me, and who I am, that's all that matters.

"So what are we talking about with William today?" she asks.

"The story we're going to give the media."

"William is involved with the media?"

"Not just him, but the entire organization. We create stories and feed them to the media. The stories make it on the news because we have members in high-up positions at all the networks. In order to control things, you have to control the messages the public receives."

"That seems wrong. And deceitful."

"It's not that different from advertising. Or political campaigns. You create a message that will convince people to buy what you're selling, whether it be a product or an idea. In this case, we're

257

selling an idea. A story that will explain why you were gone and why you came back."

"How do you know people will believe it?"

"You'd be surprised how easy it is to convince people to believe something that isn't true. Not many people question what they see on TV or read in the papers. They accept it as fact, which makes our job much easier. Add in some photos and videos and it becomes even more convincing."

I can tell she doesn't like what I'm saying, but she needs to accept it because it's what we need to do in order to reintroduce her to the world.

"Manipulating the media was how I got Garret out of his obligation," I say. I wasn't going to tell her this yet, but maybe doing so will help convince her this will work for her as well, because right now, she seems very skeptical.

"Do you mean his obligation to be a member?"

"Membership, yes, but also another obligation." I glance at her. "You can never anyone tell anyone this."

She nods. "I understand. Go ahead."

"The organization had plans to force Garret into a top political position. When I found out about this, I was determined to stop their plan. The way I did so was to create a negative media campaign with fake news stories and videos of Garret crashing cars, destroying hotel rooms, and doing other unfavorable things. The organization didn't know any of this was fake, and eventually they decided Garret couldn't be trusted with the organization's secrets and was too out of control to take part in their plans for him. So they let him go."

"You're saying people think Garret really did all those things?"

"Yes. And if you do an Internet search of him, you'll likely find some of those news stories and videos. But none of them were real."

"So his reputation was destroyed," she says quietly.

"It had to be done. And it worked, which is why I told you this. I know you're worried about being reintroduced to the world, but I promise you, this will work. People will believe whatever story we tell them."

She nods, but I don't think she's convinced.

We reach the house and go inside and see William already there, holding Abigail. Jade and Garret are standing next to him.

"Pearce." He extends his hand.

"William." As we're shaking hands his eyes move to Rachel. "Rachel, it's good to see you."

She shakes his hand. "It's nice seeing you as well."

His eyes remain on her. "Forgive me for staring. It's just so surprising to see you again."

"Papa." Abigail's reaching for me.

I take her from William and kiss her cheek. "Grandpa has some business to attend to. I'll see you a little later."

She hugs me. She's getting used to seeing me every day. She's not going to be happy when I leave next week.

"I'll take her," Jade says. I give Abigail to Jade and they disappear to the back of the house.

"Do you mind if I sit in?" Garret asks.

William looks at me. "It's up to you, Pearce."

I don't want Garret involved in this, but he at least needs to know the story we're going to tell. "It's fine. Let's go sit down."

We take a seat in the living room. Rachel's next to me on the couch and Garret and William are across from us.

William starts. "Rachel, Pearce didn't tell me the story about what happened to you. We tend to avoid talking about such things over the phone. So if you wouldn't mind, could you explain how you ended up here?"

She spends the next few minutes going over the basics of what happened. She doesn't tell him everything, and I think it's because she doesn't trust him, which is understandable. But he needs to know the whole story, so I fill him in on the rest, including Leland's role, which Rachel hadn't mentioned.

When I'm finished, William says to me, "I assume we'll discuss Leland later."

"Yes." I give him a look. He knows what it means. William knows I plan to kill Leland. He also knows I could be punished for doing so, but he understands why it needs to be done, and

259

since we're family, he'll help me do it in a way that will keep me out of trouble. "Let's discuss what to tell the media."

"I've given this some thought," he says, "and I think we should go with kidnapping and memory loss."

I nod. "Yes. I was thinking the same thing. The memory loss will keep the press away from her. The public will feel sorry for her and will be angry at the press if they try to hound her for interviews when she's in a state of recovery."

"Exactly. So let's go with that. As for the kidnapping, we could say she was at the airport that day, waiting to board, but had been followed on her way there. Someone entered the airport, injected her with a drug that knocked her unconscious, and stuffed her body in a crate, which they then loaded onto a private plane and flew overseas. When they arrived in Italy, a rival crime ring, unaware of Rachel, shot her handlers and took off. When she awoke, she found them dead and realized she didn't know who she was. Her memories were wiped clean from whatever drug they gave her."

"Why would they take her in the first place?" Garret asks.

"To get your father's money. They were going to demand a ransom in exchange for her safe return, but it never happened because they were shot and killed. And it took fifteen years for Rachel to get enough of her memory back to figure out who she was."

"Wait a minute." Rachel sits forward, glancing at the three of us. "This sounds like a Hollywood film. You really think people are going to believe this?"

"Absolutely," William and I say at the same time.

She eyes us as though we've lost our minds.

"Rachel." I put my arm around her. "Trust me, this will work. As I mentioned earlier, we've done this many times. And honestly, the more far-fetched the story, the more likely people are to believe it. It seems counterintuitive but we've found that to be the case."

"As the saying goes, truth is stranger than fiction," William says. "That's why people believe stories like this. And we'll use our resources to create evidence that supports the story."

"Will I have to go on TV and talk about this?" Rachel sounds nervous. I rub her arm, trying to get her to relax.

"You won't have to do any live interviews," William says. "Any interviews you do will be scripted and recorded by our media team."

"She could do some interviews at the house next week," I say to William. "Rachel's coming back to Connecticut with me."

"I don't know if we'll need her to record anything just yet, but I think you should make a statement we could send out. I'll tell Kiefer to get everything set up."

"Kiefer?" Rachel turns to me. "You don't mean Kiefer Douglas, do you?"

"Yes, the director. But he no longer works in Hollywood. He works for us, creating news footage and taping interviews and doing other odd jobs."

"It's another long story," Garret says.

This is a lot for Rachel to take in, but I don't have time to explain it all to her. William's time is limited and we need to make decisions fast. We need to get this story to the media soon. Making Rachel's story public will help ensure her safety. The organization would be putting themselves at risk of exposure if they did something to her once the story is out. If they killed her, reporters would dig into every possible cause, trying to find out if she's really dead this time, and if so, who killed her.

"What about our fellow members?" I ask William.

"I'm not terribly concerned about them. The older members are the ones who would've threatened her, but the majority of them are dead now, with the exception of Leland. And the younger members have no reason to go after her."

"That doesn't mean they won't. She knows about us. That alone is enough to put her at risk."

"Yes, but she also values her life and therefore has reason to keep this a secret."

Rachel tenses up and I rub her arm again. "William, perhaps you could soften your language."

"I didn't mean to scare you, Rachel. I assumed you knew the risks."

"I do," she says. "Please continue. So you're saying you think I'm safe? That none of them will bother me?"

"Yes, but I do need to know if you and Pearce plan to remarry, because that could be an issue."

"Why? What does that—"

I interrupt her. "We'll be getting married. What deal will I have to make in order for that to happen?"

"I'm not sure yet. You'll need to appear at a meeting and we'll discuss some options."

Rachel looks at me. "What deal? Pearce, I don't want you making deals with them. If that's the case, then we won't get married. We'll just live together."

"We're getting married," I say forcefully. "I'm not letting the organization stop you from being my wife. I'll do what I have to do."

"Dad, are you sure about this?" Garret sounds as worried as Rachel did.

"Everyone relax," William says. "They won't cause physical harm to him. If you'll remember, harming another member is against the rules. This deal will most likely affect your bank account, Pearce, or the company."

"That's fine. But I need more assurance that the members will leave Rachel alone."

"I will send an official warning to the lower level members telling them that she is not to be harmed. The warning will be read at the meeting that will be held to inform everyone of Rachel's return. But honestly, Pearce, I think the only member you need to be concerned about is Leland. He needs to be taken care of soon, before he tries to recruit someone to his cause."

William's right. Leland can be quite persuasive, and when he finds out about Rachel, he'll try to convince one of the other members to help him kill her, saying she shouldn't be with me and how she should've been killed years ago.

Leland needs to be killed, and fast.

"I'll get to work on this," William says. "Pearce, shall we have our private discussion now?"

"Yes. Rachel. Garret. If you wouldn't mind, I need a few minutes with William."

Garret gets up. "Mom, let's go outside. Jade's playing with Abi out on the patio."

Rachel looks at me, concern in her eyes. She doesn't want me killing Leland. She doesn't want William doing it either. But Leland has to die. If he doesn't, she'll be the one dying. Leland will make sure of it.

"Go ahead, sweetheart," I say.

She turns to William. "Thank you for helping us with this."

"You're very welcome." He smiles at her.

She leaves with Garret, and once they're gone I say to William, "I'm thinking a plane crash would be most appropriate."

He rubs his jaw as he thinks. "I suppose that would work. It's obvious, yet perhaps that's the message you want to send. The other members will suspect you killed Leland, but they won't be able to prove it. Everyone knows small planes are dangerous and they also know Leland takes fastidious care in checking his plane before he takes off. When it crashes, the members will assume he either failed to notice something during the inspection of his plane or that you rigged the plane to go down. If they assume the latter, they'll be impressed that you were able to rig Leland's plane without his knowledge, and that will make them fear you even more."

I smile. "And fear is power."

"And so it is." He smiles back.

"And I won't be punished because the cause of the crash will be undetermined."

"Correct. So shall I take care of this for you?"

"No. I don't expect you to. I'll get to work on it when I get back next week."

"That's too late. This could take some time. The steps need to begin now. The sooner, the better. Wouldn't you agree?"

"Yes, absolutely. I just feel I'm overstepping boundaries making you do this for me."

He shakes his head. "I'm happy to do it. Over the years, you have shown nothing but kindness to my family, despite all that my

263

brother put you through. I will always be grateful to you for checking in on my mother the way you did after my father died. And you've always looked out for Jade. So I owe you many favors. Consider this one of them."

"Thank you, William. If you need any assistance, please contact me."

"I will." He stands up. "I need to be going, but first I need to stop by and say hello to Mother."

"I believe she's outside. I think I just heard her voice."

We walk out to the patio and see Grace, Jade, Garret, and Rachel sitting at the table. Abigail is on Rachel's lap.

"William." Grace gets up as he approaches her. She hugs him. "How have you been?"

"Good, Mother."

She steps back. "You're staying for lunch, I assume."

"I'm afraid not. I need to get back to New York."

"William Sinclair," she scolds. "You do not come all the way out here and then turn around and go home. You will eat lunch with your mother."

Everyone laughs, including William.

"Yes, Mother."

She looks him up and down. "You're too thin. Why aren't you eating?"

He laughs again. "I thought I was, but perhaps I missed a meal or two."

Grace is always this way. Always worried about everyone, including me. She's become like a mother to me, more so than my own mother, who still shows little care or concern for me. I've come to accept that. She is who she is and that's fine. I receive plenty of love and affection from the people who are with me right now. My family now includes people I truly love and who love me back. Except the past fifteen years, someone was missing. But now she's not. Now that Rachel has returned, my family is complete.

CHAPTER TWENTY-NINE

RACHEL

I've been back in the U.S. for a little over a week now, but it seems like much longer than that. Italy seems like a lifetime ago. I wrote Celia a letter telling her I'm okay and sent her the money she gave me, but other than that, I put all memories of Italy aside. My focus has been here, with my family, and the life I'm rebuilding with them.

Pearce and I have spent every day over at Jade and Garret's house, swimming, or sitting out by the pool and talking. I'm slowly learning more about what went on while I was gone, including the story of how Garret met Jade, and the struggles they went through to be together. After hearing their story, it's amazing that everything worked out for them. I could say the same for Pearce for me, except our story isn't finished. We're hoping it will have a happy ending, but we still have a ways to go before we get there. We have to reintroduce me to the public and deal with the organization.

The story we're planning to feed the media has already been crafted and written up, and Pearce and I approved it yesterday. I've been memorizing scripted phrases to use in case I'm hounded by reporters after the story comes out. The story will be released next week, when I'm safely locked away in Pearce's Connecticut mansion. I'm hoping the story won't generate a lot of interest, but I really don't know what the response will be.

Pearce has been talking to William a lot this week, but he doesn't let me listen in on the calls. I assume they're discussing their plan for Leland. It's probably best if I don't know the details.

I don't want to think about Pearce plotting someone's murder, but I know it has to be done.

The more I learn about Pearce's world, the more I realize how dangerous it can be. I'm not just referring to the organization, but also criminals who might target him because of his money. Pearce is wealthier and more well-known than he was fifteen years ago. Back then, he lived a fairly normal life, living in a normal house and a normal neighborhood. We didn't flaunt our wealth or draw attention to ourselves. But since then, Pearce has become known as a billionaire CEO of a very large corporation, and that can attract bad people. People who might come after him—or me, once they find out I'm alive.

I've realized that if I'm going to be with Pearce, I need to learn how to protect myself. When I'm with him I feel safe, but he can't be with me all the time and I don't want to be afraid every time I go somewhere alone. For years, I lived in fear, knowing those masked men were watching me, and might kill me. I'm not going to live that way again. If anyone threatens me or comes after me, I'm going to protect myself.

That's why I asked Pearce to take me here today. We're at an indoor shooting range. I want to learn how to shoot a gun. I'll probably never need to use one, but if I ever do, I need to know how to hold it and how to shoot it.

When I told Pearce I wanted to do this, he was shocked. He knows I don't like guns. But I explained to him that I refuse to be a helpless victim, and that I want him to teach me not only how to use a gun, but anything else that will help me protect myself. He smiled when I said that, because it just proved my commitment to be with him. I know his world can be dangerous, but I still want to be part of it.

"Widen your stance a little." Pearce is standing behind me, assessing my form.

I move my feet, repositioning myself. "Like this?"

"Yes, that's good."

"Now hold the gun up, but don't shoot it yet. Get a feel for the weight of it in your hand. Hold it firmly, but don't tense your

266

body. If you're too tense, your muscles will shake and it'll affect your aim."

I do as he says, aiming the gun at the paper target in front of me. I've shot a gun before, but it was back when I lived on the farm, and it was a hunting rifle, not a handgun. My dad used to hunt, and although I never went hunting with him, I shot at targets in the yard and got to be pretty good at it.

"Now aim at the target and fire off a shot."

I hold the gun steady and shoot. I hit too high, landing above the target's head.

"I'm going to adjust your arms." Pearce steps up behind me and puts his hands on my arms, lowering them. "You were aiming too high. That's normal when you're learning."

Once my arms are in the right position, he steps back. "Okay, try again."

There's nobody else in here but Pearce and me, which is good. It would be hard to concentrate with people next to me.

I aim the gun and shoot, and this time I hit the target's chest.

"Excellent," I hear Pearce say.

"That's only because you lined me up properly."

"Yes, but now you know how to position yourself in relation to the gun. Try a couple more."

I shoot and hit the target's head. I shoot again and hit his shoulder.

"That's good, Rachel. A lot of beginners can't even hit the target."

He continues to give me tips, and after a while, I hit the target almost every time.

"I think that's enough for today," I say. "My arm's getting tired."

"I'm going to do a few rounds before we go."

I step aside and Pearce takes my place. He uses a different gun. A bigger, heavier one. He replaces the target, then aims and shoots, several times in a row. Every shot hits the target's chest, right over the heart. He continues, each shot perfect.

"You've obviously practiced a lot," I say, as we're driving back to the hotel.

"Yes, but it's much more difficult when your target is moving. That's why you have to practice. If we have time, we'll do this again when we're in Connecticut. I'll rent out the range so it will just be us."

"Because you think someone you know might be there?"

"All the members practice target shooting. It's required."

"What else is required?"

He reaches over for my hand. "Let's not discuss this."

So we don't. I've decided I don't need to know everything about the organization. Pearce can't tell me anyway so it's no use asking him questions, but sometimes one slips out.

Back in our hotel room, we're barely in the door when Pearce captures me around my waist and kisses me.

"Pearce, we need to get over to Garret's house. Dinner's in less than an hour."

"That's plenty of time."

"We need to clean up. Take a shower."

He smiles at me. "Good idea. We haven't done it in the shower for two days."

"Maybe we should slow down." I say that, and yet I'm kissing him while undoing his belt.

"Why would we slow down?" He lifts my shirt up and over my head, then yanks off his own. "You just said we had to be at dinner in an hour."

"I mean, not do this so much. We've done it a lot this week."

"And you find that to be a problem?" He undoes my jeans while kissing me and backing me up toward the bathroom.

"No." I smile against his lips. "It's not a problem."

We're in the bathroom now and he reaches in the shower and turns it on, his lips not leaving mine.

"Fifteen years, Rachel," he says, as we race to strip the clothes off our lower halves. "And watching you shoot that gun turned me on like you wouldn't believe." He backs me against the sink.

"I was thinking the same thing about you," I say, breathing hard.

"Is that so?" He lifts me up on the marble counter.

"Yes." I look him in the eye while stroking him with my hand. "I couldn't wait to get you back here so we could do this."

His fingers tangle in my hair and he tilts my head back to meet his mouth, giving me hot, urgent kisses.

"Rachel," he breathes out. "You have no idea what you do to me."

"Let's go in the shower," I whisper.

But instead, he grips my backside, pulling me into him with commanding force. I wrap my legs around him and we do it right there on the counter, the hot shower steaming up the room.

We've been like this all week and I love it. We won't be able to keep this up when we're in Connecticut. Pearce will have to return to work and we'll be living with his daughter. We're leaving tomorrow, so this is our last day to be free to do whatever we want with no one around.

Later, as we're driving to Garret's house, I check the clock and notice we're ten minutes late.

"Pearce, we should've left sooner. The kids are waiting for us. I don't want them thinking we were doing...certain things."

He chuckles. "They know we're doing those things."

"How do you know that?"

"Well, for one, they've noticed we can't take our hands off each other." He softly rubs my hand, which he's holding. "And two, our daughter-in-law has informed our son that she is quite concerned I will get you pregnant."

I laugh. "Garret told you that?"

"Yes. Just the other day. He couldn't stop laughing, then he patted me on the back and said he's hoping for a brother."

I shake my head, smiling. "Did you tell him that's not possible?"

"No. I just talked about something else. But then he asked why we never had more children. He asked if it was because I knew they'd have to be part of the organization. I just told him that was the reason. I didn't tell him what happened to you during the delivery. I wasn't sure if you wanted him to know."

"I'd rather he not know. But Pearce, is the real reason you didn't want more children because you were worried about their future?"

"Yes, but I was also concerned about your health. I didn't want you having another child after what you went through with Garret."

"If you were worried about the organization, then why did you agree to have Garret?"

"Because I wanted us to have a child. And I thought I could get him out of his obligation to be a member, which I did. But if the organization didn't exist, and if your health hadn't been a concern, I would've wanted more children."

"How many?"

"Probably three."

"I wanted three too." I smile. "Or maybe four. I love children."

He squeezes my hand. "I know you do. And you're an excellent mother."

We arrive at the house and Jade and Garret have dinner waiting.

"What took you guys so long?" Garret asks. He's smiling. He knows the answer.

"We got caught up in traffic," Pearce says as he pulls my chair out for me.

"Dinner looks delicious," I say as I take my seat.

Jade sits across from me. "Garret made it."

"Charles gave me the recipe for the barbecue sauce." Garret starts passing the food around; barbecued chicken, potatoes, and coleslaw. "Charles is going to be shocked when he sees you, Mom."

I serve myself some potatoes. "I can't wait to see him again. He was always such a nice man."

Garret takes the seat next to Jade. "Dad, have you talked to Lilly?"

"We talked earlier today. I'll pick her up Monday morning."

"When's Katherine leaving for France?"

"I believe she leaves Wednesday. She said she isn't coming back until early September."

270

"Tell Lilly she can stay with us for more than that week in July," Jade says to Pearce. "She could come here in June if she wants."

"We'll talk about it and let you know."

Pearce and I discussed Lilly earlier this week. He thinks it would be good for Lilly to stay with Jade and Garret for a few weeks while we get things settled, but I told him he should talk to her about it before he decides. I don't want Lilly to feel like she's being sent away because of me. Katherine did that with Garret by sending him to boarding school, but I would never do that to Lilly. She's just a young girl and she needs her father.

Dinner continues and we talk and laugh and just enjoy being together. When I first got here, it was awkward. My return was such a surprise that no one knew how to act. But within a few days, the awkwardness went away and now we're relaxed and just one big happy family.

After dinner, we have dessert out on the patio and remain there until it's time to leave. As we're standing at the door, my eyes fill with tears because in the morning, Pearce and I are flying to Connecticut.

Garret hugs me. "Mom, this isn't goodbye. You guys will be coming back here."

"I know, but I don't know when. And after being away from you for so long, I don't like leaving you." I hug him tighter. "I love you, honey."

"I love you too."

I hug Jade next. "Goodbye, Jade. Get some rest. I'm sure all the excitement this week wore you out."

"It did, but I loved it. It was great having you here. You guys need to move here."

She laughs as she says it, but Pearce and I do still plan to move here. We're just not sure when, so we don't want to tell anyone until we know for sure.

Pearce has already hugged Jade and Garret goodbye and is now holding Abi. She's clinging to him because she knows he's leaving.

"Grandpa has to go," he tells her. "Goodbye, honey." He kisses her cheek.

She shakes her head really fast. "No go."

"I'll come back and see you. Give Grandpa a kiss goodbye."

She kisses his cheek, then hugs him. It's so sweet.

He hands her to me and I give her a big hug and a kiss, then we head out.

The next morning, I almost can't make myself get on Pearce's private jet, knowing what happened last time I almost boarded a small plane. But I manage to get over my fear and we make it to Connecticut by the afternoon.

Pearce's black Mercedes is waiting at the airport. When I ask why he's still driving the same type of car, he tells me it's provided by the organization, but won't tell me any more than that.

"How are you feeling?" Pearce asks, as we're driving to his house.

"Sick to my stomach." I take a breath and focus on the trees that line the road. I always loved all the woods in Connecticut. I grew up surrounded by wide open farmland so when I moved here, the woods were a welcome change of scenery.

Pearce takes my hand, which was resting in my lap. "Relax, sweetheart. Everything will be fine."

"I just feel like I'm surrounded by enemies here."

"You're not. Leland lives in New York and my father is dead."

"Have you spoken to Eleanor?"

"Yes, but I haven't told her about you. I wanted to wait and tell her when I got back."

"How do you think she'll react?"

"She'll be pleased."

"I'm not so sure about that. She never really liked me."

"She liked you. She may not have come out and said it, but it was clear that she did. She's the reason my father held his tongue around you. When he criticized you, she defended you, which I'm sure infuriated my father."

"I never knew that. I'm surprised she stood up for me that way."

"She didn't at first. Those first couple years we were married, she felt the same way my father did. She didn't approve of you or our marriage. But after Garret came along and she spent more time with you, she changed her mind about you. She told me several times what a wonderful mother you were to Garret, and she knew what a good wife you were to me. My mother never liked Katherine, although she pretended she did, for Lilly's sake."

We enter a neighborhood full of gated mansions and Pearce slows down as we approach one of them. He stops at a large iron gate.

"Welcome back, Mr. Kensington," a voice says from a speaker attached to the gate.

"Thank you." Pearce waits for the gate to open, then drives down a long road that ends at a circular driveway in front of a very large mansion.

"This is quite a house," I say, eyeing the mansion. "How big is it?"

"Eighteen thousand square feet." He parks the car but doesn't get out.

"What's wrong? Aren't we going inside?"

"Yes." He gazes at the house. "I just feel odd bringing you here. I didn't expect to feel this way, but now that we're here…I don't know. It doesn't feel right."

"Why? I don't understand."

"It's not you and me. It doesn't fit us. And I know you won't feel comfortable here."

I undo my seatbelt and turn to him. "Pearce, I'll feel comfortable wherever you are."

"I've never liked this house. I never wanted it. Katherine forced me to build it. And it's full of memories I'd rather forget."

"Then why didn't you move after the divorce?"

"It was just more convenient to stay here. It's close to Lilly's school and close to the office." He opens his door. "Let's go inside."

Pearce *does* seem uncomfortable being here with me. I'm uncomfortable too, knowing that Katherine used to live here. That horrible woman stole my family, and made their lives miserable for years. I will never forgive her for that.

When Pearce opens the door, I see touches of Katherine everywhere I look. White walls. Shiny white tile floors. White furniture. Glass tables.

"I know," Pearce says as we walk in the living room. "I should've redecorated after the divorce."

I hold his hand. "Pearce, stop worrying so much. The house is fine. Give me the rest of the tour."

He takes me over to Garret's wing, as he calls it, which is a section of the house he built just for Garret. It has a movie room, a game room, a gym, and an indoor pool. It's every kid's dream, and it was nice of Pearce to build all of this for Garret, but I wish he'd been a father to him instead. That's what Garret needed, more than a game room or an indoor basketball court.

Next we go down a long hallway full of rooms that seem to have no purpose. They're just rooms with couches and chairs, and some are empty. It's strange, but I don't comment on it because I know it's all Katherine's design and I'm trying not to talk about her.

We go upstairs to the bedrooms, stopping at Garret's room first. It's a large room with its own bathroom.

"Did Garret choose the color?" I smile at the navy blue walls.

Pearce chuckles. "Yes. Katherine hated it, but I insisted Garret be allowed to choose the color."

We leave his room and pass by several guest rooms, then Pearce stops and takes me into a room that I'm guessing belongs to his daughter.

"This is Lilly's room." He smiles. "As you can see, she likes the color pink."

The room has pink walls and a white iron bed with a pink comforter. And there's a small pink couch next to a white table that has a pink lamp on it. Two of the walls are covered in artwork, mostly charcoal sketches and watercolor paintings.

I point to a painting of a field covered in wildflowers. "Did Lilly paint that?"

"Yes. She did all of these." He motions to the artwork. "The room next to this one is an art room I set up for her. That's where she does her paintings."

"She's very talented."

"Yes, she is." He smiles and I can see how proud he is of her. "Well, shall we go downstairs?"

"You didn't show me your room."

"You don't need to see it. We're not staying in that room. We'll stay in one of the guest rooms. You can pick whichever one want you'd like."

He doesn't want us staying in the bedroom he shared with Katherine, and I agree. I don't think I could sleep there, knowing she was there with him.

"I'd still like to see it if you don't mind." Then again, maybe I don't, but he's already walking me down there.

The master bedroom is huge, with a king-size bed and a sitting area off to the side. I go over to the dresser, which has photos spread all across it. There's one of Pearce, Garret, and me at Easter, when Garret was only five. He's wearing a dark gray suit that matches his dad's, and a little blue tie.

"This was always one of my favorite photos," I say, holding it up.

"Yes. Mine too."

There's another photo that shows just Pearce and me, and then some of Garret and Lilly at different ages.

"How old was he here?" I hold up a photo of Garret as a teenager.

"He was 15. I have other photos of him you can go through later. They're in a box in my office downstairs." He takes the photo from me and sets it down. "Let's go." He holds my hand and leads me out of the room.

"Should we get the luggage?"

"I'll get it later."

Pearce takes me downstairs to the kitchen. A man wearing a white chef's coat is standing at the sink with his back to us, washing dishes.

"Charles," Pearce says. "I'd like you to meet someone."

"Pearce, I didn't know you were home." Charles dries his hands on a towel as he turns around. He drops the towel when he sees me. "Rachel?"

I smile. "Yes. It's me. It's good to see you again, Charles."

He stares at my face for a moment, then hurries over to me and hugs me. "How is this possible?"

"It's a long story," Pearce says. "Let's save it for another day. Rachel and I are tired from the flight."

We can't tell Charles the truth about what happened to me. He'll be getting the same story we tell the media.

Charles steps back, eyeing me. "This is unbelievable. Did you tell Garret yet?"

"Yes. Pearce and I spent the past week with him and his family. We had a wonderful time. I can't wait to go back."

"This is amazing. I can't believe you're really here." He smiles, and it's the same warm, friendly smile I remember. His dark hair is now mixed with gray and he carries some extra weight, but otherwise he looks the same. "Let me get you something to eat. You must be starving. What would you like?"

"Anything's fine. You know I always loved whatever you made."

"Rachel." Pearce puts his arm around me. "The man is desperate to make you something. Please, tell him what you'd like."

I smile at Charles. "I always loved your grilled pizzas."

"Then that's what we'll have." He races back around the kitchen island. "I'll get the dough started. Dinner should be ready in an hour, if that works."

"That's perfect," Pearce says. "Thank you, Charles."

"Yes, thank you." I sneak around the island and give Charles another hug and say quietly to him, "And thank you for helping take care of my son. And Pearce." I step back and see him tearing up. I am too.

Years ago, I thought I was just hiring Charles for some catering jobs, but he ended up helping my family in ways I never could've imagined. He was meant to come into our lives. I just didn't know it until all these years later.

Pearce brings our luggage in from the car and up to one of the guest rooms. It's a large room with a very large bathroom. We shower and change clothes and I hang the rest of my things in the walk-in closet.

Pearce has been quiet since we arrived. He hasn't been very affectionate either. He hasn't even kissed me. It's a total contrast to how he acted in California, and it concerns me.

"Pearce, what's wrong?" I'm standing by the bed as Pearce puts his shirt on.

"Nothing's wrong." He buttons his shirt. "Why would you ask that?"

"You're acting completely different than when we were in California."

His brows furrow. "What do you mean?"

"You seem distant, like your mind is elsewhere. You're being very quiet, and you haven't kissed me since we got here."

He thinks for a moment. "You're right." He comes up to me, his arms circling my waist, and kisses me. "Is that better?"

I kiss him back. "Yes."

"I'm sorry, Rachel. It's this house. It just doesn't feel right being here. I don't like being here in Connecticut either. I want us to have a fresh start someplace new."

I smile at him. "Like in California?"

"Yes. I'm liking that idea more and more. It will be challenging working from there, but it's where we need to be. I want to be closer to Garret and Jade and the baby. Living out here, I only see them a few times a year, and that's not enough."

"How soon do you want to move?"

"As soon as possible. Once we get things settled here, I'm putting this house up for sale and we're moving."

"Where in California should we live?"

"Wherever you'd like."

"How about Santa Barbara? It's a beautiful city and a good location. It's close to Garret's house but not too close. We don't want to suffocate them." I kiss him. "And we want our privacy as well."

"Then we will live in Santa Barbara. I have a real estate agent in LA that I've worked with in the past. She can find us something."

"I don't want anything too big."

"Just make a list of what you'd like and she'll find it for us."

"I fell in love with Grace's house. If she could find us something like that, it would be perfect."

Pearce smiles. "You like Grace's house?"

"I love it. It's the perfect size. I love the layout. And her gardens are amazing. It's like my dream home."

"If you want it, it's yours."

"Pearce, we can't take her house. She loves that house."

"She's putting it up for sale later this year."

"Are you serious? Did she tell you that?"

"Yes. She was talking about it after dinner the other night. You must've been out of the room when she mentioned it. She said the house is a lot to maintain and she doesn't use it much anymore now that she lives next to Garret."

"She really wants to sell it?" I hear how excited I sound and notice Pearce smiling.

"Yes. So if you would like it, I will let her know and it will be ours."

"I don't want to buy it unless you like it too. It's so much smaller than what you're used to."

"Sweetheart, I told you, I never wanted a big house like this. I liked our old house. That felt like a home. This one doesn't. It never has."

"But do you even like Grace's house?"

"I do, but I think it could use some updating. Maybe redo the kitchen and the master bath. And the back yard definitely needs a pool."

"I agree. With all of it." I hug him. "I can't wait to move there."

"You're far too easy to please. I would've bought you oceanfront property and built you the house of your dreams. But instead you chose Grace's house."

"Because it already is the house of my dreams. I love it." I kiss him. "And I love *you*."

"I love you too, sweetheart." He checks the clock. "Let's go check on dinner."

We eat dinner with Charles and the pizza is even better than I remembered. He served it with a salad and wine and we ate outside by the pool. It's warm for May, similar to the weather we left in California.

That night, Pearce doesn't sleep well. He tosses and turns and I think it's because he's worried about how Lilly will react to seeing me here. I'm worried about that too.

CHAPTER THIRTY

RACHEL

I'm waiting inside the house, sitting in the living room, my stomach a nervous mess. Pearce just got home with Lilly and they're in the driveway. By now, he's told her about me. What if she doesn't accept me? What if she hates me? What if she doesn't want me living with them?

"Rachel?" I hear Pearce calling for me. He's in the foyer. "Rachel, are you down here?"

"Yes." I hurry to the foyer and he's standing there next to a tall, thin girl with long blond hair, blue eyes, and a very sweet smile.

"Hi," she says softly. "I'm Lilly." She holds out her hand.

I shake her hand and smile. "I'm Rachel. It's very nice to meet you."

"It's nice to meet you too." She glances down. She seems shy, or maybe she's just uncomfortable around me.

"Let's go sit down," Pearce says.

We go to the living room and Pearce and Lilly sit on the couch and I take the chair at the end. Lilly looks very similar to Katherine, but she doesn't act like her. Her demeanor seems kind and sweet, not harsh and conniving like her mother's.

"Did you have a good week with your mom?" I ask, not knowing what else to say.

She shrugs. "It's like it always is."

I don't know what that means. Is it bad? Good?

"Lilly worked on her drawings while she was there." Pearce nods towards Lilly's backpack that's sitting on the floor. "Why don't you show her?"

She shakes her head. "She doesn't want to see my artwork, Dad."

"I do want to see it," I say, "if you don't mind." I decide not to tell her that I've seen the artwork in her room. Kids her age don't like their parents going in their room when they're not home and I don't want her getting mad at Pearce for taking me in there.

She pulls some sheets of paper from her backpack and hands them to me. They're all charcoal sketches. The first one is of a little boy. It looks like a professional artist did it.

"Lilly, this is really good," I tell her.

"Thanks," she says so quietly I almost didn't hear her.

"Who's the little boy?" I ask her.

"Conner. My half-brother. He's five."

Pearce said Katherine ignores her son almost as much as she ignores Lilly. She's not even taking him to France with her this summer. She's leaving him with his father and the nanny.

I continue to look at the drawings. Some are of people and some are of buildings in Manhattan, which is where Katherine lives.

"These are amazing." I hand them back to her. "You're really talented."

"It's just a hobby." She shoves them into her backpack. "Dad, can I go upstairs now?"

"Yes. Go ahead." He gives her a side hug, then she takes her backpack and disappears up the stairs.

"She's very sweet," I say, sitting next to Pearce. "Is she always that shy?"

"No. She only acts that way when she first meets someone. Once she's comfortable with you, she's more talkative."

"What did she say when you told her about me?"

"She was shocked, but said she was happy for me. And for Garret."

"That's nice that she said that. Most children her age would be angry."

"She's not like that. She's always put others before herself. She's the complete opposite of her mother."

"Maybe you should go talk to her."

"I will, but not right now. I need to give her time to absorb this. This is a big change for her. It's just been her and me for years now. I texted Garret and told him to call her. The two of them are close and she always confides in him. He'll let me know what she says."

"Where did she learn to draw like that?"

"She taught herself. When she was younger, Katherine made Lilly stay in her room all the time, so she drew pictures to pass the time and became quite good at it."

"She's more than good. She could be a professional artist."

"Yes, well, I'm not sure what her future holds so it's best if she continues to see it as just a hobby."

"Are you saying the organization might try to dictate her profession?"

"According to the rules, Lilly will take over the company someday since Garret didn't. Or she can have the man she marries take over as CEO. She's supposed to marry one of the members someday."

"Pearce, you can't make her do that. If you got Garret out of his obligation, why can't you get Lilly out of hers?"

"Because Katherine wants Lilly to be part of it. And so does Leland. He's already trying to find Lilly a husband. It's another reason I despise that man."

Pearce's phone rings. "It's Garret." He answers the call and puts it on speaker. "Hello, Garret."

"Hey, Dad. How was the trip?"

"It was good. Your mother's here. I have you on speaker."

"Hey, Mom."

"Hi, honey." I already miss him, and hearing his voice makes me miss him even more.

"What do think of the house?" he asks.

"It's very, um…large."

He laughs a little. "Yeah, I knew you wouldn't like it. It's way too big and way too white."

"Speaking of houses," Pearce says, "tell Grace if she's still planning on selling the house in Santa Barbara, we'd like to buy it."

"Are you serious? So you're really moving here?"

"Yes, but I'm not sure when, so don't tell anyone yet, other than Grace."

"You'll only be an hour away. That's great. Hey, I was calling because I just talked to Lilly."

Pearce sits up straighter. "And what did she say?"

"That she hated being with Katherine last week. You've gotta stop making her go there, Dad."

"I can't ban her from seeing her mother. I thought Lilly wanted to see her."

"She did, but as usual, Katherine ignored her, and now Lilly's all depressed."

Pearce sighs. "She didn't tell me that. I thought she was quiet on the ride home because of the news about your mother."

"I don't think so. I think it was because she was sad about how Katherine treated her. Oh, and Mom, Lilly said she thought you were really nice."

I smile. "That's good. She was so quiet I thought maybe she didn't like me."

"She takes a while to warm up to people. When she gets to know you, she'll love you." The baby cries in the background. "Abi's up from her nap. I've gotta get her before she wakes up Jade. They were both napping."

"Give them both a hug for me," I tell him. "Love you."

"Love you too. I'll talk to you guys later."

At noon, Pearce, Lilly, and I have lunch. I ask Lilly questions about her school and her friends and she starts to relax as she tells me about them. She keeps glancing at her dad, and I can't tell what she's thinking. She does the same thing at dinner.

That night, Pearce goes into his home office to do some work and I go upstairs to talk to Lilly. I find her in her room, watching TV.

"Can I come in?" I ask her.

"Yeah." She turns the TV down and sits up on her bed. She's wearing pink pajama pants and a white tank top dotted with pink flowers.

I sit at the end of her bed. "I just wanted to say that I know this is a big change having me show up in your dad's life like this, but I'll do whatever I can to make this easier on you."

She pulls her knees to her chest, wrapping her arms around them. "Do you love him?"

"Yes. With all my heart."

She glances down at the bed and quietly says, "He loves you too. I can tell." Her finger traces over the swirling pink lines on her comforter. "He never looked at my mom the way he looks at you. Even her new husband doesn't."

I don't know how to respond to that, so I wait for her to continue.

"Dad said someone took you away and you couldn't remember who you were."

Pearce told her the fake story. He couldn't tell her the real story, given that she doesn't know about the organization or her family's involvement in it.

Her eyes move up to mine. "That must've been scary."

"It was, but it's over now."

"Did you used to know my mom? Before you were gone?"

"Yes. I went to some parties at her house. Well, her parents' house."

"So you know my grandparents?" She doesn't let me answer. "I never see them. They live in New York. They don't really like kids. Whenever I go there, they make me go in the study and read."

"Do you like to read?"

"I'd rather paint. Or draw."

"I love your artwork," I say, glancing at it on the walls. "You're very talented."

"Thanks." She hesitates, then says, "I have some more."

"More artwork? Can I see it?"

"Really?" Her face lights up.

"Yes. I'd love to see it."

284

She hops off her bed and races over to her dresser. She opens the bottom drawer and pulls out a box and brings it over to me. "These are ones I did when I was at Garret's house last summer."

She shows me drawings of Jade and Garret, and Abigail when she was a tiny infant. She also has some of her dad, and one of Pearce and Garret together.

"These are really good," I tell her as I spread them out over her bed. "You should frame them."

"I have too many. I just hang them on my walls. Do you want that?" She points to the one I'm holding, which is of Pearce and Garret. "You can have it."

"Thank you. I'm definitely framing it."

She smiles really wide. "I have ones I drew of Jade and Garret when they were dating." She returns to her drawer and pulls out another box. "I was only six when I drew these so they're not very good. I just used crayons." She takes out a drawing of Garret wearing a suit and Jade wearing a purple dress. "That was the first time I met Jade. I liked her right away. I wanted her to be my sister," she laughs a little, "and now she is."

The drawing is just another reminder of how much I missed of Garret's life. All his college years. His wedding. Just as I'm thinking that, Lilly shows me a drawing she did at their wedding. It's good for a six-year-old.

"I was the flower girl," she says proudly.

Garret showed me his wedding photos last week. Lilly looked adorable.

"Anyway, that's some of my drawings." She packs them up and stores them back in the dresser.

"Thanks for showing them to me." I wait until she comes back over to the bed, then say, "Garret said you also like to swim."

"Yeah. I'm not as good as Garret but I'm getting better. I have a swim coach."

"I'm a swimmer too. Maybe we could go swimming tomorrow."

Her face lights up again. "Okay."

She seems shocked that I want to spend time with her. She also seemed shocked when I asked to see her drawings. From what

Garret said, it sounds like Katherine ignores Lilly, so maybe she thinks I'm the same way. I'm determined to show her I'm not, and that I really want to get to know her. I just hope she wants to get to know *me*.

I stand up. "Well, I'll let you finish watching TV."

"Do you wanna watch with me?"

I smile at her. "I'd love to."

She scoots over on her bed and I sit next to her and we watch a show I've never seen, or even heard of, but it doesn't matter. What matters is that I'm starting to connect with her.

At ten-thirty Pearce finds us. "Have you two been up here all night?" He smiles.

Lilly answers. "I was showing Rachel my drawings, then we watched TV."

He comes over and kisses her head. "You need to get to bed. It's late."

"There's no school, Dad. It's summer break."

"I know, but you still need your rest."

"He's right," I say. "If you want to beat me in the pool tomorrow, you need your rest."

"We're racing?" she asks, her voice excited.

"Yes. And I used to be a very fast swimmer so you better get some sleep."

"You two are going swimming?" Pearce helps me off the bed. "What other plans did you make without me?"

"That's it." Lilly shoves her covers back, slipping under them.

"Goodnight," Pearce says as we walk out.

"Night, Dad. Night, Rachel."

"Goodnight, Lilly."

Pearce and I go to our room and he closes the door.

"I'm sorry I didn't find you earlier. I had some work issues to deal with that couldn't wait."

"It's fine. It gave me some time to spend with Lilly."

He draws me into him, his arms around my waist. "Thank you for making such an effort with her."

"She's your daughter. I want to get to know her, and I don't want her to ever feel like I'm trying to take you away from her. I want us all to be a family." I pause. "Maybe I shouldn't ask this, but how did she turn out so well? With Katherine as her mother, I'm surprised Lilly doesn't act like her."

"That was all Garret's doing. When I was working all the time, he took care of her and played with her and taught her things, like how to not be like Katherine. That's why Garret and Lilly have such a close relationship."

I smile. "We raised a good son, didn't we?"

"*You* did. He is who he is because of you." He kisses me. "Let's go to bed."

The next morning, Pearce goes into his home office to work on the plan to tell the media about me. We're telling them tomorrow. Pearce has already filmed a video of himself making a statement that will be sent to all the news outlets.

While he's busy doing that, Lilly and I swim in the indoor pool. It's not warm enough to be in the outdoor pool and the indoor pool is better for swimming laps.

"I won!" Lilly says as she reaches the edge of the pool.

We did some practice laps and just had our first race. She's a fast swimmer, but not nearly as fast as Garret. I raced him last week and couldn't keep up. But he swims all the time and I haven't been swimming in years. In Italy, I didn't have access to a pool. Garret told me Lilly swims almost every day, but not for hours, like he used to when he was her age.

"Good job, honey." I wipe my eyes and notice her giving me a funny look, then realize what I said. "I'm sorry. Do you not want me to call you that?"

She shrugs. "It's okay. I don't mind. Do you want to race again?"

"Definitely. We're just warming up."

She smiles and sets herself up in her lane. I do the same, and we race again. She beats me, but not by much.

"Can I show you something?" I ask her.

"Yeah." She adjusts her swim cap.

I demonstrate as I talk. "When you're doing the front crawl, I notice you bring your left arm up a little too high, which can slow you down. If you want to go faster, try to keep that arm a little lower."

She's quiet and I'm worried she's mad at me for correcting her, but then she says, "Will you watch me?"

"Of course. Go ahead."

She swims a lap, this time with her arm lower. I don't know if she went any faster but her form was better.

"How was that?" she asks when she's back beside me.

"Much better. Your form looked really good that time."

"My coach never told me about my arm."

"Maybe he just didn't notice it. Ready to race again?"

"Yeah, but first, will you time me?"

"Sure. Do you have a stopwatch?"

She jumps out of the pool and takes it off the rack where they keep the towels. She returns to the pool, handing me the watch, and I time her as she does another lap.

"That's faster than I do at practice," she says when I tell her her time. "Thanks for helping me."

I smile at her. "You're welcome."

Lilly's a sweet girl. Very polite. But she also seems a little sad. I think it's because of her mother. Lilly keeps making comments about how her mom doesn't like her artwork, and doesn't want her swimming, and doesn't like the way she dresses or how she wears her hair. It sounds like all Katherine does is criticize her daughter and yet Lilly seems desperate to please her, or just get some attention from her that isn't negative.

We continue racing for an hour and Lilly can't stop smiling. She said she hasn't had anyone to race with since Garret left, which is sad because Garret moved away five years ago.

"How's it going in here?" Pearce walks in, wearing a suit. He dressed casually last week, but now he's back in work mode and dressed accordingly.

Lilly swims to the edge of the pool. "Rachel helped me with my form."

He smiles. "She used to give swimming lessons. Did she tell you that?"

"It was a long time ago," I tell her.

288

"Lilly, why don't you go get ready for lunch?" Pearce says. "I need to speak with Rachel a moment."

"Okay." She gets out of the pool and grabs a towel and leaves the room.

"Is something wrong?" I ask him as I take a towel and wrap it around me. I take another one for my hair, drying it as I walk over to Pearce.

"Everything's fine. I just wanted to let you know that I have to attend a meeting for the organization later today. William has alerted them of your return and they called for an emergency meeting."

My pulse quickens. "What does this mean? Are they going to do something to you? Or to me?"

"Relax, sweetheart. I'm just going there to answer any questions they have and to tell them I plan on marrying you again."

"Pearce, maybe you shouldn't tell them that. What if they try to punish you?"

"They already punished me once for marrying you. Technically, they can't do it again. But since you're not one of us, I'm sure I'll have to give them something in return for them allowing me to be with you. They like to make deals, so we'll decide what that is during this meeting."

"I don't want you making deals with them. We just won't get married. Besides, in my mind, we're already married. We always have been. I don't need to have another ceremony to prove it."

He holds both my hands and sets his eyes on mine. "I want us to be husband and wife again. Officially. So I will do whatever I have to do to make that happen."

"But—"

He stops me with a kiss. "Don't argue with me about this. I'm marrying you." He smiles. "Unless you turn down my proposal."

"I guess you'll have to wait and see." I smile, but then frown as I remember something.

"Rachel, what's wrong?"

"I don't have my ring anymore. Jack took my wedding ring before I left. I don't know what he did with it."

"I'll get you a new one."

I nod. "It's just that I loved that ring. You went to New York and went shopping and picked it out yourself, and that made it really special."

He cups my cheek. "I will go shopping again and pick out a new one."

I laugh a little. "You hate shopping."

"Yet I will do it for you." He kisses me.

"Remember when I first made you go shopping? You were so uncomfortable. You couldn't get out of that mall fast enough."

He chuckles. "Yes. You made me buy jeans. The first pair I ever owned. My mother still scolds me for wearing them. And I've lost count how many times she's lectured me about Garret and Lilly wearing them." He gets a stern look on his face as he imitates her. "Those children should not be seen in denim pants. It's a disgrace, Pearce."

I laugh at his imitation. "And what did you tell her?"

"I just agreed with her, then let them wear whatever they wanted." His phone vibrates in his suit jacket. He checks it. "It's Kiefer. He has everything lined up to send to the networks."

"This is making me nervous. Are we going to have reporters and photographers following us around after this story comes out?"

"It depends on what other news comes out tomorrow. If it's a big news day, your story may not get much coverage." He types something into his phone, then puts it away. "Let's have lunch and then I have to go. I've instructed the security guards not to let anyone past the gate. Just stay here at the house and you won't have any problems. I can't receive phone calls during the meeting but if you need to reach me, leave a message and I'll call you back as soon as I can."

The three of us have lunch, then Pearce leaves for his meeting. I'm nervous seeing him go. I don't know what they're going to do to him. And I'm a little afraid being alone here at the house. The security guards are outside, and Lilly and Charles are home, so I'm not actually alone, but I still feel uneasy being here without Pearce. This is the first time we've been apart since I returned.

It's almost four and Pearce has been gone for hours. I'm worried about him. He told me it might be a long meeting but I'm still worried. I don't like him being around those people.

After Pearce left, Lilly and I watched a movie in the theater room on the other side of the house, and now I'm waiting for her in the kitchen. She went upstairs, but when she comes back down we're going to have ice cream out on the patio.

I didn't expect Lilly to spend all this time with me. It makes me wonder if Garret asked her to. He's talked to her several times since I arrived. When I called him this morning, he told me again how much Lilly likes me. She just met me, so I'm not sure if that's really true, but we are getting along really well. She reminds me of Garret in a lot of ways. I can see how much he's influenced her.

Ten minutes have passed and Lilly still hasn't come down to the kitchen. She was just going to change into a t-shirt, so what's taking so long? I decide to go check on her.

As I'm walking through the living room, I hear voices in the foyer. Lilly's talking to someone. A woman. I abruptly stop when I hear the voice. It's Katherine. What is she doing here? And why did the guards let her through?

"I bought you these dresses," Katherine says in a harsh tone. "And then you just left them behind. That was both disrespectful and ungrateful and I will not tolerate such behavior."

"I don't have anyplace to wear them, Mother."

"That is your father's fault, and I will be speaking to him about that. At your age, you should be attending events that require you to dress in designer gowns and be photographed for the papers."

"I don't want to go to those events," I hear her quietly say.

"It's not about what you want. It's about what's best for your family. Do you want to disgrace the Kensington name the way Garret did?"

My fists clench hearing her say Garret's name. I want to storm in there right now and yell at Katherine for how she treated my son, but I'm not supposed to let anyone know I'm alive yet, especially Katherine, who spreads gossip faster than anyone.

"Don't talk about Garret," Lilly says, raising her voice slightly, like she's defending him.

"I will not allow you to follow in Garret's footsteps. He chose to give up this lifestyle, but you are *not* going to do the same. You are my daughter, and you will take part in the high society life you were born into, and you will be happy about it. Which is why you WILL wear these dresses."

There's silence.

Then I hear Katherine again. "What did I say about wearing your hair like that?"

"I'm at home. No one's around. What does it matter how my hair looks?"

"It always matters," she snaps. "Appearance is everything. You must look your best at all times. And that ratty low-class braid is not acceptable. If you are unable to properly fix your hair, I will send a stylist to this house every day to make sure your hair looks as it should."

"Dad would never allow that."

She huffs, as though she knows Lilly is right. "Then it is up to you to make sure your hair is done properly. And while I'm away this summer, I expect you to lose ten pounds."

Ten pounds? Is she crazy? Lilly is already too thin. She should be *gaining* weight, not losing it.

"A girl your age should not still have baby fat," Katherine says. "Stop eating so much. It's not lady-like and it's a detriment to your figure."

"Yes, Mother."

I'm so angry right now. How could she talk to her daughter this way? She has done nothing but insult her and order her around. It reminds me of how Holton used to talk to Pearce years ago.

Before I can stop myself, I storm into the foyer and face Katherine.

"You need to leave." I instinctively put my arm around Lilly. I know she's not my daughter but the mother in me can't help but protect her.

Katherine's jaw drops and her stiff posture collapses as shock overtakes her.

"You…no…this can't…" She's unable to even form a sentence.

"Hello, Katherine." I smile, enjoying the shock I've caused her. "It's been a long time."

"I…I don't understand," she stammers. "You're dead."

"No. I just went away for a while. But now I'm back."

"That's not possible. I saw the plane. There were no survivors."

"I wasn't on the plane."

She stares at me, like she's seeing a ghost. Behind her I notice a clothing rack filled with ballroom gowns. Her driver must've brought those in. There's no way Katherine would've carried them. She's so skinny she looks frail, and the lack of fat in her face makes her appear much older, even older than me. She has her blond hair pulled back in a twisted knot at the back of her neck.

"Why are you here?" she demands.

"Why do you think?" I ask, glaring at her.

She straightens up, her eyes narrowed. "So you're getting back together with Pearce. In my house, no less."

"What Pearce and I do is none of your business. And this is no longer your house. Now as I said before, you need to leave."

She notices my arm around Lilly and says, "Get away from my daughter."

"If she wants to move, she can." I glance down at her, but she remains tucked into my side.

Katherine takes a step closer to me. "Let me make this very clear. Do not think for one second that you will be raising my daughter. If you and Pearce are planning to live together, I will be getting custody of Lilly."

"No!" Lilly says, panic in her voice. "You can't. Dad said—"

"Stop interrupting!" Katherine yells at her. "You're being a brat!"

"She wasn't interrupting," I say. "And stop yelling at her, and criticizing her, and calling her names."

"Don't you DARE tell me how to talk to my daughter!" Now Katherine's yelling at *me*, her face getting red.

"I'm not going to stand by and let you say those things to her. And the fact that you told her to lose weight is disgusting. Absolutely disgusting. She is a beautiful girl and extremely talented. You should be praising her, not putting her down."

I feel Lilly move a tiny step closer to me.

"Leave, Katherine," I say forcefully. "I'll tell Pearce you stopped by, although I believe doing so without telling him is outstepping the bounds of your custody agreement."

She sneers at me. "I always hated you, you piece of trash. You should've stayed on the farm where you belong." She pivots on her heels, swings open the door, and storms out to her Mercedes, where her driver is waiting.

I go over and close the door, then turn back to Lilly. "I'm sorry, honey. I didn't mean to yell at your mom. I just—"

"Thank you," she whispers, as she comes up and hugs me. Her words and her gesture make me tear up.

I hug her back. "You don't have to thank me. Your mother should never talk to you that way. No one should talk to you that way."

"She always does," I hear Lilly whisper.

I pull back enough to look at her. "Does your father know this?"

She shakes her head. "I don't want them to fight. I hate it when they fight."

"I know, honey, but your father needs to know. Would you like me to tell him?"

She shrugs. "It wouldn't do any good. Garret always says you can't change people."

I'm afraid to even ask this, but I have to know. "Did Katherine used to talk to Garret that way?"

"Yeah. But he didn't put up with it. They used to fight all the time."

What an awful life Garret must've had living here with Katherine. All his teen years were spent here in this house with that horrible woman. I could've yelled at her just now for how she treated Garret, but I didn't want to do so in front of Lilly. And besides, what good would it do? If anything, it would make Katherine happy to know I was upset about it. And in a way, I'll be getting back at Katherine by raising Lilly. She turns 13 in August and will be spending all her teen years with me. So Katherine will soon know what it feels like to have someone else raising your child.

"Garret always stuck up for me," Lilly says, "and took care of me. And now…" I see her lip quivering, her eyes damp.

"What, sweetie?" I hold her hand. "What were you going to say?"

"Now Garret is gone, and Dad has you, and…I don't have anyone left."

"Garret isn't gone. He's just a phone call away. And you still have your father. He's not going anywhere."

"What if he makes me live with her? So he can be alone with you?"

"Lilly, look at me." I wait until her eyes lift to mine. "He will not make you live with her. That will never happen. He loves you, and being with me doesn't change that. We both want you in our lives."

She sniffles and wipes the tears off her cheek with the back of her hand.

I smooth her hair. "Lilly, if things are that bad with your mom, why did you want to go see her last week?"

Her gaze drops to the floor. "Because I thought if I spent time with her, that maybe she'll like me. I try to do what she says, and look the way she wants me to look, but it's never good enough. She still hates me."

"Oh, honey." I pull her into my arms and hug her. "She doesn't hate you. She's just dealing with her own issues. But that's not an excuse for her to take her anger out on you."

We hug a moment longer, then I let her go.

"Why don't we have some ice cream?" I smile at her. "Ice cream makes everything better."

After having ice cream, we sit outside by the pool and she tells me about her artwork and some of the painting classes she's taken. She's eager to tell me, and seems surprised that I'm listening, which tells me that Katherine never does.

When Pearce gets home, I need to tell him about Katherine. Not just about how she treated Lilly, but that she knows I'm alive. By now, she's probably told everyone she knows, and I'm sure the first person she told was her father, which makes me feel like I'm not safe. I hope Pearce gets home soon.

CHAPTER THIRTY-ONE

PEARCE

This meeting has been going on for hours. The first hour was spent discussing what happened to Rachel. Everyone knows the plane crash was my punishment for marrying her, but nobody knew who was on the committee that planned it. That information was kept a secret. Even William didn't know. And until Rachel told me, I didn't know Leland rigged the plane. When it happened, we all assumed Leland was in Europe on business. He had been there that entire week and was in a meeting in Sweden when the plane crashed. So he must've flown into DC just long enough to rig the plane and talk to Jack. But since I didn't know that, I assumed a freelancer rigged the plane.

Today at the meeting, I told everyone about Leland's involvement, then asked if anyone knew who else was involved. I didn't expect anyone to come forward with information, but then Harold Knight raised his hand and admitted that his father was on the committee. Harold is my age, and was one of the people who has worked with me over the years in my efforts to keep our sons from being forced to join Dumanis. I've always considered Harold a friend, so was surprised when he said his father was involved. But he said he didn't find this out until right before his father died a couple years ago.

As he spoke, I could tell Harold felt regret for what his father had done, and in what I can only assume was an attempt to ask for my forgiveness or ease his guilt, he disclosed the other members on the committee. Although it's not against the rules to do so, it's frowned upon, and therefore could've resulted in Harold being reprimanded. But my fellow members didn't seem to care. The crash was so long ago, and the members who were on the committee were in their seventies and eighties at the time, so are now all deceased. Except for Leland.

If anyone were being reprimanded today, it would be my father if he were alive. He failed to tell anyone that Rachel didn't die, and that he'd been holding her hostage in that small town in Italy. My fellow members were shocked when I told them what he'd done, not because they care about Rachel, but because it was such a bold and dangerous move. If Dunamis found out my father had lied to them all those years, he would've been killed. But knowing my father, I'm sure he enjoyed having that secret and the risk that came with it. He was always a risk taker, and he was arrogant, always assuming he was too clever to get caught doing something he shouldn't.

"We've been informed that the media will be alerted about this tomorrow," Roger, the man leading the meeting, says. "Given that many of you are known to be friends with Pearce, you may be asked to comment on his situation. If so, you are to decline comment. We don't want this story getting out of hand. The sooner it goes away, the better. We don't want an investigation starting again regarding the plane crash."

The crash was deemed suspicious years ago by a group of curious reporters and conspiracy theorists, which caused them to look closer into what happened. Their suspicions arose because Senator Wingate was on the plane, not because of Rachel. Nobody cared about Rachel, but when a senator dies in a small plane, conspiracies abound and reporters start digging for information. They never found anything and eventually gave up.

"Who's handling the press?" someone asks.

"I am." I stand up and face the room. "I'm working with Kiefer on this. The two of us have everything under control."

I don't dare tell them that William is involved. He's not supposed to be helping me, or any of the other members. It's against the rules for someone at William's level to do hands-on work, so he's putting himself at risk by helping me with this.

"What happens now?" someone else asks.

"Pearce would like our permission to remarry the woman," Roger says.

I'd marry her even without their permission, but I have to play along with their ridiculous rules. William has been able to change a lot of those rules, but the marriage one remains. The members still insist we marry women who are approved.

"Isn't he still married to her?" I hear a man ask from the side of the room.

"Technically, no," Roger says, "given that she was presumed dead and he married and divorced someone else, so he'd like to make it official again by remarrying her."

"When this story is released to the media," I say, "the public will expect Rachel and me to be reunited as husband and wife. If we do not do so, it will generate negative press. I'll be known as the husband who rejected his wife after she returned from being presumed dead. If that happens, this story will continue rather than go away. The public likes a happy ending. It's in our best interest for me to remarry Rachel."

There's mumbling in the crowd as the members discuss this amongst themselves.

After five minutes, Roger taps his microphone, getting the attention of the room again. "What is the general consensus?"

A man in the front row says, "I agree with Pearce that it would be best if he married her to avoid the negative press that would result if he didn't. This story has to go away as fast as possible, or as you said, interest in the plane crash may resurface."

"Do others agree?" Roger asks. "Raise your hand if you do."

Most of the men raise their hands. Years ago, this would've shocked me, but now, the members are much more reasonable. Part of that is because of William's leadership at the top level, but it's also because the older members have died off. They were the ones determined to make everyone's lives as miserable as possible, even when there was no reason to do so. They just liked assigning punishments. It made them feel powerful. That was my father's generation. The people here in this room are a new generation, and the people in my age group are now the leaders, and luckily, most of them like and respect me.

"There needs to be a negotiation," I hear someone say. "If we're allowing him to go outside the rules, he needs to give us something in return."

Everyone nods in agreement. I knew this was coming and I came prepared to offer them something.

"Pearce," Roger says. "I'm sure you were aware this would be a condition of us granting you permission to marry her."

"Yes. And I'd like to present my offer."

"Step up to the microphone, please."

He moves aside and I take his place at the microphone, facing the crowd.

"In exchange for your approval of my marriage, and an agreement that Rachel will not be harmed or threatened, now, or in the future..." I pause. "I will give you my company. All assets. All future earnings. It will all be yours to do with as you please."

The room becomes silent as stunned faces look back at me. None of them expected me to offer up the company. Kensington Chemical has grown to be one of the most successful companies in the world, and everyone knows that's because of me, not my father. I grew the company far beyond what anyone ever expected it to be. I never wanted to run it, but after I was forced to, I decided to make it more successful than my father ever could. I admit, there was still that part of me that wanted to prove to him that I was a better businessman than he was, and I did. He never admitted that, but he couldn't deny the impact I had on the company.

But now? I've had enough. I achieved my goals and I have no desire to continue down this path. If my father knew I was giving away the company, he'd be rolling over in his grave, but it's no longer his company. It's mine, and I don't want to be burdened with it anymore. I don't want my children to be either.

Roger returns to the microphone. "Well...Pearce, that's quite a generous offer. Are you sure you're willing to give up Kensington Chemical?"

"Yes," I say without hesitation.

"Who would be CEO?" someone calls out.

"We can discuss that at a later time," I say. "As of now, I am willing to remain CEO until a replacement is found. I am also willing to do whatever training is necessary to help the new CEO come on board."

The CEO will have to be one of my fellow members because Dunamis uses the products we produce for their various activities. They need someone at the top to keep their secrets and allow them continued access to whatever products they need. There are several members who would be suitable as my replacement, some of whom I went to business school with.

Roger speaks again. "I think we all agree that we will accept your generous offer. I would like to suggest that you serve on a committee to help us choose the new CEO and would also ask that you remain on the board of directors." He turns to the crowd. "Do you all agree with that?"

Everyone nods their heads.

"Very well," Roger says. "Pearce, I will present your offer to the upper level members, but I'm confident they'll agree to this."

The meeting ends and I feel the urge to smile. But I don't. I want my fellow members to believe I made a huge sacrifice by giving up my company. I want them to think I'm grieving the loss of it, and will be for some time. I want them to assume my actions show my commitment and support of Dunamis.

But none of that is the truth. I'm not grieving. I'm overjoyed. I finally feel free. Like a weight has been lifted off me. I'll no longer have to spend all those hours at the office. I'll be free to do something else. Something I actually want to do, instead of a job I've been forced to do. I'm not ready to retire just yet. I'm too young, and I've never been someone who can just sit around all day. But I don't want to return to an office setting. Maybe I'll do some consulting or give speeches. I enjoy giving speeches and it's something I can do on my own schedule. I can also spend more time mentoring Garret. He and I own a sporting goods company, but I haven't been able to help him as much as he'd like.

On the drive home, my excitement builds. Soon I'll have a whole new life. A life with Rachel and Lilly. We'll live in California, close to Jade and Garret. And I will no longer be tied to the company.

But before any of that happens, I need to deal with Leland. He'll be told about Rachel any minute now, or maybe he's already been told. The thought of that makes me step on the gas, speeding to get home. I won't let Rachel out of my sight until Leland is dead.

When I get to the house, I find Rachel and Lilly sitting on the back patio, talking. The two of them are getting along even better than I thought they would. Garret used to tell Lilly about Rachel, so maybe in some ways she felt like she already knew her. And Lilly likes anyone Garret likes so Rachel was a step ahead in that regard.

Lilly stands up as I approach. "Hi, Dad."

"Hi, honey." I give her a hug and kiss her head. I've missed her after being away from her for a week. I need to spend some time with her, but I can't until things are more settled.

She hugs me tighter than normal, then lets me go and walks away.

"Lilly, where are you going?" I ask her.

"To my room to draw. I'll see you at dinner." She disappears into the house.

I take a seat next to Rachel. "Did something happen while I was gone?"

"Katherine stopped by."

"What?" I burst from my chair. "When was she here?"

"About an hour ago. I left you a message but your phone wasn't on."

I take it out and see that it's off. "Shit! I forgot to turn it back on after the meeting. Did she see you?"

"Yes. I know I wasn't supposed to let anyone see me but—"

"I'm sorry to interrupt, but I need to call William. We need to get the media announcements out right away. It can't wait. I don't want Katherine being the one breaking this story to the press." I call William's number.

"Pearce," he answers. "I heard about the company. Are you sure you want to give it up?"

302

"Yes. That's not why I'm calling. Katherine came by the house and saw Rachel. We need to get the media plan started right now. It can't wait until tomorrow."

"I'll take care of it. Everything's already in place so it shouldn't be a problem. By tonight, it should be on all the cable news channels."

I go in the house so Rachel can't hear my conversation. "Do you have an update on Leland?"

"Yes. He got back from London two hours ago and was immediately told the news about Rachel. As expected, he canceled his flight."

Leland was supposed to fly to DC tonight to meet with one of our politicians. He was going to fly himself there in one of his planes, but won't now because he assumes I rigged his plane to go down in order to get revenge for his attempt to kill Rachel. Word travels fast within Dunamis. As soon as that meeting ended, I know at least one of my fellow members alerted Leland that I knew he was responsible for the plane crash.

"Did he check his plane before he canceled the trip?" I ask William.

"Yes, and it passed inspection, but he still canceled the flight."

I chuckle. "Fear is power."

"And so it is." He chuckles as well.

"Did he try to get out of going to DC?"

"Of course, but he was told he had to be there. He's Senator Shilling's handler and therefore it's his job to be there."

"So he's leaving in the morning."

"From the hangar just outside New Haven." William laughs. "For someone who thinks so highly of himself, he's certainly predictable."

Leland has private jets in multiple locations. He assumes I tampered with the one in New York, which he keeps in a hangar just a few miles from his house, and is the one he would normally take to DC. Now he's planning to use the plane he keeps in Connecticut, assuming I wouldn't tamper with that one. But just to be safe, Leland will spend tonight inspecting the plane and then have it watched by his security team until he's ready to take off tomorrow. He could just fly commercial and not have to worry at all, but Leland refuses to fly commercial unless he's going overseas.

"Is he already at the hangar?" I ask.

"He's heading there now. His security team is already in place, guarding his plane." He pauses. "And as for yours, he did as you expected."

"Is that so?" I let out a humorous laugh. "Well, as you said, he's predictable."

In one of our previous conversations, I told William that Leland would likely tamper with the Kensington jet after he found out Rachel was alive, hoping both she and I would be killed the next time we used it.

"And you're sure about what you heard?" I ask.

William tapped into Leland's phone after our meeting at Garret's house that day and has been listening to Leland's calls and tracking his location.

"I'm certain of it," William says. "But I can play it back for you if you want to hear it yourself."

"That's not necessary."

"Now that you know this, you're not changing the plan, are you?"

"Just slightly. But the outcome will be the same."

He doesn't ask me to explain. "Good luck, Pearce. We'll talk when it's done."

We end the call and I go back outside to Rachel.

"Did you get everything settled?" she asks, referring to the media plan.

"Yes. The story will go out tonight instead of tomorrow."

"Pearce, we need to talk about Katherine." Rachel proceeds to tell me about how Katherine acted toward Lilly, then how Lilly told her this has been going on for quite some time.

I sigh. "I wish she had told me this. Lilly tends to keep things to herself, but I'm surprised she didn't tell Garret this. She usually tells him everything."

"What are you going to do?"

"I'll talk to Lilly. If she no longer wants to see her mother, that's fine with me. This isn't the typical custody agreement. Katherine has no rights when it comes to Lilly. When the organization allowed our divorce, they made it clear to Katherine that I have full control over Lilly's care and well-being. She wouldn't dare challenge them. I allowed Katherine to see Lilly because I thought it's what Lilly wanted, but if that's not true, I'll put an end to it."

"Pearce, maybe you should tell her about our plan to move to California. She should feel like she has input, and not like we're just forcing her to do this."

"She'll be happy about the move. She wants to be closer to Jade and Garret." I check behind me to make sure Lilly hasn't returned, then continue. "Now, about tomorrow. I need you to go to the airport with me."

"Why? Where are we going?"

I tell Rachel just enough of the plan for her to play along with it. I don't give her the entire plan because I don't want her body language or facial expressions to clue Leland in as to what's really going on.

"Pearce, as much as I hate Leland, I feel bad taking Lilly's grandfather away from her."

"He's not a grandfather to her. He doesn't care about her." I'll be proving that tomorrow when I carry out my plan. "Leland doesn't even spend time with Lilly when she goes to visit him at his house. He's almost as bad of a grandfather as my father was to Garret."

She nods. "Then I guess we're doing this."

"Rachel." I take her hand. "This will all be over soon. And then we can start building our life together again."

I've decided I'm not going to tell Rachel about the company until the organization accepts my offer. I don't know why they wouldn't, but over the years I've learned not to ever assume you know what they'll do.

I give Rachel a kiss, then get up from my chair. "I'm going to go talk to Lilly."

When I get up to her room, the door is open and she's lying on her bed with her eyes shut and her headphones on. I go over and sit beside her. When she feels me sit down, her eyes pop open and she yanks her headphones out of her ears.

"Can we talk?"

"Rachel told you." She sits up, hugging her knees to her chest.

"Yes. But I'm concerned you didn't tell me yourself."

"I didn't want you to fight with Mom about me."

"How I handle things with your mother is not your concern. If she's not treating you well, I need to know."

"It's not like she hits me," Lilly mumbles, her eyes on the bed. "She just yells at me."

"And says things she shouldn't be saying to you."

"It's fine. I'll just ignore her."

"Lilly." I tilt her face up to mine. "If you don't want to see your mother anymore, you don't have to."

"I still want to see her. She's my mom."

"I understand that, but if she can't be a good mother, you don't have to see her."

"Then she'll feel bad. No one likes her, Dad. She doesn't even have any friends."

Lilly has always been this way, more concerned about others than herself. And Katherine uses that to her advantage, knowing she can treat Lilly poorly and Lilly will still love her and want to see her.

"Lilly, your mother has brought that upon herself. When she treats people the way she does, they don't want to be around her. It's not your job to make her feel better." I wait for Lilly to say something, but she's quiet, her head down. "I will be having a talk with your mother about this, but I'm telling you now that if she continues this type of behavior, I will not allow her to see you."

"Okay." Lilly's shoulders relax and she drops her knees, sitting cross-legged on the bed. She's either relieved or sad or a little of both. I can't tell and she won't tell me. She always hides how she's feeling because Katherine used to scold Lilly for showing emotion. My parents did the same thing to me and I hated it and yet I let it happen to my own daughter. I wasn't around all those years to stop it. Since the divorce, I've tried to get Lilly to open up more, but she has a hard time with it. She expresses her emotions in her artwork instead, which I guess is better than nothing.

"Lilly, I have some news to share." She glances up, her expression worried. I smile to ease her concerns. "It's nothing bad. It's good. I was going to wait to tell you, but I don't really see a reason to wait, and I'd like your opinion on the matter."

"What is it?" She turns a little so she's facing me.

"I'd like us to move to California, closer to Jade and Garret."

Her face lights up. "Are you serious?"

"Would you be okay with that?"

She nods really fast. "Yes. When can we move?"

Her enthusiasm makes me smile. I haven't seen her this happy for a long time. "I'd like us to move there this summer, if possible. Rachel and I would like to buy Grace's house, the one in Santa Barbara."

"Where we had my birthday party?" she asks.

"Yes, that's the one. I'm surprised you remembered that."

When Lilly turned 7, Jade and her friend, Harper, had a birthday party for Lilly in Grace's back yard. It was a fairy theme and they dressed Lilly as a fairy. She loved it. She talked about it for months.

"I have another surprise," I say. "I'm flying you out to see Jade and Garret tomorrow. When I was with them last week, they asked if you could come out there for a visit and I agreed to it. I assumed you'd be okay with that."

"What time do I leave?" She's even more excited. She misses her brother. She hasn't seen him in months. And she loves spending time with Jade and the baby.

"You'll leave in the morning, so you should start packing your suitcase."

"Can I stay with them until we move?"

"I don't know. Let me think about it. It could be several months before we move and I'm not sure I can give up seeing my little girl for that long."

"Dad, I'm not a little girl anymore."

"You'll always be my little girl."

She scoots over on the bed and hugs me. "I love you, Dad."

"I love you too."

She sits back, a huge smile spread across her face. "I can't believe we're moving to California!"

"I'm glad you're excited, but don't tell anyone yet. Only Garret knows about this. He hasn't even told Jade. I want to get everything settled before we tell people."

"What about Grandmother?"

Shit. I forgot to tell my mother about Rachel. Katherine's probably already told her.

"Your grandmother doesn't know about the move." I stand up. "I need to go. Start packing. I'll see you at dinner."

As I'm leaving I turn back and see her with her headphones back on, dancing around her room, grinning from ear to ear. She's elated about the move. We should have done this a long time ago.

CHAPTER THIRTY-TWO

PEARCE

I phone my mother on my way down the stairs.

"Pearce, is it true?" she asks when she answers. Katherine must've told her.

"Yes. She's here at the house."

"I'm coming over."

"Why? You don't believe me?"

"Of course I believe you.

"You don't need to come over, Mother. Things are a little chaotic right now."

"I'm coming over. I'll see you shortly. Goodbye, Pearce." She hangs up.

Rachel appears in front of me. "Who was that?"

"Your mother-in-law. She's coming over to see you. Katherine told her the news."

"She's coming over right now? I have to go change." She starts toward the stairs but I grasp her around the waist.

"You don't need to change. You look beautiful." She has on a navy skirt that's full and flowing with a white cotton button-up shirt that fits her perfectly.

"This is too casual," she says. "Your mother will expect me to—"

"I don't care what my mother expects." I lean down and kiss her. "I gave up trying to please her years ago. And I love you in this outfit. You're not changing." I kiss her again. "I need to check in with the office quick. Would you mind telling Charles my mother will be joining us for dinner?"

"I'll go tell him right now."

She pulls away but I keep hold of her. "I love you."

She smiles. "I love you too."

After the plane crash, I couldn't say those words anymore, not even to my own children. And I never said them to Katherine. Doing so would've been a lie. I never loved her. But I *do* love my children. I just couldn't make myself tell them that until I saw Garret get shot by Royce. That was my turning point, when I forced myself to go to counseling and when I committed to being a better father. Since then, I make sure to tell Garret and Lilly that I love them. I never heard those words from my own parents, but I'm not going to be like them. I want my children to feel loved.

My mother shows up at five-thirty, wearing a black suit like she's going to a job interview. Maybe she plans to interview Rachel to figure out if she still approves of her. If so, I'm not putting up with it. We're not going back to that time when my mother made rude comments to Rachel while giving her disapproving looks. If my mother acts that way, she will be sent home.

"Hello, Rachel," my mother says as Rachel greets her in the foyer.

"Hello, Eleanor."

"This is certainly a surprise." My mother does a quick glance of Rachel's outfit.

Rachel seems nervous. I told her my mother had nothing to do with what my father did, but maybe she doesn't believe me.

"So how have you been?" Rachel asks my mother.

"Fine. Have you seen Garret yet?"

"Yes. I saw him last week." Rachel relaxes at the mention of Garret. "I met his wife and their baby. Have you been out to see the baby?"

"No, not yet."

My mother doesn't talk to Garret much, and she's never been out to visit him and Jade. She doesn't like Jade because Jade never tried to fit into our high society world. But that's not Jade's fault. She was never invited into that world or even exposed to it. Garret kept her out of it. When he was younger, I used to make him go to all the high society events I had to go to when I was his age, and he hated it as much as I did. When he started dating Jade, I stopped forcing him to go to those events and he hasn't gone to one since. So it's not Jade's fault that Garret is no longer part of this world, but my mother still chooses to blame Jade.

We move into the living room and my mother asks Rachel, "Will you be staying in Connecticut?"

She glances at me. "For now, yes."

"With Pearce?"

"Yes, Mother," I answer. "Rachel and I will be living together."

"I see." My mother smooths her short blond hair. "Perhaps you'll find a different house. You never cared much for this one, did you, Pearce?"

"No, not particularly. Mother, I assume you'll be staying for dinner?"

"I suppose I could." She focuses on Rachel. "Do you still enjoy cooking? I remember how you used to cook every night."

"Yes, I still like to cook." Rachel's giving me this look like she isn't sure how much to tell my mother. We should've discussed this before she arrived.

"Well," my mother says, "the weather certainly has been nice, hasn't it?"

She continues to make small talk. She avoids any questions about what happened to Rachel, so I don't offer up any information. My mother can hear the fake story on the news. That's all she needs to know.

Later, Lilly comes downstairs and we all have dinner. Afterward, I turn the TV on and see the story about Rachel. It's on all the cable news channels and is sure to be a top story on tomorrow's national morning news.

When my mother leaves, she takes Lilly with her. Now that Rachel's story is out, there will likely be reporters and photographers outside the house tomorrow and I didn't want Lilly around them. My mother will bring Lilly to the airport in the morning.

Rachel and I go to bed around midnight, and surprisingly, I sleep soundly, despite knowing what will happen in a few short hours. I feel no guilt or uneasiness about what I'm going to do. It's been a long time coming and I'm going to enjoy every second of it.

We arrive at the private airport at seven a.m. The Kensington jet is on the tarmac, fueled up and ready to go. Leland's jet is also there, surrounded by guards whose eyes are aimed at the plane, making sure no one can tamper with it.

Leland arrives at seven-thirty in his black suit and tie, his gray hair slicked back. I'm standing near the airport entrance, having a cup of coffee.

When he walks in, I approach him and smile. "Leland. We missed you at the meeting yesterday."

He did a double take when he saw me, and now he's trying to hide his shock with a fake smile. "Pearce. What are you doing here?"

"Seeing Lilly off. She's flying out to stay with Jade and Garret for a few weeks until things settle down. There are reporters and photographers waiting outside the house and I'd prefer that she not be around all that."

"Yes, I...I suppose that's wise." He's stammering. He never stammers.

"You seem ill at ease today, Leland." I sip my coffee. "Any particular reason why?"

Before he can answer, Rachel appears from the hallway, walking up to me and wrapping her arm around mine.

"Leland, what a pleasure to see you again." She smiles.

He stares at her, as though his eyes are playing tricks on him, like she can't possibly be real.

"It's been what..." she says, "fifteen years since I saw you last?"

"Yes." He tries to force out a smile but it only lasts a brief second. "I believe that's correct." His eye twitches and he blinks a few times to steady it. "How have you been?"

"Leland," I say, directing his attention back to me. "We can talk later. I believe you have an important meeting in DC to get to." I check my watch. "Rachel and I don't want to keep you." I smile. "Have a safe flight."

He glances out at the tarmac, then back at me, his eyes narrowed. "Stop playing games with me, Pearce. What did you do to my plane?

I turn to Rachel. "Sweetheart, would you excuse us for a moment?"

"Certainly." She walks over to the small waiting area and takes a seat on the couch that faces the TV.

"I know you tampered with my plane." Leland's usual cool and collected demeanor is now rattled by pure paranoia, which I find quite satisfying.

"Why would I do such a thing?" I ask calmly.

"You KNOW why!" He nearly shouts it.

I go over and refill my coffee from the pot that's set up near the reception desk. "I have no reason to seek revenge. Rachel is back and that's all that matters." I walk back over to him. "I have no vendetta against you, Leland. You simply did as you were ordered to do. If anyone deserves blame, it's my father, but he's dead now, so I no longer have to worry about him." I take a sip of my coffee.

"You wouldn't just let this go," he says, glancing at Rachel. "I know you, Pearce, and I know you'd want revenge."

"When I was younger, yes. But I'm older now, and not as impulsive or single-minded. I'm better able to step back and see the big picture, and I'm much more forgiving than I used to be. Besides, you're Lilly's grandfather. The only one she has left. I wouldn't take her grandfather away."

His body stiffens and his jaw moves side to side as he looks out at my plane. "Where is she? Where's Lilly?"

"My mother is bringing her. She'll be here any minute now. Why do you ask? Were you hoping to say goodbye to her?"

He's breathing hard, his eyes darting to the tarmac then back to me. "What did you do to my plane?" he hisses.

"Nothing," I say casually. "I told you, I have no interest in harming you. Let's just put the past behind us and focus on moving forward."

He stares out at his plane, nervously rubbing his jaw. "I checked it. I checked it multiple times. I had cameras on it all night and guards watching it."

I chuckle. "That seems a bit extreme. But I suppose if it gives you peace of mind."

"It doesn't! I know you tampered with it. Just admit it!"

"If I were to tamper with one of your planes, I would've done so to the one in New York that's close to your house. Why would I tamper with this one?"

"Because you know I'd assume you tampered with the one in New York." He straightens up, his confidence growing. "You're trying to trick me, Pearce, but it's not going to work."

"You truly are paranoid, Leland. I never knew that about you." I take one last sip of coffee, then set my cup down on the table next to us. "I'll tell you what. Just to prove my point, let's switch planes. I'll have my pilots fly Lilly to California using your plane, and you can fly mine to DC."

"No," he blurts out.

I raise my brows at his reaction. "I don't see why you wouldn't agree to it. I'm ensuring your safety here. Putting your mind at ease. I wouldn't tamper with my own plane. And I definitely wouldn't put Lilly on a plane that wasn't safe."

As I say it, she walks through the door along with my mother. My mother's driver is behind them, carrying Lilly's suitcase.

"Hello, honey," I say to Lilly. "Look who I ran into."

"Hi, Grandfather." She gives him a hug but he doesn't hug her back. He keeps his arms at his sides and looks down at her like he wants her to stop touching him.

She lets him go and steps back beside me.

Leland's eyes are on her. "So you're going to see Garret?"

"Yes. And Jade and Abi."

"I see." He glances out the window at the Kensington jet.

"Lilly, go sit with Rachel." I motion to her. "The plane isn't quite ready to leave yet."

"Leland." My mother nods at him as she goes past him, following Lilly to the waiting area.

"Well," I say. "Have you made a decision? Lilly needs to get going and so do you."

He rubs his hand back and forth over his jaw. He looks back at Lilly.

"Is something wrong, Leland?"

His head snaps back to me. "No. Nothing." He straightens up and clears his throat. "I'll take my own plane. I've checked it multiple times. I don't know why I'm doubting myself. I never doubt myself."

"Then I guess we're done here." I put my hand out. "Goodbye, Leland. Say hello to Audrey for me when you get back."

He doesn't shake my hand. He just walks out to the tarmac, not even saying goodbye to Lilly. I watch as he boards his plane.

As the plane taxis down the runway, Leland's four security guards walk back to the airport building. One of them comes up to me.

I hold my phone out to him, showing him the balance. "It's been wired to your account and will be accessible once he's gone."

The man nods and motions for the other guards to follow him to the parking lot. Their job is done and they will soon be four very wealthy men.

Those men have worked for Leland for years. But for the right price, loyalty can be bought.

"Dad, when am I leaving?" I hear Lilly ask.

"Not yet." I walk past the waiting area, down the hall to the employee break room. My pilots are sitting there, as I instructed them to do.

"Mr. Kensington." My head pilot stands up. "As you suspected, there were some serious issues with the plane. Our mechanics will need time to do the repairs. You won't be able to take it today."

"I wasn't planning to. Do you have the report?"

"Yes, Sir." He hands me a piece of paper that details what the mechanics found when they inspected the plane. There was a damaged wire near the engine that would've sparked and caused a fire soon after takeoff, leading to an explosion that would have killed everyone on board.

It doesn't surprise me that Leland wanted me dead. Or Rachel. He sees us as a threat. But what *is* surprising is that he would've let Lilly die. I thought he would try to save her. I gave him numerous opportunities to do so, but he didn't. He left here thinking she would get on that plane, knowing she would die, and he didn't even care. Hate isn't a strong enough word for how I feel about that man.

I return to the waiting area. Rachel and Lilly are talking and my mother is reading a magazine.

"Ladies," I say. "The pilot has informed me that the plane cannot be used today. Something about a wire that needs to be replaced. They'll have to special order it."

"A wire?" I hear the worry in Rachel's voice. This is the part of the story I didn't tell her. If she knew Leland had tampered with my plane, she wouldn't have been able to hold back. She would've been furious and ended up confronting him about it, thus interfering with the plan.

"It's nothing serious," I lie. "But the plane will be out of service until it's fixed."

"So I'm not going?" Lilly asks.

"Actually, we're all going. But we're flying commercial. I already got the tickets. Come on. Everyone get up. Our flight leaves in just over an hour."

My mother hugs Lilly. "Have a good trip."

"You're coming with us, Mother."

"Pearce, don't be ridiculous. I'm not flying to California."

I put my arm around her. "When I said we're all going, that included you. You're going out to see your grandson and the great-granddaughter you've never met."

"But I…I don't have my bags packed." She's flustered, which I knew she would be.

"I've asked the maid to pack your bag. It'll be waiting for us at the airport."

"Pearce." She turns to face me, her hands on her hips. "I can't just leave. I have commitments to attend to."

"Your family is more important than your commitments. You're going to see your grandson whether you like it or not. I'm not giving you a choice here, Mother."

She sighs. "I can't fly commercial."

"They're first class tickets. I'm confident you'll do just fine. Now let's go."

Lilly's giggling off to the side. She's never seen her grandmother so flustered before.

"Mother." I offer her my arm. She reluctantly takes it and I lead her out to the car. Rachel is behind us, her arm around Lilly.

On the drive to the airport, a text message pops up. It's from William and says, "And so it is."

He's telling me Leland's plane crashed. Instead of having it explode upon takeoff, I had it rigged so that Leland would see it malfunctioning while in the air and try to fix it, then realize he couldn't. Those final minutes must've been hell. Knowing you're going to die, but unable to do anything about it?

I smile at that.

CHAPTER THIRTY-THREE
Six Weeks Later

RACHEL

"Pearce, I still don't understand why we're staying here." I'm lying next to him on the bed, propped up on my side. We're back in California, at the same hotel we stayed at after I came back to the U.S., in the same suite on the top floor.

"I thought I made that clear just now." He kisses me, then deepens the kiss as he eases me onto my back. "But since you're unsure, perhaps we'll do it again."

It's morning and Pearce and I just had amazing sex. We did it last night too.

I smile. "We could have done this at home."

"The house is being remodeled." He trails kisses along my shoulder.

"Not until Monday."

He lifts his face to mine. "Are you saying you don't like this hotel?"

"No, I love this hotel. It's beautiful. And it's special because it's where we reunited after being apart."

"I agree. Which is why we're here."

"What do you mean?"

He gives me a kiss. "I'll be right back."

"Pearce, where are you going?" I call after him, but he's already gone.

It must be some kind of surprise. Pearce has been surprising me with little gifts or sweet gestures for weeks now. Flowers. Chocolate. Breakfast in bed. Massages. He's always been romantic, but he's even more so now than he used to be, maybe because he's more relaxed living out here in California.

We moved here a month ago. We bought Grace's house and live there with Lilly. The house had several small rooms that we didn't need, so the renovations will include knocking down a wall to make a bigger bedroom for Lilly. The master bedroom will also get a makeover, as will the kitchen.

We already put a pool in the back yard, which Lilly and I use all the time. The pool is surrounded by flower gardens and stone walking paths. Benches and lawn chairs are scattered throughout so you can sit among the flowers and read a book or just relax.

I love the house, and the yard, and living there with Pearce and Lilly. And I finally feel safe now that Leland's gone.

It's been six weeks since Leland died. The day of his death, the story of my return got pushed aside in the media as reporters rushed to the crash site to cover the unfortunate death of Leland Seymour, the well-known billionaire businessman who had connections to many powerful politicians in Washington.

I'm sure the timing of Leland's death was intentionally set to coincide with the release of my story. I've never asked Pearce that, but I'm sure it's true. He wanted to put the story out there, then have it be quickly forgotten and replaced by other news. But my story wasn't completely forgotten. It remained in the press for weeks, but was limited to short mentions instead of being a lead story. I had some reporters request interviews, but I turned them all down and eventually the requests stopped coming.

As for what happened to Leland, I try not to think about it. Although I didn't actually plan Leland's death, I knew it was going to happen and I was strangely okay with it. I'm not sure what that says about me. I've always been someone who has tried to help people, not harm them. But Leland was a threat and had to die, so I tell myself his death was justified. So is that how Pearce felt all those times he got an assignment? Did he find ways to justify what he did? I'm guessing he had to. How else would you live with yourself?

After this incident with Leland, I feel as though I better understand Pearce and how he was able to do the things he did all

319

those years. Someday he may have to do those things again, but I choose not to think about that.

Leland's funeral happened a few days after the plane crash. Pearce and Lilly went, along with Eleanor. Pearce said Katherine showed no emotion at all during her father's funeral, and neither did her sister or mother. It was like none of them cared that Leland died. And yet when Lilly went to give her mother a hug, Pearce said Katherine pushed her away, saying she was too distraught to deal with Lilly.

Katherine is now in France, visiting her sister. She'll be back in September, but Lilly will be in school by then so won't have time to fly back to see her mother. Katherine could easily fly out here, given that she has no job and nothing to do all day, but I'm sure she won't. She hasn't even called Lilly in weeks.

Lilly is loving her new life in California. She sees Jade and Garret all the time and often stays with them on the weekends. She loves playing with Abigail and racing Garret in the pool.

She also likes spending time with Pearce and me. We play games, watch movies, go swimming, and go to the beach. Pearce has a lot more free time now that he gave his company to the organization. That happened five weeks ago, and since then, his workload has been cut in half. A new CEO has already been appointed, but Pearce is helping with the transition. He'll be doing that for the next few months and he'll remain on the board of directors, so he'll still be involved with Kensington Chemical, but in a very limited way.

When Pearce told me he gave the company away, I knew that was the deal he made so he could marry me. Knowing how much time and effort Pearce put into building that company, I felt bad that he'd given it away, but he assured me it was his decision, not theirs, and that it's what he wanted. He'd made the company a success, but had had enough and wanted to move on and do something else. He isn't sure what that is yet, but he's excited about the possibilities.

"Breakfast is served." Pearce wheels in a cart, topped with pastries, fresh fruit, orange juice, and champagne.

"We're having mimosas?" I ask.

"We can, but that's not why I got the champagne."

"I don't understand."

Pearce stands next to the bed, wearing blue-striped pajama pants and a fitted white t-shirt that highlights his broad shoulders and muscular chest. I'm in a beige silk chemise that I slipped on when he left the room.

"Come here," he says, holding his hand out to me.

He helps me off the bed and I stand in front of him. "What are we doing?"

He chuckles. "You ask too many questions."

"I was just—"

"Rachel." He holds both my hands and looks into my eyes. "I love you more than I can ever possibly tell you." He pauses. "When you came into my life, you made me a better man, and I would not be the person I am today if it were not for you. You were the best thing that ever happened to me. And marrying you was the best decision I ever made. Which is why I can't wait another second to marry you once again. If you'll agree to it." He reaches in his pocket and pulls something out, holding it in his fist. Then he gets down on one knee. "Rachel Kensington, will you do me the honor of marrying me again?"

I nod. "Yes. I would love to marry you again." My eyes are tearing up as I watch his hand open in front of me. Sitting on his palm is my ring. My original wedding ring. "Oh my God." Tears are now pouring from my eyes. "Is that really my ring?"

"Yes." He puts it on my finger.

"But how? How did you find it?"

He stands up, his arms going around my waist. "When I went back to Connecticut a few weeks ago for work, I stopped off in Virginia on the way home. I went to Jack's daughter's house and told her what I was looking for and she gave it to me. She'd found it a few years ago when she was going through her parents' things after Martha passed away. She didn't know who it belonged to. She found it in the box that Jack used to store things from his daughters that were special to him. Cards they had made him. Drawings they had done. He put this ring in that box because you were like a daughter to him."

"Jack was a good man," I say, wiping my tears.

"Yes, he was."

"Thank you. For getting it back."

He smiles. "Thank you for saying yes."

I smile back. "You knew that'd be my answer."

He considers it. "That might be somewhat true, although I have been known to be overly confident. So much so that I have another question for you."

"Which is what?"

"What are you doing this afternoon?"

"I don't know. Why?"

"Would you like to get married?"

I laugh. "That usually takes some planning. I don't think we have time to plan a wedding between now and this afternoon."

"I might have already taken the initiative to plan it, assuming you'd say yes." His lips turn up. "I admit it was a bit presumptuous, but I did warn you of my tendency to be overly confident."

"You're not serious, are you?"

"Sweetheart, you know I've never been fond of practical jokes."

"Pearce, what's going on here?"

"I will tell you once you agree to marry me this afternoon."

I laugh again. "Okay, then yes, I will marry you this afternoon. You never give me much notice, do you? The first time you gave me a day and now I only get a few hours?"

"When I know what I want, I don't like to wait. And I wasn't kidding when I told you I didn't want to wait another second to marry you. The ceremony is taking place at two o'clock in Jade and Garret's back yard, overlooking the ocean. It will be a small wedding with just our family and friends. It's nothing extravagant, but—"

"Pearce, it sounds perfect. It's exactly what I want." I hug him. "I love you. And I'm so happy to be marrying you again."

We have some champagne and eat breakfast in bed. Before I'm able to finish my strawberries, Pearce takes my plate from me and sets it on the table next to the bed.

"I wasn't done with that."

"And I wasn't done with *you*." His hand wraps around my waist as he puts his lips to mine. He tastes like strawberries and I sink down into the bed, pulling him over me. It's only ten. We have plenty of time.

The setting is beautiful. Set far back behind the house, overlooking the ocean, a trellis covered in flowers awaits. Pearce is standing in front of it, looking beyond handsome in his tuxedo. I'm in a long, flowing, silk dress in a soft champagne color, my hair loosely knotted behind my neck.

Jade's best friend, Harper, did my hair and makeup and also helped plan the reception. It turns out Harper is the daughter of Kiefer, the movie director I met years ago. Harper and her husband, Sean, own a party planning and catering business. Sean is a chef, so he made the wedding cake and all the food for the reception. And Harper helped Grace with all the floral arrangements, including my bouquet, which is a mix of pink and white flowers taken from Grace's flower garden.

I watch as Jade and Garret walk down the aisle. Jade is my maid of honor and Garret is the best man. Seeing those two go down the aisle together, I almost feel like I'm seeing them at their wedding. They, too, got married outside, right on the beach. I wasn't able to be there, but at least today, I saw them walk down the aisle together.

Next is Abigail, our little flower girl, toddling down the aisle and trying to toss rose petals. It's darling. Lilly is walking next to her, trying to keep her on the path. When they reach the end, Lilly picks her up and they go to their seat, next to Grace. She's sitting next to William who is next to Eleanor. I was shocked that Eleanor came, but she was invited, and surprisingly, she showed up.

Logan and Shelby are also here. I've talked to Shelby a few times since getting back, but we haven't been able to see each other until now. It's so great to see Logan and Shelby again. They look as happy as ever.

Sitting next to them is Charles, and on his other side sits a surprise guest that I never expected to see again. Celia.

Pearce tracked her down and flew her here from Italy. I almost fainted when I saw her. Celia was like a mother to me, so it means so much to have her here at my wedding. I've really missed her and have thought about her a lot since I've been back.

I'm trying not to cry, but it's hard not to when I see my friends and family and all that they've done to put together this beautiful wedding.

As I walk down the aisle, I set my eyes on Pearce and smile, unable to contain the joy I feel. Fifteen years I waited, wondering if I would ever see him again, and now here we are, reunited, and getting married for the second time.

The ceremony begins and the man officiating it gives a short speech about love and how it's rare, so when you find it you should never let it go. It's probably a generic speech this man gives at all weddings, but his words couldn't be more true. Pearce and I never stopped loving each other. We were apart for a long time, but our love for each other never went away. We never let it go.

We say our vows, and I slip Pearce's ring on his finger, the same ring he wore when we were married. He kept it all these years. Then he slips mine on and I almost cry again seeing it. It brings back memories of when he first proposed to me in my apartment, and our wedding in Vegas, and our second wedding in that beautiful church with my parents there.

I feel like my parents are here again today, along with my sister. I feel like they're smiling down on us as they see Pearce and me together, reunited as husband and wife in front of all our friends and family. This is the wedding I always wanted. I wasn't able to choose the guests at our other weddings, but today the guest list includes all the people I love, which makes this one the best wedding of all.

At the end of the ceremony, the man officiating it says, "It is my pleasure to introduce Pearce and Rachel Kensington. Pearce, you may now kiss the bride."

He gives me a kiss, and as he does, I hear a squeal and look over and see Abigail clapping and giggling from the front row.

"Sorry," I hear Jade whisper, but she's laughing and so is everyone else.

Music starts playing from the outdoor speakers, and we walk back down the aisle with Jade and Garret behind us. Garret's been smiling since Pearce and I arrived here today. His parents are officially back together and he couldn't be happier.

"Congratulations," Garret says, hugging his dad. Then he hugs me, "Congratulations, Mom. You look beautiful."

"Thank you, honey." Here come the tears again.

Jade hugs us next, followed by everyone else.

"I'm so happy for you," Shelby says, teary-eyed. "We need to get together sometime. Just let us know when, and Logan and I will fly out here."

"I will. Thank you for coming all this way. Are you sure you can't stay a few days?"

"I would, but you won't be around." A sly grin crosses her face.

"Where am I going?"

"You'll find out later." She grabs Logan's arm. "Come on. You promised me a dance."

There's a small dance floor set up on the lawn next to the tables and chairs, and people are already dancing.

"Rachel." Celia hugs me. "You have such a beautiful family." She lowers her voice. "And a very handsome husband."

I laugh. "Thank you. I've missed you, Celia."

"I've missed you too. But this is where you belong."

"Yes." I glance over at Pearce, who's talking to Garret. "It's good to be home."

"Do you think you'll ever come back to Italy?"

"I'm sorry, but I don't think that I can."

"Don't be sorry. I understand."

"But you can come here. I'll buy you a ticket whenever you'd like to visit."

She smiles. "We'll see. I'm not much into traveling anymore."

Pearce walks up to her. "Celia, thank you for coming."

"Thank you for having me. Rachel is like a daughter to me and it's good to finally see her happy."

325

Pearce's smile drops. He doesn't like hearing that I wasn't happy for those fifteen years. He knows I wasn't, but to hear someone else say it makes it more real. It's not something I talk about. I've avoided telling him much about that time in my life. It's too painful to relive it and he doesn't need to know.

"You two need to dance." Celia winks at me, then walks away.

"Shall we?" Pearce asks. I take his arm and we have our first dance.

The reception continues until early evening and then everyone starts telling me goodbye. I still don't know where I'm going.

"Have fun!" Lilly says to Pearce and me.

"Don't worry about her." Garret slings his arm around Lilly's shoulder. "Jade and I will keep her out of trouble."

"Hey!" Lilly swats at him. "I never get into trouble."

"You'll be 13 in a few weeks. That's when the trouble starts."

"We'll be back in time for her birthday," Pearce says to Garret. "She should be good until then."

Garret laughs. "You guys better head out. Call us when you get there."

I'm so confused. "Pearce, where are we going?"

"To Maui. I rented a house on the beach and we're going to live there while our house is being renovated."

"The renovations are supposed to take a month."

"That's correct." He smiles, then leans down and gives me a kiss.

"We're going to Maui for a month?"

"It's going to be awesome." Lilly hugs me. "Have fun, Mo— Rachel."

She keeps almost calling me 'mom' and then stops herself. I've told her she can call me 'mom' but she's not ready to.

We finish saying our goodbyes, then head to the airport. We're taking a commercial flight this time, first class, of course.

"Why didn't you tell me about this?" I ask Pearce once we're in the air.

"I wanted it to be a surprise." He holds my hand. "Plus, I knew if I told you, you'd try to cut the trip short, wanting to hurry back to the family."

"I'm really going to miss them."

"You'll see them when we get back. For now, I don't want to share you. I went without you for years. I don't think it's too much to ask for one month alone with you."

I kiss him. "And what are we doing for a month?"

"Making up for lost time."

So we do. It's our second honeymoon. And even better than the first.

CHAPTER THIRTY-FOUR
Four Months Later

RACHEL

"Mom, do you want to do the lights?" Garret asks.

"No, you go ahead. Jade said you're an expert at it."

"I'm not exactly an expert." He starts unwinding the lights from the holder. "I just do it like you taught me."

"And it always turns out great," Jade says, handing Garret some extension cords. Jade has a big round belly in front, but the rest of her doesn't look pregnant. "He strings the lights in and out of the branches instead of just around the outside."

"I learned that tip from your grandmother," I say to Garret as I pick up another box of lights and undo the packaging. "She was an expert at decorating for Christmas."

Pearce comes up behind me, his arms around my waist. "You should've seen your grandparents' house in Indiana. They had every kind of Christmas decoration imaginable."

"I wish I could've met them," Garret says.

"Me too," I say softly. I'm sure my parents would still be alive if Holton hadn't killed them.

Pearce leans down and kisses my cheek. "I'll get the ornaments."

He's trying to cheer me up. He knows how hard this time of year is for me. Earlier this week was the anniversary of my parents' deaths and I still have a hard time accepting that they're gone. But we're honoring their memory by continuing their tradition of putting up the tree the day after Thanksgiving. Everyone's at our house this morning, and then this afternoon, we'll all go to Jade and Garret's house and decorate their tree.

"Can I unwrap them?" Lilly asks, as Pearce brings out the box of ornaments. He saved them all these years, hiding them away so Katherine wouldn't throw them out. The box hasn't been opened since I left.

"Sure," I tell Lilly, sitting next to her on the couch. Abigail toddles over and I pick her up and set her on my lap.

Pearce hands Lilly the box, then sits beside me, his arm resting behind me on the couch.

"Papa." Abi climbs off my lap and over to Pearce. She likes being with me, but she knew Grandpa first so he'll always be her favorite.

"Are you ready to be a big sister?" he asks her.

"Book." She points to the books we keep in a basket on the floor next to the couch. Pearce reads to her all the time.

"Maybe later." He kisses her head as she snuggles into his side. "Let's watch your dad do the tree."

Garret laughs. "She never answered your question. I don't think she's thrilled about the baby."

"She just doesn't understand," Jade says, leaning back and grabbing the sides of the chair as she sits down. "She'll be happy when she sees the baby."

Garret attaches another string of lights to the one he's holding. "As long as she doesn't treat it like one of her dolls."

Abi isn't very gentle with her dolls. She's always dragging them around by their hair.

"We'll have to work on that," Jade says. "We'll start practicing this weekend, okay, Abi?"

She's not listening. She's focused on the ornaments Lilly is unwrapping. She reaches across me, trying to grab one.

I take her hand and kiss her tiny fingers. "No, sweetie. You can't have that. You could choke on it."

Pearce picks her doll off the floor and hands it to her, redirecting her attention. "Here. You can practice being a sister."

She grabs the doll's long blond hair and swings her around before setting her on Pearce's lap.

"You better hope that baby's born bald," Pearce says to Jade.

We all laugh.

"Why are all of these sports?" Lilly asks, holding up a football ornament.

"Because they're mine," Garret answers.

"Every year I'd take Garret to pick out an ornament," I explain, "and he always picked ones that were sports-themed. He loved sports."

"Still do," he says. "Which is why I own a sporting goods company. Dad, we need to go over some of the numbers today. I printed out the spreadsheets. They're at the house."

"Not today, Garret. Today's about family, not work." Pearce smiles at me as he says it. He loves retirement, or semi-retirement. He still works, but not anywhere near as much as he used to. He helps Garret run the company and gives speeches at business conferences. He makes a lot of money giving speeches, sometimes as much as $50,000 a speech. It just shows how well-respected he is in the business world.

"Would anyone like a cookie?" Charles walks in with a plate of sugar cookies. He lives here now. Well, not with us, but here in town. Charles is like a member of the family, so when Pearce and I moved, Charles decided to move here as well.

Charles doesn't work for us. He works part-time at a local restaurant and does catering for the company Jade's friend, Harper, owns. He loves his new jobs and being out here in California with us. And he recently started dating someone, a woman he met at one of the events he catered.

Charles spent Thanksgiving with us and today he's making Christmas cookies. He makes the best cookies. They melt in your mouth.

"Cookie!" Abi reaches for one.

Charles looks at Jade.

"She can have one," Jade says, trying to get up. She sighs. "I can't even get out of this chair."

The poor girl. Her belly is huge and she still has over a month to go.

Garret goes over and helps her up, then gives her a kiss. "Just a few more weeks."

"That's too long. I can't take this anymore," she says. "This baby needs to hurry up."

Lilly pops up from the couch. "Okay, they're all ready." She sets the box of ornaments by the tree and Jade and her start hanging them as Garret finishes the lights.

"We need some music," Grace says. She was with us for Thanksgiving, but for Christmas she's going to William's house in New York.

Christmas music fills the air and Pearce and I watch as our three children decorate the tree. I know Garret is the only one who's mine, but I feel like a mother to all three of them. I love Jade and Lilly as if they were my own.

"This one really's pretty." Lilly holds up the crystal star ornament Pearce gave me on our first Christmas together. "I'm guessing Garret didn't pick this one out."

"Dad did," Garret says. "He always gave Mom an ornament at Christmas."

Pearce leans over to me and says quietly, "Let's go outside."

He sets Abi down and offers me his hand. I don't know what he's up to, but I follow him out to the back patio.

He draws me into him and gives me a kiss. "Remember when I gave that to you?"

"The ornament? Yes. Of course. I loved it."

"You had us make a wish. So what did you wish for?"

"A baby. I wanted us to have a child. What did you wish for?"

"For you to be safe. It was always my wish."

"You wished for that every year? Never anything else?"

"Our second Christmas together, I wished for you to be happy. You were so sad after your parents died, and I wanted you to feel happiness again. Right after I wished for that, we found out you were pregnant with Garret."

I smile. "That definitely made me happy."

He reaches in his pocket and pulls something out and hands it to me. "The tradition continues."

It's wrapped in red tissue paper and when I pull the paper aside, I see a crystal heart ornament.

"Pearce, it's beautiful."

"You've always had my heart. The first time I saw you, my heart raced in my chest because it knew that it had found its match. The person it belonged to. The woman who would own it then, now, and forevermore." He kisses me. "I love you, sweetheart."

"I love you too."

He holds me in his arms and I listen to his heart beating in his chest. He owns my heart too. He always will.

CHAPTER THIRTY-FIVE
Five Weeks Later

PEARCE

"It's a girl," Garret says, beaming with pride, as he exits the delivery room.

Lilly squeals. "Yay! Another girl!"

Rachel races up to him. "Congratulations, honey. How's Jade?"

"She's good. Tired, but good."

"Congratulations," I say, going up to Garret. "You look tired, as well."

It was a long labor and delivery. Last time, Jade had the baby in a couple hours. This time it lasted eighteen.

"I was starting to think this baby would never come," he says.

I chuckle. "I felt the same way when your mother was in labor. After sixteen hours, I was thinking it was never going to end."

"You?" Rachel kiddingly punches me. "How do you think *I* felt?"

Garret laughs. "I have to go back in there."

"Can we see the baby?" Lilly asks.

"Not yet. I gotta go." He disappears back in the room.

"Dad, can I get a soda?" Lilly asks.

"Yes." I get my wallet out and hand her some dollar bills and she takes off to the vending machine.

"He looks so happy," Rachel says as I put my arm around her.

"I remember that feeling. Seeing your child for the first time. I couldn't stop smiling."

"Garret was such a sweet baby, and so alert. He used to look at you with those big blue eyes and just watch you."

"Yes." I smile, remembering it. "He did that from the first moment I saw him."

"And then you had to take him home from the hospital all by yourself."

I nod. "I was scared out of my mind."

"You were?" She laughs. "You didn't act like it."

"I didn't want you to know. But it all worked out. I was fine after a day."

She lays her head on my shoulder. "You were such a good father. You still are."

I finally agree with that statement. When Garret was born, I had no idea how to be a father. My own father taught me nothing in that respect, other than to never act like him with my own children. So I learned from the other men in my life. Jack. Henry. And even Royce's father, Arlin. Those men were like fathers to me and taught me how a father should act. But I still struggled with it, and regret that I wasn't always there for my children. But I am now. I have been for years.

"Have you seen the baby yet?" Grace asks. She just arrived with Abigail. Charles is right behind them.

"Not yet," Rachel says.

"Come sit on Grandpa's lap," I say to Abigail as she toddles over to me, practically running. She's always so excited to see me.

I pick her up and she wraps her arms around my neck and hugs me. "Papa!"

"It's Grandpa," Lilly says to her as she returns with her soda. She sits next to me and talks to Abi. "Try it. Gran-Pa." She says it slowly.

"Papa," Abi says, kissing my cheek.

Lilly laughs. "I give up."

We remain in the waiting room until we're allowed in Jade's room to see the baby. Jade's so tired she can barely keep her eyes open.

Garret's holding the baby, a proud smile on his face. "Here she is."

We all gather around to see her.

"Aww, she's so cute," Lilly says. "Look how tiny she is."

334

Rachel touches her cheek. "She's beautiful."

"You want to hold her?" Garret asks.

"I would love to." Rachel takes her from him, smiling at the baby. "You are so precious."

"What's her name?" Lilly asks Garret.

"Hannah Julia Kensington."

"Julia was my mom's name," Jade says quietly from her bed.

"That was nice you honored her that way," Rachel says to her.

It's one of my many regrets. That I didn't do more to help Jade and her mother. If I had, her mother wouldn't have died and Jade wouldn't have grown up in poverty. When Royce told me he got a woman pregnant, I should've done some research and found out who the woman was and where she lived. I should've made sure she was taken care of, instead of trusting that Royce had done so. But I didn't, and I regret that. At least I was able to save her child, and because I did, my son now has a loving wife and two beautiful children. He has love and happiness, which is all I ever wanted for him.

"Hannah, you need to meet your grandfather," Rachel says.

I take the baby from Rachel.

"Hello, Hannah." As I say it, her eyes pop open.

Garret notices. "Dad, look at her watching you."

"You did the same thing when I held you for the first time."

"Oh, yeah?" Garret's eyes are on the baby, but mine are on him.

My son is all grown up. He's a husband and a father. Time goes so quickly. It seems like just yesterday I was holding him in my arms, and now I'm holding his daughter.

GARRET

Seeing my mom and dad together, holding my new baby girl, is almost too much. I have a huge lump in my throat, trying to control the emotion, but shit, it's hard. My emotions were already high from the birth of my daughter, but having both my parents here has got me all teary-eyed.

Sometimes I still can't believe that she's here. That my mom is back. That she's alive. She's been back for months now, so I should be used to seeing her, but I'm not. I keep thinking this is just a dream and one day I'll wake up and she'll be gone.

"Look at her blue eyes," my mom says to my dad as they both look at Hannah. "They're the same color as Garret's."

"And yours." My dad kisses my mom and they gaze at each other like they're saying 'I love you' without words. They do that all the time. It's like they have their own secret language, just like Jade and I do.

I'm so freaking happy for my dad. And my mom. I'm happy for our whole family. We're all happier now. Our lives were good before, but having my mom here has made everything so much better. My girls have a grandmother. Jade has a mother-in-law who treats her like a daughter. Lilly has the mom she always wanted. And I have my parents back.

They're even more in love now than they were when I was a kid. They were over-the-top in love back then, but now, their love is even stronger because they know what it's like to be without each other. It's changed how they act and their priorities. Now, no matter what, they always make time for each other. They never take each other for granted. They live every day like they're newlyweds. Like they can't wait to spend another day with each other.

It's a good example for all of us. Jade and I are young, and it's easy to get wrapped up in work and everyday stuff that takes us away from each other. But I don't want that to happen. I don't want Jade and me to ever grow apart or take each other for granted. When we're old, I want us to be like my parents. Still holding hands, gazing at each other, and kissing like newlyweds.

"Daddy!" Abigail is clinging to my leg.

I reach down and pick her up and kiss her. "Hey. You have a new baby sister. Do you want to meet her?" I point to Hannah, who's still in my dad's arms.

Abi seems unsure, but then she reaches out, trying to get to Hannah. I keep hold of her, not sure what she plans to do. You never know with a toddler.

"I'll let you get closer, but you have to be gentle, okay?"

Her eyes are on Hannah.

336

"Abi, remember how I showed you?" The past month, Jade and I have been trying to show Abi how to handle the baby, using her dolls for an example. It hasn't really worked. Abi still tosses her dolls around and drags them on the floor, banging their heads into things.

I bring her closer to Hannah, keeping an eye on Abi's hands so she doesn't hit the baby. She holds onto my shirt as she leans over and kisses Hannah's cheek.

My mom's watching her. "That's so sweet."

"That was nice, Abi." I bring her back to my chest and hug her. "You're a good big sister."

"Baby." Abi points to her and smiles.

"You guys still up for babysitting?" I ask my mom.

"Of course we are, honey. We love watching Abi."

"I know, but this is for a few days. You usually just watch her for a few hours. She might wear you out."

"We can handle it," my dad says. "Besides, we have Lilly. She's young. She can chase Abi around the house when your mother and I need a break."

"What did you say about me?" Lilly asks. She was talking to Jade and didn't hear what my dad said.

"Your father just volunteered you to babysit," my mom says as Lilly comes up next to me.

"Here." I kiss Abi, then hand her to Lilly. "You can start now."

"I don't mind." She hoists Abi up on her hip. "I love my niece."

My parents are going to watch Abi for a few days so Jade and I can get settled in with the new baby. It's so awesome having my parents and Lilly close by. Not just to babysit, but so I can see them all the time.

"Lee-lee," Abi says, hugging her.

"It's Lilly," she says, correcting her. "Lil-lee."

"Lee-lee." Abi giggles.

"Forget it, Lilly," I say. "You're going to be Lee-lee for at least another year. You called me 'Garrah' until you were three."

"I did?" She laughs. "That's funny."

"We should get home," my mom says to me. "Abi needs her nap. We'll stop by later tonight."

"Sounds good."

My dad hands Hannah to me. "I guess I should leave her with you."

I laugh. "Yeah, that's probably a good idea."

My parents go over and say goodbye to Jade. I hand the baby back to her and walk my parents to the door.

"Bye, honey," my mom says, giving me a hug. "Love you."

"Love you too."

I smile as I watch my parents walk away, hand in hand. Together. And in love.

CHAPTER THIRTY-SIX
Two Weeks Later

RACHEL

"Are you sure you don't want to come with me?" Pearce asks. He's leaving soon for a speech he's giving at a conference in San Francisco.

"I told Jade I'd stay and help with the baby."

"Sweetheart, she has plenty of help. She has Garret and Grace, and Frank and Karen will be arriving tomorrow."

Frank is the man who took Jade in after her mom died. Karen is his wife. They live in Iowa and are coming to help with the baby, who is now a couple weeks old.

"I'll miss the kids too much if I go," I tell him.

"What about me?" He kisses me on his way to the closet. "Won't you miss me?"

"Yes, but I'll call you on the phone." ·

"That's not good enough." He's now in the closet. "I can't find my gray tie. Have you seen it?"

"It's around your neck."

He looks down. "Oh." He comes over and kisses me again. "What would I do without you?"

"Never be able to find anything." I check the clock. "Pearce, you're going to be late if you don't leave."

"Yes, I'm going." He comes over and gives me one last kiss. "Last chance. Come with me."

"Next time. Now go."

"I'll call you when I get there. I love you." He takes his suitcase and leaves.

Once he's gone, I change into my dress, then go down to the guest bedroom and take out the suitcase I'd hidden away in the closet, already packed and ready to go.

When I get back to my room, Lilly walks in and plops down on the bed, lying back with her legs dangling off the side. "You guys are so weird."

"Why are we weird?"

"This whole surprise thing. Why didn't you just go with him?"

"Because your father always surprises me and I never get to surprise him back. So this is my chance."

"I don't get it." She takes a throw pillow from the bed and tosses it in the air.

"You will when you're older. Are you ready to go?"

"Yeah." She sits up, tossing the pillow aside. "Rachel?"

"Yes." I wait for her at the door.

She meets me over there. "I'm glad you're with my dad. He's really happy now."

"We both are." I hug her. "I'm going to miss you, honey."

"It's only for a couple days."

"I know, but I'll still miss you."

She smiles. "I'll miss you too."

Before I met Lilly, I was so worried she wouldn't accept me, but she did, and now we're closer than ever.

"When your dad and I get back, we'll have movie night, okay?"

"Can Jade and Garret come over?"

"If they're able to, then yes. You can invite him when he gets here."

We started doing movie nights again, but our family is so big now that we built a small theater room onto the house. We filled it with comfy recliners, a wrap-around sofa, and some bean bag chairs on the floor. In the back is a concession stand and a popcorn maker. The room gets a lot of use.

"You guys ready?" I hear Garret in the living room. He must've just got here. He's dropping me off at the airport, then taking Lilly to stay at his house for the next couple days.

"We're ready." I bring my suitcase to the living room.

Lilly runs up to him. "Can you guys come to movie night when Mom and Dad get back?"

Garret smiles at me, because Lilly slipped and called me 'mom' again. She alternates between 'mom' and 'Rachel.'

"Sure. We can do that." He takes my suitcase and we all go out to the driveway. "So Mom, did Dad catch onto your plan?"

"No. I'm sure he'll be surprised."

"You guys are crazy." He puts my suitcase in the trunk. "You should've just gone with him."

"That's what I said," Lilly says as she hops in the back seat.

"You two don't understand romance." I get in the front seat. "It's all about surprises."

Garret glances at me, smiling. "I'm just kidding. I get it."

We arrive at the airport and I say goodbye to the kids, then board the plane to San Francisco. It's a regular commercial jet. I avoid small private planes whenever possible.

When I arrive in San Francisco, I take a cab straight to the hotel where the conference is being held. I get there right on time. Pearce's speech started fifteen minutes ago.

PEARCE

Today's speech is on how to modify your business strategy in a changing economy. It's one of the many new speeches I developed since leaving Kensington Chemical. I've given this speech a few times now and it's proven to be quite popular. Tomorrow I'll be speaking again on a different topic.

This is a large conference, aimed at people in the financial services industry. I'm speaking to a group of at least 500 people in a large hotel ballroom.

"As financial experts, you know that you can't always predict changes in—" I stop when I see someone walk in the room. A woman. In a yellow sleeveless dress. Who is stunningly beautiful. Tall, with dark brown hair that falls in soft waves around her shoulders. And a smile that lights up the room.

She seats herself in one of the middle rows. I smile as I check my watch. She's fifteen minutes late.

341

"As I was saying..." My eyes meet hers in the crowd and my heart leaps in my chest, just like it did the first time I saw her.

Someone coughs in the front row and my mind returns to my speech.

"Pardon me." I take a drink of water, then continue on, but my gaze continues to wander to that gorgeous woman in the yellow dress. The one who agreed to marry me. Twice.

The speech goes well and prompts many questions from the audience. When my time is finally up, I see Rachel leaving. I hurry and follow her out to the hall. It's filled with people, but I spot the yellow dress in the crowd and see her turn down a short hallway that leads outside to the pool. I catch up to her before she goes out the door.

"Rachel." I hold her arm.

She turns. "Do I know you?"

So we're role playing. This is new. But I like it.

"I believe we met at Yale years ago."

She pauses, her eyes skimming up and down my suit, then back to my face. "You do look familiar. Actually, yes, I do remember meeting you."

I take a step forward, putting us less than a foot apart. "Perhaps we could get reacquainted over a drink."

"I was just heading out. I don't have time."

I place my hand on her hip and lower my mouth to her ear. "It's just one drink."

Her breath quickens. "Maybe some other time."

"I'm afraid I can't let you leave," I say, my lips brushing her ear, making her shiver.

"And why is that?"

I raise back up, my eyes on hers. "Because I know I would regret it. Many years ago, I let a girl walk out of my speech and I never got her number. She was all I could think about, but I assumed I'd never see her again."

"And did you?"

"I did. I'd given her my business card and she called me and asked me out. It was rather forward of her, now that I think about it."

She tries not to laugh. "And then what happened?"

"We fell in love. Got married. Had a son." I pause, not wanting to say what happened next.

"And were apart long enough to realize just how precious love is. So when you found each other again, you vowed to never be apart. And to cherish every moment together and fall more in love every day."

I smile. "Yes. That's exactly what happened." I lean down and kiss her. "Now how about that drink?"

"Yes. Let's go to the bar."

"Not in the bar. In my hotel suite upstairs."

"Even better." She kisses me. "I love you."

"Why didn't you tell me you were doing this?"

"That would've ruined the surprise." She smiles. "Now come on. Show me this hotel suite of yours."

I slide my arm around her waist and lead her to the elevator. As we ride up to the top floor, I keep glancing over at her in that yellow dress.

"You need to stop walking in late to my speeches," I say as I hold open the door to our hotel suite.

"Why?" She steps inside the room. "Do you find it distracting?"

"Very." I close the door, take her in my arms, and show her just how distracting she is.

Even now, all these years later, I see her walk in a room and lose my train of thought. I hear her voice and instantly smile. I feel her touch and my heart races. She's always distracted me that way, from the moment I met her.

And thank God she did. Rachel saved me from the dark, lonely, empty life I was living and replaced it with a life filled with light and love and family.

Some would say it was wrong of me to bring her into my world, but when you know you've found the one you're meant to be with, how do you let her go? Why would we have even met if we weren't supposed to be together? Certainly fate can't be that cruel.

I've pondered this over the years, especially when Rachel was gone, and the guilt over her death consumed me. I kept telling myself I should've let her go after our first date. That I never should've pursued her.

But I've come to realize that people come into our lives for a reason. Rachel saved me. Jack saved her. I saved Jade. Jade saved Garret.

These fateful encounters didn't just happen to us. They happen to everyone. We're all brought together in a way that doesn't always make sense at the time, but later, when you step back and look at how it all worked out, you see the beauty in it. The wonder. And you're amazed at how it all miraculously wove together to create a certain outcome. You realize that maybe that was the plan all along. That it wasn't up to you. That the decisions were already made. And you see how sometimes it's best not to question everything. To set aside your doubts. To go with your heart, despite your head telling you not to.

So now, finally, I've put my guilt to rest. I know for a fact that Rachel and I were meant to be together. I believe that now more than ever. She was taken from me, but she survived and she made her way back to me. Because this is where she belongs. We belong together.

She's my love. My life. My everything. My Rachel.

Made in United States
North Haven, CT
06 September 2022

23774504R00211